My Daily Prayer

Heavenly Father, walk with me today

Let me hear your footsteps and follow where you lead.

Talk to me today and let me hear your tender voice and follow what you say.

Stay with me today and let me feel your gentle presence in all that I think, or do, or say.

Be my strength when I weaken

Be my courage when I fear

Let me know that it is Your Hand holding mine, all the moments of this day.

And then when night comes, let me know that I am safe in your Loving Heart – so that I can sleep enjoying Your Peace and Love.

THE SERPENTINE WALL

THE SERPENTINE WALL

Jim DeBrosse

ST. MARTIN'S PRESS • NEW YORK

Although many of the locations described in this book exist in Greater Cincinnati, the story and its characters are wholly fictitious.

Library of Congress Cataloging-in-Publication Data

DeBrosse, James.
    The Serpentine wall.

    I. Title.
PS3554.E1768S4 1988   813'.54   88-15858
ISBN 0-312-02278-6

First Edition

10 9 8 7 6 5 4 3 2 1

To my family, Gladys, and, of course, "G"

THE SERPENTINE WALL

1

At the top of the Serpentine Wall, reporters and spectators pressed against the police barricades, vying for a view of the scene some fifty yards below. Firefighters were hacking and sifting through the rubble of a burned-out riverboat, using axes, shovels, rakes, heavy gloves. When they found a body, two or three would congregate around the spot and carefully stuff the charred remains into a rubberized bag. Sometimes they used little scoopers, not much bigger than garden tools. When the job was done, one of the firefighters would carry the yellow bag in outstretched arms, like a bride over the threshold, and lay it on the landing side-by-side with the others.

Rich Decker was one of those keeping watch from the barricades. He ran a hand over his forehead and pushed the grimy sweat back into his hair. It was almost eight A.M.—three hours since he was rousted from bed and dispatched to a four-alarm fire in the middle of the city's downtown riverfront. Nighttime had brought little relief from the late August heat, and the morning air was already beginning to stew. The acrid residue of the fire mingled with the late-summer fishhouse odors along the Ohio and the rush-hour exhaust fumes from the bridge traffic. The hazy mixture stung the eyes and filled the nostrils, like sticking your face into a steaming pot of Cajun gumbo.

Gone now were the flames and the sirens and the fireboats blasting their horns in the night. For Decker the cleanup seemed anticlimactic, as tedious as an archaeological dig. But that hadn't kept the crowds of office workers and sales clerks, some of whom held handkerchiefs over their noses to blot out the stench, from growing steadily since daybreak.

At 7:50 A.M., the unofficial tally stood at eight bags. That's when Barrett Simmons had left to find a pay phone.

At precisely eight, when she still hadn't returned, Decker tried the two-way radio again. They were hauling out body bag number nine.

"Decker to city desk. Decker to city desk."

The answer was a sound like someone balling up aluminum foil, only amplified.

He pressed down the call button again. "Yoo hoo! Anybody home?"

Static was still the answer, with the metro deadline only fifteen minutes away.

He was tempted to pitch the damn thing to the ground and dance on its electronic innards. Instead he reached for the pack of sugarless gum in his shirt pocket. He popped a strip, the first of the day, in his mouth and began working it around slowly. It was amazing how quickly the artificial flavor disappeared, and then it was just something to keep your mouth busy. He'd quit smoking more than a year ago; gum-chewing was its legacy, especially when he was antsy.

And he was getting antsier by the minute, waiting for one of the captains, or Chief Orsini himself, to climb the Serpentine's winding ledges and make a statement to the press. At one point, he considered jumping the barricade. But a half-dozen cops were holding the line. A few minutes before, he'd overheard one of them refer to the assembled members of the Fourth Estate as "a bunch of fucking vultures." He knew enough not to hassle cops in that frame of mind. Especially not Cincinnati cops. He shouted instead.

"Chief! Chief Orsini! The press would like a statement!"

That brought a ripple of applause from the other reporters. There were maybe a dozen altogether—newspapers, wire services, radio people—plus another half-dozen or so TV camera crews, including one from CNN. This was big time. The Queen City was making national news.

Orsini was on the landing, trundling back and forth in his yellow rubber boots and toting a red bullhorn that his booming voice scarcely needed. Orsini was the "papa bear" of the fire division—a hulking man gone soft and paunchy, a back-slapper, loud and self-important. On most days he loved to talk to the press. But today wasn't one of them. Decker shouted again, and Orsini continued about his business, as though directing cleanup was chief among his administrative duties.

To hell with him then. It was still three hours to home edition, and that was the *Eagle*'s biggest run anyway. Some 90,000 copies home-delivered to mostly working-class families on the West Side of town. Solid provincial folks who wanted their hometown news on the front page, and all the unpleasant business about South Africa, the Middle East, and any place that wasn't within an hour's drive tucked inside where it damn well belonged.

Decker looked beyond the crowd. There was no sign yet of Barrett, but then it was optimistic to think she would be back so soon. The closest pay phone was probably at Riverfront Coliseum, at the other end of the Serpentine Wall and a good half-mile downstream.

In the meantime, he decided to gather some "color." The *Eagle* editors were always looking for color. Set the scene. Take the reader *there*. All right, he thought, a touch of color: the boat looked like a bombed-out London cathedral in a World War Two photo, with nothing left but the low-slung hull, a half-dozen or so metal braces arching through the air, and two enormous smokestacks, like steeples, rising from the ashes below. White smoke still hissed here and there from the interior rubble. The once-proud *River Queen* was now a piece of floating trash.

"Serves him right," a man's voice behind him said, so loudly that Decker thought it was directed at him. "I hope the sleazy bastard went down with his boat. I really do." The speaker was an older man, bald and fat and wearing a blue seersucker suit, bunched under the arms like sagging flesh. He was talking to a younger, taller man stooped by his side, as though hanging on his every word.

Decker knew a quotable personality when he heard one. He switched to his interview mode, first depositing his gum between two sheets of notebook paper, then turning to his victim with an honest, wide-open smile. "Excuse me, sir. I take it you were just talking about Alvin Greenburg."

The bald man pulled up his trousers. "Who the hell are you?"

"Rick Decker. A reporter for the *Eagle*." Decker's lips curled up at the corners whenever he identified himself with the *Eagle*, as though working there was his private joke.

The man pawed the air and looked the other way. "Nah, I don't talk with reporters."

"Not even about the notorious Mr. Greenburg?" Decker smiled again, trying to appear ingenuous, and failing. At thirty, he had the impish look of a high-school trouble-maker—grown up now, but not enough. He was tall and lanky, with tousled curls of reddish-brown hair, a splash of freckles under the vivid gray-green eyes. His face was thin and almost wrinkle-free, but it was the lips, mostly, that gave him that bad-boy look: very full and pushed outward a little—like Mick Jagger's, a college girlfriend had told him once. In his mind's eye, though, he thought of himself as Jimmy Cagney, or maybe Bugs Bunny. A smartass type. Underdog. When he was being sarcastic, which was much of the time, his smile twisted into a smirk, showing lots of strong white teeth.

"I'll tell you the same thing every decent person in this town will tell you," the man said, poking a stubby finger at

Decker's opened notebook. "He had no business operating here. Not an establishment like that. That kind of stuff belongs on the other side of the river, with the rest of the trash."

There was his man-in-the-street reaction—with just the proper amount of indignation and self-righteousness. The pulsebeat of Cincinnati.

Decker egged him on. "So you're hoping Al Greenburg is among the victims?"

"If he isn't, he should be. It would be God Almighty's justice."

Decker felt a twinge of sympathy for Little Al. It was bad enough to be a midget, but then to be so utterly reviled by so many decent folk. In a way, you had to hand it to Greenburg. In a God-fearing town like Cincinnati, where people said you had to cross the river into Kentucky to have a little fun, Al had found a way to bring Kentucky—and plenty of fun—into Cincinnati.

The *River Queen* had been Al's pleasure palace—an old sternwheeler converted into a dazzling nightclub-casino-hotel and floated like an insult on Cincinnati's doorstep. The whole scheme was said to have been financed by Little Al's local chain of porno shops and X-rated movie houses. And even though the nightclub closed at two in the morning, the lights always burned in Al's private suite on the topmost deck. Rumors, of course, were rampant as to what took place there in the wee hours. High-stakes gambling? Prostitution? Live sex acts? You name it, people surmised it.

And as much as they were itching to, Cincinnati police couldn't touch the place.

"I blame the courts, all the way." The man in the seersucker suit was still in high gear. "They turned the whole damned river over to Kentucky. I mean, why call it the 'Ohio' if it belongs to Kentucky?"

Decker nodded, but couldn't help grinning. Here was the

compelling logic of the layman. Horse sense, if you will. But not the view of the Supreme Court. Ohio and Kentucky had been squabbling for decades over territorial rights to the river. By Kentucky's reckoning, the entire width of the Ohio was part of the original land grant given colonial Virginia (from which Kentucky was later carved) by His Majesty King George of England in 1792. Ohio laughed: the river had long since shifted to make nonsense of such claims. But in 1976, the Supreme Court sided with Kentucky. By George, they said, you can't argue with that much history.

Little Al had sniffed the opportunity and pounced on it. He berthed the *River Queen* in a nook between the L & N bridge and a line of abandoned pylons, just feet from the Cincinnati riverfront and five blocks from the heart of downtown. Territorially, however, the casino floated in the waters of Newport, Kentucky—"Sin City," if you please— where the police could be counted on to look the other way, just as long as the price was right and nobody got hurt. And nobody had been hurt, until that morning at any rate.

He asked Mr. Man-in-the-Street for his name.

"You mean you're going to quote what I just said?"

"Yes, sir. I told you I was a reporter."

"I don't give a damn what you are. You're not putting *my* name in the papers. No, sir. You'll have those thugs banging at my door." He grabbed his colleague by the arm. "Ron, let's get to the office."

Decker was about to select another victim when he spotted Rebo Johnson working his way through the crowd. Rebo nodded at Decker: they needed to talk. You couldn't miss Rebo, no matter how big the crowd. Six-four, black, built like a refrigerator. He wore gold-beaded dreadlocks that dangled clear to his chest, a gold stud in his left ear. A Nikkon with a huge telephoto lens hung around his neck on a stars-and-stripes band. He carried the rest of his equipment in a black-

and-yellow Nikkon bag slung over one shoulder. A white terry-cloth towel was slung over the other.

"Bozo wants you back at the corral," he said in his deep quiet voice. He wiped his face with the towel.

"Jesus, now what? I don't even have a statement yet."

"Barrett's supposed to stay. They want you for something else."

"Why can't they make up their minds, dammit?"

Rebo shrugged. Bitching was everybody's favorite pastime at the *Eagle*. "Why am I shooting pictures of body bags? You know how the goddamn place is."

It was a steamy ten-block walk back to the *Eagle*. Along the way he stopped at the pavilion in front of Procter & Gamble headquarters, a half-block square of covered arborways, perfectly tended grass, and cool running fountains. Like P & G itself, the pavilion seemed off-limits to outsiders, part of a closed corporate world where order and rationality ruled. Which is why Decker made a point of walking over the pavilion's manicured lawn whenever he was in the vicinity. This time he splashed his face in one of the fountains and doused the back of his neck, while across the pavilion a security guard watched intently, wondering, perhaps, if he had grounds to make a citizen's arrest. Decker wiped his hands on his trousers, grinned, and marched over the grass toward Broadway.

The *Eagle* building was at Eighth and Broadway. A remnant of the paper's glory days, it was a pastiche of thirties Art Deco and old-fashioned corn gone to seed. The sixteen-story tower was capped by a faded silver beacon ("Shed Light, and the Truth Will Be Found" was the *Eagle* motto) and on each of its corners stood a statue representing one of the Four Estates.

Decker rounded the revolving door and breathed a sigh of

relief. Even in the dog days of August, the cavernous lobby was cool and dark as a cathedral. The marble walls, dulled with age, were inlaid with bronze grillwork depicting eagles, gazelles, and beefy workers in heroic poses, all buried under layers of tarnish. On each of the three elevator doors was a pair of bronze goddesses in bas-relief. The one on the left held a sword and shield, the one on the right a scroll. Mother Journalism and her secretary.

The newsroom was on the fourth floor, and there was only one route for reporters to return to their desks. It meant passing through a kind of checkpoint, where an editor invariably asked, "Where have you been?" or "Where are you going?" or "What have you got for me today?" On the left side of the passage was the city desk, three desks in a row actually, all equipped with computer terminals, with Lafferty the city editor sitting in the middle, flanked by two assistant city editors. On the right was the copy desk, a U-shaped huddle of eight VDTs, the "last line of defense," where stories were given a final reading and a headline before going to type.

Decker was in the newsroom by 8:20. The place was jumping with last-minute work on the metro edition—the copy desk screaming at the city desk, the city desk screaming at the reporters, the reporters screaming into their phones. The usual big-story pandemonium at the *Eagle*. Only this morning tempers were shorter than usual: the air conditioning was on the fritz again.

Fans of every description were whipping up a hurricane around the room. Big stand-up models thundered like plane engines across the copy desk and city desk. Desk models chattered back and forth like machine guns. Extension cords snaked in every direction.

Life at the *Eagle* was never dull.

Decker looked around the room for Lafferty, the city editor, better known among the reporters as "Bozo." But he was nowhere to be found. Not on the city desk, nor in the "Bozo Box," his glassed-in office next to the doorway.

That left Barry Stein, one of Lafferty's assistants, in charge of the desk. Which only seemed right, since Stein did most of the real editing and supervising anyway, while "Bozo" shuttled back and forth between the newsroom and the office of Alexander Finch, editor and publisher, where Bozo received his minute-by-minute marching orders.

"I take it Bozo abandoned ship," Decker said to Stein. It was all right to say Bozo in front of Stein. He was simpatico. Barry should have been Lafferty's boss, instead of the other way around. But Stein had at least two strikes against him with Finch: he had smarts, and he wasn't a "yes" man.

Stein took his pipe out of his mouth—a Savenelli with a curved stem—and looked up from his terminal. Like most of the *Eagle* staff pushing forty, he looked like a refugee from the sixties. He wore round John Lennon glasses, accentuating his round chubby face. Which was further accentuated by a corona of blown-out frizz, black going prematurely gray and receding rapidly from the intelligent forehead. A smile flickered across his serene face. "Lafferty's in Finch's office for the morning powwow."

"You want my notes?"

Stein shook his head. "Barrett phoned a minute or two ago. Have anything you think we need?"

That was one of the things Decker liked about Stein: he didn't believe in makework, in bossing people around for the hell of it. He relied on the judgment of his reporters.

Decker told him the body count was up to nine. "But still no statement from Orsini."

"Thanks," Stein said. Then he stood and shouted calmly over the fan noise to the copy desk. "Mullins, make that nine bodies!"

"Nine?!" Ralph Mullins, slot man, was hoping it wasn't true.

"Yes, nine."

"Christ, not another change," Mullins whined. "We've remade the front page twice already! Give me a fucking break."

"By the way," Decker told Stein, who was busy on his keyboard again. "This radio's gone out."

Stein didn't look up. "Another one, huh? Throw it on Lafferty's desk."

He did, then circled the city desk and headed straight to "Vendville." Vendville was the *Eagle's* windowless lunch room, a cubbyhole at the back of the newsroom where a lineup of vending machines dispensed a complete array of high-sodium, high-fat junk foods and caffeine-based stimulants.

He took coffee and a carton of milk back to his desk, where he kept a box of Grapenuts hidden in a file drawer. If his luck held out, Lafferty would be tied up a few more minutes. Long enough for breakfast. He opened the milk carton, took a couple of quick swigs, then split the carton top all the way to make a bowl. In went the Grapenuts. While he waited for the coffee to cool and the Grapenuts to turn good and soggy, he went to the copy desk and found a copy of the morning's *Cincinnati Times.* Just as he had expected, the *Times* had a spectacular color photo of the *River Queen* in flames, a blaze of orange against a reddened sky.

Back at his desk, he laughed to himself. The *Times'* story was a wipeout. A six-inch bulletin didn't say much more than the sixty-point headline: "River Casino Burns, Death Toll Unknown." No body count, no IDs, no cause of fire. No juicy speculation, either. Just the official record, which was the style, of course, of the *Times.* The fire department hadn't begun the hunt for bodies until long after the *Times* had been put to bed for the night. For once, it seemed, the meat of a major story would fall on the *Eagle's* deadline. It was indeed a lucky day.

He grabbed a plastic McDonald's spoon from the collection at the back of his drawer, checked around for Lafferty, and dug into the cereal. About every other week Bozo would catch him in the act and scream, "Dammit, Decker, we don't pay reporters for eating breakfast. Feed your face *before* you come to work!"

He gulped big spoonfuls of the hearty mash, hoping to finish before Lafferty sprung from Finch's office ready to assign some wild goosechase. Like the time Decker was ordered to scare up an exposé on The Great Green Bean Shortage. The "shortage" had swept town the summer before, all because Alex Finch had found his neighborhood supermarket fresh out of green beans one night. The next morning, Laffery sent Decker to stores all over the city to find out where the world's supply of green beans had gone. Only one problem: the Queen City was awash in green beans—fresh *and* canned. Each time Decker phoned Lafferty with the bad news, Lafferty would dispatch him to yet another store. Finally, after the sixth or seventh store, Lafferty conceded: "I guess the Boss made a mistake."

Lafferty wasn't the only problem at the *Eagle*, he was just a symptom, a bubo on the plague-racked body. Like afternoon dailies all over the country, the *Eagle* was dying a lingering death, slipping by the month in circulation and advertising. The newsroom itself was testimony. Dingy and spare, with loose linoleum floors and gray office furniture that looked as though it had been auctioned from a WPA office the day after the New Deal ended. Only the VDTs were new, and in summer, those broke down on a weekly basis because the air conditioning was always breaking down, causing the microchips to wilt from heat and humidity.

He was scraping the last of the Grapenuts from his milk carton when a hand gripped his shoulder.

"Enjoying breakfast, Decker?"

You always knew when Lafferty was worked up. His pasty complexion would turn as orange as his carrot-colored hair, and his nostrils would flare and contract like the gills on a goldfish dumped out of water.

It must have been a big morning, because Lafferty dispensed with the usual Sermon on the Grapenuts.

"Now that you've finished that slop, get on the horn to Cincinnati General. Petkamp says he heard they're working on the only survivor from the *River Queen*. A woman by the name of Maisie Washington. We want an interview with that woman. Today. Home edition."

"Yes sir! On the double," Decker said sharply as Lafferty wheeled away. He caught himself before adding Bozo.

He got on the phone to Rollie Higgins, chief public relations poobah at General, and asked if the hospital was treating anyone from the *River Queen*.

"I wasn't aware there were any survivors," Higgins said in a clipped British accent, somehow acquired during his youth in Chicasaw, Ohio. "But let me make the usual inquiries. I know you're on deadline, of course. So I'll be back in a jiff."

Higgins was a pompous ass, and sometimes obstructive. But he had never lied to Decker. Or at least Decker had never caught him in a lie, which put him in a class by himself as a public relations man.

Decker went to Vendville for another coffee and returned to his desk. He flipped through his desk calendar. The date was Monday, August 31, 1982. No interviews scheduled. Only one story due—a seasonal throwaway about hayfever, which meant a couple of phone calls to the local medical college and the arboretum and a quick rewrite of last year's story. Well, it might have been a leisurely day.

He was rereading the *Times'* story, jotting down questions for any survivors, when Barrett appeared. She leaned derriere-first against his desktop, arms folded, her long legs crossed at the ankles. The skirt was snug around the smoothly flaired hips. Wisps of brown hair blew across her face in the newsroom breeze. A lovely sight, even at nine in the morning.

"Sorry to intrude on your thoughts, Ace, but Bozo said I should brief you on what Orsini had to say."

"His Rotundness graced us with a statement?"

"About five minutes after you left."

Barrett lit a Camel, the unfiltered kind, which little rich girls like Barrett smoked, Decker supposed, to dissociate themselves from the country club crowd. It was easy to see Barrett had not gotten much sleep. Her eyelids were puffy and there were circles under her dark brown eyes. Even so, the corner of each eye still had that amazing sparkle, a kind of dewy-eyed radiance, only harder, as though she'd stepped right out of a Brenda Starr comic strip.

Even tired and beat, Barrett looked gorgeous. She was blessed with the physical attributes that all little rich girls seem blessed with, either by genes or by money—creamy complexion, good white teeth, lustrous brown hair that looked and smelled clean even when it was pulled back and dirty. Which it was that morning. The clothes, of course, were impeccable *and* expensive. Barrett was dress-for-success all the way: apricot suit, crisp white blouse, little paisley tie. It was the same outfit she had worn the day before, a little rumpled by its emergency service that morning, but so well tailored she looked fantastic anyway.

"I was just—" She stopped for a minor coughing fit.

"You feeling okay?"

"Just a little run-down, I guess."

He wagged his finger in parody of his own motherly

concern. "You leave here after home edition, young lady, and go straight to bed."

"Is that an offer?" she smiled.

"Only if you don't fall asleep on top of me."

Not much chance of that. Barrett was an agile, enthusiastic lover. Yet Decker couldn't help feeling a lot of her energy in that direction was pure ego. It was another way Elizabeth Barrett Simmons could show her power in a world dominated by men. Maybe because of that—or maybe because Decker and she were so much alike, both so keyed into their careers—that they never connected, never really got beyond the motions. Although the motions were fun enough, indeed. It brought them together several times a week, usually on weekends, because neither could sleep very well—really sleep, that is—with another person in the bed. Where, or with whom, Barrett spent her other nights, Decker didn't know.

She went on. "So far, we have a confirmed body count— eleven all told—and a lone survivor, a middle-aged black woman by the name of Maisie Williams."

"Bozo said it was Maisie Washington."

"Nope, Williams. Consider the source."

"Did Orsini say which hospital they took her to?"

"She's in critical condition at General. Second- and third-degree burns over fifty percent of her body."

He looked at his watch. It was 9:15. "Dammit, Higgins was supposed to call me back. Hold a second, Barrett." He dialed the PR number at General. A secretary answered: Mr. Higgins wasn't in his office at the moment, but he would be happy to return the call.

"Sure, next year," Decker said. "Please remind Mr. Higgins my deadline is eleven-thirty."

"All right," he said to Barrett. "What else?"

"Still no IDs on the bodies, obviously, since they were 'burned beyond recognition.'" Barrett threw her head back and laughed—throaty and robust, like a true Camel smoker. He wanted her when she laughed like that.

"Don't you just love it?" she said. "'Burned beyond recognition.' Firemen are so quaint, really. Bozo, of course, will insist we use the same phrase; it sounds so much more official than 'charred' or 'burnt to a crisp.'"

"What about a cause? Any ideas yet?"

"They said that could take days. But they do know what happened after the fire broke out, more or less, and why there was only one survivor."

Barrett took a long drag on her cigarette, tilted her profile toward the ceiling, and, puckering as though she were kissing an imaginary lover, blew a thin stream of smoke that soon vanished in the circling winds.

Barrett could have been a fashion model—the type that make the cover of *Cosmo* with their boobs hanging out of slinky dresses, hair fluffed out like Medusa, makeup so thick there's no telling what's underneath. Or if she had stayed in Baltimore where she grew up, she might have been the deb who broke the heart of every blueblood bachelor in town. But she had too many smarts, craved too much excitement to be anybody's piece of meat. She made her way to the *Eagle* with no journalism background at all, straight out of Swarthmore's history department. Already, with less than a year's experience, she had proven herself more aggressive, more tenacious than most of the older "pros" at the *Eagle*, including Decker.

Barrett fired off the rest of what she knew in rapid detail, as though she were already writing her story. First the layout of the *River Queen*: Al's penthouse comprised the entire fourth floor of the boat. There were two exits, fore and aft. The fore exit led into the wheelhouse, the aft through double doors to the rear staircase. The kitchen, on the ground floor, opened on to the same staircase at the rear of the boat.

Five of the eleven bodies had been found in an area of

rubble corresponding to the rear penthouse exit. Five others were found scattered near penthouse windows, mostly in the rear. The windows were probably painted shut.

The theory was this: the fire had started in the kitchen, shot up the back stairwell like a chimney and flooded the penthouse with smoke.

Decker interrupted with an obvious question: "So why did everyone run to the rear exit, and not the front?"

"Aha," Barrett said, pointing her cigarette at Decker, "the same question investigators are trying to answer at this very moment. One theory is that Little Al had the front exit locked or barricaded, perhaps to keep fun-loving guests from getting into the wheelhouse."

"Jesus Christ, what about the fire codes?"

Barrett laughed teasingly. "Always a stickler to the law, aren't you, Rickie? There just happens to be an 'historic vessels' clause in the Kentucky fire codes. It exempts anything built before 1925.

"Anyway," she continued, waving what was left of her cigarette, "it's easy to guess what happened. When the smoke poured in through the rear exit, everybody panicked and rushed to the front. But, as we must assume, the front exit was barred. More panic. Some people tried the windows. Others went racing back to the rear exit. The double doors were thrown open, the oxygen in the penthouse met the flames in the stairwell, and boom! Everybody was hit by a blast furnace. Orsini thinks most of the eleven dropped in their tracks."

"And the lone survivor? What was she doing?"

"Cooking downstairs in the kitchen. She was probably there when the fire started, and jumped ship."

"Cooking at three in the morning?"

"Apparently Little Al was entertaining a crowd that liked to eat late," Barrett said. A vixen smile tugged at the corners of her lips.

Orsini had told Barrett it would take at least another day or two to identify the bodies, and that was an optimistic assessment, based on the presumption that Little Al had invited a select group to the penthouse for an after-hours bash. Someone, somewhere ought to have a list of guests, and from there dental charts could be checked. Most of Little Al's invitees were said to be other gangland types and high rollers who frequented his gaming tables. But there were always fresh rumors that a certain respected businessman or some other pillar of the community had been seen slinking away from Little Al's in the early hours.

"Orsini told me something else the *Times* didn't have. One of the bodies was very small, either a child's or, more likely, a midget's."

Decker grinned. "Think the mayor will declare a day of official mourning? Maybe flags at half-staff."

Barrett laughed. "No, but I think Vic Carbone will be out celebrating somewhere."

"Yeah, just as soon as he can wash the gas off his hands."

Carbone sat at the very top of Newport's underworld of gambling, prostitution, and drugs. The big-money gambling market, on both sides of the river, had been all Vic's—until Little Al horned in a year ago with the *River Queen*. If the riverboat had in fact been torched, Decker knew it was a tactic not beneath Victor Carbone. About five years before, when Vic was still consolidating his empire, two men very handy with .22 automatics burst into a full house at the Red Fox Lounge and blew away the proprietor—an ex-professional wrestler—along with his stripper wife. It was over in seconds. The patrons thought the pistols were toys. One witness said they sounded like pop guns.

The whole world knew it was Vic's doing, but there was no one who was willing, or able, to pin the deed on his head. Least of all the Newport police. By the time a squad car arrived on the scene that night, the two gunmen had a good twenty-minute jump on the trip back to Detroit.

"You know who else must be celebrating?" Barrett said. She smiled, knowing her next remark would get a rise out of Decker. "Your hero Fritz."

"Dammit, the man is not my hero."

For the last two weeks, Decker had endured a steady stream of abuse for his front-page profile on Karl "Fritz" Krieger, the Hamilton County Prosecutor. Krieger was a law-and-order man, a tireless antiporn crusader who had taken Greenburg to court time and again—and lost. To the county's thou-shalt-not voters, Krieger was a saint worthy of landslide reelection. To the *Eagle's* enclave of liberal reporters, he was an out-and-out menace to the Bill of Rights.

In July, when Krieger was tapped to head a presidential commission to investigate the social effects of pornography, Decker had been assigned the profile. He had labored mightily to find the middle ground between the two opposing viewpoints on the man—Populist Hero versus Fascist Demagogue. But falling short of the expected liberal hatchet job, it was quickly labeled puffery by his colleagues. Including Barrett.

"Face it, Rick," she said, "the man is your father figure. The daddykins you never had. And don't be ashamed. We all need a father figure."

"Geez, you must read *Psychology Today.*"

He was glad when his phone rang. It was Higgins at General.

"Christ, Rollie, I thought you died. What goes with the Williams woman?"

Barrett winked and took off. Decker's eyes trailed her as she stepped toward her desk in the corner. A confident stride, with a hint of jiggly softness. Like a promise. Yep, they would have to get together again real soon.

Higgins confirmed that a Maisie Williams was indeed

under treatment at the hospital for burns. "But I'm afraid you can't speak with her, Rick. She's quite indisposed. Besides, the police won't permit interviews with the woman until they've gathered their own statement. She's under strict security at the moment."

Higgins was sorry, sorry, sorry, but it was no go.

Decker went to Lafferty's desk, waited while he gave orders to two other reporters, then delivered the bad news. It touched off another fit of nostril flaring. "Decker, don't tell me what you *can't* do. Start showing me what you *can* do. I'm sure you'll think of something." He looked at his wristwatch. "Home edition is a good two hours away."

2

He walked briskly down the long, white-walled corridor of the UC medical sciences center, his almost brand-new RocSports squeaking on the polished floors. Past the gallery of dearly departed university honchos, grim faces fixed in glossy oil. Past the medical school library, the Dean's office, and the hallway lounge, where clusters of casually dressed med students sat joking and laughing, releasing some of the tension that went with being gods-in-training.

At the end of the hallway, he took an elevator downstairs to the basement, into the labyrinthine bowels of the medical complex. He followed a red line painted on the floor. Past boiler rooms, supply stations, a tangle of overhead pipes wrapped in oil cloth and asbestos. He ended at a second set of elevators, directly below the main lobby of Cincinnati General. Upstairs his photograph was taped to the hospital security desk, along with instructions to notify Higgins' office immediately if this man was seen unescorted on the premises.

Only Decker wouldn't be stopping in the lobby. He went straight to the seventh floor.

"ALL BURN UNIT VISITORS MUST REPORT TO THE HEAD NURSE," said a standing sign in front of the nurse's station. He paused just long enough to find a directional sign. The floors at General were H-shaped, with the nurse's station at the center of a short connecting hallway. He turned right and broke into his best doctor's strut—a cross between a swagger and an exhausted, don't-bother-me-now-can't-you-see-I'm-busy slouch. The strut, a bold tie, a few pens jammed into his shirt pocket usually took him anywhere in the hospital, no questions asked.

Down the first hallway, three different nurses, each young and willing, gave him warm little smiles. He nodded back haughtily, thinking what he would give for a blessed MD after his name.

A second right and he immediately saw the cop standing by the last door on the left. Room 706. Maisie Williams' room.

Taking a deep breath, he locked onto his target and broke into his swiftest and brashest strut, straight for the open door. It worked. The cop moved aside like a rolling boulder. Decker was about to breeze into the room when he turned and saw Higgins' pudgy frame bouncing down the hall.

"Mister Decker!" Higgins was nearly choking to keep his volume down. "*Just* a minute, please!"

The cop grabbed Decker by the elbow. "Not so fast there, buddy."

Higgins tugged at his vest and collected himself before drawing up to Decker. He was short and penguinlike in his dark suit and seething with proper indignation. "I told you no interviews. The patient is in no condition for your paparazzi stunts. Futhermore, this is the third time this year you've trepassed without hospital permission, and I'm seriously considering pressing charges. Now if you don't remove yourself from the premises immediately, I'll have you arrested."

The cop scowled and nodded as if to say, me too.

"Just doing my job, Rollie. No hard feelings, okay?" Decker grinned sheepishly as he backpedaled and turned.

Higgins pursued him down the hall. "On second thought, I'll have you escorted."

A middle-aged nurse with a face as dreary as an enema deposited Decker in the main lobby. She tipped off the security desk while Decker headed for a bank of phones by the hospital entrance. It was time to make the dreaded call to Lafferty.

"What have we got, Decker?"

"Nothing. That's why I'm calling. There's a cop stationed at Maisie Williams' door."

Lafferty wasn't impressed. "Don't you know any nurses in the Burn Unit?"

"One, I think."

"See if you can get her in there with your tape recorder. The Boss says no punting on this one. If we read it in the *Times* first, it's your head, Decker."

Decker muttered, "Yes, sir," and slammed the receiver.

From the same phone, he called up to the Burn Unit and asked for Mary Flynn. Like a lot of nurses at General, Mary hit the bars in Corryvile after a hard day on the floor, and that's where Decker had met her one Wednesday evening. Happy hour at the Silver Dollar Saloon. Drinks on him, laughs on her. They were friendly for a short time, and anyway, Mary was probably wild enough to be game for this sort of thing.

"I'm sorry," said the head nurse, "Ms. Flynn doesn't come on till next shift. Can I take a message?"

"I'll call back."

He hung up, stuffed some sugarless in his mouth, and tried to think what his next step would be. Anything but another call to Bozo. He decided to do his thinking on one of the lobby's cushy mauve sofas, and was headed there when he saw salvation in a white jacket walk through the double automatic doors. He swallowed his gum.

"Janet!"

She turned, puzzled a moment by the grinning stranger loping her way, then broke into a smile. She seemed genuinely surprised and pleased.

"Rickie Decker! Is that *really* you?"

They greeted each other with a long hug and little oohs and ahs, and afterward, he turned on the charm.

"You look fantastic," he said, stepping back and taking both her hands in his. "Just fantastic. How long has it been? Five years? Six?"

"Before I vanished into med school anyway," she smiled.

Menaced by the watchful eyes at the security desk, Decker took Janet by the arm and lightly turned her back toward the door. "Listen, Janet, could you walk with me a minute? I need to ask you something." He kept up a lively patter as they made their exit from the air-conditioned lobby into the wall of heat outside.

Kind, sweet, never unpleasant Janet Shoemaker grew up two blocks from Decker in the same Cincinnati neighborhood—a homey, blue-collar place called Cheviot, where everybody's grandparents spoke German and the yards sprouted statues of the Blessed Virgin Mary the way Florida lawns spawn herds of plastic flamingos. Janet's father had been the neighborhood doctor, and still was, as far as Decker knew, with his office in the first floor of the family's three-story brick.

His mind flashed back to when Janet was nine or ten and he was about twelve. He had just heaved an enormous water balloon, maybe half the size of a beach ball, over the Shoemakers' backyard hedge, never guessing, of course, that he would hit Janet square on the back of the head.

"Rickie!" she squealed the way all little girls squeal when they're more startled than hurt and flattered by the attention. Water poured down her pretty yellow sunsuit.

"If I catch pneumonia, Rickie Decker, you'll pay the doctor's bill!"

And now—irony of ironies—Janet Shoemaker *was* a doctor, or almost one anyway, and he needed her help in getting his ass out of a bind.

"How goes med school?" he asked when they reached the

sidewalk. Janet still looked like little Janet. Straight blond hair tied simply behind her head, a pair of big tortoiseshell glasses slipping down her nose (far more fashionable now than when she wore them as a little girl), a white cotton jacket that fell loosely over a pair of faded blue jeans. She had grown, of course, but the top of her head still reached just to his shoulders.

"Actually, Rick, I'm out of med school now. I'm a first-year resident."

"No kidding!" He laid it on thick, waiting for the right moment to pop the favor. "In what?"

"Family medicine."

"Great! That's just great, Janet. We sure need more family doctors. Too many specialists these days."

"You know, Rick, I just remembered. The last time I saw you was at your mother's funeral."

He remembered, too. Janet and her father together at the casket, arm-in-arm in silence, until Janet laid her head lightly against her father's shoulder and they moved on. It was the only time Decker could remember seeing Doc Shoemaker cry. Maybe because he blamed himself for not having found the breast cancer sooner, or for not sending her away to Sloan-Kettering or the Mayo Clinic or some other big center that would have been more aggressive in treating her advanced condition. But Decker had known it was hopeless. His mother had willed her death long before the diagnosis was known. He knew the exact day, in fact, when she had simply given up. July 8, 1969. The day his father had mailed a last paycheck from a post office in Lebanon, Ohio, and simply dropped from sight.

He changed the subject.

"Listen, Janet, I need your help on something really important." They continued slowly along the shadeless sidewalk that fronted the hospital as he outlined his predicament.

Janet listened with something more than polite interest. Her cornflower-blue eyes, alert and a bit amused by all this journalistic intrigue, widened behind her glasses. Decker looked at her, really, for the first time since they met, and was struck by the freshness of her beauty. She seemed more like a Californian than an Ohio native: a healthy, radiant blonde untouched by makeup or artifice. He wondered in the back of his mind why he'd never asked Janet out when they were both in high school. Then he remembered: his mother was always telling him he should.

"It will be a cinch," he told her. "There's only three or four questions you'll need to ask." He started jotting them in his notebook.

"I don't know, Rick. If she's been badly burned, she could be on a respirator. Or in shock. Or under so much sedation . . ."

"Just give it a try, will you, Janet? *Please.*" And playing on their shared childhood memories, added, "With sugar on it?"

It worked. She laughed away any doubts. "All right. On one condition."

"Anything."

"That we get together sometime. I'd like to know what you've been doing all these years."

"You got a deal, kid." And he pushed his minicassette and notebook into her hands. "I'll meet you out here."

She smiled a last time as she turned and marched off in her loose white jacket. Meanwhile, Decker headed for the parking garage across the street. The entrance was glassed-in and mercifully air-conditioned. He found a low wooden bench just inside the door, sat down to a view of the hospital entrance, and did what all reporters hate to be doing two hours before deadline—he waited.

He looked at his watch. It was already 9:50. He did some quick mental arithmetic. Janet would need at least thirty minutes. Add another ten to fifteen minutes for the drive back to the office, minimum, and barring a traffic backup downtown. At most, that left barely an hour to make his calls and bang in the story before the 11:30 deadline. If the Williams women knew anything at all about how the fire had started, he would have to phone the fire department for comment. If not, he would still have to reach the woman's family to nail down details about her job and her background.

He popped some fresh gum into his mouth and started chewing furiously. There was never enough time in this business to do things right. Not on an afternoon paper. He thought about the *Times* reporters and the luxury of their ten P.M. deadline. It was almost too good to imagine. He could make phone calls all afternoon, maybe even go out and visit the Williams family, and still have three or four hours in the evening to make his prose sing before Lafferty came barking at his desk.

A band tightened around his head. Demon stress—the modern condition. The stress-reduction seminars at the Y had made it sound so easy. Get your mind off your work, be aware of your surroundings. Be glad the sun is shining and the birdies are singing. He gave it a try. There were birdies, all right. A couple of fat oily pigeons plucking around at butts and wrappers in the gutter. And yes, the August sun was shining. Blazing through the hydrocarbon haze. And if somebody didn't fix the goddamn air conditioning at the *Eagle*, the whole staff would probably suffocate by noon.

Janet was back in under fifteen minutes. A bad sign. He met her at the corner. "Did she talk?"

"A little," Janet said, handing him the recorder. She was wearing a grim little smile and looking down at the sidewalk.

"Let's duck inside," he said, and she followed him into the parking garage where it was cool. There were nurses and maybe even administrative types getting on and off the elevators. It was no good for talking. So they took the elevator to the second floor and walked back toward his car.

"I asked her only one or two questions," Janet said, almost apologizing. They were standing behind his frumpy but faithful '73 Dart. "She wasn't on a respirator. But she was heavily sedated and very much out of it. It was pathetic. She stared at the ceiling the whole time I was in the room."

He played the recorder.

Janet's voice came through soft and clear, like a patient mother trying to make her child understand: "Hello, Ms. Williams. My name is Janet Shoemaker. I'm a doctor here at Cincinnati General. I know you're not feeling well right now, but may I ask you a question or two for the newspapers?"

The woman's speech was slow and slurred: "Yes, sir."

"Tell me, Ms. Williams, did you see how the fire started?"

"A man . . ." The woman gulped heavily and stopped for breath. "A man . . . You there!" Her voice rose to a hoarse shout. "Get out of my kitchen! . . . Get out!" Just as suddenly, she was mute. He could hear the sound of her breathing, quick, excited. Then, between gulps for air, she began to whisper. "Red . . . red neck . . . red hands . . . Go on, I say . . ." And shouting again, "Get out! . . . Get out!"

At that point, Janet's voice softly interrupted, "I'm sorry, Ms. Williams—"

But the woman began shouting in a deep voice, as though imitating a man. "Jump! . . . You there, jump! . . . Jump, you crazy bitch!" She coughed and swallowed, then drawing a heavy, wheezy breath, she ran off a string of frantic words, "Oh-my-God, oh-my-God-Lord-Jesus-Mercy! Fire! Fire!—"

And the tape died.

"What the hell!" He slapped the recorder against his palm.

"It's not the tape," Janet said. She was no longer apologetic.

"Rick, I couldn't do it anymore. I just couldn't. She was becoming much too agitated." She looked him straight in the eye, her mouth set hard.

"I see," he said, managing a smile. He rewound the cassette. It didn't take long. "Well, I guess you did the right thing. From a doctor's perspective."

"No," Janet said, adjusting the frames on her nose. She suddenly looked very clinical. "From a human perspective."

His face and ears were burning. He was half-angry at being lectured, half-embarrassed at seeming insensitive. "Maybe so," he said. He suppressed the urge to add, "as if doctors should brag in that department."

He thanked her halfheartedly. "We might be able to use this anyway. I'll have to see."

"Call me," she said, starting to brighten a little again. She watched him as he opened the door to his car and slid inside. He started the engine. The slant six still hummed a good tune, better than some cars half its age.

Janet appeared at his window as he backed out of the space.

"Don't forget dinner sometime. You can always reach me through the switchboard. They can page me."

"I won't forget," he said, and looked at his watch. If he made the office in fifteen minutes, he might have an hour to write the story. Some kind of story, anyway.

Lafferty was in the Bozo Box talking to Turk Nystrom, seated in a folding chair in front of Lafferty's desk. Decker stuck his head in the opened door.

"Well?" Lafferty said.

"I've got the Williams woman on tape—sort of."

"Sort of?"

"It's hard to explain. Let me play it."

Turk stood to leave when Lafferty stopped him. "You should hear this, too, Nystrom. You may need it for the main story."

Lafferty moved his desk fan to the floor and Decker set the recorder down and hit the play button.

Lafferty leaned in close. Turk sat back, staring into the gray wall behind Lafferty's head and stroking his Fu Manchu between thumb and forefinger.

Nervous habits were badges of the profession, like his own gum chewing. But Decker found it hard to tolerate Turk's endless stroking. Sometimes he wanted to slap his hand away and scream like a schoolteacher: "Get your fingers away, young man, or your face will break out."

Turk was safely beyond the acne stage, however. He was pushing forty, or looked that way at least, despite all efforts to cling to a hippie past. The high forehead was hidden underneath a wild sweep of greasy blond hair, parted on the left and tucked behind his right ear. He was tall and broad-shouldered but going soft and wide around the middle.

A true child of the Sixties, Turk had a flair for the outrageous, from the offhand remarks he made to the clothes he wore. That morning, he was wearing a pale blue guyabara over a pair of cinch-tied white pants, as though he had just stepped off a plane from Miami. On special occasions, like Veterans Day, he came dressed for work in Army fatigues— faded remnants of his Vietnam days, 101st Airborne. He also kept a toy M-16 in his desk, which he would pick up from time to time, shout, "Look! Gook babies!" and then spray the newsroom with imaginary bullets. The fear, of course, was that Turk would appear one morning with the real thing.

When the tape finished, Turk was still stroking.

"Is that it?" Lafferty wailed.

"'Fraid so," Decker said, rewinding the tape. "My doctor-friend said it was too much of a strain on the patient."

"So, what's the story?" Lafferty asked. "Was this Williams woman hallucinating or what?"

Decker shrugged. "I was told she was heavily sedated."

Lafferty shook his head, rocked back in his dilapidated typing chair. "I can't make head or tails of it. I don't see how it's anything we can use. Even for color."

Turk was mute, inscrutable. An albino Charlie Chan in a folding chair, stroking and stroking. So Decker ventured an opinion.

"It sounds to me like there was another person in the kitchen." He hit the play button again. "Listen."

"A *man* . . ." He stopped the tape.

"Those are her first words, right?" Decker said. "Then she starts shouting at him, like she can see the whole thing again in her mind."

"A *man . . . You there! . . . Get out of my kitchen! . . . Get out!*"

Decker hit the stop button. That's when Turk jolted forward in his chair, moved by sudden insight. "Yes, yes, you're right! I can see it. Play a little more."

The voice started softly this time and rose to a shout. "*Red . . . red neck . . . red hands . . . Go on, I say . . . Get out!*"

"Stop it there," Turk said.

"Red neck?" Lafferty said. "Was she calling him a hillbilly?"

"No. Absolutely not," Turk said. "A black woman, if she were mad enough, would call a white man a honky or white trash. Not a red neck. 'Red-neck' is what red-necks call each other."

Turk pointed to the recorder. "Play that part over."

Decker rewound the tape and pressed the play button. His eyes narrowed with resentment at having to play secretary to Nystrom.

"Now listen," Turk said. "She doesn't say just 'red neck,' she says 'red hands,' too." He rocked back in his chair. "You know what I think? I think our woman, Maisie Williams, caught an arsonist in the act."

Lafferty's jaw dropped. Decker asked for an explanation.

"It's obvious. She sees a strange man in her kitchen, tells him to get out. The man has a red neck and red hands. Let's assume that the red is actually scar tissue, say from a bungled torch job sometime in his past. All right, now play the rest of the tape."

It picked up where Maisie's voice deepened, as though imitating a shouting man: "*Jump! . . . You there, jump! . . . Jump you crazy bitch!*" And then the final burst of words, in her own frantic voice: "*Oh-my-God, oh-my-God-Lord-Jesus-Mercy. Fire! Fire!*"

Turk crossed his legs and began twisting a corner of his ragged mustache. "This is what I see happening," he said. "The arsonist has just finished sloshing gasoline around the kitchen. He's about to drop a match or a flare, or whatever arsonists use, when Maisie comes down the stairs from the penthouse. She finds him in the kitchen, in *her* territory—see what I'm saying?—and tells the man to get the hell out. The arsonist yells back at her to jump ship just before the fire catches and all hell breaks loose."

"A mighty compassionate arsonist," Decker said. "Why in the world would he save a witness?"

Turk shrugged and went back to his stroking.

"Well," Lafferty said, snatching up the recorder and bouncing out of his chair. "We'll have to see what the Boss says about this." He scooted out the door, looking like the messenger boy he really was.

Decker stood to leave, too. He wasn't comfortable in the same closed space with Nystrom, not since Turk took a roundhouse swing at him in a barroom. The score had never been settled.

"By the way," Turk said as Decker reached the door, "not a bad bit of reporting. How did you talk an 'M. Deity' into the interview?"

"An old friend of the family," Decker said, and added for his escape, "I better start making calls."

"Don't worry," Turk said. "There won't be a story. Finch is a damn sight too cautious to use that tape. He'll wait to hear what Orsini says first."

"You think so?"

"I know so."

"You always do," Decker said, and started to walk away.

"Wait a minute, man. Wait a minute . . ." Turk jumped from his chair. Decker stopped and turned, a mix of impatience and defiance in his face. Decker was all of six feet, but Nystrom was almost half a head taller and a good deal heavier. Both reasons why Decker didn't like his back turned to Nystrom.

"What the hell," Turk said, holding out the flats of his palms in a gesture of peace. "Let's grab a drink after work. How 'bout it? For old times' sake."

"Can't make it," Decker said.

"You name the night then."

He caved in to persistence. "All right then. Tomorrow night."

Turk had been right about Finch's instincts. In a few minutes, Lafferty came to Decker's desk and said the Boss wanted to hold back on the tape. Finch didn't think the Willams woman had said anything the paper could quote intelligently.

Decker almost blurted, "Since when has that stopped the *Eagle*?"

Lafferty assigned Decker one last duty before deadline. "Petkamp has been trying to reach the Williams family all morning. I told him to phone in his notes around ten-thirty. You take the call, feed whatever you've got to Turk."

At 10:35, Bart Petkamp, the *Eagle*'s police reporter, was on the line, calling from his cubbyhole office in the Safety Building, where he spent most of his day spreading ass in a padded chair and stuffing his face with cafeteria goodies.

"Hey, Rickie baby . . ." he said, sounding like Yogi Bear. Decker knew a totally tasteless joke was on its way. "Say, how can you tell when your girlfriend is getting too fat?"

"Let me guess," Decker said. "The answer has something to do with oral sex and not being able to hear your stereo."

"Who told you?" Petkamp was genuinely hurt. He lived to tell a good tasteless joke.

"You did, Bart. Last week. So what have you got?"

Petkamp was a lazy slug, a minor disgrace to the profession, but he was also a superb inside man. He had more good police and fire sources—high and low—than any other reporter in town. Maybe it was the jokes. On the other hand, Bart couldn't write a coherent news story if his life depended on it. Rather than deal with Bart's slapdash prose, the editors told him to phone his notes from the Safety Building. Some other luckless reporter would have to make sense of it all and write the story—with Bart's byline on top, of course.

He could hear Petkamp flipping through his notes. "Well, I haven't got much. And what I did get meant walking into the ghetto in this damned heat. I'm still sweating, for Christ's sake."

"Poor baby. Try sitting over here. We haven't had air conditioning since last night. My ass is melting into this chair."

Maisie Williams, it turned out, was a maiden lady who had lived alone in one of the publicly rehabbed walk-ups along Race Street in Over-the Rhine, one of the poorest sections of town. It was a mixture of poor blacks, poor Appalachians, and a smattering of pioneering Yuppies, stretching across the northern fringe of downtown.

Petkamp couldn't locate any family, but he checked with neighbors and found an old widow lady two doors down, an Amanda Griffith, who occasionally had afternoon coffee with Maisie and went to the same church on Liberty Street. Tabernacle of the Living God of the Most Apostolic Faith.

"The old woman said Maisie hardly ever talked about her job with anybody. Here's a quote: 'Miz Williams was a little ashamed, I do believe, working at a place with such goings-on, if you know what I mean. But I never did blame her. No, sir. Not one little bit. Jobs is hard to come by these days. You take what you gets, and let the devil take the hindmost.'"

"Good quote, Bart. Did you make it up?"

"Shut up and let me finish, okay? Like a lot of old people, this Amanda Griffith keeps tabs on her neighbors. She spends a lot of time in her rocker at the front window, looking out on Race Street. She said she sometimes saw Maisie return from work as late as four or five in the morning."

"So it wasn't unusual for Maisie to be cooking up a storm on the River Queen at three A.M.?"

"Not according to Amanda."

"Did Amanda have any idea how much Maisie was paid?"

"Paid? I don't know. Probably minimum wage. What the hell has that got to do with anything, Decker?"

"A woman burns half her body in the line of duty, you like to know how much money she was making."

"Good. Then you walk your ass up Race Street and ask the old lady."

"Okay, Bart, what else you got?"

"Not much. Except the Griffith woman is seventy-eight. Said she'd known Maisie since she moved into the apartment next to hers about five years ago. She didn't know where Maisie's family was from. Somewhere in Alabama, she thought. That was something else Maisie didn't talk about."

"Great stuff, Bart. Would you care to write the story?" Decker actually like Petkamp. But he liked needling him even better.

"No, I'll leave that to you, Decker. Wouldn't want to deprive our readers of your deathless prose."

He hung up and started working Petkamp's notes into usable form for the main story. From the corner of his eye, he saw Barrett on her way to the city desk. Ah yes, the purposeful career-woman stride, and the promising jiggle.

Barrett stopped and leaned over the top of his terminal. "And what might you be smiling at, Mr. Smartass?"

"M-e-m-o-r-i-e-s," he crooned, "light the corners of my mind . . ."

"You sound in need of servicing, Mr. Decker."

"Am I that obvious?"

"Does a moose have horns?" She broke into her best Doris Day imitation, smiling real sweet and scrunching her nose. "How about tomorrow night?"

"You've got my key."

Barret came around and leaned in over his shoulder. Her hair tickled his ear. "You heard anything from Chicago?" she said.

Chicago is where he had interviewed a few weeks before, about a reporting job with the *Tribune*. A half-dozen *Trib* editors had taken the time to talk with him, but he knew it didn't mean a thing unless the paper hired you on the spot. The *Trib* hadn't.

"No," he told her, "not yet."

She made a sad little face, then said reassuringly, "Don't worry. They will." She patted him on the shoulder and bounced away to the city desk.

It was the third or fourth time Barrett had asked about Chicago in the last week. He wondered if she really wanted him to get the job, or if she was trying to hide the opposite. Maybe they should talk about it. Sometime.

His phone rang. Higgins calling from General again, with the phony Brit accent.

"I thought you might like to update your story, old boy."

Decker grabbed a notebook and pen. "Shoot."

"Maisie Williams died here at 11:05 this morning."

3

He was out of bed early enough the next morning to catch breakfast at McDonald's. Huddled inside a bright yellow booth, he could have been in any of the four cities where he had worked the past eight years—Richmond, Wilmington, New Haven, St. Petersburg—any city at all, for that matter, scarfing down a Big Breakfast of scrambled eggs, buttered English muffin, hash browns (a greasy slab of compressed potato shavings, deep-fried, elliptically shaped), and a large coffee, heavy on the cream. While his mouth worked on the food, his mind worked on the *Times' River Queen* story. It was an eye-opener.

Seven of the eleven bodies had been identified by the previous night, in time, naturally, for the *Times'* ten o'clock deadline. One of them, as Barrett had guessed, was Little Al Greenburg, age fifty-four and now forever ageless in the annals of Cincinnati history.

But that was hardly the biggest news. Five of the bodies, it turned out, were star players on the University of Cincinnati football team, including all-American tailback Ronnie Shakes.

Five others were women, one of whom was a waitress employed by Little Al, a Sarah Lee Watson. The identities of the four others were not yet confirmed, Orsini told the *Times*. Department personnel, he said, had encountered "extreme difficulties" in locating dental records for the four women. Why? (He couldn't help grinning as he read Orsini's carefully worded quote.) "Because of the apparent transient nature of their lives." That was as far as the good gray *Times* would go toward stating outright that the four were prostitutes. Clarification, of course, would be undertaken by the *Eagle*. A nasty little job, but someone had to do it. And the *Eagle* would do it with great relish.

The cause of the fire was still under investigation. Interestingly, even though the *River Queen* lies in Newport, Kentucky's jurisdiction, city officials there had ceded the investigation to Orsini and the Cincinnati Fire Department—in part because Cincinnati firefighters had been the first and foremost to respond to the blaze. Orsini told the *Times* that neither arson nor accident had been ruled out. He was expected to make an announcement along those lines sometime that day.

Decker gulped the last of his coffee and left without finishing his slab of hash browns. He was impatient to hear what Barrett would say about the day's developments. But when he got to the *Eagle*, she was already on assignment. The newsroom was buzzing for the second day in a row. Tempers, however, seemed cooler, the shouting less audible, thanks to the return of air-conditioned comfort. A couple of workmen on stepladders were finishing up repairs in the middle of the newsroom, stuffing hoses and wires back into the ceiling like so many distended entrails.

Before Decker could hang his sportcoat on the back of his chair, Bozo collared him. "I need you to talk to the parents of Steven Mussman, one of the boys killed in the *River Queen* fire." Lafferty consulted his notepad full of orders from Finch. "Find out what the boy was doing there . . ."

"Having a good time, I suppose."

". . . and get the family's reaction."

"I bet I can guess."

Too preoccupied for the usual repartee, Lafferty ripped a page out of his notepad and shoved it at Decker. It was scrawled with an address in Norwood.

"And don't forget to ask for a recent photo," Lafferty said, and whizzed away to launch another reporter into battle.

In eight years of reporting, he had done at least a dozen knock-and-shock interviews, and the job never got any easier or any less repugnant. Over the years, however, he *had* learned a few tricks. One, always arrive unannounced. After all, if allowed time to think about an upcoming interview, the family might begin to ask, and rightly so, whose goddamned business is it anyway? Two, prepare yourself for whoever answers the door. With hands clasped politely at your waist, first offer your condolences "in this time of tragedy." Then in the same sympathetic tone, reveal yourself as a reporter. Before the victim is struck by the audacity of it all, ask if the family could answer a few *very important* questions about the horrible loss so recently visited upon them.

Nine times out of ten, if the right person answered the door (mothers and wives were always more susceptible than fathers and husbands), you would be invited inside, offered a cup of coffee or a glass of juice, and the family member would sit down with a sigh and pour out his or her soul, never thinking what it would look like in print the following day.

Norwood, the area where the Mussmans lived, was a uniformly blue-collar, lily-white 'burb. Perhaps because the town had resisted decades of annexation attempts by the city, its residents were the butt of local jokes usually reserved for maligned ethnic groups. Norwood was to Cincinnati what north Jersey was to Manhattan.

He found the Mussmans' place on Axton Street, a big white frame with a pink door, pink porch railing, pink-and-white striped metal awnings above the windows. He pushed the lighted doorbell button and a middle-aged woman in a baby-blue bathrobe came to the door. So did a German shepherd. The dog was barking with such down-in-the-canine-gut hatred that saliva sprayed across the Mussman's white shag carpet.

"Whaddayawant?"

The woman's eyes were red-rimmed, the hair bleached to a shade that nearly matched her ghost-white face. She stood at the opened screendoor and held out a varicosed leg—grudgingly—to block the shepherd from charging Decker's crotch.

He couldn't locate his funeral-parlor sincerity. Or his opening lines.

"Yes, my name is, uh, Rick Decker and I'd . . ."

"Hold on." The screendoor slapped shut, the inside door slammed. He could hear the woman shouting somewhere inside the house, her voice on the verge of tears. "Arnold! A-a-a-a-r-n-o-o-l-d! Come here and see what this man wants!"

A minute later, Arnold, minus the pooch—whose bloodlusting cries Decker could hear in the backyard—was at the door, filling the open frame with his bulk. He was a man of few words.

"So?"

Arnold might have been a big-time wrestler, Handsome Johnny division. The muscles bulged, the gut sagged, the hair was bleached colorless and slicked back à la Elvis. He was wearing white pants—beltless polyesters—and a black T-shirt with the sleeves rolled above his rock-solid biceps, one of which was tattooed, Decker believed, with a portrait of Our Lady of Guadalupe.

"I'm sorry to visit you in this time of tragedy . . ."

"Yeah, I know. Whaddayawant?"

"Well, my name is Rick Decker, and I'm with the *Cincinnati Eagle* . . ."

"You one of them reporters?"

"Yes, sir, and . . ."

"Get the hell outta here."

"But I had just a few very important questions, sir."

"Screw your questions. Get outta here. Can't you see we're grievin'."

Arnold didn't slam the door. He didn't need to. He closed it slowly, watching to make sure Decker took leave of the premises.

He did. He walked back to his car, ready to kick himself. For the second day in a row, he was returning empty-handed to the newsroom. Lafferty would be all over his case, of course, but it was his reporter's pride—and the opinion of his colleagues—that mattered most. On a big story like the *River Queen*, he itched to land the day's scoop.

In the street behind Decker's car, a teenager was working under the hood of a new Firebird, revving the overpowered engine and fiddling with the carburetor. He was blond, lean, stripped to the waist. Sweat trickled down his back and soaked into the Jockey band above his jeans.

"Excuse me—" Decker said. The boy tugged on the choke. The engine gurgled and roared like a flushing toilet, sending lots of premium unleaded down the drain.

Decker moved in close, caught a whiff of the gas fumes and summer sweat, and retreated a step. "Excuse me," he repeated, louder this time. "Did you happen to know Steve Mussman?"

The boy pulled his head out of the engine, stared at Decker quizzically. He had smudges of motor oil on his chin and nose. "Wait a sec," he said. He hopped into the front of the Firebird and turned the ignition key. The toilet stopped.

"I'm looking for people who might have known Steve Mussman."

"You've come to the right place, all right," the boy said, a little angrily. He had wide-set gray eyes—open and honest—and a thick neck like a football player's. "Steve's my older brother," he said.

Decker grinned, reached for his notebook.

"You a reporter?" the boy asked, stepping out of the car seat, a red greasecloth in his hands.

"Yeah. Rick Decker. *Cincinnati Eagle.*" He put out his hand. The boy just looked at it, wiping his hands. Decker tried a more sympathetic tack. "I'm sorry about your brother."

"I hope you go after that goddamned Greenburg," the kid blurted out.

"Greenburg's dead."

"Good. That's just what he deserved."

"Would you like to talk about it?" Decker sounded like a therapist. "I mean, how your brother came to be on the *River Queen* that night."

"Sure," the boy said. "I want everybody in town to know what a sleazebag Greenburg was." He stuffed the red greasecloth into his back pocket.

"My brother was a good guy. A straight shooter all the way. He didn't want nothin' to do with Greenburg's party, but he knew the other guys on the team would razz the hell out of him if he didn't go."

"What kind of party?"

"The big party Greenburg throws every year for the best guys on the team. The players vote on it, see, and if you get elected, you're one of 'Al's Aces.' It's a big honor. Except the only people who know about it are the guys on the team, and maybe a few coaches."

"And your brother was one of Al's Aces?"

"Hell yes. He was the best linebacker on the team. Don't you read the sports page?"

Decker smiled and shrugged. He wasn't much of a college football fan. That's what happened when you went to Columbia.

"And what usually took place at these parties?"

"Steve talked to me about it before he went. He was

| 42 |

scared shitless Mom and the Old Man would find out about it. So we made up this story about him going to Michigan on a fishing trip with the guys. Steve never lived in the athletic dorm, see. He lived right here at home, in his own room."

"And he knew what would happen at the party?"

"He wasn't exactly sure. He knew there would be a lot of women there. Some pretty wild women. He told me some of the guys who'd gone last year told him there was a strip show, and a lot of drinking. And there was supposed to be some private rooms where, you know, you could take one of the women. Steve told me he didn't want any part of that because he was afraid of picking up a disease."

"And drugs? Did Steve mention anything about drugs?"

"No, sir, he didn't. But I know he wouldn't have touched any even if they handed 'em to him. Steve wouldn't've broke training, not three weeks before the opener. Oh sure—he'd drink a few beers with the guys from time to time. But never more'n two or three."

He was about to ask the boy what time his brother had left for the party Sunday night, when his father came to the door.

"Terry!"

The boy rolled his eyes. "That's my old man screaming."

"Terry! Get the hell in here!"

"Yeah, Dad. There in a second!" And then to Decker: "I don't think the Old Man likes me talking to you."

"Listen, Terry, one last thing. Do you have a picture of your brother?"

"Yeah. Well, not right on me. But I keep one in the glove compartment. I show it to dates sometimes. To kind of impress 'em, you know."

"Do you mind if I borrow it for the paper? I'll mail it right back when we're finished."

"Sure." He slid across the front seat and got the big glossy out of the glove compartment. He sat on the edge of the seat and stared at it for a moment, then handed it over without looking up. Steve was in uniform, grinning through the blacklamp under his eyes.

Decker thanked the boy and shook his greasy palm. Then he hopped in his Dart and was about to pull away when Terry came up to the window.

"Listen, sir," he said. Decker thought he saw a tear or two in the boy's eyes. "I want you to write that Steve was a good guy. Okay? That he didn't want nothin' to do with this party or Greenburg or nothin' like that, but he had to because of the guys on the team. All right?"

"I'll do my best."

Barrett and Decker passed each other in the *Eagle's* revolving door. He pushed all the way around and joined her outside.

"Come on, Rick. I'm headed to the Cop Shop. Big doings."

She smiled and took him by the arm. In her dress heels, she stood an inch or so taller than Decker. He didn't mind. It made her a challenge, like Mt. Everest. He looked into the well-scrubbed face, unlined so far by time and nicotine and the demands of a cynical profession. He wanted to press the dimpled cheeks between his hands, kiss the smooth forehead, and tell her: "Get the hell out while you can." But he knew she wouldn't have listened. She was as ambitious as he was. Maybe more. Her dream was to work for the *Philadelphia Inquirer,* and she would probably make it long before he went to the *Tribune* or anywhere else.

"Sorry, I've got stuff to deliver to Lafferty."

"Your loss," Barrett said, and let go of his arm. "I'm getting a sneak preview of our mug shots of the *River Queen* ladies."

"Mug shots?"

"Yes indeed. Newport police sent them over to Cincinnati headquarters. Four of the five women on the boat were, in the words of Police Chief Logan, 'known prostitutes active in the Northern Kentucky community.'"

"And we're running their mug shots—next to the players'?"

"You got it, Rickie. And don't act so quaint. You know it takes two to tango in these things."

"So maybe it was a once-in-a-lifetime tango. We embarrass their families for that?"

"Oh, right. Next you'll be saying, 'Boys will be boys.' Right? Come on, let's hear the old double standard. *Boys will be boys.*" She gave him a playful jab in the ribs.

He broke into a smile. "Speaking of tangos, princess, what time tonight?" Before she could answer, he remembered his promise to Turk. "Shit. I told Nystrom I'd have a drink with him."

"No problem. I'll let myself in," she said, and in a breathy parody went on: "I shall be waiting, my dearest. It will be a test of my love."

He took her hand and kissed it. "Ah, yes, my sweet lover-until-career-paths-do-us-part."

"You're a maniac," she said, then reached around and patted him on the ass. "But a cute maniac." She patted him again. "Very cute."

"Oh, before I forget," she said, "there's something I need to talk to you about. A very strange thing one of the Newport cops mentioned on the phone."

"In Newport that could be almost anything."

"No, he said it was something on this side of the river. An underground cult that calls itself some weird name like the Pendulum or the Pentagram or something. He wouldn't discuss it over the phone. But he said we should check it out, see if it has anything to do with the *River Queen.*"

"A secret society? You mean like the Masons?"

"Don't make fun. He was serious. I'd like to meet with this guy, but I need your advice first."

"Sure you do, like Perlman needs violin lessons. All right," he waved, "catch you later."

Pressing through the revolving doors, he shook his head. If Barrett had any flaw as a reporter, it was a readiness to believe almost any crank, no matter how outlandish the claim. Like the teenage girl in Blue Ash who talked her into a story about bizarre psychic forces in the family's basement rec room. Barrett and the girl staked out the place one night, and Barrett swears she saw billiard balls migrate across the pool table. Not to be scooped, of course, the *Eagle* ran the story on page one.

In the lobby, he pulled the photo of Steve Mussman out of his notebook and studied it a second. The face was a craggier version of his younger brother's, with the same all-American good looks: deep-set eyes, sturdy chin, a smile that shouted "howdie" from the middle of an Ohio cornfield.

He weighed the brownie points of handing the photo to Lafferty against the hurt it would cause Terry Mussman. When he thought about it, there wasn't much of a debate.

He went through the lobby door marked "Dispatch" and asked one of the clerks there for a manila envelope. He slipped the big glossy inside, wrote the Mussmans' address on the outside, and dropped the envelope in the out-going box. He went back into the lobby and waited for an elevator. "Yes, Janet, from a human point of view," he said to himself, smiling.

"All right, Decker, so you didn't get to the parents." Decker smiled a little half-smile as Lafferty ripped into him. "And you didn't get a photo. Good work. So what the hell *have* you got?"

"Well," he said, flipping through his notes. "Mussman's younger brother told me about an annual shindig Greenburg throws for the UC football stars. Have we got anything on that?"

"Yeah, Al's Aces. Barrett got it all, and more, from Ronnie Shakes' parents." Lafferty waved him away. "Type your notes and feed them to Turk. We'll tuck it in the main story."

Decker knew what he would like to feed Turk, and it wasn't notes. There was no question that Nystrom was the best writer in the newsroom (some would say the best reporter, too) but Decker resented his prima donna status. Every few months or so, Turk would go on a drinking binge—disappearing for days, sometimes weeks at a time—and when he dried out and came back, the *Eagle* editors welcomed him home again with open arms. Turk Nystrom, Prodigal Son. A man of lesser talent would have been canned years ago.

He punched in his notes on the VDT, highlighting the quotes from Terry about his brother's reluctant membership in Al's Aces. It was the least he could do. When he finished, he dropped over to Turk's desk to ask what computer basket he should send his notes to. Nystrom was on the phone, scribbling on the back of a flattened White Castle bag. His desk was layered with bits and scraps of paper decorated with his indecipherable scrawl. Decker wondered how in God's name he kept track of anything.

Turk told him to send his stuff to the "metro-edit" basket, and then handed him a dusty piece of foolscap, obviously salvaged from the newsroom floor, with a footprint in the middle and a phone number written in the top righthand corner.

"Petkamp wants you to call. Says he'll be at that number for the next half hour."

"Must be the Safety Building cafeteria."

Turk laughed. "By the way, we still on for tonight?"

"Sure," Decker said, not very enthusiastically, then remembering Barrett, added, "I need to go back to my apartment first, though." He wanted to straighten a little for Barrett. At least put a roll of toilet paper on the spindle.

Turk said he'd pick him up about seven, and Decker said fine and went back to his desk and got Petkamp on the line.

"Heard the one about the whore and the French flying ace?"

"No, Bart. But let me guess the punchline: 'Madame, when Pierre goes down, Pierre goes down een flehms.'"

"Dammit, Decker, I'm cutting you off. No more jokes."

"That would be an act of mercy, Bart. Now what can I do you for?"

"No, no, no-o-o-o-o, Bobbalooie. Not for *moi* this time. No, this time I have something for *you*. Turk tells me you have a very interesting tape. Makes the *River Queen* sound like arson."

"That's Turk's interpretation. Finch won't use it."

"That may change. I have it from a very good insider here that Chief Orsini's initial report will be released in the PM."

"How nice. Just in time for the *Times* deadline."

"Lay off, Decker. I'm busting ass to break it loose. Anyway, I have a good idea of what it says already. My main man here tells me Orisini is blaming cheap aluminum wiring in the kitchen."

"No question of arson?"

"Not in the report. But that's the other thing I wanted to tell you. My man also says there's been some nasty in-fighting on this. One of the investigators, a tough lardass by the name of Milton Griswald, has some serious reservations about Orsini's report."

"What kind of reservations?"

"I don't know, because Griswald isn't talking."

"Not even off the record?"

"No on or off about it. Couldn't even get him on deep background. Bastard hung up in the middle of my first question."

"What do you want from me, Bart? I don't know a soul in the fire department except Orsini."

"Turk thinks you should play your tape for Griswald and see if you can open him up."

"Does he? Since when did Nystrom turn editor?"

"He's not an editor. But you know as well as I do, Decker, he has some damn good ideas."

"Yeah, if you run his wet brain through a ringer. So who is this Griswald character anyway? Does he have an ax to grind with Orsini?"

"Don't believe so. At least my man says not. But I've heard he isn't the easiest person in the department to work with. Not much of a sense of humor. Kind of a malcontent."

"You mean he doesn't laugh at your jokes, Bart?"

Bart laughed. "You'll pay for this some day, Decker."

"I'm sure I will," Decker said, "next time you have a big fat story to phone in." Bart laughed again, but not as loudly this time.

Decker asked for a description of Griswald.

"You can't miss him. He's huge. Like a grizzly bear with a beer gut. I'd say he's probably not past forty-five, or fifty anyway. But his hair has gone completely gray, almost white, I think, and he has a trimmed beard about the same color."

"What time does he usually leave for the day?"

"I guess the same as all of them. About five or five-fifteen."

At 4:50, he left the *Eagle* building without his jacket and started the four blocks uptown on Broadway to the Safety

Building. On the way he came across a small but spirited demonstration in front of the courthouse steps. They were Right to Lifers, with the usual placards, including a giant poster of a fetus in utero with the words: STOP THE MURDER NOW.

Right to Lifers could turn out a hundred demonstrators to picket a Cincinnati abortion clinic. But here there were only three older men, seven or eight younger women, most with toddlers who sat in shaded strollers looking confused and on the verge of tears. Their mothers were chanting: "Judge ———kills the innocent! Judge———kills the innocent! Judge———kills the innocent! . . ."

Decker missed the point, then remembered the recent court ruling, striking down a City Council ordinance that would have required the burial of fetuses. Judge So-and-So had ruled the measure unconstitutional. Council members talked tough about an appeal, but knew they couldn't win.

One of the demonstrators, an earnest young woman in a clean white pantsuit, her hair pulled back in a ponytail, stepped out of the ranks and handed him a leaflet. "God bless you," she said.

She looked like she should be home watching "The Price Is Right," but then he wondered seriously if she could have had anything to do with the clinic bombings. Who knew?

He glanced at the leaflet as he walked. Another fetus picture. A pink lizardlike thing with black eyes, a bulbous head, little hands and feet. They didn't photograph very well. But, then, neither did some people. He stuffed it in his pocket and walked on.

In the All Right parking lot across from the Safety Building, he stopped and waited by one of the honor system collection boxes. Not wanting to look like Joe Reporter, he stuffed his tape recorder and notebook into his back pockets.

He pulled his tie off, feeling cooler instantly, and stuffed that, too, in a pants pocket.

It was September first, but the dog days of summer showed no sign of breaking. The heat from the asphalt burned through his shoes, itched the balls of his feet. He noted all the signs of a classic thermal inversion. Rust-colored sky, scratchy throat, burning eyes. A few hours from now, the choked air would treat the city to a dazzling red ball of a sunset. Nature could be perverse.

5:04. Across the street, he scanned the faces and bodies of dozens of people as they filed out of the Safety Building. Young secretaries with long bouncy curls and tight skirts. Black cafeteria help and custodians with the tired look of another-day-gone-and-so-what. Beefy cops, firefighters gone gray and pot-gutted from boring desk jobs. But none was beefy or gray or pot-gutted enough to fit the description of Milton O. Griswald.

At 5:15, the parking lot was nearly empty of cars when what looked like a gorilla trapped inside a tan leisure suit left the Safety Building and crossed Central Parkway. He was carrying a luggage-sized briefcase and moving fast for a big man. He came into the lot and headed toward a red Mercury Marquis parked in a far corner. Decker rendezvoused at his door.

"Got a second, Lieutenant Griswald?"

Griswald worked a key into the Merc's door and, without turning to look, growled, "So what's your problem?"

"I'm with the *Eagle*, Lieutenant. I got your name from Bart Petkamp, our police reporter, and I was just wondering . . ."

"You were just wondering," Griswald laughed. When he turned and straightened, it was like standing in front of a stuffed polar bear at the Naval History Museum, with your eyes staring straight into the massive chest.

"Why is it," he said, "that you reporters are always wondering? It must be wonderful to be wondering all the time."

"I have something, sir—"

"Forget it, son. I told Bart this morning I'm not talking to nobody—and I mean nobody. No TV people, no newspaper people, no-o-o-body. So leave me the hell alone. I'm late for dinner."

Griswald tossed his briefcase in, piled inside, and slammed the door. He powered the window down and was positioning the tilt-wheel over his gut when Decker pulled out his microcassette and put his head in the window. "Listen, Lieutenant. I have two minutes of tape here you'll find very interesting. An interview with the last survivor from the *River Queen*, less than an hour before she died."

Griswald turned the ignition. The big engine hesitated a second, then roared. "Too late now," he said. "It's all in the chief's report. You'll get your copy in the morning."

"Hold on just a minute." Decker was shouting over the engine. "This lady died a slow and very painful death, and the least you can do is listen to what she had to say."

It worked. Griswald cut the engine.

"All right, all right, goddammit. Get the hell in and let's have a listen."

Griswald heard the tape without expression, hands clasped over his enormous belly, like a churchgoer about to nod off halfway through a sermon.

Afterward, he stared out the tinted windshield into the asphalt and heat, his underlip curling through the beard.

Decker primed him. "Does that sound like somebody's faulty aluminum wiring to you?"

He frowned, shrugged his shoulders, still looking through the windshield. He dropped his chin to his chest, and the fat bulged like the bellows on a bullfrog.

"I can keep your name out of it," Decker said.

The big man grunted. "It wouldn't make a damn bit of difference. They'd know where it came from."

"Why?"

He turned and looked at Decker for the first time. The gray eyes were very bright, very hard in the fat ruddy face. "Because the chief and I were the principal investigators."

"All right, talk to me on deep background only. Nothing you tell me is printed unless we confirm it somewhere else."

"No notes?"

"No notes." He sunk his pen into his shirt pocket, but held onto the notebook and, below it, the tape recorder. His finger was on the recording button. He suffered a twinge of ethical doubt, then hit the button.

"If one goddamned word of this is attributed to me, I'll deny everything." He stuck a finger two inches from Decker's nose. "And the *Eagle's* ass will be grass with the entire department. You hear me?"

"Loud and clear."

"Okay. I'll tell you everything I know right now. No questions. Just open your ears." He stared out the windshield again.

"There was no mistaking the burn pattern on the kitchen floor. It had to be gasoline or some other flammable liquid. If you'd ever seen what I'm talking about you'd know. Gasoline leaves a pattern on a wood floor that looks something like a lace curtain. The liquid seeps down through the cracks in the boards, collects there in little pools and keeps those parts of the board from burning. Most people don't realize it, but it's gasoline fumes that burn, not the liquid."

He looked at Decker again. "Well, the chief says I'm full of shit. He claims the burn pattern was probably from oil in the furnace tanks that exploded and oozed all over the floor. But, hell, those tanks were way toward the middle of the boat, and that wood floor would have burned a long time before those tanks blew. So I asked Orsini, could we run a lab test to see if it was gasoline or oil that soaked down into those boards? He says no need to, the tests were already in and they were negative all the way.

"I couldn't believe it. So I took my own piece of wood from the kitchen floor, near the back where the liquid would have pooled, and sent it off to the arson lab in Columbus. And you know what? They found enough gasoline in that wood to run a goddamned Buick."

He stared at Decker a moment, letting his words sink in. But Decker was frantic by then, thinking he might have pressed "play" instead of "record" on his microcassette. His head throbbed trying to remember the order of the buttons.

"Now do what you will with that, but don't you dare quote me," Griswald said. "Like I told you, I'll deny everything."

He turned the ignition key, and the surge from the big V-8 rocked the Mercury like a boat on choppy water. Decker pushed the door open and hopped onto the asphalt. He watched the Marquis lumber across the lot and turn right on Central Parkway, pulling away with a throaty roar.

When he lifted the notebook, he found his worst nightmare confirmed—the play button was down and the microcassette was reeling through blank tape, playing the sounds of silence. The sound, too, of his own stupidity.

4

Thanks to a last-minute assignment from Lafferty, Turk didn't pick up Decker until almost eight. They rode together in Nystrom's battered white Civic, vintage '74, when Hondas were still shaped like aphids and offered about as much room. Turk's arms and shoulders seemed to hang outside the car. His knees scraped the underside of the dashboard.

From Northside, they headed south on I-75, took the Vine St. exit, and turned right toward the Suspension Bridge to Covington. The car hummed onto the bridge's metal grating, and Turk cranked up the volume on his four-speaker Alpine system, drowning the insides of the tiny Honda with organ music. E. Power Biggs himself could have been in the backseat, fingers racing over keys, feet flying across footpedals.

"Bach!" Turk shouted over a bass note that rattled the car windows with its mighty undertone. He was heady, wound up. "Prelude and Fugue in A Minor," he shouted again. Decker caught the mood. It was good music for crossing the Ohio in early September twilight. A crimson sunset glinted off the river. A few stars pierced an indigo sky. And far off on the southern horizon, clouds began to gather, black-bottomed, brooding. Could God Himself be far off?

"Imagine," Turk said as the music took a subdued, melancholy turn. "You go back two hundred fifty years or so and you find Johann sitting in a dark corner in some chapel and he's writing music by candlelight, right? And you say, 'Johann baby, did you know that two hundred fifty years from now people are going to be driving around in little Japanese cars and blasting your music from cassette tapes no bigger than

your goddamn prayer missal—hell, smaller than a fuckin'
rosary case.' So you ask him, 'Johann, can you imagine? Can
you even conceive of it?' And what do you think the old man
would have said?"

He turned and grinned, waiting for an answer.

"You got me," Decker said finally, and Turk was silent
while the notes of the fugue began chasing one another round
and round like a whirlpool in the river below, descending
deeper and deeper into some unfathomable mystery. And just
when it seemed like the notes couldn't plunge any deeper and
you felt like you had to come up for air—Ba-a-a-r-u-u-u-m-
p!—the bass pedal rattled the windows again like a blast from a
barge horn.

"I know what the old geezer would have said." Turk
smiled, his greasy hair scattering in all directions from the
window breeze. "He would have said, 'Sure, I knew that. And
three hundred years from your time, they'll be playing my
music on teeny-tiny recorders you just plug in your ear and
throw away when the music's over. And, hell, a thousand
years from now, come Judgment Day, you'll hear my music
when Jesus Christ himself steps down from the clouds and
says, 'I want you and you and you, and to hell with you over
there, motherfucker.' You know what I'm saying?"

Decker smiled a little and looked out his window and
watched the clouds rolling in. A hell of a storm was on its way.

The fugue built to a finish with a flurry of keyboard notes
spilling and tripping one over the other. And underneath the
seeming confusion, like a deep and mighty current, the big
bass pedal pumped out the same dark note again and again,
until all of the notes—high, middle, low—were joined in one
majestic harmony, held together for a fragile moment, and
then sucked into the dark whirlpool where they disappeared
and drowned.

"Now think, Rickie," Turk said, flashing his Cheshire

grin—the all-knowing grin he always wore when he was wound up like that. "Think about what you and me do all day. How we bust ass to make a little sense of things, to get at something we call truth. And how long does the product last? Twelve hours, maybe a day. And then it's bingo!—out to the trash, or into the bottom of the old bird cage. Am I right? Tell me, Decker, am I right?"

Decker nodded, again and again, thinking, "Oh Lord, it's sure to be one of those nights with Turk."

Steamboat Willie's was the first of five boats in Newport's Riverboat Row, moored along the Ohio riverbank from the mouth of Licking up past the Big Mac Bridge. It was Decker's favorite because it hadn't succumbed to the yuppie demand for stained glass, hanging plants, and ceiling fans. It was a comfortable floating dive—the last place left on the river where you could sit outside and have a cheap drink and maybe a sandwich without making a dinner reservation.

They found an empty picnic table on the top deck of the riverboat, next to a railing that overlooked the water. A nice steady breeze moved upstream from the storm front, clearing the air and carrying off the day's heat. Decker thought he could smell the rain coming.

Overhead, cars moved along the Central Bridge, their tires making a sad kind of droning, like a symphony tuning up. Across the river they could see the winding contours of the Serpentine Wall, with the shell of the *River Queen* where the serpent's head would be, and the tail pointing downstream to the coliseum and the stadium and the densely clustered boxes of the Cincinnati skyline, now fading pink in the sunset.

Traffic on the river was light. A few houseboats on leisurely evening cruises. A hellion in a speedboat spraying past the Serpentine Wall, trying to impress the women who sat watching from the ledges. Upstream, beyond the yellow arches of the Big Mac Bridge, Decker spied a towboat downbound with fifteen open barges, three across, five deep, each piled high with coal.

Suddenly a Dixieland band somewhere down Riverboat Row struck up a fast rendition of "Sweet Georgia Brown," kicking off the night's entertainment.

"All right!" Turk joined in. "Blow dem crazy horns!"

The waiter came and they ordered a large mushroom pizza, extra cheese. Decker asked Turk if they should get a pitcher of beer to go with it.

"Go ahead," Turk said, "I'll have a Coke."

Decker's jaw was hanging when the waiter turned and left.

"Yeah, I'm on the wagon," Turk said. "Almost three weeks now." He broke into a wry smile, as though he found it hard to believe himself.

"Remember the last time we had a drink?" Turk said. "Do *you?*"

Turk's smile turned pensive. "Yeah, I guess I was pretty wasted at the time."

It was the summer before, the Friday night after Turk's divorce. He called Decker at home and said, "Let's get wasted." They crawled to three or four bars when Turk started on double martinis. That's when his gray eyes took on that look—like a bank of storm clouds building on the horizon—and Decker knew trouble was on the way. Nystrom, the somber Swede, was about to turn Viking throwback.

He started in by calling Decker a fucking wimp and a lazy-ass, silver-spoon-in-the-mouth Ivy League boy who never did a goddamn thing to help his country (meaning Decker hadn't made the trip to Vietnam like Turk). In rebuttal, Decker said he didn't give a goddamn how many rotting jungles and flooded rice paddies Turk had chased Charlie through, that didn't make Turk any better than him—just less fortunate, and maybe a whole lot dumber.

Turk let go a roundhouse at Decker's jaw. He missed by inches, thanks to the width of the tabletop. His rage still not satisfied, he flipped the table, drinks and all, onto Decker's lap. It took two bartenders and the manager to show Turk the door.

At Steamboat Willie's, the new Turk—Turk the Teetotaler—was wearing what he called his "summer uniform." Tan guyabara with balsa buttons, cinch-tied white baggy pants, a straw fedora with a wide black band. Add the scraggly Fu Manchu and he looked more like a funky sax player than a journalist. People, of course, stared, but when you kept company with Nystrom, you got used to it.

"So," Turk said, laying his folded hands on the table, "what's your theory on the *River Queen?*"

Glad for the chance to unload, Decker told him about the interview with Griswald, and how he missed getting any of it on tape. "I haven't said a word to Lafferty yet. What's the use?"

Turk blew air out of his cheeks, then asked the question that had gnawed at Decker since leaving Griswald: "If Orsini's covering something up, then who the hell torched the *River Queen?*"

"If you want my guess—Victor Carbone," Decker said. "Who else could have gotten to somebody as high on the ladder as Orsini?"

Turk nodded slowly. "Makes sense."

Decker went on. "Or a less sinister possibility. Maybe Orsini and crew simply botched the investigation. What about those firebombings at the two abortion clinics last spring? The department still hasn't turned up a thing in either case. No suspects, no motive, no anything."

"Reasonable," Turk said, stroking upward on the Fu Manchu, standing the blond hairs on end. "Very reasonable. But let me run one more idea past you. What about Krieger?"

"Krieger? Come on now."

"Would you agree he had sufficient motive?"

"Sure I do. Every nun, priest, and fundamentalist Bible beater in town had sufficient motive to burn down the *River Queen*. But it takes more than motive. You need a criminal frame of mind, which surely Krieger doesn't have. You're talking about a family man." Turk smiled a little at the quaintness of the expression. "All right," Decker said, "let's talk about his professional record. Krieger would nail the Pope himself if he broke the law, and you know that as well as I do. Look at the Brinkman case."

Arnold Brinkman was a lawyer from one of the best-connected German families in Cincinnati—and practically a neighbor of Krieger's in Hyde Park. But that didn't stop Fritz from investigating, and successfully prosecuting, an embezzlement case against Brinkman that involved some $200,000 in securities belonging to a widow's trust fund.

Krieger's unwavering adherence to the letter of the law—that was one of the traits Decker's profile had hammered away at. Krieger seldom settled for a plea bargain. In most every case, he pushed for the maximum charge and the maximum penalty—a tactic that would sometimes backfire when he didn't have all the goods on the accused.

But there could be a pettier and more vengeful side to Krieger's inflexibility, and Decker's profile had mentioned this as well. Like the time Krieger busted one of Greenburg's X-rated movie houses, filing obscenity charges not only against Little Al, but also against the theater manager, the old lady ticket-taker, and a sixteen-year-old who was selling popcorn and Cokes in the lobby. It was the boy's first week on the job.

The waiter came with the Coke and a sweaty pitcher of beer and said the pizza would be out in a minute. Tilting his beer glass to hold down the foam, Decker filled it to the top and took a sip. It went down ice cold, crisp. Just what he needed. Turk seemed indifferent to his Coke. He swirled the ice with a straw.

"Maybe you wouldn't need a criminal frame of mind," Turk ventured. "Maybe all you really need is some chink in the armor, some freaky neurosis. I mean, this town, for all its funky conservatism, all its tightass veneer, can be pretty damn kinky behind closed doors. The police raid a whorehouse, and find out the mayor's been paying by check. Is he ruined? Hell, no. He says a few public mea culpas and people vote him right back into office. 'Hey, no problem, pal. Everybody does it, only you were stupid enough to pay by check.'

"Then you come to the tightass of them all—Fritz Krieger. So what's his problem? you ask. Nobody could be that hung up on skinflicks and jack-off mags unless he was holding back some pretty weird shit of his own. It's all part of the internal dynamic. The yin and the yang, man. The yin and the yang."

Decker bristled at the smug tone. "You say skinflicks and jack-off mags like it's all some innocent diversion, like reading the funnies. Have you seen some of the shit they're peddling these days?"

"Can't say I've had the time."

"All right then," Decker said, folding his arms across his chest. "I'll tell you about a film Krieger confiscated in a raid. An eight-millimeter peep show. You know how they work— you go into a private booth at a porn shop, drop in a quarter, get two minutes of viewing time. Ten quarters buys you the whole wad, so to speak. Anyway, this was one of the most popular peep shows ever made, a little film called *First Communion*.

"Opening scene. You got three little girls in white communion dresses kneeling at an altar. All of seven or eight. Long blond hair, rosy cheeks, sweet, virginal—what else at that age, right? The ceremony is just underway when a motorcycle gang rides into church on their bikes. They grab the priest, beat the shit out of him, chain him to one of the bikes. Then they go after the little girls. It's a silent film, so you can't hear the screams, but you can see the terror in their eyes. Wide-eyed, totally hysterical. All right, so the bikers get the girls down on the altar floor, rip off their white dresses, rip off their panties, and take turns raping them. All in all, a nice diversion, wouldn't you say?"

Turk winced a little. "You say Krieger got that from one of Greenburg's shops?"

"No, never made it that far. Krieger's office got wind it was in town and shook down a distributor. But that's not the point. The point is, where do you draw the line? Where does it say in the First Amendment that slimebags have the right to make money portraying women and children like hunks of meat? Slice 'em, dice 'em, anyway you like 'em. I sure as hell don't agree with everything Krieger does, or how he does it, but at least he's taking a stand. I think somebody has to."

"And that's the problem," Turk said. "Where do you take a stand? With Krieger, it's banning bra-and-panty ads in Sears catalogs, for Christ's sake."

An implicit truce was declared as the pizza arrived, steaming hot and swimming in melted cheese and olive oil. Turk asked for another Coke. Decker topped off his beer glass and took a long gulp before putting it down. The evening with Turk, sober or not, promised to be rough going.

The tow Decker had spotted upriver was broadside now with Steamboat Willie's, and it was bigger than he'd imagined. The first barge was nearing the Central Bridge while the towboat was still straining its diesel guts under the L & N crossing, three football fields upstream. The hoppers were piled so high with coal they seemed to be diving into the water. They kicked up a mean wake as the towboat plowed ahead.

"Hold on," Turk said, and Steamboat Willie's began to rock like an English Channel ferry on a stormy crossing. Decker grabbed the pitcher of beer before it sloshed all over the table. Two more waves passed, but neither carried the jolt of the first. Life at Steamboat Willie's returned to normal.

Turk drank his Coke in long, infrequent gulps, the same way he used to knock back glass after glass of Rhine wine or house bourbon and soda. He glanced across the river to the *River Queen*. "I heard Finch was crazy about your Krieger profile."

"As a matter of fact, he was," Decker said. "He sent me a note saying I'd been fair and to the point. How did he put it? Oh yes, he said I'd 'captured the essence of a man with a mission.'"

Turk grinned his know-it-all grin.

"All right, dammit," Decker said, setting his glass down hard. "So it wasn't a hatchet job."

He had written that Krieger was "perhaps a man born of our times," and by that he had meant a prosecutor with an overwhelming mandate to swing the courts back to common sense and stability after two decades of trying to "rehabilitate" violent, hardened criminals.

"No, not a hatchet job," Turk smiled. "More like a blow job."

Decker pushed his glass away and jumped from the bench. "I'll leave before this gets any worse."

"Hold on a second," Turk said, motioning him to sit again. "I'm not blaming you."

Decker sat and sloshed some more beer into his glass.

"It's not you, man. It's the nature of the newspaper business," Turk said. "We either paint some guy as a complete fucking villain, or a complete fucking hero. You know what I mean? There's no middle ground. Editors don't want reality, and readers sure as hell don't want reality. It's just too damn boring. God knows I've written profiles I'd just as soon forget.

"But I'll tell you, man, the thing that scares the hell out of me is exactly what Finch said about Krieger. He's a man with a mission. Remember, LBJ had a mission, too—stop the Commie threat in Asia, keep the dominoes from falling or we'll be fighting Chinks on Malibu beach. Right? And it was suckers like me had to wade through blood and shit up to our eyeballs so he could say he fulfilled his goddamn mission . . ."

"All right," Decker interrupted. "Next you'll lay it on me about how you went off to war while college boys like me lived off the fat of the land. Forget it. We've had that argument."

Turk glared from underneath his fedora, as if he was considering how quickly his fist might travel the distance across the table. But then he leaned back, finished off what was left of the Coke, and fingered some ice out of the glass.

"I'd like to be buddies again," he said matter-of-factly, chewing on the ice. He kept his chin up, but his eyes dropped to the table. "I'll be honest. I don't have many. Not since Caroline and I split."

Then he laughed mirthlessly. "I know what they think at the *Eagle*. They think I'm fucking crazy. You know, a bad case of delayed stress syndrome. Tsk, tsk, tsk. Poor boy killed too many Gook babies in 'Nam, and now he can't live with it. I see it in their fucking eyes all the time. Real edgy, like they expect I'll freak out any second and start biting people." Turk pushed his glass away, grinned. "Watch out. It's Mad Dog Nystrom."

Decker laughed a little and drank some more beer and looked out across the river. The approaching storm still seemed far off, but the breeze was picking up now that the sun had set. As darkness gathered, the downtown lights bled across the water's jagged surface. A big tree limb, looking for all the world like a sea serpent, humped and bobbed its way downstream.

Decker did his best thinking on the river. Some people say an ocean is the best place to think things through, but he would take a river anytime. Stand on a beach and send out your anger, your hope, your melancholy, any emotion at all, and the wind and surf throw it back in your face just the way it was. Or maybe the immensity of the ocean simply crushes what you feel, leaving you as empty and passive as a Zen master.

But a good wide river—well, a river is quite a different thing. A river carries your emotions, cradles them in its flow, lets them drift and whirl for as long as you want. And then when you want those feelings again, they flow back to you— tempered, mellowed, but still of a piece, still definable, like a gentle, distant memory of the feeling that you had. And then you know just what to do.

"All right," Decker said, extending a hand across the table. "We're friends."

It was 10:50 by the time he reached his apartment, and it was pouring rain. He was hours late, but he knew Barrett would be waiting—all curled up in his wing chair reading a detective novel, or maybe soaking in the claw-footed tub, pampering herself after a hard day's work.

Barrett loved his apartment almost as much as she had grown to hate her trendy bachelorette pad in Clifton. It was the Old World charm. Three rooms tucked in the rear half of a long, narrow brick house. High ceilings, hardwood floors, cedar closets that still smelled like cedar, and a couple of wood-burning fireplaces in the living room and kitchen. Very cozy. Barrett called it his "troll house."

After a couple of misses, he slipped his key into the deadbolt. The lock was already open.

"Hel-lo-oh!" he sang out as he stepped inside. He was soaking wet without an umbrella, and a little lightheaded—full of himself—from the beer. "Sor-ry I'm la-ate."

He shivered. The central air was running, still coping with the day's heat. He took off his jacket and hung it to dry on the doorknob and went to the living room: the floor lamp was on, but the wing chair was empty. He paused a second, closed his eyes. There was something different about the room, but his mind wouldn't focus. He went back to the hallway and popped through the double doors into the bathroom, next to the kitchen. No Barrett.

She was already asleep, he thought. Another victim of uncompensated overtime at the *Eagle*. And for what? He yawned violently, belched, then went to the kitchen for a glass and back to the bathroom for aspirin.

He swallowed two with cold water, then downed the rest of the glass. He wished he hadn't stayed out so long with Turk. Or drank so much. But with Turk no celebration was ever cut short.

He decided to brush his teeth—for Barrett—and squirted out a good long strip of Adult Strength Gleam.

He looked vacantly in the mirror as he brushed. He wasn't getting any younger, that's for sure. He grinned, mocking himself. There were tiny crow's feet now around the eyes, a growing fleshiness in the smooth cheeks. How much longer could he pull off the boyish good looks?

He kicked off his shoes in the hallway and headed through the kitchen to the back bedroom. The room was dark, but he had no trouble distinguishing the contours under his sheets. Barrett was on her back, knees bent and turned demurely to one side. She had the blankets pulled to her chin. He almost chuckled at the sight—Barrett Simmons, tough chick reporter, tucked into his bed, a little girl gone nighty-night after a long hard day. He undressed quietly in the dark, put his wallet, keys, change, twelve-dollar Casio on the dresser top. Then he went to the bed, lifted the covers, and slipped quietly across the mattress.

He decided not to wake her. There would be plenty of time to play in the morning, or the middle of the night, if they both happened to wake and were in the mood. He lay on his side for a second, close but not touching her. But it was no use. Being so near he couldn't resist. He turned onto his stomach and slid his left hand across her smooth curved tummy and wrapped his fingers around the firm swell of her hip. Then he slid his other arm under the pillow where her head lay, and brought the hand around to rest on her far shoulder. Supporting her, protecting her. He liked that. Then he placed his head on her pillow, put his cheek against the clean smell of hair, yawned again. His head was spinning from the beer. Just a little. A nice gentle buzz, with no aftereffects, he hoped.

In seconds, his brain was ready to shut down for the night. The cortex plunged toward sleep, but some part of it rebelled, nagged. He stirred and twisted, clung more tightly to Barrett, but something wasn't right. He lifted his head from the pillow, swirled his hand over Barrett's tummy, then up her rib cage. He cupped her breast. She was cold. Incredibly cold.

"Barrett."

He shook her gently.

"Barrett, wake up."

He reached across the bed, turned on the tablelamp.

"Barrett, come on. What's the matter?"

He straddled her legs, lifted her by the shoulders and tried to pull her close. But her head snapped backward from the bruised neck, slack and heavy as a rock.

5

When the knock came at the door, he was still sitting in the wing chair in front of the fireplace. It came a second time, louder and more insistent, and he suddenly jumped to, moved to the door, flipped the deadbolt.

A small thin man in a blue suit was standing on the porch, breaking down an umbrella in the rain. Decker was disappointed. He had expected someone bigger, someone more robust. He didn't know why.

"Are you the police?"

The man reached inside his coat pocket, flashed a badge. "Detective Frank Ellway, Cincinnati Homicide Division." He pointed up the pathway toward the street, where another man in a suit was poking around in the trunk of an unmarked gray car. "My assistant is Detective Ronald Berringer. He's bringing in the gear."

Decker found himself staring at Ellway, who looked almost bloodless in the cold porch light. The lips were pale and meaty, the chin recessed. He didn't look like a cop at all.

"You going to let me out of this rain?" Ellway asked.

"Yes, I'm sorry."

He stepped by Decker into the hallway and leaned his wet umbrella against the wall. He was late-fortyish, slump-shouldered, tired-looking. His head was almost completely bald, with a fringe of coarse brown hair, scalp flakes showing through. The eyes were flint gray, unsmiling—honed tools of the trade, nothing more. He peered into every corner of the apartment, his head swiveling with a ratchetlike motion.

Living room to bathroom, bathroom to kitchen, then back to the bedroom door.

"The body?"

Decker led him into the bedroom. The tablelamp was the only light in the room, making two cones of wan yellow, upper and lower, in the corner by the bed. In the bottom cone was Barrett's face—eyes opened, lips slightly parted and turning a grayish-blue. She was still on her back, a green thermal blanket pulled to her chin.

Berringer bustled into the room carrying an olive duffel bag. He was pudgy, nervous, maybe twenty years Ellway's junior. He dropped the rain-splattered bag by the door, unzipped it, pulled out a Polaroid. He brought the camera up to his tortoise-shell glasses and snapped off a shot. Flash, click, whir.

"Is this exactly the way you found her?" Ellway asked.

"No— Well, yes. Pretty much the same. I threw that blanket over her. Then I—I guess I brushed the hair out of her face. It was down in her eyes."

Ellway stepped over to the bed, pinched the top edge of the blanket and startled peeling it back slowly. Decker wanted to leave the room, but felt he shouldn't, that he should be there with Barrett. He focused on Ellway's eyes, watched them move down the body, inch by inch, like a scanning machine. Then Ellway stepped back and Berringer snapped off a second shot, a third. He held the drying photos between the fingers of one hand.

"Ron, get somebody from the coroner's office out here."

Berringer looked quizzically at Decker.

"In the kitchen," Decker said.

The body seemed burnished in the lamplight. It was unmarked, pristine, except for the two purple bruises, almost elliptical in shape, on either side of her throat. The marks were nearly symmetrical, like the wings of an exotic butterfly.

Berringer returned and started rooting in his duffel bag. Ellway was at the back window of the bedroom. He put both elbows against the top frame, careful not to smudge any prints, and tried to pry it open.

"Locked."

"I keep it locked," Decker said. "Somebody could slip in from the backyard. The alley's behind it."

He walked into the kitchen and signaled Decker to follow.

"I sure could use some coffee," he said. The meaty lips turned even paler as they stretched toward a smile.

Decker started the coffee, then joined Ellway at the kitchen table. The questioning began. When did Decker return home? Where had he been? Who was he with? How long had he known the deceased?

Ellway asked every question in the same official-sounding monotone. Most of the time he kept his eyes fixed on the pages of his notebook, where he carefully penciled each answer in longhand.

"And your relationship to the deceased?"

"We were friends."

"You mean lovers."

"If that's the word you want."

"You were sleeping with her, weren't you?"

"Sometimes."

"How often?"

"Is that important?"

"Listen, Mr. Decker, you can either answer the questions here, or we can go downtown, book you, and ask you questions through the cellbars. What's your choice?"

"All right. Once or twice a week. But we saw each other almost every day. At work, I mean."

"Anything in the apartment missing?"

Decker pressed his fingertips to his forehead. The skin seemed to vibrate. There was ringing in his ears.

"Mr. Decker, I asked you a question."

"I don't know. I haven't checked. I haven't even—"

"Okay, we'll look around."

They walked into the living room first. Decker stared into the empty corner to the left of the fireplace.

"The TV," he said.

"What kind?"

"A Panasonic."

Ellway put it down in the notebook. "Look around. Anything else?"

The cabinet doors to the right of the fireplace were open. The stereo components were missing—amplifier, turntable, tape deck, everything except the tangled wires.

"They took the stereo."

"Who do you mean 'they'?"

"They? I don't know. I was just talking. Whoever."

"Let's check the bedroom."

Berringer was on his knees, holding a can of something in one hand, a small paint brush with the other. He dipped the brush first, then lightly coated the neck of the tablelamp, squinting up into the harsh light with one eye closed.

Ellway pointed to a metal security box on the dresser. The lid was open.

"What about that box there?"

Decker took a look inside. "Someone's been in it, but there's nothing to steal. Just receipts and bank statements, things the IRS would want."

"Any CDs?"

"No, I don't have any CDs."

Decker checked his top dresser drawer. His checkbook was still there. So was a raft of credit cards he rarely used— Penney's, Firestone, Amoco. His penny bowl was upset, the change scattered all over the bottom of the drawer. He tried to think what else he kept inside.

"My tape recorder."

"You keep a tape recorder in there?"

"Yes, I think that's where I put it. Before I went out, I mean. I keep it in this drawer when I don't have it at work."

"And you're sure that's where it was. Not somewhere else."

"Yes."

"You didn't leave it at work?"

"No."

"What kind?"

"A little microcassette. A Sony."

Ellway brightened a little. "You partial to Japanese?"

"What?"

"Forget it."

Ellway led Decker out to the kitchen again, and Decker poured him some coffee. The captain fixed it the way he wanted, heavy on the half-and-half and sugar. They sat at the kitchen table. The questioning went on and on.

Had Decker seen any signs of forced entry?

No, he hadn't. The door was unlocked.

"So it was a habit of Miss Simmons to leave the door unlocked when she was waiting for you?"

"Yes—I mean I don't know. She never had to wait on me before. Not as late as eleven."

"That was late?"

"Yes, for us."

Exasperated, Decker stood to pour himself some coffee. The questioning continued.

"Do you think your next-door neighbors might have seen anyone?"

"I doubt it. They're an older couple. In bed by nine most of the time."

Ellway took down their names anyway.

"Has your apartment been broken into before?"

"No, not since I moved in. But across the street—about two or three months ago, I think—somebody broke through a back screen. They—the people who live there, I mean—were both gone at the time."

"Did Miss Simmons have any enemies that you know of? Anyone who might want to do her harm?"

Decker was putting the half-and-half back into the refrigerator. "Everybody liked Barrett. She was kind, full of energy. A fun person to be with."

"I'll bet," Ellway said under his breath.

Decker caught it. "What the hell does that mean?"

Ellway kept his eyes in his notebook. "Nothing. Were you two on good terms?"

"Yes. Why do you think she was spending the night?"

Ellway lifted his face. "I'll ask the questions, Mr. Decker. Do you lift weights?"

"No." Decker sat again and stared at Ellway. There was nothing to see in the flat gray eyes.

"Do any of the martial arts?"

"The martial what?"

"Forget it. Do you exercise? Swim, jog, work out on Nautilus?"

"I like to swim. I do about a half-mile at the Y every other day."

Ellway pushed out his lips. "Not bad."

The questioning continued while Berringer began poking around the living room, brushing for fingerprints, collecting bits and pieces of things with tweezers, dropping them in zip-lock bags. He took Decker's fingerprints to match them against others in the apartment.

A half hour later, an ambulance arrived from the coroner's office. Two male attendants in white polyester uniforms wheeled a stretcher-cart through the kitchen, into the bedroom.

One of the two attendants mumbled something in a deep voice. The other laughed nervously. In a minute or two, they wheeled the cart out. The body was wrapped in white plastic sheeting, strapped down in three places and covered completely, except for the curved fingers of one hand—white and lovely as sculpted marble—poking through an open fold.

Berringer came from the living room, his duffel bag packed and slung over a shoulder. "I think I got all I need for now."

Ellway pocketed his notebook and pencil stub and joined Berringer at the door. Berringer had Ellway's umbrella ready and handed it to him.

"You staying here tonight?" Ellway asked Decker.

"I don't know. I may."

"It's okay. Just stay out of the bedroom. For a day or two anyway. Detective Berringer and I are just the advance men. We'd like to get the boys from the crime lab here first thing in the morning. Go over this place with a fine-tooth comb. You have an extra key?"

"Yes, of course." Decker pulled one out of his wallet and handed it to Ellway.

"You have any plans to travel soon?"

"No, not until the holidays."

"Good. It would be a good idea to stick close until the investigation is closed. You're not currently under suspicion, but things can change. You never know."

Berringer pushed through the door with his gear, and Ellway turned and followed. Decker was glad to see the cold little man leave. Ellway had made him feel sleazy, ashamed. Why?

From the porch, he watched the two of them walk through the drizzle along the narrow pathway to the street. He looked at his watch. It was 1:30 in the morning. He stepped back into the apartment, shut the door, and listened to his ears ringing, like someone slowly scraping the insides of a metal pot.

He went to the bedroom door and poked his head in. The bed was uncovered, the sheets smooth and bare. No bloodstains, no rips, no tears, no marks of any kind. It seemed impossible that Barrett had been killed there. Barrett was a fighter. She would have clawed the son of a bitch, bitten him, thrown something at him.

But she never had the chance. He must have found her sleeping, broken her neck and strangled her before she could even wake.

He looked at his hands. They were balled into fists. The fingers were throbbing, the knuckles almost white. He felt the urge to smash a fist into the wall, to drive it clear through the plaster. But for what? Everything that raged in him seemed futile, senseless. Barrett was dead. Her warmth, her energy, her intelligence gone. Exchanged for a few piddling scraps of hardware. Absurd.

He turned and went to the kitchen phone, stood there a moment. He thought about calling Stein, or even Turk. But he felt too ashamed. Of what? What the hell had he done?

He went to the cabinet over the sink and pulled down a half-gallon plastic jug of vodka and a big tumbler. He filled the tumbler halfway and took it into the living room and set it on a folding tray next to the sofa. He sat down. When he was comfortable, he picked up the tumbler and sipped the vodka until his whole mouth burned with the liquid. He waited a few minutes until the burning stopped, and then filled his mouth again. In a few minutes, he repeated the dose. It wasn't doing much good. He still wanted to smash his fist through the wall.

He got up from the sofa and started for the kitchen again when it hit him, like someone kicking out his knees. He stumbled back to the wing chair and sat down. He was crying now, big sobs heaving out of his chest like ghosts he couldn't control. He gripped the armrests as tight as he could and let his head fall loose over the back of the chair. The ceiling was a blank sheet of white, a voyage into endless nothingness.

6

Decker was at work the next morning. Only the death of a relative warranted time off at the *Eagle*, and he wasn't about to test company policy under the circumstances. Word had gotten around the paper, of course. But since he and Barrett had been a newsroom "item" only, there were no official condolences, only embarrassed little "hellos" as the other reporters gave his desk a wide berth.

He tried to read the *Times'* profile on Little Al—the shady life and times thereof—rereading whole paragraphs that didn't sink in. His brain was still lubricated and slipping gears from the vodka tumblers the night before. Words echoed in his brain. He left his desk and went to Vendville for a third cup of ersatz coffee—the only real cure he'd found for a hangover.

He found Turk there, at one of the folding tables, eating microwaved pancakes slopped with packaged syrup. Decker's stomach soured.

"Have a seat." Decker brought his coffee over.

"You shouldn't have come in today," Turk said.

"Yeah, sure. I could've stayed home and punched holes in the wall."

Turk sliced into the stack of pancakes with a plastic knife and fork, then swirled the wedge in syrup and stuffed it in his mouth. Syrup clotted on the ragged edges of his mustache.

"The *Eagle's* doing a story, you know."

Decker wasn't surprised. "Whose assignment?"

"Mine. Just the straight stuff. Names, addresses, times, dates. Finch said not to play it big."

"Shockingly tasteful." Decker sipped at his coffee. Just the bitter taste of it seemed to clear his head a little.

"Something else," Turk said, "I was looking over the police report this morning. It doesn't make sense."

"What doesn't?" He waited while Turk swallowed a mouthful of pancake, wiped the Fu Manchu with a crinkly paper napkin.

"That somebody would kill for your Sony. And kill damned professionally."

"So what are you saying? You think *I* did it?"

Turk shook his head, wiped his mouth again. "I'm saying I don't think robbery was the motive. I think somebody was in your apartment looking for something. Something very specific."

"Like what?"

"Like your tape of Griswald."

"But I blew it. There was no tape."

"How could the person tailing you know?"

"Tailing me?"

"Decker, wake up, for Christ's sake. I'm being hypothetical. Trace your route yesterday. You met Griswald in the parking lot. You had your tape recorder with you. You went straight home. A couple hours later, I pick you up, we go out drinking. The tail follows, sees we're settled down for a long evening. Then he either phones one of his cronies or doubles back to your apartment looking for the tape and . . ."

"All right," Decker stopped him. He shut his eyes. "I can fill in the rest."

They were both quiet for a few seconds, and then Decker stood up and threw his paper cup against a vending machine. Hot coffee splattered everywhere. He sat again facing sideways and felt his eyes beginning to sting. He blinked hard, once, and the tears were gone. But not his rage.

Turk laid a hand on his shoulder. Decker shrugged it off.

"Why get mad? Get even. Tell Finch you want the *River Queen* story full time. That's what you want, isn't it? You'd like to nail their goddamn asses to the wall. Well, let's do it. You and me. We'll nail ass like nobody's ever nailed ass in this town. You hear me?"

He nodded and jumped from his chair. By the time he reached Lafferty's desk, he had a grip on himself again. He knew how to handle Bozo. He leaned over the top of Lafferty's VDT until Bozo looked up, startled.

"I got to Griswald yesterday," Decker began. His eyes narrowed with a kind of angry cunning.

Lafferty settled back in his chair. "Well?"

Decker gave him a quick sketch of the interview. The rush of adrenaline helped him recall details that had escaped him before. He was repeating whole sentences verbatim.

Lafferty's nostrils were in a frenzy by the time Decker finished. "Dammit, Decker, if you knew all this yesterday afternoon, why didn't you file an overnight story?"

"Griswald wouldn't go on the record."

"You mean you let Griswald rattle on like that *off the record?*" His voice was caught somewhere between wrath and incredulity.

"He wouldn't have given me a damn thing otherwise."

Lafferty shuffled his notes from the morning meeting. "What are you asking then?"

"I'm asking for time—a month or so—to really dig into the Orsini report. Find out what the hell is going on."

"A whole month? When we're already down a reporter?"

Lafferty caught himself the instant he said it, and blushed to his carrot-colored roots. Decker felt like throwing a punch across the VDT, but remembered what Turk had said. *Don't get mad, get even.*

He grinned and said, "You know, I'd hate to see the *Times* beat us on this one."

Lafferty was silent. Decker knew what the tiny brain was working on: Finch's reaction to losing a major exposé.

"Well," he said finally, doodling on his notepad. "Let me talk to the Boss. It's not what he had in mind, you know. He was all set to have you and Turk start a series on aluminum wiring."

"Aluminum wiring?"

"It's here in Orsini's report." Lafferty tossed a thin stack of Xeroxed eight-by-elevens across the city desk. The cover page was stamped "Preliminary" in big red letters.

He skimmed the introduction, flipped back to the one-page summary. Lots of technical terms. "Circuit branches." "Oxide deposits." "Electrical resistance." What it came down to was this: "old technology" aluminum wiring—the kind used in the *River Queen*—has been known to overheat and melt at connecting points. If the broken connection sets off an electrical arc, the heat can ignite nearby flammable material. In the *River Queen*'s case, the report said, the nearby material happened to be especially flammable—a pocket of natural gas from a leaky stoveline inside the kitchen wall.

"There may be thousands of homes out there wired with aluminum, and their owners don't even know of it," Lafferty said, his eyes wide with the secret horror of it all.

"Yeah. And maybe arsonists out there, too, nobody knows about."

The nostrils went to work again. "Can't resist being the smartass, can you, Decker?" He reached across his desk and started flipping through his desk calendar. "What about that hayfever piece you promised me weeks ago."

"Oh heavens," Decker said, "that's right. Hayfever season in the Ohio Valley is almost upon us. I'll get cracking on that right away, sir." The "sir" had a good deal of military snap.

"I want it for tomorrow's city edition."

"City edition. Yes, *sir*."

At his desk, he pulled his file marked "seasonal stuff," laid it in front of him, and, in a moment or two, stuffed it back into the bottom drawer. His mind was made up: It was either the *River Queen* story or he would quit. His head was crammed so full of questions he could feel the vessels throbbing. If Turk was right, then who would have killed to get his tape of Griswald? Who had the most to fear? There was only one man, and around every corner his thoughts turned, they ran straight into the bulldog face of Franklin T. Orsini.

He dialed the arson division, asked for Griswald.

"I'm sorry," a receptionist said in a singsongy voice. "But Lieutenant Griswald called in sick this morning."

"Do you expect him tomorrow?"

"I'm sorry, sir. I have no idea." The same singsong voice, but now a touch exasperated.

"Do you have a home number for the lieutenant."

"I'm sorry. We can't give out that information."

He slammed the receiver. The phone rang out almost at the same instant.

"*Cincinnati Eagle.* Decker here."

"Is this Richard Decker of 321 Pullan Street?"

"The same."

"Joe Benoit of the *Times.*"

Decker hung his head and closed his eyes: Joe Benoit, a total jerk-off if there ever was one. He strained to be pleasant. "What can I do for you, Joe?"

"I was hoping I could ask you a few questions—about the murder last night in your apartment."

"No need to hope, Joe. I have no comment. None at all."

"Is it true, Mr. Decker, that you and Ms. Simmons were, shall we say, close personal friends?"

"Listen, Joe—can I call you that, Joe? Good. You can call me, Rick. All right, Joe, here's a quote for you. You got

your pen ready? Okay. Here it is: 'The *Cincinnati Times* can kiss my sweet fucking ass.' You get all that? Good."
He treated himself to a second phone slamming.

Entering Finch's office from the newsroom, Decker knew how Ming Dynasty slaves might have felt leaving the slums of Hunan and stepping inside the walls of the Emperor's Forbidden City. Instantly, linoleum floors were covered by thick carpeting, metal furniture metamorphosed into fine old oak, bare walls sprouted mahogany panels, rows of book shelves, oil paintings.

Turk was sitting uneasily in the back of the office, as far from Finch's desk as possible, hands gripping the arm ends of a brass-studded red leather chair. Lafferty and Stein were there, too, on either end of a comfortable chintz sofa near the front of the room. Decker took a chair opposite the sofa and, glad to see his closest newsroom ally in attendance, nodded across at Stein, who nodded back.

Finch would be the last in order to make a grand entrance—something he must have learned in a management seminar, Decker supposed. As they waited, the detainees indulged their respective nervous habits. Decker popped gum into his mouth. Turk stroked his Fu. Lafferty crossed and uncrossed his legs and fidgeted with his notepad. Only Stein, sans pipe, sat calm and stolid as a Buddha, his hands clasped over a comfortable tire and his coal-black eyes hardly blinking as he stared somewhere into the carpet. Stein was on another wavelength. Decker sometimes wondered if his Brillo-pad hair pulled in vibrations from a parallel, but mellower universe.

At 10:10, the editor-in-chief marched in, circled his big desk, and mounted the throne.

"Well, gentlemen," he said, surveying the room from his black leather chair, "let's not waste time."

Alexander Finch was pushing retirement age, but he was

damned if he was going to look like it. He wore big aviator glasses and European-cut suits that did more than just hang on his jogging-trimmed body. The thinning hair was slicked back over his head, the roots no strangers to Grecian Formula. But age will out. It showed in the wild gray eyebrows, the watery blue eyes, the neck wattle that hung over his narrow, starched collars.

"Gentlemen," he started again, this time suddenly leaning forward from his chair and dropping his folded hands on the desk, thumbs in the air. Turk called it "The Big Lunge": that's when you knew Finch was getting down to business. "This will be brief," he said. But it wasn't. Finch recapped everything the *Eagle* had learned so far about the *River Queen* "enigma," as he put it, then finished with a rallying cry.

"Gentlemen, we are going to dig deep into whatever shit Mr. Orsini has landed himself in."

He divvied up assignments. "Mr. Nystrom and Mr. Decker, the two of you are swinging the shovels in this enterprise. Mr. Decker works the fire department. Mr. Nystrom pokes his nose into Greenburg Enterprises and all its fulsome operations. I will leave the details of your assignments to Barry, whom I have chosen to coordinate the investigation. Both of you will report to him on a daily basis. Any stories you file will be edited by him."

It was exactly what Decker had hoped for. A chance to work with Stein.

"You have six weeks, gentlemen," Finch concluded. "During that time, I've asked that you be freed from your regular newsroom duties. Any questions?"

Lafferty shook his head, although Decker knew he couldn't be happy about losing two of his best reporters for a month and a half. Stein sat motionless, still void of expression. The group was about to leave when Turk spoke from the back of the room.

"Sir," he said, a hint of contempt in his voice, "six weeks is not a lot of time."

Finch hunched forward again into The Big Lunge, a look of pained sincerity behind the aviator glasses. "I know that, boys. But this *is* a daily newspaper, and that means we put out a product every day of the year, not every week or month. Lafferty and I have talked at some length about this, and six weeks is all we can spare you from the newsroom. I'm sorry, gentlemen, but those are the realities, as it were."

The issue was settled, although Turk stewed in his chair a moment as the others got up to go. When Finch laid down reality, "as it were," there was no use arguing.

Ten minutes later, Stein, Turk, and Decker—or "the team," as they came to call themselves—met again in what was known as the *Eagle's* "conference room." It was a corner of the newsroom, set off by partitions and furnished with a long folding table and six folding chairs.

"Congratulations on the promotion, Pops," Decker said as Stein pulled up a chair. Turk chuckled. "Pops" was Decker's affectionate dig at a man who had three boys, all in the hyperkinetic age bracket.

"Some promotion," Stein smiled. "Baby-sitting for a couple of prima donna reporters." He pinched some shredded Cavendish from his leather pouch and tucked it loosely into his pipe bowl, then lit it with one of the Rosebud matches he kept in his shirt pocket. The room filled with the tobacco's thick sweet aroma as Stein launched into the mechanics of the investigation.

The team would keep joint files of their notes. Absolutely everything would be dated and cross-filed. Any important leads, theories, hunches would be put in memos and also filed. Finally, they would keep a master index of all sources, with names, addresses, phone numbers, profiles, connections to other sources. The meeting was conducted in typical Stein style—a minimum of words and fuss. In ten minutes, it was over.

"So, gentlemen, what's our first move?"

Turk said he would begin at the federal courthouse, checking bankruptcy and tax records on Greenburg Enterprises, in line with a Nystrom dictum: sniff the scent of money and the trail leads to shit every time.

"It won't hurt to begin dropping in on some of Mr. Greenburg's store clerks and theater managers, either," Stein said. Turk nodded.

Decker said he would begin casing the other investigators in Griswald's department, to see if any would talk about the Orsini report. Or about their boss.

"Good. Keep it on the record if you can," Stein said. "We meet again at five, or just as soon as I can wrap up the final."

Decker was back at his desk by 11:40, in time to catch Petkamp by phone before he left the Safety Building for his usual ninety-minute lunch hour.

"Yeah, I can give you the names and numbers of the other arson investigators," Petkamp said, "but as far as I know, Orsini and Griswald were the only ones involved in gathering evidence. I've been told Orsini took personal charge of the case, said he didn't want anybody fucking things up. Which didn't sit very well with Griswald. There was a little scene between the two, I've been told. Griswald supposedly bust into Orsini's office and said he would damn well be part of the investigation or his whole team would walk. That's when Orsini backed down. Or a little anyway. I don't think Griswald was ever privy to everything in the report."

"In other words, Bart, you're telling me I'm up a creek."

"Well, you could go around to the fire stations and ask some of the rank and file if they know anything. But I doubt it.

You'll probably get a whole lot of speculation, and a shitload of grief from Orsini's office if they find out what you're up to."

"Thanks a million, Bart. Any other good tips?"

"Wait a minute." Petkamp shifted gears. "I just thought of one thing. The prosecutor's office. Hell, if there was any talk of arson, Krieger would have heard, right?"

"Maybe so, Bart. It's worth a try."

"Sure it is. Besides, after that profile last week . . ."

"Just give me those names and numbers and shut the fuck up, Bart."

Decker dialed Krieger's office and got his secretary on the line. She was one of those who get their jollies keeping little people away from the Big Man. Petty power brokers. But you learned to treat them nice, or you got nowhere at all.

"Hi, Alice." He made a point of remembering secretaries' names; few people did. "Mr. Krieger available, by any chance?"

No, he certainly wasn't. He was leaving early that afternoon for a law enforcement conference in San Fransisco. A 1:20 flight. He would be gone until the end of the week.

"Has he left yet for the airport, Alice?"

"No, Mr. Decker, but he's not in his office at the moment."

He paused, hoping Alice might volunteer her boss's whereabouts. Not a chance. "Is Mr. Krieger anywhere I might reach him?" His tone was suppliant, almost desperate. "I really need your help."

It turned the key.

"Well, let me think," Alice said. "Mr. Krieger did mention he would be attending Mass prior to his flight. He hardly ever misses a day, you know. You might possibly catch him after the service."

"Saint Xavier Church?"

"Well, yes—"

"Noon service?"

"Yes, Mr. Decker. You are familiar, then, with Mr. Krieger's habits."

He certainly was. His research for the Krieger profile had been exhaustive. One of the questions he had asked the prosecutor, hoping to unlock some secret guilty compulsion, was why he made the trip to church every day.

"Because it makes me so very happy," he had answered, smiling benevolently. Then he pressed his palms together, like a priest in the midst of a sermon. "Thomas Aquinas once said that human happiness is not to be found in sensual pleasures. Nor in honor, glory, riches, or worldly power. Not even in the exercise of moral virtue. No, he said, it is found only in the knowledge of God. So you see, Mr. Decker, my church-going is really quite selfish."

That's when Decker had felt the hair tingle at the back of his neck. The moment reminded him of a high-school history teacher he'd had years ago—a dandruff-ridden old man who would start reading from the Declaration of Independence or the Gettysburg Address, then veer off on some misty-eyed tangent about "this great country of ours." The speeches, as silly as Decker knew they were, had never failed to elicit the hair-tingling response. He couldn't really explain it, except to say he was sometimes charmed by people who believed strongly in something—anything at all.

He thanked Alice and hung up when he noticed his hands were shaking. A classic case of coffee overdose, complicated by lack of food. He decided to grab some lunch before meeting Krieger.

The weather had broken after the storm of the night before. The air was clear and gusty, the temperature around eighty—cool in comparison to the string of nineties that had baked the city for the last week or more. Maybe the dog days of summer had finally come to heel. People on the street were smiling, like actors in a Dristan commercial—they could actually breathe again. Barrett would have grabbed him on a day like this and insisted they eat takeout in Lytle Park among the zinnias and marigolds.

He tried not to think about that. He stopped at a pizza parlor on Seventh Street, ordered a slice of plain, and held it down by sipping a Diet Coke.

From the pizzeria, it was only four blocks to Saint Xavier, one of the oldest churches in the city, and the first to offer boarding school to the children of the working poor. Decker arrived at 12:25 and waited outside on the sidewalk.

In the sixteen years since his father had disappeared, Decker had seen the insides of a church maybe two or three times. (His mother's funeral had been one of those.) He hadn't been particularly close to his father, expecially as a teenager, but it had been part of his unquestioned system of beliefs that his father would always be there. When he vanished, something cracked deep within the foundation, and soon the entire edifice came tumbling down.

Still, Decker could always appreciate a good gargoyle. He spotted some intriguingly nasty ones jutting from the corners of Saint Xavier's steeple. They were sticking their tongues out, sending raspberries to the far quarters of the city.

A little after 12:30, the church began to empty. Krieger was one of the last to step through the double wooden doors. In the sunlight of a clear day, his silver hair gleamed like a halo. His face was a picture of perfect inner peace. The eyes blinked softly, the corners of his mouth lifted into a smile, infinitely assured, infinitely gentle, like a blue-eyed portrait of Jesus in a children's missalette.

Decker met Krieger on the sidewalk.

"Rick, what a pleasant surprise!" They shook hands and without wasting time, Decker said he needed Krieger's comment on something important.

Krieger dropped a hand to Decker's shoulder. "Do you mind if we make this a strolling interview?" he said, asking, not insisting. "I'm in a bit of a hurry to catch a plane."

"I know. The one-twenty to San Fransisco. You're cutting it close."

Krieger laughed. "So Alice has told me."

Decker was almost six feet, but in the shadow of the mighty Krieger, he felt like a mutant slob. The prosecutor was six-three or six-four, broad-shouldered, dignified in the warm, quiet way of Gregory Peck, with the same unruly black eyebrows. At fifty-nine, he carried himself like a twenty-five-year-old. He had no intention of retiring. In his own mind he was probably still the boy commander of a tank division, helping Patton drive the Hun back to Berlin. Krieger didn't just walk, he assaulted the space in front of him—long, powerful strides, arms and shoulders swinging in sync with each step. Behind his back, Krieger's less reverent underlings called him "The Tank Commander," or simply "Treads."

They joined a lunch-hour crowd waiting for the walk sign on Seventh Street. Not a car in sight, but that was Cincinnati.

Decker got to his point: had Krieger's office been approached about the possibility of arson in the *River Queen* fire?

Krieger smiled, but kept his stride. In profile, the long classic nose, the jutting chin were like the prow of an Athenian warship.

"Arson? Oh, I'm quite certain there must have been some discussion of that. But I'm afraid I'm not the person you should be talking to. Ethan Nottingham, my special assistant, is our liaison with the fire division. My understanding, of course, is that arson has been ruled out. By the way," he said, cold blue eyes peering down the lengthy nose, "have you read Chief Orsini's preliminary report?"

"Yes, sir, I've done my homework, but I—"

"Very thorough job, it seemed to me. Chief Orsini personally supervised the investigation, I understand."

"But are you aware, Mr. Krieger, that at least one person in the department disagrees with the report?"

The bushy eyebrows lifted. "No, as a matter of fact, I was not. Of course, I am not always privy to such internal affairs. Perhaps Nottingham can help you there as well."

There was a short silence while Decker caught up on his note-taking. Then Krieger started in again, his eyes narrowed in a tense, troubled look.

"There is one thing about the *River Queen* affair that does worry me, Rick. May we go off the record for a moment?"

Decker grimaced. "I need information I can use, Mr. Krieger."

"Indeed, you may be able to use this at some point. But for now, I simply want you to be aware."

Decker sighed and closed his notebook. "All right. Off the records."

Krieger continued the brisk pace as he talked in a hushed, almost melodramatic tone. He told Decker that for the last month his office and the FBI had been probing links between Greenburg Enterprises and the Carbone family.

"We have good inside information that, several weeks before his death, Mr. Greenburg struck a major underworld deal with Victor Carbone."

Decker flipped open his notebook, then remembered this was off the record. Krieger went on. About a month ago, he explained, Greenburg had agreed to supply his porn shops with hard-core material distributed by friends of the Carbone family in Cleveland. In return, Carbone would launder a big chunk of the *River Queen's* gambling take through the family's business front, Amex Vendors.

"Amex as in A-m-e-x?" Decker asked. The Vendville machines were Amex.

"Yes," Krieger said. "I believe they own nearly every vending machine downtown."

Krieger returned to his subject. "Evidently, Mr. Greenburg was having more success with the *River Queen* venture than he knew how to handle. He was finding it increasingly difficult to hide the profits in the books for his porn operation."

Kreiger dropped a hand on Decker's shoulder again. "Do you recall the confiscated film I showed you a few weeks ago, *First Communion?*"

"It's not easy to forget."

"Indeed. It was part of a large shipment of material on its way from Cleveland to Greenburg Enterprises. Our office was tipped by an anonymous caller we believe may have worked inside the Greenburg organization. Someone, it seems, who was not happy with the deal Greenburg had struck with Carbone and his Cleveland connections."

"But why?"

"We're still working on that. Two things we do know for certain. For the last several months, an organization in Cleveland has been trying to monopolize the distribution of pornographic material throughout the Midwest. And they've been very successful. In cities like Cleveland and Detroit they're putting out harder-core material and in greater quantity than anything we've seen in this town. Some magazines and films, but more and more we're seeing videocassettes. Over the counter, under the counter. It doesn't matter. They're out to control the business."

"Let me get this straight," Decker said. "You're suggesting that this Cleveland outfit burned the *River Queen* because they thought Greenburg was playing footsie with your investigation?"

Krieger smiled again, but shook his head. "I'm not suggesting anything about the *River Queen* at this point.

Certainly not on the record. Until a case for arson is established, the investigation is entirely in the hands of the fire division. What concerns our office is that Carbone's associates may now find their way into the local market, and with material far more insidious than anything we've seen before. I'm talking about child pornography, what they call 'chicken stuff' in the industry. South American snuff films. Sexually violent material that would make your stomach turn."

"So why tell me all this?" Decker was flattered but also surprised to be treated like an insider.

Krieger clamped a hand on Decker's upper arm. They were suddenly partners. "Because I think you can be trusted," he said evenly, "and because someday I may need your help in this fight."

They reached Krieger's car—a gunmetal-gray Mercedes. It was parked in a reserved space next to the courthouse steps on Sycamore Street. The insides of the 450 SL looked cool and inviting through the smoked glass.

They shook hands. Krieger's shake was firm, with a slight pause at the end. Just enough to make it personal.

"Before I go, Rick, I must tell you how much I enjoyed the profile last week. An absolutely splendid job."

Decker mumbled a modest thanks, and then realized to his discomfort that the profile might explain Krieger's sudden trust in him. He squirmed as Krieger rattled on about the piece. Another Nystrom dictum: When sources began praising your work, you knew it was turning to shit.

"I must admit, when you first called me with the idea I was a bit troubled. The press has not been entirely fair to me in the past, as I'm sure you're aware. I am not complaining, of course. Attacking public figures is one of the most cherished prerogatives of the Fourth Estate. A mainstay, in fact, of our free democratic process." Krieger smiled, winked. "But your profile was more than simply fair, Rick, it was filled with insight. In fact, I feel I learned a few things about myself. About 'my mission,' as you say. If anything, it has hardened my resolve.

"And I might add," he said playfully, "you passed the very toughest test of all—my wife Marcie. She simply loved the article. Everything, that is, except the business about my shirt collars being—how did you phrase it—'starched to priestly proportions.' She launders them herself, you know."

"Hoo, boy."

Krieger grinned this time, and wrinkles bracketed his thin, angular face clear to his eyebrows. "But you needn't worry. In fact, Marcie suggested I invite you out to the house sometime."

"Sounds terrific." Decker smelled a possible inside story.

"Good. As a matter of fact, Marcie has something planned for this Friday evening. A little cookout. Very informal, just a few of our friends and neighbors. Do you think you can make it?"

"Wouldn't miss it."

Decker dropped a quarter into the coffee machine and pressed the button marked "freshly brewed, cream only" and watched the paper cut drop down and begin to fill with a stream of hot brown liquid that was anything but "freshly brewed."

Turk was sitting behind him at one of the Vendville tables, drinking a can of Cherry Coke.

"You know," Decker said, "we should have our own coffee maker in here. Why give our quarters to a scumbag like Carbone?"

"As a matter of fact, we had a Mr. Coffee in here once," Turk said drily. "Plugged it next to the microwave there. It lasted about two days. Somebody ripped the cord clean out of the machine."

Decker brought his coffee over to the table. "No shit?"

"No shit. Any other brilliant ideas, Mr. Columbia grad?"

"Nope."

Turk's shoulder stiffened as his eyes fixed on the Vend-ville door. It was Lafferty, notebook in hand, coming their way with a carrot-head full of steam.

"Sorry to interrupt the extended lunch hour, boys, but one of you is working for me this afternoon."

Turk crushed his Coke can in one hand. "What about our reprieve from the newsroom?"

Lafferty ignored him. "The Christian Unity League is holding a rally in Fountain Square at one o'clock." Decker glanced at his watch; it was already five till. "The Reverend Bevis is giving a speech about the *River Queen*. Finch wants one of you there, in case things get out of hand."

"What does Bevis care about the *River Queen*?" Decker asked.

Lafferty smiled. "That's why we pay reporters."

"The great den of Satan has burned, gone forever in fire and smoke! Alleluia, brothers and sisters! Alleluia!"

The booming voice with the slight Southern drawl reverberated around the square, chasing pigeons in wide sweeping circles. Two, maybe three, hundred bodies were jammed in front of the dais where the Reverend Roy L. Bevis, leader of the Christian Unity League, was holding forth in one of his shiny blue suits. He was a short man, not fat, not thin, with a square jaw, a horizontal mouth full of perfect capped teeth, and a cresting wave of dark brown hair that man, not God, had given him.

"Let me read to you now from the Holy Scripture. A prophesy, I daresay, of our times. Revelations, nineteen, and one. 'After this I seemed to hear the great sound of a huge crowd in heaven, singing, "Alleluia! Victory and glory and power to our God! He judges fairly, he punishes justly, and he has condemned the famous prostitute who corrupted the earth with her fornications; he has avenged his servants that she killed." They sang again, 'Alleluia! The smoke of her will go up for ever and ever and ever.'"

Bevis pulled off his half-glasses before poking a finger in the air and delivering the coup de grace. "Yes, brothers and sisters in Christ. The *River Queen* is gone, and her captain is no more. Mr. Alvin Samuel Greenburg has met his eternal reward, and I trust, dear brothers and sisters in Christ, that it is a just one."

At that, the mixed crowd of housewives, teenagers, men in business suits, and assorted hangers-on let out with "Amens" and wild applause. Bobbing in the air were the Unity League's equally diverse signs: ABORTION IS MURDER. NO MORE SMUT. BACK TO A NATION OF CHRIST.

Turk leaned toward Decker, who was scribbling furiously in a notebook. "Man, this is sick." They were standing at the back of the crowd, not far from the Tyler-Davidson Fountain, where the spray from the Water Goddess's outstretched hands sent a fine cool mist into the air. Decker could feel it on the back of his neck.

"What about the kids on that goddamn boat?"

"Shut up," Decker said, "I'm trying to get it down."

"The Serpentine Wall!" Bevis thundered. The feedback from the speakers was so sharp it seemed to pierce the eardrums. "Why do you think they call it *the Serpentine Wall?*" He spat out the words. "No secret there, my brothers and sisters. At the bottom of that winding wall lay the serpent's den itself. A den of gambling, of prostitution, of drugs. Of depravities so sordid it is beyond the power of true Christians to imagine. Into that serpent's den were drawn five of our children, like lambs to the slaughter, and they, too, were asked to pay the wages of sin."

"This is too fucking much," Turk said.

Decker kept scribbling, his messy shorthand about a half-sentence behind the sermon. Bevis went on to recite what was now the litany of the unity league: The pornographers, the abortionists, the liberals, and the secular humanists were in consort against the Christian nation, and only through a unified ecumenical front—Catholics, Protestants, Fundamentalists—could America's soul be won back to its Christian roots.

"There are some, you must know, who say *we* are to blame for what happened a month or two ago at the Majority Center and the Planned Parenthood Clinic." Bevis sneered as he named the two abortion clinics, as though the names themselves were part of a cover-up.

"They have said to me, Reverend Bevis, you are as guilty as anyone who threw those bombs. *You* have helped create this atmosphere of hate and violence. *You* have encouraged the righteous to defy the law and take matters into their own hands."

Bevis stepped away from the podium and smiled. "I have to laugh, dear brothers and sisters. For why would *we* need bombs when *we* have the power of the Lord Jesus Christ . . ."

Turk elbowed Decker. "Hey, take a look!"

A small group of counterdemonstrators had appeared just to the right of the podium. They were holding a half-dozen handmade signs. One said, "Free Speech, Free Choice, Your Constitutional Rights." A larger sign in red letters said, "Bevis Is No Christian."

The crowd started booing. A man shouted, "Go home, baby killers!"

Bevis pointed to the protestors and thundered: "Pay no attention to these people. The Lord will see to them in His own good time, as He sees to all things."

"Free speech! Free choice!" a woman's voice cried out. The crowd booed again. There was a surge toward the counterdemonstrators. Decker saw their signs go down.

"Let's go," Turk said, and they circled fast around the crowd. When they got to the scene, six or seven policemen were already there, pushing apart demonstrators and counterdemonstrators.

"They're taking our signs!" a young woman shouted.

Decker saw one of the cops grab the "Bevis Is No Christian" poster. He threw it behind him to the ground. In an inverted flying wedge, the police started pushing the counterdemonstrators away from the crowd. A chant went up: "Free Speech! Free Choice! . . ."

Turk tried to run around the wedge for a closer look, but two cops took hold of his arms and dragged him off.

"Get your goddamn fascist hands off me!" Turk screamed. A billy club was poised over Turk's skull when Detective Ellway appeared. The club froze in midair.

"All right boys!" Ellway ordered. "That will be all."

The two cops stood at attention while Turk adjusted his hat and guyabara. Decker stood by with his notebook.

"Go on," Ellway said to the police, "everything's under control here."

The cop with the billy club rammed it through his leather belt loop. He traded glares with Turk before he and his partner stomped away.

Decker looked back to where the police had corralled the counterdemonstrators. The police were leading two men and a woman in handcuffs toward a paddy wagon on Walnut Street.

"Nice day for a police riot, isn't it?" Turk said.

Ellway was wearing a tan plainclothes suit, his eyes hidden behind aviator shades. Decker had recognized him only by the Elmer Fudd chin. But if Ellway recognized Decker, he didn't acknowledge it. His meaty lips were fixed in a calm smile as he spoke to Turk. "You'll have to forgive the boys if they seemed a little overzealous. We had reports there might be violence here today. We wanted to nip anything in the bud."

"You nipped it, all right," Turk said. "And you nipped the First Amendment, too."

Ellway continued to smile. "We broke up a potentially violent situation, that's all. Trying to protect the public safety. You're free to file a grievance with the mayor's Human Rights Commission if you'd like."

"You bet," Turk said. "And maybe with the FBI."

When Ellway quit smiling, Decker decided to interrupt. "Come on, Turk. We've got twenty minutes to file for the final."

7

Decker hammered in the Bevis story while Turk was on the phone with Petkamp at the Safety Building, seeing if Bart could reach the three demonstrators who were arrested.

The story would make front page of the final, along with an *Eagle* editorial decrying "the increasing polarization of the community" over the abortion issue.

Police Chief Logan defended the confiscation of the counterdemonstrators' signs. "They might have been used as weapons," he told Decker over the phone. "There were sticks on them."

Decker was typing in Logan's quote when Turk came over with his notes from Petkamp. He gave Decker the names of the two men and woman arrested at the rally. "All three were charged with disorderly conduct—nothing about resisting arrest—and released on their own recognizance. Petkamp says none of 'em would talk to the press."

"Great. So we don't know if they were demonstrators or counterdemonstrators."

"The woman works for Planned Parenthood. A counselor. I called there."

"The two men?"

"Nothing. But there's an interesting footnote here. According to Petkamp, a fourth person was brought in for questioning, but not formally charged. A teenager by the name of Charlotte Krieger."

"Krieger? Any relation to Fritz?"

"Yes, if we can believe Petkamp, it's his daughter.

Petkamp says he tried to talk to her before she left the building, but the cops wouldn't let him anywhere near the girl."

Decker scribbled a quick note on a legal pad. "Sounds like a black sheep in the Krieger family. I'll tuck it in our follow-up file."

At two that afternoon, Decker drove out to visit one of his best sources, and favorite people—Gert Larsen. Gert had been editor of the *Eagle*'s society page for almost thirty years, back in the days when it still carried fearful clout. A single line in one of Gert's column's could make or break the social aspirations of a young deb; a feature could do the same for the entire season of an established matron.

She lived alone in a big stone house in North Avondale. It was set back a good fifty yards from the street, behind a row of giant blue spruce. The space from trees to house was solid overgrowth: Queen Anne's lace, cornflowers, and tall grass, all gone to seed. The air was filled with the rasping of insects as Decker walked the driveway from his car. Gert threw open the door before he made the front steps.

"By God, there's my Rickie bird!"

She was wearing a long green dress with padded shoulders, and as always, a string of pearls around her neck. Her silver hair was fresh from its weekly coiffing.

"Get your buns in here, young man!"

He stepped into the foyer and the two of them hugged. Decker wagged his finger at her. "Gert, you've been nipping at the sherry again."

"Awwwww, a little pickerupper in the afternoon never hurt anybody. What can I get you, Rickie?"

"Just some of your famous herbal tea, Gert. I'm pressed for time."

Gert wagged a finger back. "Rush, rush, rush. That's all

you young ones do. How many times have I told you—let the damned stories come to you."

"Sometimes you have to meet the big ones halfway." He winked.

"Go on. Make yourself comfortable in the library. I'll be out of the kitchen in a jiff."

There were few places in the world he loved more than Gert Larson's library. It was worthy of a Renaissance monk. There was a big tile-covered fireplace at the far end of the room, and walls and walls of bookshelves all around, interrupted only by the slenderest of stained-glass windows. The books, of course, were all hardbound, and stacked in every conceivable position and in no apparent order. Yet Gert knew exactly where each one was.

On either side of the entry were black file cabinets, six drawers high and eight rows across. That was the famous Larsen "morgue," crammed full of newspaper and magazine clippings dating back to the early thirties, when Gert was getting her start in journalism. Gert had kept files on every person of any prominence in the city, as far back as their grandparents. But her own memory was an even richer gold mine of information. It was full of gossip, new and ancient, and unequaled by the recall of any six society matrons put together.

Gert came bustling in with two settings of tea and handed one to Decker. He was sitting in a corner of the sofa next to her rolltop desk. She pulled a high-back chair away from the desk and sat with her knees properly together.

"Now," she said, arranging some folders on her desk. "I have everything here you asked for. Let's see. We have Karl F. Krieger, Franklin P. Orsini, Victor A. Carbone, and, last but not least, Alvin S. Greenburg."

He watched Gert sort through the clips. She was a big-boned woman, tall and imposing, and full of vitality. Her eyes were flashing brown like Barrett's.

"Now, first of all—" She caught him blinking at the floor.

"All right," she said. She leaned from her chair and took his hand softly in hers. They were warm and vibrating with energy. "I was going to save this talk until later, but let's get it out of the way. What happened to the Simmons girl was an awful, senseless, brutal thing. And one never knows what to think, much less say, about awful, senseless, brutal things. Tell me, Rickie, did she mean a lot to you?"

He smiled a little. "I don't know. I was just thinking how much you remind me of her."

"Well, then," she said, slapping him smartly on the thigh, "she wouldn't have tolerated this moroseness for a minute. Now let's get down to work and get to the bottom of this sordid business. I can already see what you're driving at from the names you gave me over the phone. It's the *River Queen*, isn't it?"

"Gert, you're a whiz."

"Ha. I'm not so senile that I can't read the newspapers."

"Only every word and missing comma."

"Damn straight. Now let's see about these men and what makes them tick."

She picked up the Orsini file first and launched into a quick biography. The son of a West Virginia coal miner ("a bad start, but after the war, he had the damned good sense to leave the mountains and move to Newport, Kentucky. He was only sixteen at the time"), young Orsini worked in a brewery by day and finished high school at night. He was bright, he was a hustler, and he made friends quickly, especially in Newport's closely knit Italian community.

In 1955, he found his way into the Newport fire department, rose to lieutenant, then to captain. Six years later, in 1966, he had a falling out with the Newport fire chief, Roscoe Ubrizzi ("who was some damned cousin or other of Victor Carbone's. The Carbones ran the town at the time. Still do, only they're more subtle about it these days"). Orsini moved his family across the river to Cincinnati, where he joined the department as a firefighter, first grade. He worked his way into the arson division, became division leader, and was later appointed chief by City Council in 1981.

Decker was impressed by the research. "You got all that from the clips?"

Gert let out a short haughty laugh. "Hell, no. I've made a point of learning as much as I can about Orsini. The twerp fascinates me."

"Why?"

"Because he happens to be one of Karl Krieger's closest friends."

Decker looked up from his note-taking.

"You didn't know that? They're next-door neighbors. Their families barbecue together, vacation together, practically sleep together, and nobody can understand why."

"Why not?"

"Rickie, honestly. You're such a plebe. Because Krieger belongs to one of the oldest and wealthiest German families in Cincinnati, for God's sake. Nobody can understand why he would take up with an Italian hillbilly who puts out fires."

"All right, so why does he?"

Gert threw up her hands. "Your guess is as good as mine. They've been like that for the last two years."

Decker jotted down some quick notes. "Okay, how about Carbone?"

"I'm afraid I haven't much on that one." She picked up a manila envelope and pulled out a loose handful of clips. "Mostly business briefs about Carbone's little front operation—Amex Vendors. You realize, of course, the man owns half the vending machines in Cincinnati."

"I'm a regular contributor to the Victor Carbone Sleaze Fund."

"You and anybody else who wants a cup of coffee in the morning. You realize, don't you, why there are so few clips on our friend Mr. Carbone?"

He nodded. Carbone hid from the media the way a scorpion hides from the desert sun. He never gave interviews, never answered reporters' queries, never allowed pictures. Vic let his family do his public bidding. His brother-in-law, Tom Barrens, was twice elected mayor of Newport, and Vic's brother Tony still sat on City Council. Another Carbone relative, a cousin by the name of John Petalla, was a captain in the police department. And Carbone's only son, Vic Jr. (there were six daughters), was head of the city's sanitation department.

"The joke, of course, is that Newport will never have a dog catcher until Mama Carbone produces another boy," Gert laughed.

She sifted through the clips and handed Decker one from the *Eagle* that had been folded several times. It was dated May 10, 1979. "Bar Owner, Wife Gunned Down." A teaser added: "Dozens of Patrons See Shooting." Deep into the story, an FBI agent is quoted as saying "certain figures with ties to the underworld, including Victor Carbone," were suspects in the shootings. The killers were never found, and Carbone never indicted.

The Greenburg file was jampacked. Most of the material was common knowledge—nay, legend—in the *Eagle* newsroom. Gert kept an entire folder on the courtroom battles between Little Al and Krieger, filed under "Free Speech versus Community Standards."

She lifted a photo from one of the folders. "This says it

all, doesn't it?" Little Al was standing on a chair in the witness booth, pointing a tiny finger into Krieger's stony face.

"Here's another treat. I must say, the little man was quite photogenic." It was a gutter-level shot with a fish-eye lens. Little Al seemed a towering giant, his face a devilish mask as he grinned below an X-rated cinema marquee. The caption: "Porno King Alvin Greenburg stands tall after winning federal court fight."

In May of 1981, the grand opening of the *River Queen* merited a full-page spread in the *Times'* lifestyle section. The story ballyhooed the restaurant's New Orleans-style cuisine, the boat's lavish and painstakingly restored interior. There were crystal chandeliers in the dining room. Brass fixtures on every door and wall. The private suites brimmed with mahogany, inlaid teak, ironwood, and oak.

Gert sighed. "And now, nothing but ash and rubble."

The Krieger file, too, was bulging. The early years: local rich boy goes to war and returns a decorated tank commander in 1945. ("I remember how it was when he came home. For months, every society gal in town was in an absolute tizzy. You would have thought it was Caesar returning from the Gallic Wars.") He enrolled in Xavier University's theology department the same year. Three years later he had both undergraduate and master's degrees. ("Get this, Rickie. The title of his thesis was 'The Spirit of Thomism in the Jet Age.'") Then on to UC law school and the top spot on the law review. He graduated second in his class, 1952, and immediately joined one of the city's oldest and most prestigious law firms— Becker, Diehl, Simpson, and Rausch.

Gert picked up a second folder. "There's nothing in the clips for five years or so, until Fritz announced his engagement to Marcella Diehl. Talk about a match made in society heaven. Marcie was the reigning princess of the deb circuit. A Grace Kelly look-alike, everybody said. Tall and blond, but not as icy. Had a brain, too, although she's tried her best to hide it since marrying Fritz."

Gert held up a photo of Marcie in a strapless black gown. "Quite a dish, hmmmmm?"

"I think they'd call her a fox nowadays, Gert."

"A fox? Is that the latest? My God, I'm still learning to say 'chick.'"

After the wedding Krieger launched his political career. In 1960, a successful run for County Board of Education. 1974: his first bid for county prosecutor, followed by the landslide reelection of 1978. A footnote to 1979: the Hamilton County Bar Association awards Krieger its highest honor, the B. Morgenstern Award, for vigilance in upholding the law.

Six months into his first term, Krieger tried to stop *Last Tango in Paris* from playing at the Palace Theater, and was laughed out of court. The *Eagle* headline was a laughter, too: "Fritz Falls Flat in Tangle over 'Tango.'" Krieger was unfazed. Two weeks later, he shut down the opening night production of *Oh, Calcutta!*—five minutes into the first act.

Gert slapped her knee. "My God, Rickie, you should have seen the audience that night. I thought they would riot. All those Mercedes liberals howling and jeering as the police came on stage. After all, they'd paid twenty-five dollars a pop for an evening of artistic titillation."

Gert pushed the Krieger clips aside and picked up her tea cup.

"What do you know about Reverend Bevis?" Decker asked.

"What *is* there to know? A loudmouth and a phony. A Bible thumper with political aspirations. But I don't think anyone—anyone who counts, that is—takes him seriously."

"Do you think he could have put someone up to torching the *River Queen*?"

Gert sipped her tea and thought for a moment. "He's a bit

too dim for that, I'm afraid. He might have prayed for a fire, perhaps. But that's certainly not a crime."

"Funny. Turk said the same thing."

Decker sat back in the sofa and rubbed his itching eyes. He was worn out, drained but still driven. When he opened his eyes again, he said, "So tell me, Gert, where do I go from here?"

"You mean in this *River Queen* business?"

He nodded.

Gert set her tea down, smoothed her dress in a preoccupied manner, and spoke, as she would put it, in no uncertain terms. "My advice to you, young man, is to butt out. Leave it to the proper authorities. A Pulitzer won't mean a damn thing if you're not around to enjoy it."

He cracked a thin smile and rose from the sofa. "Well, Gert, I knew I could count on you."

Decker was back in the newsroom by three. He was organizing Gert's folders and photos, getting the whole mess ready to Xerox and drop on Nystrom's desk, when his phone rang. It was Ellway.

"Just wanted you to know the lab is finished with your apartment. We still have the key."

Decker told him the old man next door, Charlie Hobbs, would hold it for him. Then he asked if there were any leads.

"Are you inquiring as a member of the press, or as a friend of the deceased?"

"Both, I guess. But don't worry. The *Eagle* is shying away from this one."

"Wish I could say the same for the *Times*. I've had a fellow by the name of Joe Benoit pestering me all day."

"Me, too. I told him to kiss my sweet ass."

"Well, I leave that sort of thing to our public relations people." There wasn't a trace of humor in his voice. "You were asking about leads. Well, there aren't any. Except we know this must have been done by a big man, a strong man, judging from the marks on the neck. By the way, we talked to your neighbor Hobbs. Says he didn't see or hear anything that night. Don't think he would have even if he'd been awake at the time. Feeble as hell."

"Tell me," Decker said, "does this look like a professional job to you?"

Ellway was silent a moment. "At this point, I'd say no. A true professional would have cased the place better. No offense, Mr. Decker, but he would have known you didn't have much worth stealing. The real smoothies go after the big layouts in places like Hyde Park and Indian Hill. And they make damn sure nobody's home at the time."

"Then what about the murder? Would some punk off the street break somebody's neck that cleanly?"

"Mr. Decker, I suggest you leave the theorizing to us."

"I'm just asking."

Ellway settled down. "Yes, it's possible the theft was a cover-up for the real motive—murder. We'll know more about that when we've had a chance to talk to Miss Simmons' parents and a few of her friends. But we're not ruling out the possibility that a burglar was surprised in the act, and panicked."

"I just don't buy it," Decker said, his voice pitching higher with emotion. "Barrett would have fought like hell. I know she would have."

"You say that, Mr. Decker, but listen for a minute. It's hard to know someone's reactions when it's dark, when they're half-asleep, and when they've left the front door open for someone they're expecting to join them in bed."

"You're pretty hung up on that, aren't you?"

"On what?"

"On Barrett being in my bed. What's your problem, Detective?"

"I've got no problem, Mr. Decker. You just leave the investigation to us."

The law-and-safety complex was on the northeast fringe of downtown—about as far from the river, and the soul of the city, as you could get. Far from the riverboat jazz, the ballpark, the party boats and the barges, all the funky sounds and smells of the Ohio. At the center of the complex was the Hamilton County Courthouse—a perfectly square, perfectly gray stone building, five stories tall and spread over a whole city block. It had that neo-imperialist look so popular for public buildings in the thirties. Massive, bunkerlike. The only softening touches were the Ionic columns built into the upper three floors—far above the street. On the ground, there wasn't a tree or a touch of greenery in sight.

Decker arrived at five minutes to four for his interview with Ethan Nottingham and plunked down in one of the plastic-molded chairs provided for visitors in the secretarial pool. It was a dingy, worn-out room. Cheap paneling, gray carpeting with coffee spills. It might have been somebody's basement rec room, only it was occupied by an army of secretaries—typing, filing, bustling in and out.

On the double doors at the back of the room was a black-on-gold plaque: KARL F. KRIEGER, HAMILTON COUNTY PROSE-CUTOR. There were smaller plaques for each of the four assistants, including Ethan Nottingham, whose door was first on the right.

Nottingham had surprised him by agreeing to an interview that very afternoon. Even more incredibly, Decker had gotten the assistant prosecutor on his first call, in clear violation of the Professional Phone Call Pecking Order, in which reporters are near the bottom of the list. Just above life insurance salesmen.

Nottingham surprised him a second time. He burst out of his office two minutes early and put out his hand.

"Glad you could come over." The voice was as smooth as a shot of Dewar's—with just a splash of water, thank you. Nottingham was younger than Decker had expected, a shade under thirty. His blond hair was cut Seventies style, stopping modishly, but precisely, at the bottom of his ears. He was short and almost delicately built. He put you in mind of an altar boy. Side by side with Krieger, who had the stature and bearing of a cardinal, he'd look even more like one.

Nottingham led him to a small black swivel chair in front of his desk. His office was an improvement over the secretarial pool, but a far cry from Finch's Forbidden City. He sat behind what looked like an old teacher's desk—heavy oak, lightly stained. His jacket was off, his shirt sleeves rolled up. He was ready to get down to business.

"How may I help you?"

"I'm wondering, sir, if you've been close to the *River Queen* investigation."

"No, not close, actually. But I was allowed to review the preliminary report before it was made public."

"Did you have any concerns or problems? I mean, with the report?" Decker clenched his teeth. He hated himself when he beat around the bush.

"Problems? How do you mean?"

"I mean, sir, do you think there was any chance of arson?"

"That possibility was certainly discussed between my office and Chief Orsini's. But, as you know, it was not the finding in the report."

"I see," Decker stalled. "You're aware, of course, that there is at least one person in the department who disagrees with the report."

"I believe you're talking about Lieutenant Griswald." Nottingham laughed softly.

"I'd rather not say." Decker knew it was a weak attempt to protect a source.

Nottingham leaned forward, elbows on his desk and hands touching at the fingertips. *(This is the church, here's the steeple . . .)* His voice turned confidential. "Actually, Mr. Decker, Chief Orsini has told me a few things about Lieutenant Griswald. Things that bear rather directly on his criticisms."

"Such as?"

A cherub's smile flickered across Nottingham's face. "I'd rather not go on the record."

"And I'd rather not go off," Decker said. "I've been fed too much off the record as it is."

"From Lieutenant Griswald, I assume."

Decker shrugged.

"All right, then," Nottingham said. *"On the record,* I can say that certain information has come to this office that would tend to discredit whatever opinion Lieutenant Griswald has in the *River Queen* case."

"And what is that information?"

"That," he smiled, "is off the record." His babyish cheeks now had a tinge of pink in them, as though he'd just come from a quick game of racquetball at the club. He seemed to thrive on verbal sparring.

"Okay," Decker said, "off the record. Is this deep background only?"

"For now, yes. But the time may come when we could allow quotation, say, from someone close to the case."

"I'm all ears."

Notthingham propped his chin on two index fingers. "Do you recall the firebombings that destroyed the Majority Center and the Planned Parenthood Clinic?"

"The abortion clinics. They happened on the same night."

"That's correct. Both bombings occurred in the very early hours of April seventeenth, about five minutes apart."

"And still no suspects," Decker said.

"That also is correct. Would you like to know one of the principal reasons why?"

"Yes, I would. On or off the record?"

"Everything I say from this point on is off the record. I thought we had made that clear."

Decker grinned. "Just checking."

Nottingham smiled, too, somewhat exasperated, as though dealing with an incorrigible child. "I'll continue then—off the record. In both fires, Lieutenant Griswald was in charge of the investigation, and for a number of reasons, he botched them badly. Chief Orsini, of course, would have the details. But I know one thing. Lieutenant Griswald failed to secure the damaged areas during the investigation. As a result, vital evidence was taken—stolen, to be more precise—from the scene of both fires by unknown parties. As to exactly what kind of evidence, once again, you would have to consult the chief."

Nottingham pushed out his chin. "Naturally, when the *River Queen* caught fire, Chief Orsini took personal charge of the case. There was no room, he maintained, for any more bungling. Not on a case of such proportion."

Decker played dumb. "So what does all this have to do with Griswald's criticism of the *River Queen* report?"

"I think it's obvious." A trace of condescension slipped into the smooth voice. "Lieutenant Griswald wants to embarrass Chief Orsini in order to strengthen his own badly damaged position in the department."

He decided to make a quick visit to the fire department's arson division. It was near quitting time, but the office was just across the street in the Safety Building. Sally Eckes was eating carrot sticks one at a time from a plastic bag as he pulled up a chair next to her reception desk. Sally was tall and trim and fit nicely into a satiny white blouse and a tight navy skirt. He smiled like a friendly enough fellow and identified himself as a reporter.

"Is that late lunch, or early supper?" Decker asked. He sometimes wished he was more gifted at small talk.

"Breakfast," she said, with the well-practiced drop-dead tone of receptionist-secretaries. She was young, probably too young to remember Motown music. Her brown hair was long and curled and dramatically styled. A "Dallas" fan, no doubt. She'd have been cute, in a synthetic kind of way, if she'd broken the stony face with a smile.

"Mind if I sit for a second?" He crossed his legs and pulled out a notebook.

"Do you have an appointment to see someone, Mr. Becker?"

"That's Decker, Rick Decker. And no I don't. I was hoping we might talk a little."

She frowned at her watch. "I leave in five minutes."

"Don't worry. This won't take long. I was wondering, what can you tell me about Lieutenant's Griswald's handling of the firebombings this spring? You remember, don't you— the two abortion clinics?"

"What do you mean, what can I tell you?"

"Well, what did the guys in the department think? Did they think Griswald did an okay job?"

"Why are you asking me? Why don't you ask the men in the department?"

"I intend to," he told Sally. "But Bart Petkamp told me it might be a good idea if I talked with you first—you know—to sort of break ground. He says you know more about what's going on in this department than most of the investigators."

"You know Bart?" She smiled at last.

"Oh, yeah. Bart and I are great buddies."

"Isn't he an absolute *riot*?" She grabbed another carrot stick and started nibbling on the end of it like a gerbil.

"A real card," Decker avowed. "Did he ever tell you the one about the French flying ace and the prostitute?"

"Oh God, that one." She laughed, and held up her hand to cover her mouth.

"Bart told me you had a great sense of humor. I can see he was right."

"Okay," she said, nodding and smiling at the same time. "You can stop buttering up Little Sal. I can't tell you what I've heard from people in the department. You'll have to find that out yourself. But there *is* a little something I can show you."

She stood and walked to some file cabinets behind her desk, venting a generous slit in the back of her skirt. She returned with a single sheet of paper and slapped it on the desk.

"Take a look."

He read greedily. It was a letter of reprimand, addressed to Lieutenant Griswald and signed by the chief himself, blasting the lieutenant for "dereliction of duties in the handling of a major arson investigation."

He looked up. "So the lieutenant has a fan club."

"Yeah, but take another look. See the date there?" Sally pointed to the letterhead. "It says April nineteen. Would you like to know when this letter was filed?"

"When?"

"About a half hour ago." She gave him a sidelong glance.

"Sally, could I Xerox this letter?"

"No way," she said, slapping a hand over the sheet.

"All right. Then let me copy it in my notebook."

She thought about that for a second. "Okay. But do it quick. And remember, you don't know who showed you this."

He wrote fast, longhand not shorthand, taking backward glances at the reception-room door. The three paragraphs seemed to take forever.

"You know," Sally said as he wrote, "I asked the chief about the date on that letter, and why it hadn't got to me until today. Well, he got all uppity and told me his secretary had misplaced it or something. And then you know what he said? He said he didn't think it was any of my damned business. How do you like that?"

"I like *you* a lot, Sally." He blew her a kiss as he let himself out the door.

8

Stein called a six o'clock team meeting in the conference room. Decker, beat from the hectic day, slumped into a chair as Turk was spreading a half-dozen Xerox copies across the table. Stein and Decker hunched from their chairs for a closer look. They were tax records, each showing thousands of dollars in donations from Alvin S. Greenburg to All Children's Medical Center.

"One hundred and fifty grand in all," Turk said, sitting back in his folding chair and looking a bit smug, Decker thought. Turk said the hospital confirmed the information, reluctantly. "The money helped build the new genetic research and counseling wing."

"Interesting," Decker said, "but is it relevant?"

Turk grinned and stroked the Fu. "Sometimes little surprises lead to big ones."

Stein took a final glance at the scattered sheets. "Doesn't surprise me a bit," he declared, and went back to puffing his Savenelli.

When it looked as though he would leave it at that, Decker spoke up, "Well?"

Stein removed the pipe. "The donations are consistent with the character of the man and his deformity."

Decker and Turk swapped glances: Stein was a man of few words, until you got him started on the subject of character. Good reporting, Stein always said, was nothing more, nor less, than the study of human nature in action.

He held the pipe bowl in his right hand, the stem pointing outward, which he stabbed in the air for emphasis as he spoke. "Let's start with the fact that Little Al was a midget. True, an intelligent, rich, and powerful midget, but that only made his physical grotesqueness all the more insufferable.

"Ergo, the need to surround himself with perfect physical specimens. Star football players. Exotic strippers. In his theaters and porno shops, he peddled the images of sexy, willing young women, healthy young studs. It's easy to understand. Here was Little Al's means of both denying and transcending his physical stature. That he, Al Greenburg, could have so much perfectly formed flesh at his command made his shortcomings, so to speak, less painful to bear."

He stopped and relit his pipe, striking one and then another of his Rosebud safety matches and dropping them in the Styrofoam cup he carried around with him for just that purpose.

Decker grew impatient. "Brilliant, Barry. Now what about the donations to All Children's?"

"I was coming to that," he said, dropping his fourth and final match into the cup. "The donations represent another side of Little Al. His conscience, if you will. Despite all his nose-thumbing, Greenburg must have felt some twinge of guilt for incurring so much community wrath. The new wing at All Children's did two things to alleviate that guilt. One, it proved to Greenburg that he was really, deep down, a good guy, despite what decent folk thought of him. And, two, by supporting research into genetic defects, the money from his ventures might someday prevent deformities like his own." Stein took a couple of puffs, and mumbled, "End of discourse."

Turk and Decker traded glances again, smiling and shaking their heads with amused admiration.

"All right," Stein said, "what else have we got?"

Before Turk could open his mouth, Decker brought up the interview with Krieger earlier in the day. He told them about Krieger's joint investigation with the feds, the suspected ties between Greenburg and Carbone, the outfit in Cleveland looking to monopolize the porn trade. When he finished, Stein and Turk were sitting closer to the edge of their seats.

"Yet Krieger won't dispute the Orsini report," Stein said, pushing out his lower lip in puzzlement.

"I think I know why," Decker said, then followed with Gert Larson's tip that Krieger and Orsini were next-door neighbors and bosom chums.

Turk brought up an obvious question. "How the hell can Orsini afford to live on Grandin Road?"

Decker nodded. "I'll follow up on that."

He moved on to his postscripts on the Nottingham interview, and finished by reading out loud Orsini's letter of reprimand to Griswald.

"My, my, you've been busy today," Stein said. "So it sounds like our Lieutenant Griswald has an ax to grind."

"Hold on," Turk said. "Aren't we forgetting Nottingham is one of Krieger's toadies?"

"I've got more," Decker said defensively. "The date on Orsini's letter to Griswald was April nineteen. But the secretary in the arson division said it wasn't filed until today."

Turk clapped his hands. "Bingo!"

"One last thing," Decker said. "The other morning, Barrett wanted to talk to me about something a Newport cop had told her. Something about a secret outfit calling itself the Pentagram or some damn crazy thing. The cop thought there was a link to the *River Queen*. I know it sounds crazy, but Barrett seemed to think the guy was on the up-and-up."

The team was silent for a long while. Stein was the first to speak up. "She had a good nose for these things," he said in the gentle tone of a eulogy. "But it's not much to go on." He turned to Turk. "It's something you might keep in mind."

* * *

By late afternoon, the air had gone stagnant again, and the temperature, oddly enough, seemed to be rising as the sun was falling. Turk slipped some Bach choral preludes into his tape desk as he and Decker rode uptown on Vine Street through Over-the-Rhine. What was once a ghetto for German immigrants was now a mix of poor Apalachians and poorer blacks. Kids darted in and out of the narrow street. Curtains gasped for air through screenless windows. On the stoops of government-rehabbed rowhouses, women sat spraddle-legged and motionless under the weight of an endless day, while the men gathered in macho clusters on street corners and in front of bars, some with bottles in their hands.

"O, the humanity!" Turk wailed, and cranked up the stereo until the door panels vibrated. He shouted over the fluttery organ notes: *"Kommst du nun, Jesu, vom Himmel herunter auf Erden?!"*

I was old J. S. at his jauntiest. But it was no antidote for the sense of hopelessness that sinks in while cruising a ghetto on a hot summer evening.

The Discount Book Store was located near the top of the hill on Vine Street, not far from the campus of the University of Cincinnati. There was a twenty-four-hour "Washateria" on the left, a liquor store on the right.

Turk squeezed his Honda into half a metered space on Vine Street and they walked downhill a block to the bookstore. The storefront was windowless and paneled with unfinished cedar gone dry and gray. Nailed to the paneling on both sides of the door was a giant hand-lettered banner: GOING OUT OF BUSINESS . . . ALL ITEMS HALF PRICE!

"Looks like we got here just in time," Turk said. He pulled open the red sheet-metal door and they stepped into a room about the size of a candy store. There was no one there. To the left the walls were covered with magazine racks that, glanced at quickly, formed a solid blur of pink flesh. Straight back was a narrow doorway covered by a grimy turquoise curtain. Above it, another hand-lettered sign: PRIVATE VIEW-ING BOOTHS.

Running the length of the right wall was a glass case that could have been found in any candy store, only the shelves were lined with dildos in all shapes and sizes. Vibrating dildos, pump-action dildos, dildos with fantastic knobs and lethal-looking attachments.

"War supplies," Decker said. Turk laughed and headed for the magazine racks, where he began sampling the goods.

Decker hesitated to touch anything. A layer of grime and fingerprints seemed to coat everything, even the revolving racks in the middle of the room that were loaded down with videocassettes and reels of sixteen-millimeter film.

He grinned at some of the titles: SUZIE SUCKS A BIG ONE, RIDING THE CHOCOLATE HIGHWAY, WENDY WHIPS WALL STREET. On the last was a jacket photo of Wendy dressed for the occasion. Crotchless leather panties, black leather boots, whip in hand. Wendy was standing spread-eagled on a desktop, while a Wall Street type cowered in his chair, a look of delicious terror in his eyes.

"Christ, would you look at this," Turk said, holding up a magazine called *Mothers*. "It's nothing but beaver shots of pregnant women. Dozens of 'em. Redheads, blondes, brunet-tes. Man, the stuff some guys get off on." He shook his head as he leafed through the pages. "This shit is unbelievable."

"Yeah, so why are you still looking?"

Turk was putting *Mothers* back on the rack when the turquoise curtain snapped open. A man, hugely obese, angled sideways through the doorway. He stopped and glared at the two as though they were desecrating a shrine, then lumbered across the room and squeezed behind the glass case.

"Help you, gentlemen?" The voice was hoarse, husky. A beer drinker's voice. A beer drinker's body, too—puffy red face, swollen gut, breasts big and floppy enough to fill a C-cup bra. Yet, for a human slug, he was oddly fastidious. The white short-sleeved shirt was spotless and tucked neatly into chocolate polyester pants. His flattop was freshly mown.

Turk told the man they were reporters.

"You sure you guys ain't cops? Hey, I don't want any trouble with cops," he said, holding up his palms in a backing-off motion. "I'll be outta here within the week."

"We're not police," Turk said, and located his press card in one of his guyabara pockets. "We just have a few questions. For starters, why the big rush to move out?"

The fat man was incredulous. "You guys don't know much about the business, do you?"

"Fill us in," Turk said.

The man smiled and looked at Turk and Decker like two kids on the first day of kindergarten. He pulled a white handkerchief from his front pants pocket and ran it over the flattop and down the back of his neck. The room was air-conditioned, but the fat man was coated in sweat. A fat, glistening slug.

"I can put it to you in one word," the man said. "Krieger."

"Okay, try a few more words," Turk said, pulling out his notebook.

The fat man glared, ready to walk away, but Turk held him there with a stare of smoldering intensity, a look that spoke untapped reserves of violence.

"All right, dammit. Let me put it this way—with Little Al gone, I got no protection money. Not a penny." He waved a puffy hand around the premises. The fingers stuck out like tiny Viennese sausages. "And I don't mean money to buy off cops, because they're not the real problem. No, sir. The real problem is Krieger, and you've got to have money—big money—to fight that Nazi bastard in court."

Decker spoke up. "But didn't Greenburg win in federal court?"

"That don't mean it won't happen again. Krieger can come back with a whole new set of obscenity standards and pack us off to court again. And if that don't work, he'll have cops swarming all over the place, citing us for everything they can think of—illegal street parking, creating a public nuisance, contributing to the delinquency of minors. Hell, I've seen him send out building inspectors to shut a place down on code violations."

"Any visitors yet?" Turk asked.

"No, Krieger's laying low for now. Besides, he knows most of the shop managers will do like me. Get the hell out before there's any trouble."

A customer walked through the door. He wasn't what Decker would have expected—no greasy hair or thick glasses or trench coat buttoned to the collar. He was a fortyish, well-groomed man in a tan business suit. Probably someone who had a little time to kill before going home to the wife and kids. He froze for a second when he saw Decker staring, then walked back to the magazine racks.

"Ten-minute browsing limit," the fat man growled. Then to Turk and Decker: "Got to have a limit. Otherwise, some of these guys will come in here, jerk off in their pants, and leave. I'd never sell a thing that way."

"Some people have no class," Turk said. The jab flew over the flattop without ruffling a hair. Turk asked, "Why don't you get legal backing from somewhere else? Why not Carbone?"

"Carbone?" The fat man laughed and jiggled, his jowls flopping like sacked jelly. That's when another customer walked in. A tall, pimply college kid, wearing a store-bought UC football jersey. Decker sympathized. The lonely hell of the college freshman.

The kid handed the fat man a five-dollar bill, got a fist full of quarters in return, and disappeared through the greasy curtain. The fat man shouted after him:

"And don't make a mess back there. We got Kleenex, you know."

"Why not Carbone?" Decker asked. "Weren't you being supplied by friends of Carbone in Cleveland?"

The fat man held up a hand. "Buddy, you just left me way out in left field. I don't know nothin' about those kinds of arrangements. I'm just the little guy in a big operation."

"But you'd know if you were getting chicken stuff and snuff films from Cleveland," Decker said.

"Go ahead. Take a look for yourself. See if you can find any of that crap here."

"What about under the counter?"

The fat man went red in the face. "Get . . . Just get the hell out," he sputtered. "I'm busy."

Turk and Decker didn't budge, but the man in the business suit dropped his magazine on the bottom shelf and went quickly on his way.

"Damn," the fat man said, "you guys cost me a sale."

Turk smiled and slapped Decker on the back. "Let me apologize for my colleague here. He's been a little overworked lately, that's all. You see, what we really came here to talk about is the *River Queen*. We happen to think it wasn't an accident, and we need your help."

The fat man roared with laughter, and pulled out his handkerchief again for a quick swipe over the flattop. "I've answered enough questions for today, boys. Why don't you two just move along, okay?"

Turk went into his stare again. "Come on, who did the torch job? Was it one of Carbone's boys?"

"Ha!" the fat man erupted.

Turk hit him with another quick question. "You don't think Al was cutting into Carbone's trade?"

"Sure, the gambling some," the fat man said, serious now. "But it was strictly business between Al and them boys over there. Hell, Al had a policy: any customer that asks, you send 'em to all the right places in Newport. Girls, boys, drugs, anything they wanted. Al didn't deal in them things anyway. All he really wanted was to run a nice clean gambling operation, free of the law."

"Then why the porn shops?" Decker said.

The fat man laughed again. "You know," he said, still chuckling, "you got me there. There ain't much money in these places. Pin money compared to your gambling and your drugs."

"Then why?" Decker said. "So he could launder his gambling money?"

The fat man's eyes popped. He turned to Turk. "Sounds like junior has done a little homework."

"Some," Turk said, folding his arms across his chest and beginning to look impatient. Six feet, four inches of impatience. "Why don't you fill us in some more?"

The fat man mopped his head again, and his eyes seemed to take a fresh look at Turk. Appraising, suspicious, more than a little fearful. When he spoke again, it was to Decker. "Take my word for it, Al Greenburg was a strange man. Mighty strange. He wasn't what most people around this town would like to think—it wasn't just the money. Hell, sometimes I think he ran these places just to piss off Krieger. Hated the man's guts. Al never called him by name, not in private. It was always 'that fuckin' Nazi.'"

A grin of secret knowing spread across the fat man's face. "There's another reason for these shops that might surprise the hell out of you."

"Have anything to do with donations to All Children's?" Turk said.

The fat man's jaw dropped.

Decker followed with, "One hundred fifty grand in the last three years."

"Hell, it was more than two hundred fifty grand over the last five," the fat man corrected. "And every penny of it from Al's shops and screens."

"A strange little man," Decker said to no one in particular.

"One last question," Turk said. Decker suspected it probably wasn't. "Who do you think wanted the *River Queen* torched?"

The fat man examined his spotless nails. "You'd have better luck with that question over at the courthouse."

"You mean the prosecutor's office?"

"I mean I ain't saying any more than what I just said." The fat man turned and started for the curtain.

"One more question," Turk said.

The fat man kept going. Turk shouted after him. "We think the arsonist is burned around the neck. You know anybody who fits that description?"

He disappeared into the back room, but when Turk and Decker opened the door to leave, he poked his head through the curtain.

"You fellows might just ask one of Carbone's boys. I hear they like to play with matches from time to time."

"And your name, sir?" Decker was never one to forget the basics.

"Are you out of your fucking mind?"

It was 7:20 when they returned to the newsroom to file their notes. Getting it down fresh was important, even though it meant unpaid overtime. That was the way it worked at the

Eagle: if you wanted to do things right, you did them on your own time. Exhausted as he was, Decker didn't mind. It was the thought of returning to his apartment, and the memories there, that filled him with dread.

He was typing out a short memo on Griswald's letter of reprimand when the phone rang. It was almost 8 P.M.

"Hello, Rick?" It was a young woman's voice, very perky. It seemed to come to him from some benign universe alien to his own.

"Have you forgotten already? Janet Shoemaker."

"Ohhhh, Janet. Why yes. How goes med school?"

"You mean my residency. It's hectic, but otherwise fine. I was calling about the interview with the burn patient, Maisie Williams. Did the tape help at all?"

"Oh, yeah, I was about to call you on that," he lied. "The editors decided it was too sketchy. The woman didn't seem in control of her faculties."

"That's exactly why I couldn't go on with it, Rick. The poor woman. God, what an awful thing. I don't think there's anything worse than a burn. Nothing, really. You know, she died not long after I talked to her."

"I know. She must have been badly burned."

"Sixty percent of her body—torso and lower extremities," Janet said clinically. "The chief resident said he could smell the gasoline in her shoes when they brought her in."

"Gasoline!?" It was almost a shout.

"Yes. Most severe burns *are* gasoline-related."

"But Janet, Orsini is saying— Forget it. Do you have a name and a phone number for this chief resident?"

"Of course, Wiley Thompson. Let's see if I can find him in the residents' directory." He took a couple of deep, measured breaths while Janet looked. "Oh, yes, here it is. He even lists his home number." He took down both of them.

"Thanks, Janet. Gotta run."

"You've forgotten, haven't you?" She was only half-faking her little-girl disappointment. "You promised me dinner sometime."

He lied again. No, he hadn't forgotten. Then Janet said she was on call for the rest of the week. They agreed to meet Monday night at seven o'clock.

"I know this very cozy Italian restaurant," she said.

"I'll bet you do."

Dr. Wiley Thompson was not used to being disturbed at home. Especially by nosy reporters. "Who told you about the shoes?" he snapped.

Decker said a friend.

"Well, I certainly have no comment one way or another, Mr. Decker. I'm a doctor, not a policeman or a fire chief. And to tell you the truth, I can't recall making such a statement to anyone. If you want information along those lines, I suggest you contact the fire department."

Thompson hung up.

Turk was digging in the team's file cabinet, next to the conference-room entrance, when Decker called him over and told him the news.

Turk gave a low whistle, then said: "Better get on the horn to Stein. They may want something for first edition."

Stein's wife Barbara answered. She strained to be pleasant, but sounded edgy and fatigued. It was suppertime. In the background, Decker could hear the clatter and scrape of dishware, an overlay of little boys' voices, shouting and squealing.

"Boys! Boys! Now be quiet, *please.* Your father's going to use the phone."

Stein came on the line in the same soft voice he always used. Decker gave him a quick rundown on Janet's offhand disclosure and the doctor's weak denial.

"Should we write for the early edition?" Decker asked.

"No, it's too big for a rush job. What you *can* do tonight is reach Griswald. Go out to his house if you have to, but give him the goods. Tell him we have too much information now to keep his suspicions off the record. Either *we* go with it, or someone else will."

"Gotcha. What about Turk?"

He was standing by Decker's desk, listening to half a conversation.

"Jeff!" Stein's attention was elsewhere. "Take your hands *off* your brother's food. You hear me? Jeff!" Then back to Decker, "I'm sorry. What did you say, Rick?"

"Turk's here tonight, too."

"All right, see if he can get a response from Orsini. Ask the chief if he can explain this little discrepancy with the shoes. If not, we'll try again in the morning."

"Roger dodger, Big Daddy. Over and out."

"Decker, you're worse than my kids."

There was no listing for Milton O. Griswald in the phonebook, but he checked the city crisscross directory and found a number and an address: 1080 Cascade Drive, North College Hill. He went quickly to his desk and dialed.

In the middle of the first ring, a woman's voice answered, tense and expectant.

"Hello?"

"Is Lieutenant Griswald home?"

"No, who is this, please?" The voice was heavily accented. Japanese? Filipino?

Decker identified himself. "Is this Mrs. Griswald?"

"Yes. But, please, you must talk later. I am expecting a most important call."

"But it's important that I talk with the lieutenant tonight. Do you know where I can reach him?"

"No, I cannot." Suddenly the woman let out a sob. "No

I 128 I

one has seen my husband since he left this morning. So please go away."

"Wait, Mrs. Griswald. Please. Maybe I can help. I talked to your husband just last evening."

He heard her softly blow her nose, and when she spoke, her high thin voice was close to breaking. "I don't think you can. Miltie was home last night. Now he's gone. He should have come home two, three hours ago. This is not like Miltie. No, not like him at all."

"Have you called the police, Mrs. Griswald?"

"Yes. Now please, you must—"

"Do you have any idea where your husband might have gone?"

"He was dressed for work. He left early. At seven, I think, instead of eight o'clock. He said he could not sleep. Then this afternoon, his secretary called me here. She asked why Miltie did not come to work today. I said—" Mrs. Griswald sobbed again, hard. "Oh, please! Someone please find my husband!"

Decker tried to say a few comforting words. He left his number and a message in case Griswald called home. Then he phoned Stein.

"Well, well, this gets curiouser and curiouser," Stein said. "All right. Tomorrow we see if anyone in the Safety Building knows about the lieutenant's sudden disappearance. But knock off for the night. You hear me? You sound pretty frazzled."

"What if the *Times* knows about the gas in Maisie's shoes?"

"Go home, Decker."

It was past midnight when he reached his apartment. He stepped out of his car and looked up and down Pullan Street, checking one last time to see if he was being followed. But the street and the sidewalk were empty, save for the usual pack of teenage boys who hung out on the porch steps of the double across the street. He could see the tips of their cigarettes in the dark, glowing hot orange and then fading again like tiny pulsars. It was reassuring to hear their smart-alecky tones, the contrived huskiness of their laughter.

He opened the wrought-iron gate and trudged back to his apartment at the rear of the narrow brick house. He had met with Turk again at Steamboat Willie's, talked and drank, and was more than a little drunk, not to mention bone-tired. So tired his thoughts at times seemed more like snippets from a dream. Almost anything would pop into his head. Like the face of Hera on his door knocker suddenly coming alive in the light from the porchlamp, winking at him playfully. He shook the image out of his head and unlocked the door. Where had he seen that bit before? Oh, yes, A *Christmas Carol*. Scrooge's house. And God bless you, one and all.

He stepped inside, closed the door and immediately turned the deadbolt.

Snapping on the hallway light, he half-expected to find Barrett in the living room, sunk comfortably in the wing chair in his velveteen bathrobe and reading an old *Esquire*. But the chair was somber and empty, and the next thing to pop into his mind were the bruises on her neck, like butterfly wings, and the body, strangely luminous and cold, like polished marble.

He avoided even a glance at the bedroom door and from the hallway went straight to the living room. It looked untouched despite the work of the lab techs that morning. He yawned. His joints ached. He was hot and sticky, but he hadn't the energy for a shower.

He untied his tie, flung it over the back of the wing chair, and dumped his keys, wallet, pocket change on the folding tray next to the sofa. He didn't need an alarm. In late summer, the sun always woke him about the same time—6:45. He turned off the overhead light, kicked off his shoes, and sprawled on the sofa in his shirts and pants.

He lay motionless, the sheets pulled to his chin, his eyes fixed on the white light that flickered now and then from under the bedroom door. His heart was pounding, the bedsprings creaking audibly with every beat.

There were footsteps—light and quick—down the hallway, down the stairs, gone.

He went softly to the bedroom door, opened it a crack, listened. No more footsteps. But downstairs, what? Mumbling? A sibilant, whispery voice, like a nun in chapel. "Oh God . . . please dear God . . ."

He tiptoed to the stairs, took three steps down. He could see the light flickering again, playing against the walls. He recognized the whispery voice.

She was in the living room in her chenille robe, a flashlight in one hand, a rosary in the other, kneeling before the gold-framed photo she kept on the TV set. She spotted the flashlight in his face as he approached.

"Rickie," she said softly, and sniffled. "Oh, dear Rickie." She stood and went to him, taking his hand in hers and gently tugging as she knelt again.

"Rickie," she pleaded, "pray with me, Rickie. Pray that he'll come back . . ."

"But I don't care, Mom. I don't care if he ever comes back . . ."

He woke with a start and lay there until his eyes could make sense of the blackness. He got up from the sofa and stepped carefully through the dark into the kitchen. His stomach let out a growl, long and hard. A convulsion of angry juices. In the refrigerator, he found some three-day-old Colonel Chicken in a grease-soaked box. He grabbed a thigh and started gnawing with the refrigerator door wide open. The chicken was tough going—crusty and dry and hard to swallow. So he crouched and searched the low shelves for a stray can of beer. None. Not even a soda. But there was a brand-new jar of Grey Poupon. He snapped it open, dunked the thigh, gnawed some more.

He was debating whether he needed a second piece to stop the growling when he heard the bedroom door creak. He turned his head, froze, listened. Silence. A heartbeat later, he heard the faint rushing of wind outside. The door creaked again.

He shut the refrigerator and stared into the gloom. The silence was cold and palpable. It tingled on his skin, droned in his ears.

"All right, who's in there?" he called out with as much force as he could muster.

He dropped the chicken bone to the floor, reopened the refrigerator door, and in the light, went to a kitchen drawer and pulled out a butcher knife. He moved quickly to the bedroom door. It was half-open. He listened. Again there was nothing. Only the thrashing of wind through the backyard trees. Holding the knife in front of him like a sword, he reached beyond the doorjamb and hit the wall switch.

The back window was open. Probably the way the idiot cops had left it. The wind stirred again and the curtains were sucked outside. The screen was gone. He shivered, and then he saw the bed. The mattress was covered with slash marks. Dozens of ragged punctures, the stuffing coming out. At first, it seemed random—the work of a crazy man. But when he stood at the foot of the bed, he could see it. A jagged pattern of lettering—YOU NEXT.

9

Decker balanced the gun on the flat of his palm, hefted it gently up and down, impressed with its weight, its utter absoluteness. He thought of Ben Johnson kicking his foot against a rock and shouting at Berkeley, "I refute you thusly."

"Now if you're looking for something to keep around the bed, I'd recommend the baby you got right there—a Taurus thirty-eight," the salesman said. He was a stocky man with red hair and a fifties-style burr, white walls around the ears. He was wearing a green Banlon shirt, snug around the biceps, and his right forearm was tattooed "Semper Fidelis."

"Now you can look at our Smith and Wessons over there, but you'd be getting into some big bucks," the salesman said. "The price is right on this one."

He rubbed his fingertips over the cross-hatched wooden handle, then across the cylinder—black and oily—and down the snub-nosed barrel. It felt odd and, yes, sinful in a way, to be buying a gun. To be admiring its craftsmanship, discussing its reliability, like any other consumer item.

"Go ahead," the salesman said. "Take it by the handle. See if you like the feel. It's got a real nice balance."

He gripped the wooden stock, but kept his finger outside the trigger guard. He had never fired a gun, but he had seen plenty of movies. He pointed the gun vertically in the air and then slowly straightened his elbow until shoulder, arm, and barrel became one extended line. He took aim. There was a Confederate flag behind the counter. In his mind's eye, he pulled the trigger, drilled a neat hole dead center through the intersecting bars.

But what about a living, breathing man?

He lowered the gun and set it carefully on the counter-top. The barrel was stamped MADE IN BRAZIL.

"Does it have much of a kick?" he asked.

"Nah, but it gets the job done. Especially at close range. A lot of your off-duty cops carry a piece like this."

He stared at the gun. Would he really need it? Would he even know how to use the damn thing? It wouldn't have saved Barrett, he realized. She never had a chance. But it might make him feel less naked, less vulnerable.

"Of course we got cheaper," the salesman said. "But if it's life and limb you're protecting, you don't want some cheapass Saturday Night Special. You know what I'm sayin'?"

He looked into the salesman's eyes for the first time. There was no con there, no ingratiating grin. Only a look of intense sincerity, of shared defiance against punks, burglars, all the bogey men who scared and preyed upon the little people. This was their revenge.

"I'll take it."

"Not very subtle," Stein said, lighting his pipe and quickly filling the conference room with a dense blue cloud of smoke. Turk feigned a hacking fit, but Stein only smiled at him.

"So, do I go to the police?" Decker asked.

Turk shook his head no. "They're trying to scare us."

"I *am* scared, goddammit. You'd be, too." He thought of the gun he now kept in the glove compartment of his car. No, he wouldn't tell them about that. It seemed a private matter.

Stein scratched his scalp, yawned. It was 10:05.

"I think you should," he said. "But only so there's a public record."

"I get it," Decker said. "In case somebody *does* wipe me out, is that it?"

Stein changed the subject. "You have a place to stay?"

"Sure, I was at Turk's last night."

"Good."

"Yeah," Decker laughed. "If you can stand the snoring."

"Close your door," Turk said.

"And suffocate?"

"Shit—"

"Boys!" Stein crossed his hands in the air like a referee signaling time out. He dropped them and smiled. "Sorry. Sometimes it's like I'm still at home."

Turk tossed the A section of the *Times* across the table to Stein. "You read this yet?"

"Aluminum Wiring: The Hidden Hazard" said the headline on the day's top story. It was the first of four parts. Stein cocked an eyebrow as he puffed and read. Decker couldn't help chuckling. The *Times* was tilting at windmills again, while the real villains—whoever they were—were inside the windmill and bollixing up the whole damn works.

Stein was smiling in self-congratulation when he finished the piece a minute later. "Good. At least we can forget about the competition."

Dottie, the *Eagle* receptionist, interrupted the meeting: Mr. Finch was ready now to see Mr. Stein in his office.

"Well," Stein said, rising from his chair, "we'll soon have a verdict."

While Stein was in the inner sanctum, Turk visited Vendville for microwave pancakes and Decker sat at his desk reading, and rereading, Joe Benoit's story on Barrett's murder. It was front page but under-the-fold, with a discreet one-column head, no pictures.

Ellway hadn't given Benoit much he could use; Decker could see that. The story was written mostly from police reports, a few long-distance calls, a smattering of gossip. Barrett was described as a Phi Beta Kappa graduate of Barnard

College, in New York City, in case readers didn't know (he rolled his eyes: "It was Swarthmore, you asshole"). She was further pigeonholed as a former debutante from the Baltimore area. He groaned: it was exactly the label Barrett would have scorned.

There were no references to a relationship between him and Barrett. But the story was quick to point out that "Miss Simmons' unclad body" was found in his bedroom. "Mr. Decker refused comment to the *Times.*" (Yes, and how, he thought.) Buried at the bottom of the piece was a quote from Ellway: "Mr. Decker is not under investigation at this time."

All in all, it was typical *Times* "crapmanship"—plenty of "facts" for the record, little digging into the truth.

In less than fifteen minutes, Stein was back in the newsroom. Turk and Decker met him at the city desk. He was smiling and slowly nodding his head.

"He wants it. Today. Home edition."

Decker's heart squeezed inside his chest like a clenched fist. "All right!" Turk shouted, then clapped and swirled his palms together.

Annoyed by the outbursts, Lafferty turned from his VDT. He had the half-hurt, half-angry look of a little boy left on the sidelines during the big game. "Hey, keep it down. Some of us have work to do."

Stein winked at Turk and Decker and said. "Finch wants us in his office."

The Boss was in rare macho form. Like a much younger man, he was sitting on his glass-covered desktop, hands gripping the edge, Guccis crossed.

"Gentlemen," he announced as soon as the team was seated, "I am going to lay this paper's balls on the line." He paused to let that bit of bravado sink in, then resumed at a clip. "After talking with Barry, I've decided it's time to run with everything we've got on the *River Queen* story. Everything—which is, of course, far from the whole story. But what we have is damned powerful, and what's more, it's not available to the *Times*."

Finch slapped a fist into his palm, clearly on a roll now. He was Bogie in *Deadline U.S.A.*, Katie Graham in *All the President's Men*. "The time to press our advantage is now, gentlemen, before the boys on Vine Street wake up and smell the coffee."

Beating the *Times* seemed even more imperative in the last week. The most recent circulation figures showed a quarterly drop of three thousand for the *Eagle*, a gain of almost five thousand for the *Times*. The *Times* now outsold the *Eagle* almost two to one in the suburbs, and the *Eagle*'s slight advantage inside the city was beginning to erode as well. Further proof the *Eagle* was dying.

"Secondly," Finch said, "and Barry and I agree entirely on this, we need something to give this investigation a push. We can't afford to sit back and let Orsini think he holds all the cards. If the chief has struck some kind of deal with Carbone and the boys in Newport—and I strongly suspect he has—this story ought to make him squirm."

He shifted gears; there was a fleeting moment of moral angst. "The hard decision, of course, is whether we use Griswald's off-the-record comments. Under normal circumstances, I would say no. Absolutely not. It would be unethical and risky. But these are not normal circumstances, gentlemen. Our most valuable source has suddenly and unexpectedly disappeared. Therefore, to make a long presentation short, we go with it."

Finch looked around the room with fire in his eyes. Decker wondered if they were supposed to clap. He glanced at his watch and took a deep breath. Almost 10:30. The team had little more than two hours to put together a very complicated and potentially libelous story.

"Nystrom will write the main story," Finch said. "Decker, you'll do a sidebar based on a complete transcription of our tape of Maisie Williams—grunts, moans, and all. Neither story should be very long. Keep them brief and keep them simple. No speculation, no theorizing. We'll let our readers put two and two together. Then tomorrow we run an editorial asking the department to reopen its investigation—in light, of course, of new evidence obtained by the *Eagle*. So there we have it, gentlemen. Questions?"

Decker thought of one. "What about the visit to my apartment last night? Do we mention—"

Stein cut him off with a quick wave of his hand.

"Nothing, sir," Decker said.

"All right then, gentlemen." Finch slammed fist into palm again. "Let's do it."

The moment they were back in the newsroom, Decker grabbed Stein by the arm. "What the hell was that hand signal all about, Barry?"

Stein kept his voice low. "Finch would blow the mattress story sky-high. It's just the angle he loves—*Eagle* reporter martyred for investigation. We don't need that kind of attention. Not yet."

Decker got to work. His first call was to Orsini. As expected, the chief had no comment.

"Chief Orsini is extremely busy right now," his secretary snapped. "But he wants you to know that he stands by every word in his report."

"Then why the hell can't he come to the phone?"

The next sound he heard was a dial tone.

Taking a tip from the stress-management seminar, Decker sat back, closed his eyes, and took a couple of deep slow breaths. Don't get mad, get even.

He cranked out the sidebar in no time at all—a little under an hour—and then joined Turk at his VDT to help piece together the main story.

He loved to watch Turk working against a deadline. Nystrom became a man possessed, flailing at the keyboard like a concert pianist performing one long scherzo. He didn't let up until he had a complete first draft. Then he would stop to check the story against his notes, and with few exceptions the facts were the same, down to the exact wording of the quotes.

In three or four places Decker suggested slight changes in phrasing. Turk stopped in mid-frenzy, briefly considered the change in silence, then either made the change or shook his head and moved on to the next sentence. Mostly, though, Decker kept his mouth shut and let the story unfold—and from a respectable distance, too—because Turk reeked. Decker recognized the smell: the sour odor of a hung-over journalist working under the gun. Nystrom was off the wagon and drinking again, heavily. He had seen signs of it the night before when he arrived at Turk's apartment. An empty fifth of Jack Daniels on the floor next to the La-z-boy. A tray of watery ice cubes on the kitchen counter.

Turk finished a good fifteen minutes before deadline. The story sang. It was simple, it was clear, it was all there.

Stein breezed through the main story without a change. Then Mullins, the slot man, read through it again—picked over some grammatical nits—and slapped a head on it: QUESTIONS RAISED IN RIVER QUEEN FIRE.

Turk wasn't impressed. "What the hell does that tell the reader?"

"Beats me," Mullins said, "but that's the head Finch asked for." He pressed a red button along the top row of his keyboard and sent the story and headline to electronic never-never land. In seconds, a machine in the composing room would spit out neat strips of newspaper type ready for paste-up.

At 12:15, Turk and Decker were about to leave the newsroom for a long congratulatory lunch when Dottie yelled from her desk that Decker had a call on his line.

"Can you take a message?"

"He won't. He says it's very important."

"Who is it, Dottie?"

"He won't say."

"Oh, for Christ's sake." Like most journalists, Decker was a sucker for anonymous calls. It wasn't just the mystery, it was the drama. He returned to his desk and picked up the line.

"Hello, Decker here."

"Mr. Decker, this is Chief Franklin Orsini."

He quickly sat down, rummaged over his desktop for a notebook and pen. "Yes. How can I help you?"

"You can help me by not printing lies."

"How, sir?"

"I mean this shit Griswald has been feeding you. It's a pack of lies and he knows it."

"Remember, Chief, anything you say can be quoted."

"I don't want to be quoted. I just want to knock some sense into you, goddammit. Griswald is a vengeful, misguided man. He's mad because I shook him down for a royal screw-up, and now he's getting even. There's a big fat letter of reprimand sitting in his file any time you'd like to take a look."

"I'm already familiar with that letter."

"Well, how can you believe the man then?"

"Nobody's taking sides, Chief. We're just raising questions that need to be raised." Feeling in control now, Decker thought he'd try something. "For instance, why was gasoline found in the soles of Maisie Williams' shoes?"

"Who the hell told you that?"

"It doesn't matter. Do you have any comment, sir?"

"It doesn't prove a damn thing. There was plenty of

gasoline in storage on the *River Queen*. Big tanks of it for the shuttle boat. It's all in the report."

"According to Lieutenant Griswald, the tanks were in the mid-section of the boat, and they didn't blow until long after Miss Williams jumped ship."

"I don't give a goddamn what Griswald said. It's one man's opinion. A very vengeful man's."

"Is that for quotation, Chief Orsini?"

"Never mind, goddammit. I'm sorry I called. Fritz told me you could be reasoned with. I can see he was dead wrong. I warn you, young man, if these lies are printed, you and everybody else at the *Eagle* will live to regret it."

"Is that a threat, Chief Orsini?"

He hung up. Decker was two for two that morning.

Turk was waiting at the newsroom exit. Decker waved him over, told him the news, and they both went to see Stein on the city desk. Decker ticked off his notes on the chat with Orsini, then asked Stein if any of it should be inserted into the day's stories. Stein shook his head immediately.

"Not worth it. First of all, he didn't tell us anything we don't already know. Secondly, he wanted it off the record, so we keep it that way. Besides, we're not through with Mr. Orsini by any means. He'll have plenty of chances to tell his side of the story. Go to lunch."

Turk and Decker sat at one of the round metal tables in the courtyard at Arnold's Bar and Grill. It was Decker's favorite summer lunch spot: a converted airshaft, surrounded by walls of mossy brick, filled with a jumble of mismatched tables and chairs. A lone tree of paradise, strung with Christmas lights, grew defiantly from the cracked cement. Even on the hottest days, the air in the courtyard was cool and a little damp, like a wine cellar. The food was hearty, good, reasonably priced.

When the waitress showed, Decker ordered iced tea and

Nona's spaghetti with meatballs. Turk ordered chili and a double martini.

Decker slipped the menu back between the salt-and-pepper shakers and the open bowl of dill pickles. He went straight to what was on his mind. "So you're off the wagon?"

Turk shot a glance across the table that closed the subject. Temporarily, anyway. Decker knew he would have to bring it up eventually. If not with Turk, then Stein. There was too much at stake for both of them now. It was no time for Nystrom to go off on one of his binges.

Decker changed the subject. "Did you ever file your complaint with the Human Rights Commission?"

"You mean about the fucking cops in Fountain Square?"

Decker nodded.

"Nah, what's the use? They'll say I was obstructing officers in the line of duty. That's what they said when Rebo got his skull creased trying to take the pictures of Reagan. You remember that?"

"Yeah, good old Rebo."

"Where the hell have you two been?" Lafferty held up his wristwatch. "It's almost two-thirty."

"Discussing strategy," Turk fired back. Decker cringed at Turk's slurred speech, but Lafferty was too stupid to notice anyway.

"The Boss wants to see both of you. Pronto. Orsini was in his office a minute ago, raising all kind of hell."

They found Finch sitting rigid in his big leather chair, but far from his usual picture of composure. There was still some red in his face, and a sliver of hair—oily with Grecian Formula—had fallen down over his forehead.

Stein arrived a second later and closed the door behind him.

Finch waved him in, dropped forward into The Big

Lunge, and started off. "Gentlemen, I have just had a most interesting conversation with Chief Orsini. The chief, it seems, is ready to play hardball."

"He's going to sue," Turk said as though it was no surprise. Decker winced. Surely Finch would notice Turk's condition.

"Of course," Finch said, "but that's not all. Lieutenant Griswald has evidently skipped town with some important documents from the arson division. There's a warrant out for his arrest. Orsini insists that we know where Griswald is hiding, and that if we refuse to disclose that information, he'll have us arrested, too. Furthermore, he was fairly apoplectic that the *Eagle* would stoop to hearsay, as he put it, by referring to the gasoline in Miss Williams' shoes. I informed him that we did not print that bit of information, but he didn't seem to hear."

Decker mentioned quizzing Orsini about the shoes earlier that day. "I was just fishing."

"Fine. Let him think we know more than we actually do."

"Is he bluffing about the arrest?" Stein asked.

"There's good reason to believe that. I told him we were looking for Griswald ourselves. I also told him that even if we did know the lieutenant's whereabouts, we would protect him as a source—even if it meant you boys would go to jail."

"Thanks," Decker smiled.

Finch laughed a little. He was regaining the old composure. "I doubt anyone but Orsini is going to jail."

Finch moved on to his biggest concern: how would the *Times* play its story the next day? "Orsini is certain to peddle his side of things on Vine Street, and in great detail, hoping to make us look reckless and naive."

"Ha!" Turk erupted, and Decker could see from Stein's fixed stare that he had guessed Nystrom's state.

Finch continued in a low voice. "Gentlemen, I needn't tell you how vulnerable the *Eagle* is at this point. We haven't a single shred of solid evidence to contradict Chief Orsini."

He bore down first on Decker. "We've got to confirm Griswald's arson theory, or else. I don't care if you have to visit every fire station in the city."

Decker tried to interrupt.

"Please," Finch said, shutting his eyes in irritation. "Let's not make excuses before we've even begun."

Then he turned to Turk. "And Mr. Nystrom, you must find the man who actually spilled the gasoline and threw the match. It *can* be done. Somewhere, sometime, the punk will brag he set fire to the *River Queen*. It's too damn big for anyone to hold back."

The idea flashed into his brain the instant the team reassembled in the conference room. Finch had triggered the train of thought: "Not a shred of solid evidence."

"Don't laugh until you hear me out," Decker began, "but I think it's time for some hands-on reporting. I suggest we get our own material evidence. We could grab a piece of wood from the *River Queen* and send it off to the arson lab in Columbus. Just the way Griswald did."

"Why not?" he repeated as Turk let out a short, derisive laugh. Stein puffed on the idea for a while, then said evenly. "The boat's under twenty-four-hour armed guard. They won't let our photographers near enough for pictures."

"That's right," Turk said. "I've been over there. They keep a cop at the Serpentine Wall, right in front of the boat's gangplank."

"Only one?" Decker asked.

"As of yesterday," Turk said. He was stroking the Fu now. A good sign, Decker thought. Turk was beginning to take life seriously again.

"Fantastic," Decker said. His mind, and mouth, went racing ahead. "Then it's simple. We create a diversion. We send one of our photographers to the *River Queen* and have him demand to take pictures. He raises all kinds of hell about the First Amendment, the public's right to know. Truth, justice, the American Way. Okay? Meanwhile, we sneak up in a boat, slip onto the back of the hull and take some wood." Decker was slightly breathless, his eyes appealing to Turk and then to Stein.

"You mentioned 'we'?" Turk said.

"Of course, you and me. We'll find somebody who can lend us a rowboat. Then we row out—" Turk rolled his eyes. "Dammit, Turk, give it a chance. You're an expert at this commando stuff."

"I was never a commando."

"You know what the hell I mean."

"Yes, I do, and it's crazy," Turk said. And then he broke into his biggest grin. "But I fucking like it."

They both turned to Stein, who was puffing on his pipe, trying to look impassive.

"A couple of things," he said. "One, this venture was never discussed in my presence. Two, if you're caught in the act, the *Eagle* never authorized your actions. In short, you two are on your own."

At nine P.M. sharp, they launched their gray wooden skiff from a clump of bushes underneath the Big Mac Bridge, several hundred yards upstream from the Serpentine Wall and the wreck of the *River Queen*. Decker manned the oars while Turk sat in the prow.

Decker was having second thoughts, an uneasiness that seemed to settle in his abdominal muscles and thighs, all of which quivered as he rowed. Turk was edgy, too. He seemed irritated with everything Decker did.

"For Chrissake, did you think this was a Sunday outing? You're shining like a goddamn beacon."

Decker was wearing a gray Columbia T-shirt, beige camping shorts, and white tube socks with blue Nikes. Turk was in camouflage fatigues and a black pullover cap.

"Excuse me, Sergeant Rock. My commando outfit was at the cleaners."

Decker eventually found his rhythm on the oars, and the muscle spasms in his thighs began to ease. He looked around him. The night was warm, breezeless, the water black and smooth, a mirror for every light on the riverfront—a fact that didn't escape Turk's notice.

"Fucking Reds game," he mumbled. Downstream, a quarter mile past their destination, Riverfront Stadium was lit up like a giant birthday cake. For hundreds of yards in either direction, the stadium glow laid a wash of white across the river's surface.

"Dammit, I knew we should have crossed from Kentucky," Turk said. "We'll cut right into his line of vision."

"Too late now." Decker had been the one to veto the idea of launching from the Kentucky shore, fearful of how the small skiff would perform crosscurrent. He still thought he was right. By comparison, rowing downstream was a cinch. It was a matter of keeping the boat aimed in the direction of the stream and avoiding the abandoned pylons along the river's edge.

The plan was to work this way: when Turk and Decker reached the L & N Bridge, near the start of the Serpentine Wall, that was the photographer's signal to engage the guard. They were confident they had the right man for the job— Rebo Johnson. Rebo's dreadlocks alone were enough to set most cops reaching for their nightsticks. And he was the kind of photographer who wouldn't take no for an answer; he'd been kicked out of more hospital emergency rooms and detained at more disaster scenes than anybody else on the staff.

As he rowed, Decker concentrated on letting the current do the work. The river was strangely quiet for a Thursday night. A houseboat was the only other vessel within sight, slowly churning upstream near the Kentucky shore. Even Riverboat Row was silent, with another half hour or so before the jazz bands kicked off the night's entertainment, and at least two hours before the aftergame crowds jammed the riverboats.

The skiff reached the L & N Bridge just as Riverfront Stadium erupted with an electronic bugle call and a shout of "Charge!" There were probably men on base, the Reds at bat.

A hundred yards or so ahead, the blackened hull of the *River Queen* was barely visible above the waterline, its rounded bow facing upstream. The ship, a football-field long, ran parallel to the promenade at the bottom of the Serpentine Wall, which wasn't a wall, actually, but a series of winding concrete ledges leading up to a grassy park called Yeatman's Cove.

In the half-darkness, the ledges seemed gray and almost vaporous, like a giant cascading waterfall descending to the river. A couple sat at the very top, huddled against a backdrop of city lights.

Barrett and he had huddled there once, too, on a chilly September night. He remembered now having a sweater and wanting to leave, but Barrett had laughed and said no, they couldn't, the great river god Polluto would be angry if they left without an offering. An offering of what? he said. And then she kissed him so hard they both fell backward onto the pavement. They rolled one over the other, clutching and devouring each other like Burt Lancaster and Deborah Kerr on the beach in *From Here to Eternity*. When they stopped, Barrett was breathless and laughing. She was still laughing as he hustled her off to his car and took her back to his apartment.

Turk tapped Decker on the shoulder and pointed downstream to the policeman on guard duty. They were a good thirty yards upstream, but they could make him out. A hefty one. Broad in the shoulders, just as broad in the ass. He was facing downstream toward the stadium, sitting on a metal gangplank that led into the bow of the *River Queen*. The plank sagged underneath his weight.

But where was Rebo?

The plan was to board the *River Queen* somewhere near the stern, as far from the guard as possible. But it was no go without Rebo's diversion.

"What do we do now?" Decker whispered.

Turk tapped him on the right shoulder. "Take us wide into the river. We'll cut back when we're past the guard."

That hadn't been in the plan. "What if a barge comes through?" Decker whispered. "We'll be swamped."

"We worry when it happens."

Turk started rustling in the trash bag where they had stowed their gear—a heavy-duty flashlight, a pair of hand-held suction cups, a first-aid kit. Decker turned his head. Turk was dabbing his face from a tin of shoe polish.

"You're kidding," Decker said.

"Shut up and row."

He did, but his muscles began to quiver again as he realized how dangerous and absurd it was to be navigating an eight-foot skiff down the middle of the Ohio without lights or horn. They were sitting ducks—not even that, he thought, because ducks could float and neither of them was wearing a life preserver. Turk said they would be too bright.

When the skiff was even with the smokestacks of the *River Queen*, Turk tapped his shoulder again.

"Okay, we cut back. Easy does it."

He sunk his left oar deep and nosed the skiff around into the current. It was tricky. He needed enough power to pull them against the current, but also enough balance to keep the bow pointed in the direction of the *River Queen*. After a bit of flailing, he got the rhythm—two hard pulls on both oars, then a soft tug on the left seemed to keep them on course.

They were no more than twenty or thirty yards from the *River Queen* when they heard an echoing thunderous roar, like half the field at Daytona starting their engines at once. The sound was coming from the public landing downstream.

"Turk!" Decker pointed.

"The son of a bitch!"

It was a nasty speedboat, one of those long, twin-engine jobs that red-necks love to slice up and down the river when they're good and plowed. It was on a course somewhere between the skiff and the *River Queen* and kicking up a wake like a tidal wave.

Turk gave him a push. "Into the bottom."

He swung the oars inside and fell backward. He was looking at the tops of Turk's muddy combat boots when the speedboat passed so near he could feel the engine vibration through the planks of the skiff. The wake hit a half-second later. It rocked the skiff high on one side, then the other like an amusement park ride. The river came sloshing in, cold and slick and smelling of gasoline.

By the time the skiff settled, Decker's face and torso were buried under water. The boat was sinking. They would have to swim for it. He poked his head above water, took a deep breath, a quick look. It was a miracle. The skiff was more than half-filled, but somehow, they were still afloat.

He sat up and spat to get the oily taste of the river out of his mouth.

"Oh, shit," Turk said. He was sitting in the bow and looking upstream toward the Cincinnati shoreline. Decker looked, too. They were now a hundred yards or more downstream from the *River Queen*.

"Let's go," Turk said. "We got to move, or we'll miss Rebo."

Decker shivered in his wet shorts and T-shirt. He slid back onto the bench, swung the bow of the boat around and started upstream again. With the extra ballast, the skiff was harder to pull, but easier to steer. They kept a slow but steady course.

He listened for the speedboat, but it appeared long gone, probably up the Licking into Kentucky. All they could hear now was the dipping of the oars, the creaking of the oarlocks, and the occasional roar of the crowd from Riverfront Stadium.

When they had closed within ten yards of the *River Queen*, they heard something—angry voices. One of them was unmistakably Rebo's. It boomed with mighty indignation.

"I'm telling you, *s-i-i-i-r*"—and the "sir" was stretched into a sarcastic slur—"I have every right—"

"And I'm telling you, buddy, I got my orders. Now I don't give a damn if you're black, white, or polka-dotted, one more word from you, mister, and you're under arrest."

"Under arrest!?"

"One more word—"

"This is an outrage—"

"That's it. Turn around."

"Sir, I hate to inform you, but this is a free and democratic nation—"

Decker and Turk were within arm's reach of the *River Queen's* stern, hidden behind the boat's hull, when the handcuffs clicked.

Rebo was incredulous, his deep voice suddenly two octaves higher. "You can't do this! You haven't read my rights!"

The cop radioed for assistance, then told Rebo to move it.

They watched from the skiff as the pair climbed the Serpentine Wall. The cop had his nightstick in Rebo's back, prodding him every step of the way. But Rebo moved at his own pace, back straight, head held high, dreadlocks dangling over his broad shoulders. He looked powerful and majestic, almost superhuman, like Samson in chains ascending the steps to the temple.

"An Oscar-worthy performance," Turk whispered.

"I hope Stein can bail him out."

"Are you kidding? The jail will beg somebody to bail him out."

They prepared for boarding. Decker rowed the skiff in tight on the port side of the *River Queen*, a foot or so from the stern, then tucked his right oar inside the skiff while he steadied with the left. Turk handed him the big suction cups. Decker dunked one, then the other in the ballast, pressed each snug against the charred metal hull, and, pulling in his other oar, held onto the suction grips with both hands. He kept the skiff tight against the *River Queen*, but not bumping it.

The empty hull stood a good seven feet above the waterline, and from the vantage of a half-sunken rowboat, it loomed like a black granite cliff. Turk stood slowly from the skiff's watery bottom, reaching for the top edge of the hull, a metal lip about two or three inches wide.

"Careful," Decker said as they began to rock.

Turk tested his grip, then lifted himself chin-up style until his eyes peered just over the hull. Then, bending his knees and lifting both feet from the skiff, he tried to swing his left leg up and over the hull—and missed, by several inches.

"Dammit!"

Turk let himself slide down the hull, slowly, until his feet touched the skiff's bottom again. He rested a moment, panting.

"You want me to try?"

"Shut up. I'm going again."

With a mighty heave that nearly capsized the skiff, Turk landed his left knee just over the lip of the hull, but lost his right grip. Suddenly he was dangling from the *River Queen* by one arm and a leg, like an orangutan from a tree limb. Decker couldn't help chuckling.

"Goddammit, give me a push."

He tried, but couldn't get enough leverage. Not without sinking the skiff.

Turk grunted and wheezed, straining upward with his left arm and groping with the right. Decker shoved from below, and with a final grunt, Turk was straddling the hull like a jockey on a horse. Decker whispered a cheer.

Turk took a moment to catch his breath, then disappeared with a thump and a clatter into the innards of the *River Queen*.

"Toss the flashlight," he said.

"I can't see where you are."

"Toss it anywhere, dammit."

The flashlight landed with a soft thud, into a pile of ashes, Decker hoped.

"Good throw," Turk said sarcastically. Decker could hear him slipping and clattering over debris with every step.

"It's a god-awful fucking mess in here."

"What did you expect—the *Queen Mary*?"

Turk ventured a few more steps, and then began rooting around for a sizable chunk of floorboard, per instructions from the arson lab in Columbus. They wanted a piece that was charred, but not so ashen it couldn't retain traces of gasoline.

"Turk, hurry it up. The cop will be back any second."

He heard the splintering crack of dry wood.

"Got it!"

"All right then. Get a move on."

The sliding and clattering began again as Turk made his

way back to the edge of the hull. At that moment, Decker saw the guard appear at the top of the Serpentine Wall.

"*Turk*. He's here."

A black cap and a pair of eyes were all that showed above the hull. He handed Decker the flashlight.

"Where is he?"

"He's coming down the wall."

The skiff was hidden behind the *River Queen*, but Decker wasn't so sure about Turk, black face or not.

Turk handed him the length of the floorboard—longer than Decker's forearm—then balanced his stomach and chest carefully along the edge of the hull. Slowly, quietly, he slid his left leg down toward the skiff, and gripping the edge with both hands, let the right leg drop as well. For a breathless instant, his legs and torso swung free against the hull like a pendulum. And that's when he lost his grip.

He dropped like a sandbag. The skiff rocked, the oars clattered, and Decker thought the boat was going down this time for sure.

"Hey! Who's there?" The cop wasn't deaf.

Turk lay flat in the bottom of the skiff where he'd landed. Decker had somehow kept his grip on the suction cups. He was crouched low with his face pressed agains the hull.

They could hear the cop's heavy footsteps as he walked the embankment, first to the *River Queen's* bow—where Decker knew they could never be seen—then back to the stern. He stopped. They waited, afraid to move or breathe, and kept on waiting—for a shout, a light beam, a gunshot. Finally, there was the sound of footsteps again, slow and easy, followed by the groan of the gangplank as the cop resumed his station.

Turk nudged Decker's shin with his foot, and whispered: "Let's get the hell outta here."

A mighty roar swelled up from Riverfront Stadium.

Bench had probably clobbered one into the green seats, or Seaver had struck out a batter to end the inning. It was a good time to make a move. Decker popped the suction cups and Turk pushed them away.

They hid in the bottom of the skiff, lying face-to-face in the cold viscous water. Like a schoolkid who had just pulled off the prank of a lifetime, Turk broke into an enormous grin, his blackface half-hidden in the water. Decker grinned back and they gave each other a high-five as the river took them gently downstream.

10

Friday morning at 8:30, the floorboard sample was dispatched to Columbus. The lab results would take at least forty-eight hours. That meant waiting out the weekend, and Decker dreaded any lull in the investigation. Work was the only thing keeping a lid on his rage and anxiety, but that still left the nights, when it all came bubbling out of his unconscious.

He had dreams now of being chased by a faceless horror he could hardly describe, a menace that he couldn't see, only feel, like a cold current under his flesh. When he woke, he could never remember where he was being chased, or why. Only that his legs were like lead, pumping and pumping, but never moving fast enough, until he could feel the awful thing chasing him sink its cold vibrations into the back of his neck, up into his skull. And that's when he woke, exhausted and slick with sweat.

Turk had a promising lead. Late Thursday night, while Decker returned the skiff to a friend's garage, Turk had visited the strip joints along Monmouth Street in Newport. A bartender dropped the name of Vernon Walker, a small-time hood who sometimes started fires for local merchants who wanted to cash in on their insurance policies. He also believed Walker had done a number of jobs in the past for Carbone.

"How much did that piece of information cost us?" Decker asked when the team met the following afternoon at 4:30.

"Nothing," Turk grinned, "except a thirty-dollar bar tab."

Late Friday morning, Turk had also paid a second visit to

the Fat Man at the Discount Book Store. "His real name is Howard Nussbaum, which he doesn't want printed for obvious reasons. Anyway, Nussbaum says he thinks Walker was burned pretty badly in a torch job a couple years ago. The problem is, nobody I've talked to has actually seen Walker— just heard of him—so I still don't know if he fits our description."

Turk was stroking the Fu again, not nervously, but with a quiet preoccupation, a smooth motion down the left side of his mouth with all four fingertips of his right hand. "I asked for an audience with Carbone," he announced matter-of-factly. "His secretary said he'd get back to me in a couple of days."

"I wouldn't go alone," Stein said.

"I doubt if he'll talk. It was probably a put-off," Turk said. He seemed unusually subdued, and Decker wondered if it was an extended hangover or something nonalcoholic preying on his mind.

For his part, Decker had little to report. It had been a day of working in circles, going round and round the stony walls of silence at the Safety Building and Cincinnati General, trying to find a crack in the mortar. No one, not even sweet receptionist Sally Eckes, knew where Griswald had disappeared. And none of Griswald's cronies were taking calls—not even on their direct lines. At General, the gasoline in Maisie Williams' shoes was starting to seem like a figment of Janet's imagination. No one at the hospital seemed to know what he was talking about.

With nothing else going, he asked Stein if he could begin working on a follow-up to his Krieger profile. He laid out a number of reasons. One, the team needed a story on Krieger's reaction to the demise of Greenburg Enterprises (seven of nine porno shops and all five cinemas had closed in less than a week, just as the Fat Man had predicted). Two, if Krieger was indeed a key figure in the arson and its cover-up, the team needed to learn as much as possible about the character of the man and his friendship with Orsini. (Stein, of course, would agree.) Finally—and this reason he kept to himself—he believed Krieger was untainted by the *River Queen* mess and, to strengthen that belief, he wanted to talk with the man again.

Stein nodded. "Call him today."

"It so happens I'm invited for din-din tonight." Decker hadn't forgotten Krieger's invitation, delivered on the courthouse steps.

When the meeting ended just after five, he tried again to reach Janet Shoemaker. She, too, was on the trail of Maisie Williams shoes, trying to find someone other than the chief resident who might have noticed the gasoline smell. But for the fourth time in seven hours, Decker was told that Dr. Shoemaker was assisting with a delivery and couldn't come to the phone.

By 5:30, his head was throbbing and his hands were shaking from a coffee overdose. He was about to call it a day when the phone rang. He plucked at the receiver, dropped it, grabbed it off his desktop, and growled hello. On the other end was the voice of an older man—pleasant but businesslike—with a clipped accent that was almost British.

"Mr. Decker, this is Theobald Simmons."

He didn't recognize the name.

The voice said, "I am the father of Miss Elizabeth Simmons."

Decker nearly said "Elizabeth who?" when his mind engaged: it was Barrett's father. The coffee shakes suddenly disappeared. He sank back in his chair with the weighty dread only guilt can induce.

"Mr. Simmons, you have my deepest—"

"No, please," Simmons interrupted. "No condolences. I only wish to talk with you. In private. A half hour or so of your time is all I ask."

"You've got it."

"In person, Mr. Decker. My wife and I are taking the next plane back to Baltimore in preparation for tomorrow's funeral. I believe it's an eight-thirty flight. Could we possibly meet before then? At your convenience, of course."

At 5:45, he met Simmons in the lobby of the Vernon Manor Hotel. Their handshake and greeting were quick and formal—two men with serious business to conduct. Decker, however, was feeling very ill at ease. On the drive over, he had begun to wonder what this man could possibly want from him. Revenge for his daughter's death? Details about Barrett's love life?

After the introduction, they went straight into the bar, a cozy carpeted place with glass tables and wicker chairs. They found a quiet spot in a corner. Simmons apologized for his wife not being there.

"She said she preferred to stay upstairs until we leave for the airport. She's not particularly fond of your fair city, as you might imagine."

Simmons was exactly the way Barrett had always described him—the original aging preppie. Outside the temperature was in the seventies, but Simmons was wearing a wool suit, a blue Oxford shirt, and a wool regimental tie that could be found only at Brooks Brothers. He seemed a big hearty fellow. Squared shoulders, a wrinkled, suntanned face, and tangled gray-brown hair that looked somehow windblown, as though he had just breezed in from the tennis courts. His manner, however, at least at that moment, was reserved. His eyes alternated between quick glances at Decker and a steady gaze at the glass tabletop between them. Decker couldn't decide if the man was angry, embarrassed, or both.

The waitress appeared. Simmons ordered a perfect Manhattan, straight up, while Decker asked for a soda with a twist. The waitress disappeared. Silence ensued.

Barrett would have been amused by the scene, Decker thought. Her father and her sometime lover thrown together to discuss matters of weighty importance concerning one Miss Elizabeth Barrett Simmons. Yes, it might have been funny, if Barret had been there to laugh at it.

Simmons leaned forward, hands clasped on the tabletop, and leveled his clear green eyes, trying to look sincere, composed, assured. But the tension in his brow, the tiny furls in his forehead, gave him away.

"First of all, Mr. Decker—"

"You can call me, Rick."

"Yes, perhaps that makes sense under the circumstances. All right then—Rick—why did I ask you here? It's hard to say exactly, except that I need to know more, much more than the police are telling me. And I assume you are the man who can help me."

"I'll try my best."

Simmons, too, had noted the discrepancy between the murder and the value of what was taken from the apartment. But he couldn't understand how his daughter could possibly have had any enemies.

"Yes, she always spoke her mind. And she pushed herself very, very hard," he said proudly, straightening in his chair. "Elizabeth expected a great deal from those she loved, because she expected so much from herself. But the idea of her having enemies—mortal enemies—is inconceivable."

Decker agreed and, as delicately and efficiently as he could, told Simmons about the *Eagle's* investigation, about the slashes in his mattress, about the team's suspicions. By then, their drinks had arrived. Simmons downed half his Manhattan in the first swallow. For a second or two after, Decker noticed the anger in the clenched jaw, the sudden twitch in the temples. Then it was gone. WASP rage.

"You're telling me that my daughter was most likely a victim of organized crime?"

"To the best of our knowledge, yes. She just happened to be in the wrong place at the wrong time."

"Meaning your bed."

"Yes." Decker shut his eyes a moment to hold back a torrent of emotions—anger, self-pity, shame.

Simmons swirled a fingertip around the edge of his glass before downing the last of the Manhattan, cherry and all. Decker saw the temple twitch again.

"Forgive me, Rick. I'm not here to attack you for—how can I put it delicately?—for not making an honest woman of my daughter. I realize that would have been quite an undertaking for any man. Elizabeth was fiercely independent, as much or more so than any man who would have tried to hold her."

Or men, Decker thought. He always wondered if there were others. He had been too afraid, perhaps, to find out.

Simmons looked at his watch and motioned for the waitress to bring the check.

He turned to Decker with an air of unfinished business. "Actually," he said, "Elizabeth seldom mentioned her men friends to Martha and me. She was very private about such matters, perhaps because she believed we would have disapproved. She was wrong, though. All that ever mattered to us was that she be happy with whomever she chose and under whatever circumstances. We never told her that, but now I wish we had. It is, of course, too late for that."

"It's too late for a lot of things, Mr. Simmons. But maybe not too late to find the killers."

"Revenge?" Simmons chuckled without mirth, shook his head. "There is no adequate revenge. None at all." His tone was accusing, and somehow Decker felt like the accused. He looked at his watch and stood to leave.

"I've got to get back to the office."

"Please. Sit for one last question." Simmons motioned with his hand. Decker sat. "I want you to be honest. For the sake of an old man who has lost his only daughter. Tell me, Rick, was Elizabeth happy? I mean, was she happy with her arrangement with you?"

Decker saw the green eyes fix on him, unblinking, demanding.

He didn't know where to begin. He and Barrett had never discussed their "arrangement." They had fun together, and if things weren't going so well, they didn't see each other for a while. They coasted. They didn't ask questions, they didn't make demands.

"She was very happy with her career," he answered, thinking of nothing else he could say.

"But that's not what I'm asking." Simmons frowned and turned his head away. "Forget it. Please. I had no right. I just wanted to make some sense of all this."

The temples twitched again, but now the eyes were going moist, too. He turned them on Decker. "Can't you see, if Elizabeth had good reason to be in that bed—your bed, any man's bed, I don't give a damn—then the horrible thing that happened to her won't seem so—so unspeakably senseless and, yes, tawdry. What I am asking, Rick, is this: did you and my daughter love each other?"

Decker felt confused, numbed. An obvious question, and yet it was one he had never asked himself or Barrett. Before she was killed, he would have answered, "Yes, no, maybe . . . What the hell difference does it make?" But the man was right. It *was* different now—and too late. Simmons deserved an answer. But what answer?

He looked at the older man's face: the green eyes closed for a second, expecting the worst, then opened again, expecting no answer at all. Suddenly, from some region of heart or mind Decker had never called on before, the answer surfaced in a flash. It wasn't a thought so much as a mental reflex, an intuitive grasp of what was true.

"We just never let it happen."

Simmons' eyelids fluttered, then narrowed with contempt. He started to say something, stopped himself, then turned his head away and waved for Decker to leave. It wasn't an angry gesture, but one that simply said he wanted to be alone.

As Decker left the bar, he glanced back to see Simmons still motionless at the table, his head bent over an empty glass.

The Krieger residence was at the end of a long private drive, marked NO OUTLET, off Grandin Road in Hyde Park. It was a Tudor castle of heavy stone and gray stucco, with enough chimneys, in Decker's estimation, to fill a block of London rowhouses. Evening swallows (or were they bats?) dipped and scissored above the slate rooftop.

Decker was flattered and a little intimidated to be greeted at the door by both Kriegers. Fritz introduced his wife as "Marcie dear" and Decker recognized her instantly as the kind of woman who throve in the shadow of her husband.

She was wearing a white apron over a khaki jumpsuit and looked like her name, a petite thing with hair tinted rich lady's blond and tucked behind her ears in a pageboy. A braided gold necklace, gold bracelet, gold earrings further established her station in life. She was a fitting trinket for Krieger to dangle before guests.

"It was such a lovely article you wrote, young man," Marcie said after the introduction. And then looking up at her husband with adoring eyes, she added, "Of course, we've known all along what a wonderful man our Fritz is." Her eyes were fixed somewhere on the entryway carpet as Krieger wrapped his arm around her tiny shoulders. Decker swore she blushed.

"Well, now," Krieger said, slapping Decker on the back. "We have Christian Moerlein on ice out back, and a couple of lawn chairs with our names on them."

Poplar trees rimmed the far edge of the back lawn, as tall and gracefully proportioned as Greek columns. Past the trees, a steep hill covered with bramble and vines dropped off to a wide bend in the Ohio, where pleasure boats skimmed the water like so many insects. Beyond the river rose the hills of Kentucky, dotted with tiny houses and churchsteeples, and silhouetted by a band of deepening red orange sky.

That was the view to their right as Decker and Krieger lolled in chaise longues by the pool. Krieger looked sporting if not quite relaxed in a striped green-and-white rugby shirt and go-to-hell-yellow golfing pants. Decker was still dressed in his work clothes, although he had loosened his tie and left his poplin jacket in the car. The air was warm, but not stifling, and clearer perhaps than in the valley where the poorer classes dwelt. They both drank cold Moerleins from designer plastic cups, waiting for the other guests to arrive, while Charlotte Krieger, all of sixteen or seventeen, took diving practice.

She was a veritable machine, executing every dive with the same smooth, crisply compact motion. Toes to the edge of the board, knees loosely bent, arms lifted and—sproing!— lightly, every so lightly, into the air. At the very top of her ascent, the lithe body folded in two and then dropped straight as an arrow into the pool, piercing the water without stirring so much as a bubble.

Krieger applauded loudly, and when his daughter surfaced, shouted: "Lovely, Charlotte! Absolutely lovely!"

Smiling proudly, Krieger turned his cool blue eyes on Decker. "You know, of course, that Charlotte was runner-up in the state diving competition this year. Actually, she would have won first place if the meet hadn't been held in Cleveland," he said, then added good-naturedly. "All those damned Cuyahoga County Democrats, you realize."

Decker laughed on cue. "Naturally."

Social occasion or not, Decker still had work on his mind. For the last half hour or so, he had been trying to quiz Krieger about the closing of Greenburg's porn shops, but the prosecutor's attention was focused on his daughter. Nor had Decker forgotten about Charlotte's arrest at the Christian Unity rally earlier in the week. Did her father know she was there?

Charlotte climbed the ladder out of the pool, tossed her long wet hair behind her head, smoothed it back with her fingers. She was a sunny blonde, long-limbed like her daddy, with the same almost-haughty bearing, although there was a touch of youthful uncertainty in the way she kept her eyes cast to the ground. She wore a swimsuit that Decker hardly expected to see on Fritz Krieger's daughter—a black one-piece that clung like an extra layer of skin, cut high at the hips, low at the chest. Perhaps it was the type worn by all competitive divers.

As Charlotte emerged from the pool, Krieger applauded again, more loudly this time. "Marvelous! Much better line, my dear."

But if Charlotte was heartened by the praise, she didn't show it. There was no smile for her proud Daddy, not even a nod. She padded on wet feet to the board, where she repeated her machinelike execution. Decker watched carefully this time, but couldn't tell if the line was marvelous or not.

"Tell me, Rick, do you find my elder daughter attractive?"

Decker could feel himself blush, although he hadn't been

thinking about Charlotte in that way. Not consciously, that is. He cleared his throat. "Well, Mr. Krieger, I—"

"Don't be ashamed," Krieger said. "It's only quite natural. Thomas Aquinas himself writes in the *Summa Theologica*, 'Men alone take pleasure in the beauty of things; their faces uplifted, not downcast.' You see, Rick, I'm not the boring prude that my critics have made me out to be. If I am anything, I am an utter realist."

Decker was about to ask for an elaboration when Mrs. Krieger appeared at the backdoor. "Fritz, dear!"

"Ah, yes. Time to do the honors," he said, rising spryly to his feet. "Would you care to join me?"

Marcie was waiting at the door to hand her husband a large platter of brats, Italian sausage, and thick red patties of ground fillet. "Fritz doesn't have to do this himself," Marcie told Decker. "But no one else does it quite so well."

Krieger gave him a broad wink. "Wonderful psychologists, these women. I believe they invented positive reinforcement." Marcie laughed and went inside.

A safe distance from the house, Krieger doused the charcoals in the portable grill with enough lighter fluid to trigger an explosion, and then told Decker to stand back as he threw a match into the sodden mess. The flames shot two feet into the air and out through the ventilation holes in the bottom of the grill.

"Only way to do it, really," Krieger said. "Too many people dillydally around, wasting matches and time. The charcoals never burn evenly that way."

Krieger was silent a moment watching the flaming charcoals. Decker took the opportunity to ask what he had meant by declaring himself a realist.

"Exactly what the word implies. I understand that men are both angels and beasts. And the beast, so long as it is properly controlled and directed, is a natural and healthy part

| 165 |

of us all. I know you must tire of my continual references to Aquinas, but allow me one more: 'The soul does not take an airy or heavenly body, but a human constitution composed of flesh and bones.' The great monk recognized long ago that one's moral powers depend in large part on the direction of one's psychic and physical energies. It is for that reason I abhor pornography—it diverts and drains moral energies. And I daresay I am years ahead of my time."

As though looking at a child from dizzying philosophical heights, Krieger patronized Decker with a smile, then resumed. "Over the years, I have prosecuted dozens, possibly hundreds of cases involving sex crimes—child abuse, rape, rape-murders, sexual violence you wouldn't imagine in your wildest and most sordid dreams. And what do you think was the common link among all those behaviors? Pornography. Indeed, in almost every case, the investigating officers found that the men who committed these crimes had pornography of some kind in their possession."

On some gut level, Decker agreed with Krieger, but he also knew the liberal argument: you can't corrupt those already corrupted.

"It's not just the criminal element that concerns me," Krieger said, as though he had been reading Decker's mind. "The real tragedy is that pornography has saturated our media. It's become a societal obsession. Destructive and energy-depleting. The celebration of the flesh has come at the expense of so many deeper values that once made this country great—the value of hard work and a job well done, of learning and intelligence, of dedication to family, and most important, to the untiring search for God . . ."

Krieger was on a roll when he stopped in mid-breath. Decker turned and saw Charlotte standing at attention before her father, her knees and feet touching primly together, a large white towel wrapped around her shoulders. Her eyes looked as blue and shimmering cold as the water in the pool. Krieger peered down at her, his nostrils still flaring some from the tirade.

"Father," she said evenly, as though to no one in particular, "I've practiced more than an hour now. I'm going in to change."

"Yes, dear," he said, reaching for the towel around her shoulders. "But how many times have I told you you mustn't walk about like this without toweling your hair."

He draped the towel over her golden head, like a terry-cloth veil, and when she looked down, he put his hand lightly under her chin and lifted it. When her eyes met her father's, Decker saw for an instant an icy glare so filled with loathing that he, too, felt its force. She pulled the towel around her shoulders again and walked away.

Krieger called out, "Charlotte, why don't you wear that lovely gingham affair of yours? It would be just the right mood for this evening."

"Yes, father," she said without turning around.

"I supervise every hour of her training, you know," he told Decker proudly, as though he were talking about a different person than the young girl who had just shot him dead with her eyes. "We're looking toward the Olympics, of course."

Mrs. Krieger called from the door. "Fritz, dear, the guests are arriving."

"Yes, honey, we're ready." He began to heap the brats and burgers atop the glowing briquets, careful to space them evenly across the grill. While Krieger was occupied, Decker popped another question. "Tell me, what was your reaction when you heard of Al Greenburg's death?"

Decker studied the chiseled face, looking for the tiniest display of emotion. But there was no change in the haughty mask, just the same quiet intensity as Krieger forked more brats onto the grill.

"I'd rather not be quoted on this," he said with a conspiratorial air, meaning Decker was being treated like an insider again.

Decker reached for the Bic in his shirt pocket. "I'd rather keep everything on the record, if you don't mind." But when he searched his back pockets for his notebook, he remembered he'd left it in the car.

Krieger smiled, and handed him a paper napkin. "All right, I'll say it anyway. I believe a true menace has been removed by the hand of God."

Decker jotted it down. It sounded like Reverend Bevis all over again.

"What what about the kids on the football team? Was that the hand of God?"

Krieger closed his eyes in a kind of silent prayer and slowly shook his head from side to side. "Tragic," he said, opening his eyes again, "simply tragic."

Krieger sighed and went on, turning the sizzling brats and hamburgers as he spoke. "But the boys should not have been there to begin with. They should have been home safe with their families or in their dormitories. And I am sure their parents would agree with me on that. But please—don't quote me out of context. I am not suggesting those boys deserved such a horrible end. Deserved, that is, in the sense of retribution. We must remember that God works in ways not always known to us. Nevertheless—"

Krieger's face lit up as his attention turned toward the back door: "Frankie! Glad you could make it."

Decker didn't recognize Orsini at first when he burst through the door with a beer in his fist. Going toward the grill was the same bulldog face he had seen at countless press conferences, but animated now by a puppyish grin and big brown eyes that seemed to say, "Hey, let's have us some fun."

Orsini was still grinning when they were introduced. He took Decker's hand and pumped it hard several times before letting go. Decker forced himself to be agreeable, trying to clear his mind of suspicions that Orsini lurked behind Barrett's murder. Innocent until proven guilty, he told himself. He was soon reminded that Orsini harbored his own vengeance.

"So you're one of the folks trying to make my life miserable, huh?"

Krieger wagged a finger at Orsini. "Now Frankie, remember our agreement. Rick is our guest tonight. We're not to badger him about the *River Queen*." Then to Decker, "And in fairness, Rick, I expect the same from you. This is a social occasion, not an opportunity for a verbal brawl. Agreed?"

"Of course," Decker said, pulling his lips into a smile.

He knew it wasn't the time to press Orsini anyway, not until the team had something solid to confront him with. Like the lab results from Columbus. Or maybe the reason Orsini could afford that big fancy house next door to Fritz's. "Actually," he said to Orsini, "I was hoping we could talk at a later time about the *River Queen* case. At your convenience, of course."

Orsini shook the bulldog head. There was moisture in the puffy creases around his eyes. A beer drinker's sweat. He was breathing hard. "Don't bother," Orsini said. "Hey, as far as I'm concerned, the case is closed. Open and shut. Everything I got to say is right there in the report."

"And quite a thorough report," Krieger added. "I can assure you, Frankie didn't get much sleep those nights he was playing the sleuth."

Orsini laughed. "You been looking in my bedroom window again, Fritz?"

"Frankie, I suspect prime-time television offers racier fare."

After the boys finished yukking it up, Orsini lumbered

away with his beer and plunked himself in a folding chair by the pool. Out of uniform and dressed in short sleeves and baggy shorts, Orsini somehow seemed more fit, Decker thought. The enormous paunch was still there, but there was a solidity to his big frame that suggested a good deal of muscle underneath—the hidden muscle aging bouncers rely on to whip the shit out of surprised young punks.

Krieger concentrated on his grilling while Decker stood close by. Suddenly, Krieger's younger daughter—Melissa— tore out the back door with her pigtails flying. Puffing and following on her heels was a pudgy dark-haired boy, unmistakably an Orsini.

"Ralph!" the chief yelled at the boy, but he continued bouncing after the little girl, past the pool and along the edge of the yard. "Settle down, Ralph! We're eating in a few minutes."

"That damn kid," Orsini said, shaking his head. "He knows he gets a bellyache if he eats after all that running around. It's bad for the digestion." Orsini then swallowed deep from his beer glass. He was either potted, Decker decided, or determined to get there shortly.

Decker wanted to talk philosophy again with Krieger, but Fritz and the chief were nearly inseparable that evening, even after the other dozen or so guests arrived, parking their Mercedes and Cadillacs on the Kriegers' manicured front lawn.

Gert Larson was right: Krieger and Orsini were an unlikely pair—the one tall, dignified, and Teutonic, the other effusively Mediterranean, uncouth, and built like a butcher block. It was obvious that Orsini looked up to Krieger. He was in awe of the prosecutor's urbanity and intellect and, of course, the old Cincinnati money that Fritz represented.

But what did Orsini offer Krieger? That was harder to answer, but it became clearer to Decker as he watched them together that evening. Orsini was the "pal" that Krieger could never have found among his snobby peers. He was the adoring sidekick with whom Fritz could drink a few beers, trade jokes, and steal some moments away from his wife and girls and the sheer drudgery of being a Krieger.

As his wife claimed, Krieger was, indeed, a master grillsman. He browned his brats until the skins split, and then steamed them in a tray of beer to keep them plump juicy. He insisted Decker load his brat with plenty of horseradish and brown mustard. Decker liked the results, even though his sinuses were seared open more than a few times. He might have asked for seconds if his mood had been right. Certainly everyone else's appetite seemed intact. The guests were jammed around the long patio table, fussing over an assortment of Mrs. Krieger's homemade fare that included baked beans, hot German slaw, hot German potato salad, and spaetzle.

Decker again tapped the keg of Moerlein, discreetly hidden in half an oak barrel, and retreated to an empty chair by a corner of the pool. He was glad to be alone. Mingling with the Hyde Park crowd was more work than pleasure, especially when he was asked about his job. He was forced to listen to several gratuitous sermons on yellow journalism and the scandalous behavior of the press.

After he'd had a few minutes by himself, Charlotte surprised him by sitting in the next chair. She was indeed wearing the "gingham affair" that her Daddy had suggested, and she looked cool and lovely in it. Her long hair was even more blond, almost straw-colored, now that it was dry.

Charlotte smiled briefly and said hello, and then dropped her gaze to the plate of food balanced on her knees. She was an impressive beauty, something she herself seemed to take little note of. She ate slowly and without talking while Decker plotted a smooth way to bring up the subject of her arrest. He broke the ice by asking where she went to school.

"Mother of God Academy."

"You like it?"

"Just fine," she said, then stared at her food again. "We have brothers teaching us for the first time this year."

"At Mother of God?" He was, in fact, surprised. In his day, "The Mother," as the boys at St. Ignatius called it, was run by a group of iron-fisted nuns.

"It's just a one-year trial."

He feigned indignation. "Well, Mother of God, what's this world coming to?"

Charlotte laughed, and it was like a rush of air through the poplar trees—light and cool and quick. He moved in for the kill. He was about to ask if Charlotte shared her father's political views when she put down her fork and said, "Father tells me you're a reporter."

"True," he said, lifting his beer in the air. "Know how you can tell? My tie's pulled way down like this, see, and my collar's unbuttoned."

Charlotte broke into an amused smile, a kind of half-sneer that marked her as a Krieger. It wasn't the reaction Decker had wanted.

"Actually, I think I'd like to be a reporter someday," she said, as though this was an outrageous idea that had just popped into her head.

"You would?" He feigned amazement this time. "It requires a calling, you know. Like a priest. You take a vow of poverty and then write epistles all your life that nobody reads."

Charlotte laughed, open and unguarded this time. But she stopped as suddenly as she had started when Krieger walked up to where they were sitting. He had grill tools in both hands. "Eat up, dear," he instructed his daughter. "Remember, you're in training."

"Yes, Father," she said, returning to her oddly detached tone of voice. She took another bite of potato salad and stared into the pool.

Krieger turned his attention to Decker. "I don't know if my daughter has told you, Rick, but she scored seven eighty in math and eight hundred in English on her SATs last spring."

Decker whistled, duly impressed. Then he turned to Charlotte, "I'd say you could just about name your college next year."

"Very true," Krieger interrupted. "But Marcie and I would like very much for her to attend Edgecliff. We both feel it is perhaps the most suitable institution in the country for young girls with Charlotte's Catholic upbringing. Besides, Charlotte could spend her weekends here, close to her family," Krieger said, studying his daughter's downturned face. "Unfortunately, Charlotte doesn't see things our way."

"I would prefer Radcliffe, then Columbia for journalism," she said matter-of-factly. Her eyes were turned toward Decker, but her voice was unquestionably directed to her father. Decker felt trapped in the role of referee.

"Ah yes, the fatal attraction of the Ivy League," Krieger smiled. "The prestige and the tradition. But Marcie and I are more than a bit fearful of the influences she'll find there. Cambridge is an entirely secular world, not to mention a hotbed of Eastern liberalism. Unfortunately," he repeated, with more vigor this time, "Charlotte doesn't see things our way."

Charlotte continued eating as though she hadn't heard. The conversation ended as Mrs. Krieger crossed the patio carrying an enormous chocolate cake covered with lighted candles. Behind her was a string of guests singing "Happy Birthday."

"Dear, you shouldn't have," Krieger said as his wife

presented him with the cake. The assembled crowd was shouting, "Make a wish! Make a wish!"

Fritz swelled his chest and, with the proper proportions of dignity and humor, dispatched all fifty-nine candles. The guests applauded.

"I know what the wish was," Orsini volunteered. "His first eighty-shot golf game."

Everyone laughed, with Krieger loudest of all. "No, Frankie," he said, "I only *pray* for that." That brought another round of applause. A moment later Decker saw Charlotte slip away from the back of the crowd and disappear into the house, perhaps to hit her books for the next day of classes at Mother of God. After all, you don't land near-perfect SAT scores without a little sweat—not even a Krieger could manage that.

He cornered Fritz one more time that night. It was after the cake had been cut and passed all around, and Orsini had drifted inside the house. He found the prosecutor standing alone on the steep edge of his back lot, hands clasped behind his back, and looking intently into the deep starlit sky above the Kentucky hills.

Decker stood beside him, looking into the same patch of sky between the poplar trees. After a moment of shared silence, the prosecutor spoke softly as though Decker had been there all the time.

"You know, son, I was thinking about your article again this evening. What you called 'my mission.'" Krieger's gaze was still fixed somewhere cross-river and heavenward as he laid a hand on Decker's shoulder. Decker stuffed his hands in his pockets, a little embarrassed by the instant intimacy.

"Yes, 'a man with a mission.' Some of your more liberal colleagues, I am certain, must laugh at that notion. Prosaists so easily ridicule the profound. But I think you struck at the heart of something, Rick. Something I have known about myself for quite some time, and see more clearly every day."

Decker was afraid to turn his head; he could almost feel Krieger's eyes peering down at him. The hand on his shoulder squeezed once, and let go.

"Aquinas once said that the man of office should be the best man for the task, not necessarily the man of finest character. I would add nothing to that, except this: I feel strongly that I am the right man, at the right time, for a task that many other men simply could not face."

And as Krieger's eyes wandered back to his patch of sky in the distance, Decker shivered and quietly walked away.

11

Monday morning, Turk and Decker took the one-page letter into Vendville, where they could savor its contents over the first coffee of the day. Turk started reading the highlights as Decker fed the vending machine. "The volume of gasoline saturating the wood was unusually high, indicating a direct application of the flammable liquid prior to oxidation . . ." Turk looked up from the letter and grinned. "Translation: somebody sloshed around a shitload of gasoline before tossing a match."

Decker laughed, really laughed, for the first time in days as he brought the coffees over to their table. If certain ominous signs could be ignored—such as Turk's renewed drinking—things were at last looking up. The team now had its "shred of solid evidence," a letter from the chief chemist at the Columbus lab confirming that the wood sample "was positive for the presence of leaded hydrocarbons."

"Let the *Times* stick *that* in their aluminum wiring," Decker said, and leaned over the table to sip his coffee without lifting the hot paper cup.

Turk had other interesting news. Friday afternoon, he had checked the real-estate records on Orsini's Hyde Park home. It was purchased by Orsini less than a year ago, and valued at $375,000. A mite steep for a public servant earning less than $60,000 a year. But not, as Turk had found out, if you could swing the right financing. The mortgage on the home belonged to Newport Savings and Loan, at an APR less than half the current market rate. It just so happened, too, that the S & L's CEO was Tom Berrens, Victor Carbone's brother-in-law.

The downside that morning was that Griswald was still missing. Turk expected the body would soon wash up somewhere along the Ohio, "so bloated it will be reported as a whale sighting." His grim theory had a corollary: the files that Griswald allegedly stole before disappearing were actually sensitive documents that Orsini himself had destroyed.

Meanwhile, Stein and Decker clung to the slim hope that Griswald was hiding out, with the stolen files as a bargaining chip to protect himself and his family.

By nine that morning, Turk and Decker were already at their keyboards. Turk was working the main story on the floorboard sample, billed in his lead as "startling new evidence in the *River Queen* mystery, recently obtained by the *Eagle*." The story would leave out the details, of course, of just how the evidence was obtained. (Finch had insisted that no one tell him, either, in the event that any team member were brought to trial.) Decker's job was to write a sidebar on the sudden disappearance of Lieutenant Harold Griswald, outlining his dispute with Orsini.

Turk and then, later, Decker tried to reach Orsini for comment, but his secretary insisted he was out of town and wouldn't be back until early next week. Decker called Petkamp at the Safety Building to see if that was true.

"If he is out of town, he's not very far," Bart said. "I saw him in the cafeteria early this morning, palling it up with a couple of assistants."

Petkamp could be tenacious when he wanted to be—as long as it didn't interfere with his lunch hour. He spent the rest of the morning camped outside Orsini's office, then called Decker five minutes before home edition deadline. "The chief either has a private bathroom or one hell of a bladder. His secretary keeps going in with coffee, but Orsini won't come out."

At 11:45, when the story was punched in and edited, Turk and Decker took off for Arnold's. They found a table under the tree of paradise in the courtyard, which was still damp and cool from the rain of the night before. In the noonday sun, the surrounding brick walls seemed to breathe a mixture of moist plaster and warm moss. It reminded Decker of trips to New Orleans.

While they waited for their food, Turk started on a double martini, and his hand visibly shook each time he lifted his glass.

There was no question now that Turk was on a full-blown binge. His gray eyes were red-rimmed and glazed, his complexion the color of sodden ash bark. The usually crisp guayabara was wrinkled and sour-smelling. It should have been buried deep in the bottom of a laundry hamper.

Decker was still sharing Turk's apartment, and hadn't seen him come in the night before. He worried that, next time, he might not see Turk for days.

He was careful how he broached the subject. "You feeling okay?"

"Just a bad cold," Turk sniffled, and glanced nervously around the courtyard. "I'll get over it."

When their orders came, Turk picked up his fork, took a small bite of his jambalaya, then thought better of it and went back to the martini.

"On a liquid diet, I take it," Decker said, angry enough now to be a smartass.

Turk put down his glass, signaled the waitress for another. The watery gray eyes squinted across the table. "I know what you're thinking, buddy, and you can just cool your heels. I'll hold up my end of the investigation," he said, stabbing a finger at himself, then at Decker. "You worry about yours."

Decker considered a comeback, then decided to drop it and went back to eating his turkey sandwich. Another time. But was there ever a good time to approach an alcoholic about his alcoholism? Maybe Stein would know what to do.

While Turk sipped his second martini, Decker started a quick rundown on everything he had seen and heard at the barbecue Friday night, but focusing mostly on the odd-couple friendship between Orsini and Krieger.

"They're like a couple of good old boys on a fishing trip," Decker said. "I think Krieger would honestly believe anything Orsini told him. He's blind to the whole *River Queen* cover-up."

Turk threw his head back and laughed, loud and raucous enough to draw stares from the other tables. He downed the rest of his martini and said accusingly, "You just can't accept Fritz's role in this shit, can you?"

Decker tried to stay cool. He was dealing with a drunk.

"And why are you so convinced he has one? Whose ax are we grinding here?"

Turk leaned across the table, red-rimmed eyes burning. "Never—and I mean *never*—underestimate the brutality of the righteous."

Turk ordered a third martini as the waitress came to clear their table. His jambalaya was hardly touched, the rice and bits of meat and vegetable congealed into a solid brown mass. Decker finished off his iced tea in silence. There was no sense trying to communicate with Turk now.

Turk set his fedora on the table with one hand, slicked back his long hair with the other. "You know, Rickie, I thought I'd taught you better by now. But you will see every goddamn thing in black-and-white, just like every other stupid shit in this town. Nobody wants to live with the process. And that's what it is, man, it's all process. But you can't live with that, Rickie, can you? Black or white, man. Black or white."

Decker signaled the waitress for the check. "I haven't got time to sit here and argue."

Turk leaned across the table, whispering gin vapors into Decker's face. "You know the problem with you, Rickie? You still haven't shaken the Catholic thing. You still got your God back in the fourteenth century. You know, the Old Man with the beard who's supposed to take charge and, abracadabra, everything will be all right. But we're in the twentieth century now, Rickie, and *we* are the gods. You and I and everybody else in this fucked-up world. We are the gods and nobody wants to accept that. Nobody except Krieger. He plays God for all of us. And it's people like you that let him."

"This is a newspaper, dammit, not a stage set!"

Finch was yelling at a TV camera crew that had somehow sneaked into the newsroom and was busy taping reporters and editors at their desks. There were hot klieg lights set up all over the room. "Clear the premises! All of you!"

One of the cameramen protested, saying the crew had gotten permission to do the taping.

"From whom?" Finch boomed.

The camera man pointed at Lafferty, who was sitting at his terminal, trying to look busy.

"Harry!" Finch shouted, jerking his thumb. "I'd like to see you in my office."

It was a little past 2:30. The *Eagle's River Queen* story had been on the streets less than an hour, but Decker had already fielded a dozen calls from the electronic media. Radio stations wanted on-air interviews. TV stations were asking to set up minicams in the newsroom for live reports.

The question of the day, of course, was how the *Eagle* had obtained its wood sample from the *River Queen* when the boat was under armed guard. Finch had instructed the team to have no comment on that question, except to say that the *Eagle* could verify the sample's origin.

Decker might have reveled in all the crazy attention, or at least laughed at it, if he hadn't been worried about Turk. At 1:30, Decker had left him sitting in Arnold's courtyard with his fourth martini. At two, when Turk still hadn't showed at the *Eagle*, Decker called Arnold's. The bartender said he was gone.

When Decker informed Stein of Turk's AWOL status, he looked grim and said, "We'll just have to wait and see."

"Well, that's reassuring," Decker snapped, and he stormed back to his desk wondering why he was so upset. True, he was worried about Turk, and the outcome of the team's investigation, but he was forced to admit that it was more than that. He was frightened for himself. The thought of continuing the *River Queen* story alone was a terrifying prospect. No matter how much they disagreed and bickered and competed with each other, Decker needed Turk. He needed his toughness, his cynicism, to give him the guts to see this through.

Just before three, after the TV and radio people had disappeared, Joe Benoit phoned from the *Times*.

"Yes, Mr. Benoit," Decker said with saccharine sweetness, "so we have the pleasure of talking once again. What's doing these days at the paper of record?"

Benoit cleared his throat. "Mr. Decker, I'm calling to see if you have any comment on what we have been told by a senior ranking official in the fire department."

"Come, come, Joe. You mean Chief Orsini. Shoot away."

Benoit cleared his throat again. Maintaining one's *Times* professionalism wasn't always easy. "We've been informed that the *Eagle* obtained its sample from the *River Queen* illegally, and that you and Mr. Nystrom will soon face charges of tampering with state's evidence."

"No shit," Decker said with mock surprise. Then he

| 181 |

began talking in quietly patient tones, like father to small son. "Well, why not wait until the charges are filed, Joe? Then it's a matter of public record. The *Times* won't even have to sweat itself about a libel suit. Okay? Now you go back to writing about the perils of aluminum wiring, like a good little journalist."

A second or two later, the phone rang again. He assumed it was Benoit.

"Joe, you really have to stop this now."

"This isn't Joe," the young man said. The voice was smooth and polite, and just a bit chummy, making Decker all the more curious about the caller's identity. "I was very interested in your *River Queen* story this afternoon, Mr. Decker. I have something that may interest you as well. Some rather intriguing photographs."

"Who is this?" Decker reached into his drawer for his tape recorder and phone pickup.

"Are we on a private line?"

"Of course. *Who* are you?" Cradling the receiver between his chin and shoulder, he quickly plugged the pickup jack into his recorder, then attached the suction cup to the back of the earpiece. He jammed down the red recording button.

There was a long silence, then the voice said, "Ethan Nottingham. We've talked before. Can you be here in ten minutes?"

"For what?"

"You'll see."

The girl couldn't have been more than twelve or thirteen, all gangly limbs and bone, with tiny swollen buds for breasts. Her hair was long and blond, reaching almost to her waist. What waist there was, anyway. You couldn't see the face. The straggly hair fell over most of it, over the eyes and around the puffy cheeks. But you could see the lips, loose and parted. Was she crying or moaning? Perhaps either would be part of the game.

But there was no mistaking the face that showed behind the girl's. A look of concentrated ecstasy in the raised brow, the half-closed lids. Man at his piggiest and, in an amusing way, his most sublime. It would have seemed comical if it hadn't been so grotesque, so pathetically tragic. Franklin Orsini holding a lanky little girl in his fat lap, making love in a straight-back chair.

Decker slipped the photo back onto Nottingham's desk and sat again. "How do I know this wasn't doctored?"

Nottingham pulled open his desk drawer, a look of grave concern on his cherub's face. "There are more here if you care to look."

Decker shook his head. He'd seen more than enough. He pulled out a notebook and pen. "Where did you say you found these?"

"As I told you at the beginning of the interview, everything I say must remain in strictest confidence until formal action has been taken against Chief Orsini."

"All right, I got that," Decker said. "But I'm still not clear how you came across the photos."

"I believe Mr. Krieger has already told you that our office is working closely with the FBI in an investigation of interstate pornography traffic. These photos were among material confiscated from a distributor's garage in Newport."

"And this distributor has connections to the Carbone family?"

"We believe that's the case. It appears that extortion was the aim."

"All right, so why are you showing me these photographs?"

Nottingham smiled conspiratorially. "Because I think

that both of us could benefit from an exchange of information at this point."

"You mean you want whatever we've got on the *River Queen* cover-up."

Nottingham smiled and nodded. "You see, Rick, our office is at a distinct disadvantage in all this . . ."

Decker finished for him. "Because Mr. Krieger and Chief Orsini happen to be very good friends. Is that why you waited until now to show me these photographs?"

"Let's say it took Mr. Krieger a bit longer than the rest of us in this office to see the light. Like yourself, Mr. Krieger was skeptical of the authenticity of the photos until very recently. We had an expert examine them for evidence of retouching."

"So what happens now?"

"It's hard to say. The FBI would like to keep our joint investigation under wraps for as long as possible. On the other hand, it would seem that the *River Queen* case would have to be reopened. Not only because of these photographs, but because of your excellent story today."

Decker took a long look at Nottingham, who was smiling now as though the two of them were about to become partners in a fantastic coup. "If we hadn't run the story, would you have shown these photographs to anyone?"

Nottingham rolled his eyes, stuck out his lower lip playfully. The Pillsbury doughboy, Decker thought. Just add some red to the chubby face, top the round head with a chef's hat.

"I'll say this. Your story certainly hastened the process."

Stein was sucking on the stem of an empty pipe, shaking his head in wonderment and confusion. "This whole thing is getting more bizarre by the minute," he said. "I don't know what to think." He pulled the pipe out of his mouth. "Did

Krieger know Nottingham was showing you those photographs?"

"I didn't ask. I assumed Krieger was too embarrassed to do it himself."

"Did you call the FBI to see if they'd confirm any of this?"

"Yeah, I talked to Masterson again. But you know how the feds are. They won't confirm or deny a damn thing until they're ready to bring charges."

Stein rapped his pipe softly on the edge of the conference table. "What did you tell Nottingham about sharing information?"

"I told him I'd have to talk with my editors first."

"Good. Because we're not giving them a thing. If Krieger looks like a fool, it's his problem."

Decker tossed his notebook on the table and ran his hands over his face and through his hair. He felt suddenly drained, suddenly touched by the absurdity of it all. "Can you believe it, though? That fat sonuvabitch hitting on little girls."

"That may be just the beginning," Stein said. "Turk has stumbled onto something that could put us light years ahead of the *Times*."

Decker's spirits lifted. "You heard from Turk?"

"He was here for a few minutes while you were gone. He looked shaky, so I sent him home."

"Barry, we've got to talk about Turk . . ."

Stein raised his palm. "Never fear. I'm meeting with him first thing in the morning. In the meantime, I need you to cover for Turk on something important. You look pretty wiped. Are you up to it?"

Decker picked up his notebook from the table. "When and where?"

"This evening, the Hot Box Lounge in Newport. It could lead us to Vernon Walker."

*　*　*

The Hot Box was near the south end of Monmouth Street, popularly known as the Strip, a five-block stretch of bustouts, back-room gambling joints, and nudie bars. It was a gaudy length of real estate, most of it owned or managed now by Victor Carbone. Colors on the Strip ran to hot pinks, screaming reds and yellows. Lights flashed, signs shouted. EXOTIC DANCERS! DAY AND NIGHT ENTERTAINMENT! GIRLS! GIRLS! GIRLS!

At 7:30, Decker swung his Dart into the first curb space he could find, about a half-block north of the Hot Box Lounge in front of an Army-Navy surplus store. For a second or two, he sat and watched the line of cars that drove by, looking for anyone who might have followed from the other side of the river. He made a habit now of remembering makes and colors of cars that stayed with him more than a block or two. Especially those with more than one man inside.

Reasonably certain he hadn't been tailed, he tucked his recorder and notebook in his coat pocket and then reached down and felt under the front seat. The gun was still there. He still wasn't sure why he'd bought it, or whether he could hit anything beyond point-blank range, but he liked knowing it was there. He left it in the car. Gun-toting customers weren't welcome on the Strip. In that respect at least, Victor Carbone was a pillar of law and order.

The Hot Box was one of the classier establishments along Monmouth Street. You knew by the New Orleans-style motiff. Black curlicue ironwork. Pink stucco walls. A blood-red double door with pull handles the size of barber poles. And unlike some of the bars along the Strip, no sleazy hawker outside waving in customers and promising "we show it all."

Decker waited a moment inside the door and let his eyes adjust to the smoke and gloom. Then he walked straight to the bar on his right and sat in one of the high-back swivel stools in front of the bartender's station. The edge of the bar, like the stools, was covered in red padded vinyl. He wondered if this was a decorative touch, or a safety feature for drunks.

It was Monday night, still early, and business was slow. Decker sat alone while the bartender worked on orders for a cocktail waitress. She was standing a few feet to Decker's right, an oversized blonde shoehorned into a blue satin teddy. She was chewing gum, not nervously, but slowly, contentedly, like a cow. She smiled and said she would be with him in a minute.

Decker looked to his left toward the dance runway, which jutted out from the back of the lounge. Two college boys in Izods and shorts sat at the very end of the platform, hunched over beers and waiting for the next dancer. Decker guessed they were about his age the first—and last—time he had visited a nude dance joint.

To the right of the runway was a handful of convention types in their best polyesters, on the left a couple of Snappy Lube mechanics still in their white jumpsuits. Behind them, at one of the little tables against the wall, sat a fat man in a dark suit. He was trying to look prosperous and bored while a B-girl cozied up, stroking his face and cooing in his ear.

The furnishings were all of a piece. Spanish lanterns. Flocked red-and-gold wallpaper. Smoked marbled mirrors. There was a sweet, musky odor about the place. Eau de Genitale?

The bartender cocked an ear in Decker's direction.

"Dewar's and water, please."

"Sorry, bud, house Scotch is all we got."

"Fine."

Decker dropped a five on the bar, and peeked at the rest of the money in his wallet, including a couple of fifties and a lone hundred. Normally, he never carried anything larger than a twenty; it made him nervous. But Stein had insisted he take plenty of green along to flash for the benefit of Miss Kristi McLain.

Decker took a good look at the bartender. He fit Turk's description of Jack Murray, all right. Fortyish, medium height, massive arms and chest, no gut. Murray didn't flaunt it, though. He wore a loose gray bowling shirt, a white T-shirt underneath, and a folded apron over an old pair of jeans.

Murray picked up a glass from the drain rack and flipped it right side up in one hand. He loaded the glass with ice, poured in a quick dab of Scotch, and filled the rest with water. He plunked down the drink and picked up the five.

"Keep it," Decker said.

Murray didn't smile. "Drinks are five dollars."

"Oh."

In a minute or so, the music started. From a dressing room behind the runway, one of the dancers came strutting out. She was a biscuits-and-gravy-fed teenager, a washed-out blonde already going slack around belly and thighs. Decker recognized the breed. She was probably just off the morning bus from Hazard or Perry or places so deep in the Kentucky hills you had to hitchhike to the nearest Greyhound stop. She wore high heels, little metallic pasties, and a gold G-string cut within a millimeter of the legal essentials. She didn't dance so much as offer a kind of kinetic anatomy lesson. Bumping, grinding, kneeling, squatting.

The college kids hooted, but looked a little dazed by the rawness of it all. The mechanics sat quietly with their beers, concentrating on the entertainment. But the conventioneers got most of the dancer's attention. She twitched her bottom just inches from their faces, and they reached out with folded bills and tucked them inside her G-string.

The next two dancers featured more of the same. Teenage losers on the run. But the fourth was a different story. She was a little older than the rest, in her mid-twenties or so, with a trim figure and a proud strut that showed the proper amount of contempt for her audience. She had the guts to be a brunette—not bottled, either—and Decker admired that. She could actually dance, too. She moved down the runway as though she owned the place. Her movements, like her body, were tight and controlled. She never missed a beat.

Decker signaled the bartender and put down a ten. When Murray came with his drink, Decker jerked his thumb toward the runway. "Kristi McLain?"

Murray nodded and took the ten.

"Keep it," Decker said.

Murray slipped the ten into the register, took out a five, and stuffed that into a beer glass next to the register. He came back to where Decker was sitting and said, "She takes a half-hour break after this."

"Thanks."

Kristi zeroed in on the college kids. She strutted to the far end of the platform, then leaned back from the lean hips and broke into a neat little trick that must have been her specialty. Rocking her torso lightly from the hips, she could make the gold tassels on her pasties spin in opposite directions. And all the while the tassels twirled, the firm, high bosoms hardly bounced. The college kids fumbled in their wallets for spare bills.

Decker saw his chance. He scribbled in his notebook: "Can we talk?," then ripped out the page, and took the hundred from his wallet and folded it inside. Just as he approached the runway, Kristi started to retreat, but shouts of "More! More!" brought her back to the spotlight. This time she turned her back to the college boys, spread her legs, and reached to her toes without bending the knees. Nice view, Decker thought, but a bit like a proctological exam.

Tired of being left out, one of the mechanics and a couple of the polyesters jumped up from their seats and joined the college boys at the far end of the runway. They were waving their bills and Kristi, still bent in half, reached between her legs to collect the offerings in her hands. Decker was the last to approach the altar, and he made certain Kristi got a good look at his face when he slipped her the note with the hundred curled inside. Then he returned to the bar and ordered another Scotch and water.

Kristi danced a second encore before another of the washed-out country girls took her place. Or tried to, anyway. He looked at his watch and frowned. He remembered he was supposed to meet Janet Shoemaker at eight—four minutes away. He started to swivel off his stool when he bumped into something soft and warm.

"Excuse me." He smiled. "Have to make a call."

"Why call, honey? Everything you want is right here waitin' for ya."

The B-girl climbed on to the stool next to his and wrapped her arm around his shoulders, pressing a friendly breast against his arm. She was plump, but not fat, with a head piled high with Dolly Parton curls. Her smile showed even rows of stained teeth. She couldn't have been more than eighteen.

She whispered in his ear. "Anybody ever tell you, honey, you look just like Mick Jagger? I mean, if you didn't wear no jacket and tie and all."

"Every day," he said, trying to get off his stool again. The B-girl tightened her grip around his shoulder and licked the inside of his ear.

"Why don't you relax a little, honey, and buy me a drink?"

"No, thanks," he said, inspecting his near-empty glass. "I'm waiting for somebody."

"Another sucker for Kristi, huh?" She wriggled against

his arm, whispered again in his ear. "She can't show you half as good a time as I can, Mr. Jacket and Tie."

He slapped a twenty on the bar and gestured to the bartender.

"Woo! Now that's more like it, honey."

Murray finished an order for a Seven and Seven and came over.

"Two drinks for the lady," Decker said. "And do me a favor. Serve them at the end of the bar."

The B-girl slipped off the stool. "You little shit," she snapped, tugging at her pink Teddy (there was a firm bulge at the midriff). She picked up the twenty and dropped Murray a ten before waddling back to the conventioneers. Decker swore she was pregnant.

He left a message for Janet's answering machine and came back, but there was still no sign of Kristi. He began to worry that he had scared her off, looking too much like a cop. Or maybe he was just too damned wimpy for Miss Kristi's tastes, loaded with C-notes or not.

A few minutes later, when the music started thumping again, he decided the *Eagle* had kissed its money good-bye. He dropped off his stool and was about to leave when he spotted her stepping through a door to the left of the runway. She worked her way toward the bar.

She was wearing an oversized Bengals T-shirt, number sixty-nine, with the collar cut out so that it sagged nicely down one shoulder. There was nothing else to the ensemble, except the spike heels that clicked along the wooden floor, attracting male attention like a mating call. Without so much as a glance in Decker's direction, she climbed the stool to his left. The moment her ass touched vinyl, Murray had a drink in front of her. Then he brought her a long filtered cigarette and lit it.

Kristi swirled a red straw in what looked like a double Amaretto in heavy cream. She took a couple drags on the cigarette before turning her eyes on Decker with something like contempt. "So what is it you want to talk about?"

He could barely hear over the music. He leaned in close and said, "Is there some place a little quieter?"

Kristi shot him an icy stare that would have stopped a moose mid-coitus.

"Listen, Mister, I'm here to talk, and that's it."

Decker nodded several times in perfect agreement. "But I need quiet or it's no good." He wanted the interview on tape.

Kristi swiveled in his direction and crossed her legs, and the Bengals T-shirt took a nice long hike up the slender thighs. She broke out laughing.

"No," she said, shaking a fringe of sheep-dog curls, "you can't be a cop."

"I'm a newspaper reporter." He was almost shouting to be heard. "I need to talk with you about Vernon Walker."

He got the icy stare again. "Why should I talk to you about Vernon?"

"Because there might be another hundred in it for you."

She smiled and slipped off the stool with her drink in one hand and the cigarette in the other. He followed her past the runway, clickety-clack across the wood floor, and back to a door marked EMPLOYEES ONLY. A warning was scribbled underneath: TRESPASSERS WILL HAVE THEIR BALLS BUSTED. He followed her in.

The room looked, and smelled, like a basement locker in a downtown Y. Brick walls smothered in gray paint. Bare overhead bulbs. Folding chairs scattered across a cement floor. To the right, a row of banged-up lockers leaned at an angle from the wall. On the left stood a spattered, full-length mirror, and next to it, a low sink where one of the dancers had her foot propped, and, with a pink-handled razor, was carefully shaving the inside of her right thigh.

Kristi motioned with her cigarette. "Beat it, Amber."

Amber looked up, her leg still arched over the sink. "You know what Jake said about bringing johns in here." Decker was standing sheepishly just inside the door.

"Fuck Jake. He doesn't own the place."

Amber threw her razor in the sink. "No, but you sure as hell think *you* do."

"Just move it, Amber."

Amber snatched a T-shirt off one of the folding chairs and headed for the door. Just before she stormed out, she turned to Decker and sneered. "I hope you get your money's worth."

Kristi sat in a chair almost dead-center in the room. She crossed her legs, and set her drink on the floor beside her. Decker pulled up a chair facing her. The naked light was not kind to Kristi. Her face was pretty, dominated by big brown eyes and wide arching brows, but below the cheekbones, the skin was badly scarred and pocked. The makeup was just there for the ride. In a flash, you saw back in time to the teenage Kristi, who drew wolf whistles in the high-school parking lot, but never the second look that might have generated something more promising, more tender. And here she was now, nightly at the Hot Box Lounge, taking belated revenge on all the nice boys who had never asked her out, and the bad ones who did.

"All right," she said impatiently. He had expected a sharp Appalachian twang, but her Southern accent was more like Georgia clay, rich and smooth. "What do you want to know about Vern?"

He fumbled inside his coat and pulled out his microcassette.

"Uh-uh," she said, shaking her head and drawing on her cigarette. "No tapes."

"Fine with me." He slipped the recorder back, pulled out his notebook, and perched it on his knee.

"I understand Vernon Walker spends a good deal of time with you, Ms. McLain."

"Yeah. Sometimes." She shrugged, as though the mere memory was a bore. "When he feels like partying."

"What about Monday night, a week ago. Was he with you then?"

She shook her head no and reached down for her drink. "You sure you're not a cop?"

"Do I dress that bad?"

Unamused, Kristi looked suspiciously at him for a second, and having made up her mind about something, took a sip on her drink, a draw on the cigarette, and flicked the ashes on the cement floor.

"All right," she said, getting down to business. "I saw Vern last Wednesday night, and I haven't seen him since. So I ain't much help to you there."

Decker got down to business, too. "Both you and I know how Vernon makes his living. I've already heard from several people who think he torched the *River Queen*. What do you think?"

She sipped again and shook her head. The tousled bangs swayed across her forehead. "Vern never talks to me about his jobs. He's too smart for that. And I'm too smart to ask."

"All right, then, what about his mood the last time you saw him. Was he depressed? Excited? Did he brag about anything?"

She glanced toward the door. "Listen, sweets, I have to go soon. I'm missing tips."

He got the message and pulled out the two fifties in his wallet, one at a time. He tucked the bills under his notebook so they hung just over his knee, dangling like bait.

Kristi scootched her behind into the back of the chair. She took a last deep drag on the cigarette and dropped the butt nonchalantly on the floor. It rolled under her seat, where it continued to smoke.

"Yeah, Vern was pretty moody that night. He kept talking about those college boys who burned up. On and on. He said anybody who would set a fire like that should go straight to hell. I don't know. I think it's the torchman's code or something to make sure nobody's inside when it burns. And anyway, Vern knows what it's like."

"So he's been burned?"

"You've never seen him?" She seemed surprised. She leaned forward to pick up her drink from the floor, this time making a casual show of the inside of her T-shirt. Decker kept his eyes on his notebook.

"Yeah," she said, straightening in her chair. "Vern got burned real bad about two years ago. Almost died, he said. It was mostly his chest and arms. You don't see much when he's wearing a long-sleeve shirt. Just the hands and around the neck is all. But most girls can't deal with it. Burn scars are a pretty ugly thing, you know. Like pink meat or something. Anyway, that's why he comes to me sometimes."

When he has the cash, Decker thought.

"I understand Vernon was flashing a lot of money that night. Do you have any idea how much?"

She looked at Decker over the edge of her glass, and then at the door behind him. She was getting impatient again. "It must have been thousands the way he was throwing it around. He was buying the girls drinks all night. Then we took a yellow cab over to the Travelodge, and he tipped the driver a twenty. I told him that was a damned fool thing to do, and he said, 'Don't worry, so-and-so's goin' to take good care of old Vern.'"

"So and so?"

"I can't hardly remember. I think he said some weird name, like Ethan."

Decker uncrossed his legs. "Ethan? Ethan Nottingham?"

"I told you, I never ask those kinds of questions. But I'm pretty sure that's who he said. Ethan."

He wrote Nottingham in big caps in his notebook, then collected himself. "You say you haven't seen Vernon since the Wednesday after the fire. Do you know where he might have gone?"

Kristi didn't say anything while her eyes settled on Decker's notebook, or rather what was tucked underneath. He put one of the crisp fifties in her palm. She hiked the front of the Bengals T-shirt and snapped the money inside her G-string.

Like one of Carbone's vending machines, she started dispensing information again. "I can't tell you where Vernon went, because I don't know. But he left in the middle of the night, still half-tanked, and in one hell of a hurry after he got this phone call."

"From whom?"

"I don't know that, either. But I can tell you this: there's only one person in this town who can reach people in the middle of the night in a motel room."

"Victor Carbone."

Kristi nodded. "Him, or one of his boys."

He thanked Kristi and slipped her the other fifty. In the middle of the exchange the dressing-room door flew open.

"Kristi, where in goddamn hell . . ."

The intruder stopped just inside the door and took a long, mean look at Decker. He was a short, wiry man in tight jeans and a flannel shirt with the sleeves rolled up. He looked like a displaced mountain man, someone wild, with long tangled black hair and an untrimmed black beard that crept over his cheekbones like moss.

"Kristi, I thought I done told you no johns in here."

Kristi stood up and smoothed her T-shirt over the essentials. "He ain't no john," she said defensively. She strutted toward the door. Decker stood motionless in front of his chair, facing the wiry man. The sunken blue eyes seemed to burn inside a nest of black hair.

The man grabbed Kristi by the upper arm. "I seen him give you money, bitch. Now what's going on here?"

Kristi yanked her arm away and rubbed the muscle with her hand. In heels, she was half a head taller than the man, but she was clearly intimidated. "For Chrissake, he's some kind of newspaper reporter. I don't know. He gave me money to talk."

"About what?" He grabbed her by the arm again.

"Dammit, Jake. I don't know." She struggled to pull loose.

Decker spoke up, trying his best to sound forceful even though his breath kept catching. "About Vernon Walker, thank you. And I was just about to leave." He slipped the notebook inside his jacket and, keeping up the show, made slow, confident strides toward the open door.

Jake pushed Kristi ahead and she disappeared into the bar. He blocked Decker's path and the two were face-to-face, or more like face-to-chest, given Jake's diminutive stature. Decker stood his ground, but smiled as though the whole scene was a joke in a bad movie. He held out his hand and loudly introduced himself. "The name's Rick Decker. I'm with the *Cincinnati Eagle*."

Jake looked at the hand as if it were gangrenous and then up at Decker. There was a coiled-snake defiance in the little man, something instinctively suspicious, perhaps, of anyone in a jacket and tie. He was a mountain man, all right.

"I know who you are," he said with slow venom, pointing a finger at Decker's face. "And I don't want you fuckin' around here again."

12

Decker arrived at Janet's apartment building in Clifton at a little past nine, a half hour later than Janet was expecting him. He spent another five minutes going around and through the yellow brick box, trying to find apartment "A." He settled finally on what looked like a service entrance to the basement. Down the stairwell next to the door, he found a rusty mailbox with a white index card taped to the front: J. SHOEMAKER.

The curtains were drawn, and a light shone dimly somewhere in the back of the apartment. He knocked hard on the screen-door frame and waited, glancing over his shoulder up the stairwell. He had been on edge since leaving the Hot Box, wondering what the hell the mountain man had meant by "I know who you are."

"Just a minute," a voice sang from deep inside the apartment.

He remembered the last time he had waited on Janet, in the parking garage at General Hospital, and her stinging words: "No. From a human point of view."

Well, from a human point of view, he was in no mood for lectures that night. Sensitivity was not a character trait he had seen much of lately, and his thoughts returned to the sad pictures of Orsini with the little girl. And to Barrett.

He was on the verge of just walking away when Janet came to the door. She was smiling as though nothing else in the world mattered at that moment, except forgetting everything that mattered. The night air stirred faintly with perfume as she stepped outside.

"You don't want to go in there," she said in mock horror,

slamming the door and turning the key. "It's been officially declared a national disaster area."

Decker's mood snapped and he smiled. "Your place too, huh?"

For the evening, Janet had traded her "uniform" of blue jeans and button-down shirt for a cool white cotton dress and sandals. Her long hair was combed out and fell around the stems of her glasses and down her shoulders. She took him lightly by the arm. "You're in for a treat. I know this wonderful little Italian restaurant right around the corner."

"Do they have booze?" He was quite serious.

She didn't answer, but let go of his arm and walked beside him along the driveway and out to the sidewalk, where they were greeted by a gentle breeze. It was September seventh, and the warm air of late summer had turned sharp and moist after a weekend of rain, hinting of damp bark, dying leaves. A harbinger of fall.

"So your day was bad, too?" she said.

He laughed mirthlessly. "Just the usual confusion, rushing around like an idiot, and being lied to. And then there was this red-neck at a Newport bar who wanted to rearrange my face." He turned to her and said, "By the way, I'm sorry I was late—"

"Don't apologize," she broke in, "I'm glad you were. I tried to reach you. I didn't finish at the Free Clinic until eight-thirty."

"You're working at the Free Clinic? In the middle of your residency? You must be crazy."

"I know," she smiled, flattered by the underhanded compliment. "But it's just one afternoon a week. And the patients there are so grateful—I mean absolutely *bonkers*—for anything you do."

She walked ahead on the narrow sidewalk, where the gas lamps of Clifton were spreading soft circles of light up and down the tree-lined street. Soon they had turned the corner onto Ludlow Avenue with its shops and restaurants and trendy boutiques.

There was just a trace of a breeze, enough to make Janet's dress flutter softly around her hips and knees, defining a shape he tried not to notice at first, out of a sense of devotion, perhaps, to Barrett's memory.

But the visit to Monmouth Street had put him in a certain frame of mind, and he eventually found himself sizing up what was inside the dress—not all that consciously or lustily, but in the way most men do when their line of vision is presented with the opportunity. Like most men, too, he assessed by way of comparison. Where Barrett had been all sleek curves and dark-haired chic, Janet had the healthy blonde's rounded, sturdy softness. The hips were amply proportioned, but not fat. And the behind . . . Well, the behind looked very comfortable.

At the Italian restaurant, they were seated at a small corner table by a window with red half-curtains. The restaurant was small and cozy, as Janet had promised, with an Italian mama for a waitress who pampered and abused them as if they were guests in her own house. Decker ordered linguine with red clam sauce—his favorite in any Italian restaurant—and he wasn't disappointed. Janet ordered the basics—spaghetti and meatballs. But first they shared a bottle of Valpolicello.

He started off the evening with business, asking Janet if she had learned anything more about Maisie Williams' shoes.

She shook her head. "You can't mention the woman's name now unless you want your head chopped off. The chief resident circulated a memo last week, reminding the staff of the confidentiality rules. No one is to speak to the police or the press without the hospital's clearance."

Decker said it didn't matter that much anyway, because it looked as though the *River Queen* investigation would be reopened soon. But he refrained from telling her about the interview with Nottingham, the pictures of Orsini and the girl, and changed the subject to something more suitable.

"So, how many years has it been?"

What seemed like centuries ago, he and Janet had gone to the same Catholic high school. Or almost the same. In those days, Catholic boys and girls were still corralled into separate institutions, like ponies waiting to be bred. Janet's high school, Mount Saint Mary, had been the sister school to Decker's. The distance between the two was a five-block walk, but if you were really cool, you got in your car and "cruised the Mounties" just as classes there let out.

For a half hour, they traded gossip about old classmates. Then it was Janet's turn to change the subject.

"You know, the last time I really talked to you, Rick—at your mother's funeral—you said you'd never come back." She broke into a gently ironic smile.

He finished off his wine. "I should have followed my own advice."

"Is it really so bad?"

He told her briefly what had happened to Barrett, and maybe why. When he had finished, Janet was staring wide-eyed behind her glasses, ready, it seemed, to accuse him either of lying or of suffering from paranoid delusions. She blinked a couple of times.

"Rick, I'm sorry. I had no idea. I simply don't have time to follow the news anymore. Are you certain she was killed because of this—this investigation you're doing?"

"Who knows? But it's the only thing that makes sense right now. One of the few things that's made any sense since we started working on the story."

He dug into his linguine. He hadn't eaten since noon, and after the dry red wine, he was ravenous. Barrett would have been ravenous, too, at a restaurant like this, on a night like this.

"Did you love her?" Janet asked.

He put down his fork and spoon, sat back, and sighed in frustration.

"Forget it, Rick. It's none of my business."

"No, no, it's not that. It's just a damned hard question to answer, that's all. And you're the third person to ask this week."

"Well, then don't answer," she said firmly. And in a while, Janet was smiling her smile again, the one that said nothing else mattered in the world right now, except their being together and having a good time.

And that they did. When they left the restaurant, they decided to do something crazy in homage to their shared childhood, and so they drove out to Westside Bowl-A-Rama, the old neighborhood haunt. They rolled two games, drank a few beers, and laughed so hard at times it put knots in Decker's stomach.

He loved watching Janet bowl. She would bounce up the lane in her white dress and her floppy red bowling shoes as if she didn't know what she was doing. And then suddenly at the throw line there was a transformation from giggly little girl to resolute woman. She would lunge forward from the hips, swing the ball straight back from the shoulder, and then fling it down the alley with a mighty swoop of her arm. *Kablam!*— the pins flew in all directions. On strikes, she would jump up and down and dance back to her seat, her cheeks flushed from the exertion. After one such celebration, he kissed her on the cheek, and was immediately embarrassed by what he had done. She took his hand and squeezed it.

Without much effort, Janet scored 180 while Decker squeaked into the hundreds. His performance, however, supplied most of the laughs. Third frame of the first match, he rolled a gutter ball that somehow skipped into the next lane where some good old boys were playing a deadly serious tournament game. Decker sauntered over and asked if anyone had happened to see his ball, and when one of them handed it over in stony silence, he slapped the ball and wagged his finger at it: "Bad boy!" Then to the stunned onlookers: "I'm very sorry. He's not entirely trained yet."

He drove Janet back to her apartment just after midnight, and they were loose enough by then that the usual shy awkward task of walking a date to the door was not so awkward. Janet slipped the key in the lock and invited him in.

It was a small, stripped-down basement apartment in a corner of the building, with linoleum floors and exposed pipes running across the ceiling. The entrance led into a tiny open kitchen. To the left was a small dining area, straight ahead the living room, and to the right the bedroom and bath. And, yes, the place was a disaster area, as Janet had said. The kitchen table was a bounding sea of textbooks, notebooks, medical journals. The sink was teeming with neatly stacked but unwashed dishes. In the living room, the sofa was piled high with clean laundry waiting to be folded and put away.

Janet grabbed a double armful of clothes from the sofa and told him to have a seat. "What would you like to drink?" she said as she hurried off to the bedroom.

"Let's see, what does one drink after an evening of Valpolicello and Hudy Gold . . ."

"How about Amaretto?" she called from the bedroom. "It's all I have."

He laughed out loud, recalling Kristi's favorite drink.

But while Janet was busy in the kitchen, his mood somehow snapped. He sank back into the sofa, thinking now that Janet had schemed to land him here from the moment she'd met him at Cincinnati General and insisted they have dinner. Why, he didn't know. But he felt as though a trap was being laid. That Janet was just one more person who was lying to him, who wanted to manipulate him, use him in some way. He knew his suspicion had no basis, but distrust had almost become a sixth sense. He couldn't shake it, any more than he could stop being a good reporter.

Janet handed him a tumbler filled with two fingers of Amaretto and set her own glass on an old children's schooldesk next to the sofa. "Isn't it a little warm in here?" she said.

"I think it's the alcohol."

"Hey," she said, playfully tugging at his arm. "Leave the medical observations to me."

She went to the corner windows opposite the sofa and threw both wide open. A breeze stirred the curtains, bringing inside the soft whooshing sound of neighborhood traffic. Returning to the sofa, she kicked her Dr. Scholls on the floor and, tucking her feet under, cozied into a corner of the sofa next to him.

"Ahhh," she purred, "what a nice way to end an evening."

He nodded without smiling.

Janet draped her long hair over the back of the sofa and rested her head there. Her neck was long and lovely. She took a sip of Amaretto and he watched the smooth pulsing of her throat as she swallowed. She turned her head and saw him staring. She smiled, teasingly, like little Janet again, and turned away. He forgot about traps. He looked at Janet's profile and how her face was still flushed from the craziness of the bowling, and he found himself wanting to stroke the warm glow of her cheek, to touch its almost childish freshness. So when she set her drink down and settled into her corner again, he did, lightly. Janet swirled her cheek in small circles against his hand. He leaned toward her and kissed the cheek, gently, then reached for the big glasses and lifted them up and away.

With the glasses gone, the blue eyes were suddenly naked, more naked and alive than if he had torn her clothes off and she were standing goosefleshed in the middle of the room.

He kissed her on the lips this time, and her eyes half-closed, fluttered, then opened wide again with a new awareness, a new resolve. They kissed again, so eager at first they bumped teeth and laughed into each other's open mouths. Then Janet moved from the corner of the sofa and wrapped her legs around his lap and began kissing his neck, ears, face, lips with a seeming intent to devour. She moved her hips and the cotton dress bunched around her waist.

He was just as intense, pulling at her dress-top and kissing her shoulders and all around her neck. He was stroking the softness of her skin there when suddenly, in his mind's eye, he saw the awful purple marks appear like butterfly wings on either side of her throat. He trembled so violently that Janet stopped and looked into his eyes. When he turned away, she slid off his lap and curled next to him, her forehead resting against his shoulder.

"I'm sorry," she whispered. "I didn't mean to— I thought I could help you forget."

He patted her cheek and got to his feet, trying to be cheery, trying to be pals again. "Hey, don't be sorry. Lust is never having to say you're sorry."

Janet smiled grudgingly from the sofa. She lay curled on her side, her head propped on an elbow. "I think maybe I'm just a little bit loaded," she said dreamily. She hiccuped, and they laughed, and he was about to kneel and hold her again when the phone rang. It rang a second time before Janet sat up and smiled sarcastically, as though to say such awkward disturbances were a normal part of her life. She smoothed down her dress and padded in bare feet out to the kitchen. She put on her best physician's telephone voice—alert, authoritative. "Doctor Shoemaker here." And in a second: "It's for you, Rick."

"For me?"

"Yes, someone named Barry Stein."

Decker was still breathing a little hard when he took the phone.

"Sorry to interrupt your bachelor escapades, Rick. Something big's come up. We need you in the newsroom."

"What's the deal?"

"The police found Orsini in his backyard about an hour ago. He blew his head off with a shotgun."

13

Turk arrived in the newsroom at 11:20 A.M., just as Decker was putting the finishing touches on the home edition update of the Orsini story. He looked pale and a little shaky, but he was wearing clean clothes (a yellow tennis shirt and navy jacket instead of the guyabara) and judging from the nicks on his jawline, he was freshly shaven. He pulled up a chair next to Decker's terminal, and quickly scanned the six paragraphs on the screen.

"So," he said, "the boys have finally begun to turn on each other."

Decker bristled at the breezy pronouncement, especially since Turk had been nowhere to be found while Decker was up half the night trying to piece the story together.

Orsini's body was found next to the barbecue pit in his own backyard, the top of his head blown off by a twelve-gauge shotgun normally reserved for turkey hunting. His wife and two sons had just returned from grocery shopping around eight that night when they heard the shot.

According to Mrs. Orsini, her husband had left no suicide note, had shown no signs of despondency and no indication that he was about to take his life. In their final conversation, Orsini had called his wife from the office to say he'd be late for dinner that evening. He hadn't said why.

"Maybe to get those photos back from Nottingham," Turk said with his know-it-all grin.

"Maybe," Decker said, "or maybe to plead for his job."

He went back to writing, but Turk continued to hover at his side. Decker hated to be watched as he wrote; it made him self-conscious and nervous, especially on deadline. He un-wrapped a stick of sugarless, then stared at the newsroom clock, hoping Turk would get the message. He didn't.

"Mind if I read the rest of it?"

Decker pushed away from the keyboard. "Just make it quick."

Turk moved his chair over and started pressing the roll-up button, nodding his head vigorously as he read the rising column of type.

"You got all this from the police?" He seemed genuinely impressed.

Decker shook his head, then told Turk about having met Mrs. Orsini once before at Krieger's cookout. When he heard about the suicide, he went straight to the Orsini residence. "She was ready to unload, and I guess I was a familiar face, that's all."

"Timing is everything," Turk said, and Decker stiffened as Nystrom patted him on the shoulder. "By God, we blew the *Times* out of the water on this one."

Decker let pass the reference to "we" but asked dryly, "So where were *you* last night?"

Turk missed the implied insult, or chose to ignore it. He was all grinning enthusiasm. "In about every dive in Newport. I'm hot on the trail of Vernon Walker."

"I thought you were ailing."

"I was, until late last night. I couldn't sleep, so I headed out to some joints on Monmouth Street."

Decker brightened a little. Maybe Turk was still in the game after all. He turned around to his desk and grabbed a notebook and, laboring to decipher his own shorthand, started briefing Turk on the Kristi McLain interview. Turk stroked his Fu as he listened.

"All in all, we didn't get a whole lot for two hundred

bucks," Decker said. "Except one possible clue: Vernon told Kristi someone named Ethan would take care of him."

"Nottingham," Turk said evenly.

"That was my guess, too, but Kristi was in the dark."

Turk was grinning again when he said, "We may have some answers by tonight, anyway."

"Meaning?"

"Meaning I've got an interview with somebody who says he can put us in touch with Vernon Walker."

"Incredible," Decker said, caught up in Turk's enthusiasm now. "Who?"

"Anonymous. But I think he knows what he's talking about. He gave me a good description of Walker over the phone, said he knew where he was hiding. He claims Walker is eager to talk now that the arson is out in the open."

"Where do we meet this guy?"

"The Blind Lemon. And it's not 'we,' it's me. Alone."

"Bullshit, I'm going with you."

"Forget it. The man said come alone or not at all. He's scared shitless of Carbone. That's why we're meeting on this side of the river."

Decker wouldn't let him off the hook. "Are you out of your mind? Look what happened to Barrett—"

"For Chrissake, what can happen at the Blind Lemon? The place will be crammed with Yuppies."

"All right, dammit. Call me when you're through."

Turk got up slowly from the chair, grinning again, but there was an uneasy tension in the confident mask. "What are you, my friggin' mother?"

The sleep was so hard it felt as though he was submerged in black flowing water, only it was thicker and warmer than that, and he could draw the viscous ooze into his lungs and breathe it out again as freely as air.

As the phone rang, he rose unwillingly through the ooze, higher and higher toward the surface, where everything was bright and cold and painful. And when the ringing stopped, he dove again into the warm darkness, trying to sink deeper into the current, only to be sucked back toward the surface again by the next nagging ring. On the third ring, he opened his eyes to a different kind of blackness. He lurched from Turk's over-stuffed sofa, trampled and almost fell over the shoes he'd left on the floor, and moved quickly to the kitchen phone.

"Hello?" he croaked. The sound seemed to come from his ears and nose instead of his mouth.

"Rick? Are you awake?"

He was still in his work clothes, and the bottom of his Oxford shirt was twisted oddly around his waist. With his free hand, he straightened things and tucked the tails inside his pants. "No—I mean, yes. Yes I am." He didn't recognize the voice. "Who is this?"

"Thurston—"

"Oh, God, yes. So what's up, Darrell?" Thurston worked nightshift. He was one of the newer reporters at the *Eagle*.

"I think you should get down here. Turk's been in an accident. A bad one." Decker could hear the wailing of sirens in the background.

"Where, Darrell?"

"Are you awake?"

He had to think for a second, and after shaking his head a couple times, said, "Yes. Very awake. Just tell me where."

"The retaining wall below Mount Adams. It's off Eggle-ston. You can't miss it with all the cruisers and fire trucks."

"I'll find it."

Thurston was right. There was no way to miss the scene, even in the dead of night, even in the middle of a no-man's-land of bridge approaches, cloverleafs, tangled interchanges. A half-dozen or so cop cars, ambulances, pump trucks were pulled into a semicircle in front of the massive thirty-foot retaining wall. Red lights, blue lights whirled and strafed the scene, creating an eerie shadow-play of men and machines that flickered against the wall.

He parked on Eggleston behind a string of TV news vans, and ran up a gently sloping hill toward the lights and confusion. He was panting when he reached the semicircle of trucks and cruisers. He looked but couldn't find Turk's car. Everywhere TV crews were jockeying minicams and lights into position for spots on the eleven o'clock news. A Channel 6 reporter was already into his stand-up routine.

"John, Action Eye News is here live at the scene of a most bizarre and tragic accident—"

Decker moved frantically around the semicircle, seeking a view and yet afraid to see. His skull seemed to vibrate with the sounds of disaster—the pulsating rumble of diesel engines, the crackle of radio transmissions, the deep-throated, self-important shouts of rescue workers in their element. And beneath it all was another sound that didn't seem quite possible. A lovely melodic undertone, pure and crystalline as a winter's night.

He pushed aside a cameraman.

"Hey, asshole, we're shooting live here!"

The still-smoldering wreck was flipped bottom side up, its roof smashed to the door handles. Decker let out a burst of laughter, harsh and forced, as though someone had punched him in the gut. It was too absurd. From inside the pancaked shell the tape player was blasting the Toccata and Fugue in D Minor, its majestic notes rising above the chaos and carrying on the warm night air clear to the stars above Mt. Adams.

He clamped his hands to his ears, but the Bach—and the Bach alone—came through.

He ran across the clearing to a fireman who was winding hose on a truck winch.

He pointed and screamed. "Why don't you stop that music!"

The fireman gave him a puzzled look. There were black smudges on his cheekbones and brow. "What music?" he said indifferently, and went back to working the winch.

"The goddamn music in the car, you idiot!"

A lieutenant in a white helmet came out of the truck's cabin and stepped off the running board. He was tall and collegiate-looking and his face was clean. "What's the problem here?"

"For God's sake, stop that music!"

The lieutenant tugged at the bill of his helmet. "We do one thing at a time, buddy. Now clear the hell out, or you'll be taken out."

Someone grabbed Decker by the shoulder. He whirled, ready to throw a punch, and there was Darrell Thurston, both hands in the air.

"Whoa! I'm not the enemy," he said.

Decker stuffed his fists in his pockets and mumbled an apology. Thurston took him by the elbow, and the two of them started away from the noise and the diesel fumes and the dizzying swirl of lights.

"Tell me what the hell happened, Darrell."

Thurston shrugged his big shoulders, then threw his cigarette butt down the grassy slope toward Eggleston Street. He was a young black man, dignified beyond his years, and he was trying his best to look unshaken—shoulders thrown back, head held high. But sweat was trickling from his sideburns in a thin stream. His round meaty face was lined with tension.

"I talked to a couple of cops. They're not saying. But one of them told me it looked like he lost it on Monastery Road. There's a steep curve just above the wall there." They stopped walking as he pointed, but the street was obscured by tall weeds and shrubs. "They think he was hightailing it. Maybe fifty or sixty."

Thurston pulled a pack of Salems from his shirt pocket, looked inside the empty package, and crushed it in his fist. "You have a cigarette?"

Decker shook his head.

"God, I need a cigarette."

They returned to the crash site and watched as four firemen brought the "jaws of life" from a pumper truck. It took two men to carry the heavy steel pincers, two more to carry the compressor engine and the hose lines. They set the machine next to the driver's door of the flattened wreck and started the compressor.

It was over in seconds. They stuck the tip of the jaws just inside the door crack, then released the pincer arms. The door popped open like a lid, and the Toccata and Fugue came spilling out. Ripples of piercing high notes, crystalline and cold, that made your hair stand on end. Thundering blasts from the bass. Just the way Turk liked it.

A paramedic with a flashlight got down on his hands and knees on the scorched grass and crawled inside the body of the car. Three TV crews surged forward with their cameras and their lights. The police pushed them back. "Give 'em room! Give 'em room!"

While the first paramedic rooted in the belly of the carcass, a second knelt by the door. They shouted to each other over the organ music, and in a minute or so, the first paramedic backed out of the wreckage empty-handed. He stood in a glare of the TV floodlights, swishing debris from the knees of his jumpsuit, then motioned to the two firemen standing by with the "jaws of life."

After talking with the paramedic, one of the firemen got on his hands and knees and dragged the pincers inside. In a little while there was a loud metallic crunch, like an explosion, followed by a second and a third. And then there was no more Bach, only the drone of the compressor and the rumble of the big truck engines.

The firemen crawled out, the rescue worker went back in. A few seconds later, he poked his head out the door.

"I need a bag in here!"

The young lieutenant came from his truck and started yelling at the two policemen holding back the TV crews: "Get these vultures outta here! I want them back. Way the hell back!"

The fireman who had been working the winch came with a yellow rubber bag and unceremoniously dropped it on the ground. He unrolled it, unzipped it, and with his foot, pushed the bag inside the car to the rescue worker.

Thurston looked at his watch and started taking notes, and that's when Decker felt the acid rise from his stomach. He swallowed hard and turned away.

"You all right, man?" Thurston said.

He ran down the hill, away from the awful din, the flashing lights, the smashed car that was now a coffin. As he ran, his ears filled with the whirring and rasping of insects, of life's incessant mindless hum. When he reached Eggleston Street, he leaned against a No Parking sign, gasping for breath. He fell to his knees and, doubling over, splashed the acid in his stomach into the gutter.

He cleared his throat and spat again and again, but there was no end to the burning metallic taste in his mouth. He held onto the No Parking sign and straightened himself on shaky legs, clutching his gut. He remembered Turk in the moments before he left the newsroom. The high spirits, the enthusiasm, the uneasy grin that betrayed both.

So they'd gotten him. Whoever it was, they'd gotten him and gotten him so good there was nothing left now but some burnt pieces to stuff into a bag. It was no accident. He was sure of that. No more than Barrett had been the hapless victim of a burglar.

He shook the metal signpost as if he were strangling an enemy, then pulled and bent it toward the sidewalk. He slammed his fists together. He wanted to kill. But for God's sake, how did you kill something you could not see, could not even name?

He threw his head back and saw above him the skyline of the city—a jeweled canyon of lighted glass and steel and concrete. Pristine, orderly, compact. But somewhere inside the facade was a menace that had no face. He raised his clenched fists to the sky and screamed, "Come and get me, you fuckers! Come and get *me*! Why not *me*!"

It was past midnight when Decker reached Stein at home. He sounded as calm and alert as if he were answering a call in the newsroom. "What's up, Rick?"

He was still winded from the run up Eighth Street and into the *Eagle* Building. His sentences spilled out between breaths. "Barry, they got Turk. His car crashed and burned at the bottom of Monastery Road. Barry, we've got to stop these bastards. They took the body away in a bag, Barry. In a fucking *bag*!"

"How did it happen?"

"Christ, Barry, I don't know. He said he was meeting some guy at the Blind Lemon tonight. Said he had to go alone. Then I get this call from Thurston . . ."

"Listen," Stein said firmly. "There's no time to lose. Get up to the Blind Lemon. Talk to bartenders, waitresses, anybody who might have seen Turk with this man. See if anybody knows the guy. If not, get as complete a description as you can. And another thing—find out exactly when Turk left, and whether he left alone. You got all that?"

Decker was jotting it down.

"Check."

"Good," Stein said. "You sound better already. Remember. There's nothing more we can do for Turk, except get to the bottom of this mess."

The Blind Lemon was hidden along Hatch Street in Mt. Adams. To get there you had to duck between a pizza parlor and an Irish pub and down a narrow set of sidesteps, careful not to hit your head on the overhang. It was a rite of passage for the chic.

The rear courtyard was already closed for the night. Decker pulled open the heavy beveled-glass door and stepped into the barroom. It was a slow night, even for a Tuesday. Across the room to the right a hip, thirtyish couple sat at a small table in the corner, touching fingertips in the air. To the left, sitting on a barstool, a young man in a salmon V-neck sweater and no shirt gave Decker the eye as he loped past the bar and into the adjoining room looking for the bartender. Decker found him sweeping under one of the tables. The chairs were stacked on top.

"Sorry," the bartender told him. "We're closing early tonight." He was in his mid-twenties, tall and skinny and, by Cincinnati standards, punked-out. He had a spiked crewcut, wore cheap black shades and a white T-shirt under an oversized black jacket.

"I'm not here to drink," Decker said, pulling out his notebook and identifying himself.

"Say, you're not the guy who does the restaurant reviews, are you?"

"No," Decker said, sensing what was next. "That's somebody else. I'd like to ask—"

"Jesus, I'd like to punch out the sonuvabitch jerk. Said

my Bloody Marys were over-iced. Got me in a hell of a lot of trouble with the manager."

"I'm sorry about that, but I'm here about something entirely different." To emphasize the point, he lifted his notebook. "Do you remember seeing two men here earlier tonight?" Decker gave him a detailed description of Turk. No one could miss the man easily.

The bartender rested his folded hands on the tip of the broom handle and thought for a second. He bunched his eyebrows, adjusted the shades on his nose. He seemed very young. "Yeah, I remember the two. Especially that guy you call Turk. Jesus, could he put away martinis."

"What about the man Turk was with? Can you describe him?"

"Oh, yeah. April called in sick, so I was waiting the inside tables tonight. The two of them had about the same coloring. You know, blond hair, kind of pinkish skin. He was balder than this guy Turk. Shorter. Maybe ten years younger. Or he looked that way anyway. Kind of a baby face. No beard or mustache, real clean-cut, and dressed in a blah gray suit or something. I figured him for a lawyer, or maybe a P & G man. I don't know. We get a lot of that kind in here after working hours."

"What time did they arrive?"

"Your friend Turk was here first, about nine or so. At that table there." It was the first table inside the second room, underneath an Audubon print of two Mallards winging over a marsh. "Then the other guy shows maybe a half hour, hour later. I remember because there weren't a whole lot of people in here tonight. Everybody's at the big-screen bars watching the Reds game."

"How long did they stay?"

"They called it quits just before eleven, I think. The

other guy kept calling me over, but it was your buddy Turk did most of the drinking. I don't know how he walked outta here."

"And you let him drive?"

The bartender turned defensive. "Hey, I asked if he wanted a cab, and he looked at me like I was a piece of shit or something."

"Forget it. Who paid the tab?"

"The lawyer-looking guy."

"Did he use plastic?"

The bartender thought a moment, then broke into a smile. "Say, that's pretty smart. But no. He paid cash."

"You remember anything peculiar about the other man? Anything that stuck out?"

The bartender cocked his head to one side, rubbed his cheek. "Nah. He was your average-looking lawyer or CPA type."

"Just average-looking?"

"Yeah."

He got the bartender's name—it was Alf Banecke—and started to close his notebook.

"Wait a minute," Alf said. "I do remember one thing. He was carrying this big, fancy-ass briefcase."

"What did it look like?"

"Well, it was huge, almost like a traveling bag. Leather straps, gold buckles."

Decker looked up from his note-taking. "The soft kind—half-leather, half-tweed?"

"Yeah," the bartender said. "It was a real production."

Decker remembered one other question. "Did Turk leave alone or with this other man?"

"Alone. Definitely. On his way out he crashed into one of the chairs. That's when I asked him about the cab. Like I said, the other guy, Mr. CPA, squared away the bill. Left a fifteen percent tip to the penny, which is why I think he might have been a CPA."

"How much later did the other man leave?"

"Just a few minutes or so. He didn't seem like he was in much of a hurry. Not like your friend Turk—he buzzed right outta here."

"Angry or upset?"

"No, just like he had some urgent business to take care of."

Decker thanked him and turned to leave. His hands were trembling a little as he stuffed his notebook inside his jacket.

"No problem," the bartender called after him. "Just tell your restaurant critic to keep his ass outta here, or I'll see that it's kicked."

"It's a she," Decker said over his shoulder, and left the bar.

It was 1:10 when he reached the newsroom and called Stein again from the city desk. Thurston was sitting next to him, banging in his story and smoking a fresh pack of Salems.

"We could have done worse," Stein said after Decker finished with his notes. "It was lucky for us the place was empty."

"Yeah, fucking lucky for Turk, too."

"Listen, Rick . . ."

"I'm sorry. I know what you meant. I just . . ." He massaged his temples and felt the blood pounding there, as though his entire head might explode.

"Forget it. What I wanted to say was, Why not come stay with Barbara and me tonight? We have a guest room, if you don't mind sleeping in a room full of books. And I promise not to let the boys near you until at least seven. How 'bout it?"

He thought about it a moment. Stein's kids were a rush, like a shot of adrenaline, and they could help take his mind off things. But he had been thinking of someone else since leaving the Blind Lemon. "Thanks, Barry. But I've got some place I can go."

When he hung up, he dialed Janet's number. A sleepy voice yawned softly and said, "Doctor Shoemaker . . ."

He closed his eyes and listened to his own words come out, as though someone else was speaking in a hoarse, dry voice.

"Janet. I need to see you."

14

"The cops are still saying reckless driving or suicide," Thurston said. "They claim they checked the length of Monastery Road and couldn't find a single skid mark."

Thurston looked heavy-lidded and groggy. Nine A.M. was the wee hours for a night-shift reporter. He was wearing a fresh cream-colored shirt, but the same suit he had had on the night before—a gray-green summer-weight, tailored to his thick proportions. His arms were folded as he leaned his behind against the edge of Decker's desk.

"But what if he had no brakes?" Decker asked. His voice was accusing, although not toward Thurston.

Thurston cleared his throat. "The police say he could have downshifted or used his parking brake."

"Right," Decker sneered, "or opened a parachute."

Three other reporters were standing behind his chair, drawn to the conversation by a mixture of curiosity and awe. Working on the *River Queen* story had become a newsroom curse, and mere survival, Decker realized, had made him a hero among his colleagues. Only he didn't feel much like a hero. Earlier that morning, before driving to work, he had lifted his car hood looking for a bomb, then realized he didn't know where to look, much less what to look for.

"And if he was run off the road?"

Thurston shook his head. "No witnesses. That stretch of Monastery is nothing but trees and empty hillside. The police say it's abandoned at night."

More to himself than anyone, Decker almost whispered, "So we'll probably never know, will we?"

Thurston lowered his head and walked quietly away, and so did the others, leaving Decker alone in his chair with his hands clasped behind his head. In a kind of numbed trance, he could feel the others drift away, as though they belonged to a reality separate from his own. The barrier was almost palpable, this fear and anger and grief that now isolated him from the others. Turk would have understood, but Turk was dead. And so was Barrett. There was no one now but Barry, and he had become so much the man of action now, the Great Avenger, that any philosophizing, any sharing of feelings made him impatient.

Decker realized he was drowning in a kind of self-pity. But he was prepared to go on feeling that way the rest of the morning, until he remembered, in a rush of warmth, the night before.

Without questions, without a word spoken between them, she had taken him in, set him up on her sofa, tucked him in. When he woke, there was hot coffee, fruit, and fresh bagels (none of which he could eat) along with a note that said, "One lifetime pass to the Shoemaker Hotel. Bearer welcome any time, day or night."

On the strength of that memory, he roused himself from his chair and went to the vending room for coffee. When he returned to his desk, ready to tackle the remainder of the morning, Lafferty was there waiting.

"Meeting in the Boss's office, el pronto!" He jerked his thumb and walked away. Decker smiled to himself, pleased that at least some things at the *Eagle* hadn't changed.

When he stepped into Finch's office, Stein was already in one of the red leather chairs, puffing on his pipe with his eyes closed, seemingly anesthetized by a cloud of blue tobacco smoke that hung about his head. Finch was pacing the carpet in front of his desk, hands behind his back. He acknowledged Decker's entrance with an impatient flick of his hand toward one of the chairs. He continued pacing as he spoke, deep-throated, chin thrust in the air. This was truly his finest hour.

"Gentlemen," he began, "I know you must feel, as I do, not only grief but outrage at the loss of one of our finest reporters. Now, whether Mr. Nystrom alone was responsible for his death or whether, as I believe, there were elements of foul play, is an issue yet to be resolved. But what must never be questioned is our resolve as a newspaper to continue this investigation to the very end." Finch stabbed the air to emphasize his point. "We will not be bullied. We will not be frightened. And to make that clear, I am ordering all stops pulled on the *River Queen* investigation."

All stops pulled, they soon learned, was the addition of a second reporter to the team—Darrell Thurston. Decker was happy with the choice. Thurston was a good man. He had been on the paper less than a year, but he had already proven himself one of the more aggressive reporters on the staff, and a solid writer. He was a survivor from the ghetto of East St. Louis, educated in a minority program at Berkeley, and hungry for a big story. Big enough to buy his ticket back to the West Coast.

Thurston would be digging deeper into Turk's accident—hounding the police and fire departments for details of the investigation, combing Mt. Adams for anyone who might have seen the crash or what led up to it.

Decker, of course, was annointed to take up Turk's quest where it had abruptly ended.

For the next six hours, Decker and Stein pored over Turk's notes, memos, tapes, the scraps of paper on his desk, looking for some mention, even a hint, of whom he had met the night of the accident.

As he sifted and analyzed, Decker found himself trying to think in ways that Turk might have thought. It wasn't easy. Some reporters' minds instinctively dig through the bullshit that buries a story, straight down to the hard nugget of irreducible truth. Which is maybe not the whole truth, but the truth that can be capsulized in a single sentence or a single phrase, which is the truth according to daily newspapers. Turk's mind had always gone straight for the nugget. Decker's, on the other hand, would scoop around until it found an interesting artifact, but not necessarily the nugget, then worry it for a while before finally giving it the toss and digging a little deeper. Decker's mind was the type that left a scattered trail. Turk's didn't.

At the very back of Turk's top drawer, buried under some pension-plan brochures, Decker found something. It was an AA pamphlet. A phone number and the name "Ron" was penciled across the top.

"Look at this," Decker said, his eyes stinging a little.

Stein nodded silently, then went back to sifting through the Indian River citrus carton where Turk stashed his old notebooks.

Later, Decker tried the number on the pamphlet, just to make sure. It checked out, all right. "Ron" was a local AA member. Yes, he remembered Turk, and said that he had come to a couple of meetings over a year ago. But that was the last anyone had seen of him. Yes, he had read the news about Turk.

"It's sad," the man said with an air of resignation. "But it's not the first time it's turned out that way."

It was almost three when every tape cassette, notebook, and scrap of paper had been exhausted. Decker rubbed his eyes. They seemed to ache clear back to his brain from all the searching and skimming. Stein pulled up a couple of typing chairs next to Turk's desk and they sat.

"Two possibilities," Stein said, lighting his first pipe of the afternoon. "He either took the pertinent notes with him—

which no one will ever see again. Or there were no notes to begin with."

Decker frowned and pushed a toe into one of the piles of paper they had left scattered on the floor around Turk's desk. "He shouldn't have taken the chance, Barry. I told him."

"But we both know that taking chances is sometimes the only way to make things happen," Stein said. "Which brings me to an idea I've been toying with the last few hours."

He puffed hard a few times on the Savenelli and then plunged in. "The way I see it, our bits and pieces of circumstantial evidence are beginning to tie together at least four people—Walker, Orsini, Carbone, and Nottingham."

"Nottingham? You mean what Kristi said about an 'Ethan'?"

"Yes, flimsy but what I like to call intriguing, especially when you consider . . ."

But Decker wasn't in the mood for one of Stein's circuitous analyses. "All right, so what's the plan? Where the hell do we go from here?"

"The question, I'm afraid, is where *can* we go. The only witness to the arson is dead. So is the fire chief who covered up the arson. That leaves just one other investigator, Griswald, who could prove there was a cover-up—dead or hiding. The same for the man suspected of setting the fire."

"It's a bitch," Decker said, thumping his palm on Turk's desktop. "Something's rotten to the core and we're just nibbling around the edges. There's no way to get at it."

Stein took some more quick puffs, sending smoke out both corners of his tightened mouth. "Maybe there is a way. Maybe what we need to do now is bite right into the core. Bite down hard and see how rotten it really is."

"I'm sorry I started the metaphor."

Stein smiled and went on. "This is what I mean—it's time to take on Krieger."

"Krieger?" Decker's voice was incredulous and strained. "But with what, Barry?"

"You're right, 'with what?' We don't have a thing on Krieger himself. But we have a strong motive—Greenburg's empire has been shut down, his porn shops are dead. And we might have something on Nottingham. Which, if true, is the same as having something on the county prosecutor's office."

Decker's nerves were as jumpy as the half-dozen secretaries busily engaged outside Krieger's office. They were typing and Xeroxing, hopping in and out of chairs, running from desks to file cabinets or out the door and down the hallway into neighboring rooms. The working day was building to an end. It was 4:25 P.M.

One of the secretaries, a middle-aged woman with half-glasses and a motherly air, stopped by his chair on one of her trips out.

"Could I get you some coffee, honey?"

"No, thanks. You seem to have your hands full anyway."

"Oh, it's like this every day just before court filing time," she said pleasantly. "Does Mr. Krieger know you're waiting?"

"Yes, thank you."

"I know he had just a few more things to finish up. I'm sure he'll be with you soon." And she was out the door with a stack of legal papers in both hands.

For the fifteenth time, he went down the list of points he wanted to make with Krieger, scribbled on a page torn from Turk's desk calendar earlier that afternoon. The important thing, of course, was to speak and act as though he knew more than he did—without being trapped into in an outright lie.

It wouldn't be easy, he knew. Especially not for him. Decker's interview style, like his personality, was tentative and questing, hardly ever confrontational unless pushed. Playing dumb was what worked best for him, since people seldom failed to hang themselves with their own words. But now he was confronting Krieger, someone sharp, highly respected, and savvy to the tricks of the media game. And confronting him with what? The boozy recollections of a G-string queen.

But Stein had been right about one thing: there was nothing to lose. If Krieger was clean, he would immediately launch an investigation into his own office. If he wasn't, they might at least scare him into a move they could jump on.

Decker was tucking his list back into his shirt pocket when Ethan Nottingham breezed into the waiting room, straight past Decker's chair. He shouted a friendly "Hello, I'm back" to the secretarial pool, then stopped in front of his office door and announced that he was absolutely *not* to be disturbed for the remainder of the day.

"Mr. Nottingham, do you have that brief you wanted typed? The Mueller case?" one of the secretaries asked.

He rolled his eyes in his little cherub's face. "Oh, yes. I nearly forgot."

He dumped his briefcase on the secretary's desk and unbuckled the leather straps. That's when the bag impressed Decker the same way it had impressed the bartender at the Blind Lemon. It was a busy design, part canvas, part leather, with lots of buckles and straps. Like a fancy book bag some kid would carry to school to wow his friends. In a flash, he recalled the bartender's description of the man—a CPA type, blond hair, pinkish skin. He felt the blood tingling in his scalp.

For the first time, he studied Nottingham's face, really studied it, as the face of a deadly enemy. But how could that be? It was such an angelic visage, in the truest sense—glowing with innocence, good spirits, keen intelligence. It was a face that could smile and spin out downhome Cincinnati expressions like "okey doke" or "jeezul pete" and no one would think to laugh, because corniness was part and parcel of the persona.

Decker took another look at the briefcase. His jaw

muscles flexed and tightened. He had more now than just smoke to blow in Krieger's face.

Nottingham handed the secretary the brief, handwritten on a yellow legal pad, thanked her, and slipped into his office. A moment or two later, the matron who had so kindly offered Decker coffee said Mr. Krieger would now see him.

Decker jumped from his chair, double-checked his shirt pocket for pens. As she ushered him toward the door, he slipped his microcassette out of his coat pocket and tested the battery light one last time.

Stepping inside Krieger's office was like entering the vestibule of a medieval rectory. It was musty and dark and lavishly furnished, with the only light coming from a pair of desklamps under heavy green shades. Decker took a few more steps into the room, waiting for his eyes to adjust. It was by voice alone that he recognized Krieger, his words cutting the gloom like a beacon of warmth.

"I'm sorry I kept you waiting, Rick. But as you must know, the wheels of justice never stop turning . . ."

Krieger came around the desk to greet him with a firm handshake, a fatherly grip on the shoulder. Decker smiled out of politeness. Krieger's familiarity used to flatter him. Now it made him uneasy.

Decker was seated on a long burgundy sofa only a little wider than Krieger's massive wooden desk.

"How do you like my little nook?" Krieger said, settling into a tall, straight-back chair behind his desk.

In a sweeping glance, Decker tried to take it all in. The ribbed walnut paneling, suitable for a Bavarian palace. Oil portraits hung between shelves of thick lawbooks. A high, wood-beamed ceiling. Behind Krieger was a stone-carved fireplace—a fake, unless the courthouse roof had suddenly sprouted a chimney. Front and center on Krieger's desk was a family photo in an old-fashioned wood frame. The rest was covered with neatly stacked piles of papers and books.

"Very cozy," Decker said.

"I think so, too. Almost womblike, you might say. I don't like distractions when I'm working. There are far too many of those, I'm afraid, in our media-saturated world." Krieger leaned forward in his chair, hands folded on his desktop, so that only his face and hands showed in the lamplight, like those of a mime against a black background.

"Excuse me if I seem withdrawn today," he said softly. "I'm still very upset, as I'm sure you must understand, about the sudden loss of Frankie. Over the years of a close friendship, you believe you come to know a man. You believe you know his character, something of his values. In the end, though, we never really understand anyone. Do we, Rick?"

"Not always."

"There has been talk, of course, that it was the *Eagle* who drove Frankie to such—" Krieger chose his words carefully, "desperate action. But I find that rather too simple, don't you agree?"

Decker shrugged noncommittally.

Krieger leaned back in his chair, and his face half-disappeared into blackness. Decker could see the sharply protruding nose, the two black hollows under the bushy brows, nothing more. The prosecutor sighed from the shadows. "I pray that some good will come of what happened to Frankie. Perhaps now we can finally get to the bottom of this sordid *River Queen* affair, and begin to restore the city's confidence in its public servants."

Decker saw his opening. "Sir," he said firmly, "that's why I'm here."

Decker crossed his legs, planted his elbow on his knee and his chin in his palm and pretended he was Mike Wallace—hard-nosed, self-assured, with every question plotted in his brain. But there was a chink in his armor: he could feel his arm trembling under the weight of his chin.

"About the *River Queen*?" Krieger said, with seemingly minor interest. He receded farther into his chair and his face now vanished altogether. Decker was a little unnerved. It was like talking to a headless man.

"I'm afraid it's bad news," Decker said, not sounding afraid at all. "It concerns a certain member of your own office, sir." He knew he was using too may "sirs" for the effect he wanted, but it was a hard habit to break when addressing someone as imposing as Krieger.

The prosecutor leaned forward again into the light. The eyebrows were lifted in a look of puzzled concern. "I'm sorry, Rick, but I don't quite understand. The *River Queen* case has yet to be prosecuted by anyone in this office."

"That's exactly it, sir. There's been a cover-up. In fact, we have evidence that one of your own assistants has had contact with the man who started the fire."

Krieger snorted, and crossed his long arms on the desk. In the tight circle of light, his face looked cold and slightly translucent, almost like marble. He spoke sharply. "May I remind you, Rick, that many prosecutors are well known to arsonists simply because they prosecute them."

"But we have good information, sir, that the assistant in question made payments to the arsonist."

Krieger retreated again into darkness. Only his hands showed on the desktop now, one laid flat upon the other, perfectly still. The fingers were long and tapered, yet thickly jointed, thickly veined. "Are you saying, Rick, that someone in my office *paid* to have the *River Queen* set afire?" He laughed haughtily, and when he spoke again, his tone was threatening.

"You'd better have some damned good information, young man."

"We have more information than some might think, sir." Decker let the half-bluff sink in. When there was no response from the shadows, he resumed. "The assistant we are talking about, of course, is Ethan Nottingham."

"Nottingham?" Krieger's voice was full of incredulous irony. "My God, young man, he doesn't pay arsonists; he puts them in jail. His record is outstanding. Absolutely spotless."

"That may be true, but our sources—"

"Your sources," Krieger said contemptuously, leaning into the light. His face was no longer cool as marble, but a little red in the creases now, and leering at Decker like a cathedral gargoyle. "What *sources* could possibly have told you such lies as this?"

"I'm not at liberty to say." Decker crossed his legs and propped his chin again. It was time for the coup de grace.

"Mr. Krieger, I should tell you I'm not here to confirm the facts one way or the other. I'm here, in good faith, to offer you the chance to comment on a story that involves *monstrous* wrongdoing in the county prosecutor's office." The "monstrous" was emphasized as though Decker had told only half the story.

"You mean to tell me the *Eagle* plans to print these lies?" Krieger shook his head in disbelief. Then, regaining some of his earlier composure, he said almost jokingly, "Please tell Alex Finch that I hope his paper can stand up under a multimillion-dollar libel suit."

"Is that your comment, sir?"

"No," he said coolly. He was in perfect control again. "My official comment, is no comment."

"Thank you, sir." And Decker dug himself out of the burgundy sofa and rose to his feet, suddenly lightheaded and dizzy. The bluffing had been a bigger strain than he had realized. Still somewhat unsteady, he started for the door, and to his surprise, Krieger came around the desk to escort him, wrapping an arm around his shoulder as though nothing at all had changed between them.

"I understand how it is," Krieger said soothingly. "You have a job to do, and so do I. No hard feelings then?"

"No." But he was thinking differently. "No hard feelings."

Decker could feel his hand trembling when he extended it to meet Krieger's. The prosecutor's grip was firm and warm, and in its enveloping dominance, Decker felt something inexplicable happen almost against his will. The trembling stopped.

15

Decker sat in front of his humming Selectric and stared at the blank sheet of memo paper, its whiteness screaming for what was inside his head. But the words came only in disjointed spurts, incomplete thoughts. A sign to call it quits. He filed his notes on the Krieger interview, checked in with Stein, and left the *Eagle* building a little after 5:30.

The Dart was parked at the end of a long alley that ran beside the *Eagle* building—a kind of free zone for reporters where the traffic cops ignored the No Parking signs. He pumped the accelerator three times, turned the key, and gritted his teeth as the ignition warbled its high-pitched tune. Reeta-da-DEEE, reeta-da-DEEE . . . On the fifth da-DEEE, the slant-six wheezed and turned over. He smiled. It usually took eight or nine, and more when the weather was damp. Maybe his luck was beginning to change. Maybe the worst was over.

He didn't bother with the unpredictable air conditioner. It had been cloudy and blustery all day, and the air had cooled toward evening. He rolled down his window, then leaned across the bench seat to the broken handle on the passenger side in time to see a sedan turn into the alley from Eighth Street and abruptly stop.

He sat up and pretended to adjust his rearview mirror. He saw a powder-blue Fairmount with a tinted windshield. Nothing a reporter would drive, unless it was a rental. Two men were in the front seat, or two heads anyway, but he couldn't see much more than that. He revved his engine, stalled it, started it up again, sneaking glances in the mirror. In a second or two, the Fairmount slowly backed up the alley and into Eighth Street, where it headed uptown.

He dropped his head back against the headrest, eyes closed, then suddenly shivered as though something had crawled up his spine. He leaned forward and reached under the seat. The gun was there. Illegally concealed, of course. He laid it on the seat beside him. Snapping open the glove compartment, he got out the box of shells and spilled them next to the gun. It didn't seem real that he was loading a revolver, like John Wayne hiding behind a rock, waiting for the Commanches to charge him. He shoved a shell into each of the five slots in the cylinder, locked it, and stuffed the gun into his inside coat pocket. Then he quickly gathered the shells, put the box back into the glove compartment, and drove away.

The gun hung heavy under his arm, and its swaying at every stop and turn reminded him to check his mirrors for the powder-blue Ford. It never reappeared, although at Knowlton's Corner, he had seen a white Fairmount with two men inside that made him wonder if they were changing cars. Then, too, he could be lapsing into paranoia. He hoped to God it was paranoia.

It took just under fifteen minutes to reach his Northside apartment on Pullan Street. He parked in front of the Hobbs' place next door, got out and looked up and down the street, then walked back to his side entrance. His mailbox was bursting; he hadn't been home in more than a week. Among the bills and the junk mail and the magazines he found a letter from the managing editor of the *Chicago Tribune*.

He tucked the other mail under his left arm, ripped open the letter and read it. The *Trib* was offering him a job. He broke into a grim ironic smile, thinking what a difference a few weeks would have made. He read on. It was a bureau position, probably in the middle of nowhere, but it was still a job on a first-class newspaper and there was always the chance, of course, of advancement once he had proven himself. He quickly reread the letter and then stuffed it folded into his shirt pocket. He liked the feel of the paper against his chest. His ticket to Chicago. For now, though, it would have to wait, just as everything else in his life would have to wait, until he had some answers.

He was at his door, fumbling in his pants pockets for his keys, when he saw it a second time. The powder-blue Ford. Cruising slowly up Pullan Street like a reconnaissance ship.

He quickly stepped inside, threw the deadbolt, and went straight to the kitchen phone. He nearly groaned when the hospital operator told him Dr. Shoemaker would have to be paged. While he waited, he tossed his mail on the kitchen table and pulled out his gun and placed that, too, on the table. He wished now he had taken some target lessons. He'd never fired a gun in his life.

"Hello, this is Doctor Shoemaker."

He tried to speak slowly as his mind went racing ahead. "Janet, Rick. Listen, can you steal away for a minute? I need someone to pick me up."

"Is there something wrong, Rick?"

"I'll tell you all about it when you get here. Only I don't want you to pick me up at my apartment. There's a laundromat at Hamilton and Pullan. Can you meet me there?"

"Yes, but I need about ten minutes to finish up with a patient. Rick, are you sure you're all right?"

"Just hurry."

He hung up, picked up the gun from the kitchen table and stuck it in his coat pocket again. Then he went into the bathroom for his shaving kit, took it to the bathroom and packed the kit and some clothes into an old vinyl shoulder bag, making sure he had the same number of socks and underwear.

He tried the back window, but it wouldn't budge. He grunted with the effort, then swore at his own stupidity. The window was locked, not stuck. He twisted the rusty tab and flung open the window. Tossing his bag out first, he crawled over the sill and dropped to the flower bed below, where he landed on a patch of once-promising white mums. Retrieving his things, he headed fast across the backyard and into the alley that ran behind Pullan Street.

"I don't care what Barry says. I still think you should go to the police," she said. He suppressed an urge to chuckle as he watched her pull a quiche from the oven with gloveless hands and drop it with a clatter on the stove. Janet the Domestic.

For the first time in days, he felt safe, almost cozy. He was sitting at Janet's kitchen table drinking a bottle of Molson Golden. The little table was covered with a checkered cloth and set for two. In the center was a tennis ball can stuffed with day lilies that Janet had been delighted to find at the edge of a supermarket parking lot.

"But it makes sense, Janet. We can't go to the locals until we're sure they're not involved. I'll just have to hide out for a while."

"For how long? The rest of your life?" Now she was rooting through the bottom of the refrigerator, stalking vegetables for a salad. Her hair was still pulled into a bun from work, and she was wearing a pair of soft faded jeans and a lavender tie-dyed T-shirt, a hand-me-down relic from her older brother, but now almost fashionable again.

He sniffed, feigning offense. "What's the matter? You don't want my company?"

She smiled playfully. "Listen, Toots, you have no idea what it's like to live with a doctor. Now get off your tush and chop these veggies."

In a while they sat down to dinner. But first Janet turned

off the kitchen light and lit a single red Christmas candle, plastic holly still attached, and placed it on the table between them.

"Doctors are such romantics," he said.

"Do you realize," she said, slicing the quiche with a tableknife, "that you're the only man to share a meal with me in the last six months?"

"You mean you don't know any other freeloaders?"

"No," she laughed, then seriously: "It's just that the only professional men I ever meet are other residents. And they're positively terrified of women in their field."

"And I'm not threatened?"

She pushed the big frames back on her nose and considered the question thoughtfully. "No, you're not," she concluded evenly, "not in the same way, at least. It's not an ego thing with you."

"*Moi?* Without an ego?"

She laughed as she served up the quiche, his plate first, then hers. "I guess it's because we go back together. I mean, we're so relaxed with one another, so—I don't know, I guess the word is comfortable. Like when we were kids." She smiled wistfully for a moment, then began to eat. He was already two bites ahead of her. The quiche was smooth and creamy and full of his favorite ingredient—cholesterol. There was also a fresh salad loaded with spinach, mushrooms, tomatoes, and shaved carrot, and some of Decker's homemade vinaigrette dressing. Not to mention the cold Molson.

He finished off his bottle and went to the refrigerator for another. Janet was drinking spring water. "Are you sure you feel comfortable with me," he said, "or with the Rickie Decker who lived down the street twenty years ago?"

"Is there that much difference?"

He sat down again and grinned. The letter from the

Tribune was still folded in his shirt pocket. He showed it to Janet.

"So it's back to your life of wandering," she said, handing the letter back.

"Wandering? I wouldn't have come back here in the first place if it hadn't been for Barry." And his mother, whose cancer had brought him home. But Stein had convinced him to stay. The *Eagle* was on the way up, on the verge of Big Things, Barry had told him, and someone like Decker, with his drive and his Eastern education, could make a difference in his hometown. Some difference. He was hiding to save his own skin.

He pulled out the front of his shirttail and used it to help grip the Molson's cap. It wouldn't budge.

"Dearest," she said teasingly, "it's not a twist-off."

"Oh." He got up to find an opener, but she stopped him and got up herself instead.

"You don't feel the need to maybe sink some roots?" she said. She handed him the opener and sat again.

"No more than anybody else. What are the statistics? The average American moves once very three-point-five years or something."

"I suppose you're right," she said evenly, and they both went back to eating.

More for himself than for Janet, he dominated the conversation by laying out the unanswered questions in the *River Queen* case. Janet listened attentively, a look of concern on her face.

When he began recounting the details of Turk's crash, she reached across the table and took his hand in hers. He wondered why she had done that, until he realized his voice was going hoarse with emotion. He stopped in mid-sentence. "I'm sorry," he said. "You've heard all this."

She started clearing the table. He rose to help, but she waved him back.

"First meal is on the house," she said. "Tomorrow *you* get to make dinner."

"Great. How do you like your Spam?"

She laughed and went to the freezer, where she pulled out a pint-sized carton of Graeter's double chocolate chip, setting it on the kitchen counter.

"None for me, thank you." He finished off the Molson's and went for a third. Janet shot him a disapproving glance.

"Is drinking an occupational hazard among journalists?" she asked, injecting enough whimsy in her voice to avoid sounding like a nagger. She was hunting for a spoon in one of the kitchen drawers.

"No more than doctors," he said, grinning defiantly.

She came to the table with her small dish of ice cream and started licking her sticky fingers. He watched, a sly grin on his face.

"Stop that," she laughed, "and drink your dessert."

Janet started talking about her father, and with such open admiration that Decker felt a twinge of jealousy. He wondered for a moment where *his* old man was these days, and whether he ever wondered about Decker, too. Or perhaps he could forget just as easily as he could disappear.

Decker never knew why his father had vanished. His mother had never talked about it, although Decker suspected there might have been some connection to his mother's rigid Catholicism. To birth control. To S-E-X. All topics that, with his mother, were strictly *verboten*.

"A couple of weeks ago," Janet started brightly, "Dad thought he'd be modern, so he hired one of these high-powered consultants to see how his practice could be improved." She laughed out loud. "Well, the consultant took one look at the books and nearly passed out. In one month,

Dad had given away something like thirty-five percent of his fees in charity work."

Doc Shoemaker was indeed something of a local saint. He was an affectionately gruff, outspoken man, with hands as big and rough as a farmer's, but deft and gentle in the handling of his patients. He had kept his practice in the heart of Cheviot, steadfastly refusing to abandon his inner-city patients while most of his colleagues were following the money out to the surburbs. During the years that Decker's mother was trying to get on her feet, the family's medical care had been free. Decker had tried once to pay Doc Shoemaker then, just before he went off to Columbia, for spearing a boil on the back of his neck. The doctor had laughed and told him, "I don't charge for the fun things."

Decker told Janet the story and she laughed with her hand over her mouth. "I just pray there's a few paying patients left by the time I leave school."

"You're taking over the practice?"

"Haven't I told you? Dad can hardly wait. He says he's going to retire to Florida and play so much golf people will think he's a lawyer."

They both laughed, and then he said, "Promise me one thing, though. For God's sake, keep the dum-dums in the waiting room."

"You mean the suckers in the old apothecary jar?"

"They pulled me through many a visit."

"Oh, if you knew how many dentists have complained—"

"Hell, let 'em complain. You'll be the new Doctor Shoemaker."

And that's when Janet's eyes misted over behind the glasses. She blinked fast a couple of times and said, "You know, I just hope I can live up to the name. I worry about that sometimes."

"Nonsense," he said loudly. "Of course you will—"

But before he could finish, the phone rang. Janet sighed and stepped toward the kitchen.

"It's for you," she said, holding out the receiver. Then in a very bad Bogie imitation: "I think it's rewrite, *shweetheart.*"

"What could they want now?" He looked at his watch. It was almost nine P.M., beyond even the *Times'* deadline.

"Sorry to bother you on a big night out." It was Donnelly, the night city editor. He didn't sound very sorry. In fact, Decker could almost see the smutty grin on his fat Irish face. "Stein said we might reach you at this number. Anyway, about fifteen minutes ago, this guy called the desk and wouldn't give his name. Said he absolutely had to talk to you tonight. Could be another crazy, I don't know. I wouldn't bother you with this bullshit, except he sounded pretty spooked." Donnelly gave him the number, a Newport exchange. Decker thanked him and hung up.

"This will only take a minute," he told Janet and started dialing.

"Good. I'll put on water for tea."

The phone wasn't through its first ring when someone picked up. "Who is it?" The voice was petulant, nervous.

"Rick Decker, returning your call."

"Hey, you and me, we gotta talk, buddy. And I mean tonight." He spoke in a slightly wheezy Appalachian twang, anxiety pitching it even higher. Decker had an inkling. "Is this Vernon Walker?"

"You bet, pal. We got lots to talk about. I'm upstairs at the Kentuckian Cafe. Monmouth Street. You know where that is?"

"Yeah, I can find it. But I'd rather meet on neutral ground. Can I suggest a place?"

"Ain't no suggestin' about it. If I leave here tonight, I'm

deader than a fuckin' doornail. No, you gotta come here, or there's no talkin' at all."

"All right," Decker said, "but I'd like to bring someone with me. Just for the record."

"No, just you, nobody else. Two would look like cops. Come alone, or I don't talk at all. And don't come lookin' like a reporter, neither."

"What does a reporter look like?"

"You know what I'm sayin'. No fancy threads. And don't be flashin' a tape recorder."

"What's in it for me?"

"Just the story of the century, pal. Just the story of the fucking century. You come up here and I'll burn your ears off with all I got. Now I got to get off this line. You comin' or not?"

"How do I find you?"

"Go to the bar, ask for Roger. And don't attract lots of attention. Buy a drink or somethin', then slip up the back. But you gotta make it quick now, or you won't find nobody here."

"Half an hour," Decker said, but the line was already dead.

He hung up the phone, looked at Janet. She was sitting at the table with her bowl of ice cream melting and mostly uneaten.

"So what did rewrite want, sweetheart?"

"I could use some coffee," he said abstractedly. "You have any instant?"

"Sure." She gave him a concerned look before getting up and going to the cabinet above the sink. "Who was that on the phone, Rick?"

He was still standing by the wall phone, rubbing the back of his neck. "In a half hour, I talk to the man who set fire to the *River Queen*. He wants to meet in a bar in Newport."

"Alone?"

"Yeah," he laughed. "I've been to bars alone before."

"That's not what I meant, Rick, and you know it. What about Turk?"

"I've got no choice. If I want the story, I go alone."

Janet went to the oven and removed the tea kettle, now whistling, from the burner. Suddenly, she slammed it on the counter and whirled around. "The story! Is that all you can think about?"

"Listen, Janet, it's too late to run scared now." Although he *was* scared. He could feel the muscles quivering along his jawline, like a current of electricity. "Too many people have given too damn much."

"All right," she said. "I go with you and wait in the car."

He folded his arms and shook his head. "On Monmouth Street, sitting by yourself? Forget it. I'm going alone."

"I can take care of myself."

"And, goddammit, so can I."

"Compromise then. You give me a call the second you're out of Newport."

"Agreed." He looked at his watch. It was almost 9:15. "If you don't hear from me by eleven, phone Barry and tell him where I am." He wrote Stein's number on a phonepad hanging on a string from the phone, then looked up the address of the Kentuckian Cafe and wrote that down, too.

"Whatever you do," he said, "don't call the police. Not in Newport. Not in Cincinnati. We don't know who we can trust."

She nodded. He went to the door; he was anxious to leave. His jaw muscles were still quivering. He tried to cover up with a bad John Wayne imitation. "Just make sure you're here when I get back, all right?"

In a rush, she came to the door and hugged him, and he folded his arms around her. She pushed him away and said, "Dammit, Rick, don't take any chances."

"Don't worry. I'll be totally gutless."

She grabbed him by the arms and shook him in mock anger, making a kind of growling noise, then nestled her cheek against his chest. "You know I care about you, don't you?"

"Yes," he said softly. He was trying to imagine how good it would be when all this was over.

She pushed away again and said, "Go on, then."

He beamed at her and she sniffled a little and smiled back.

"Go on," she said.

That's when he slipped the big glasses off her face, and in the sudden nakedness of her eyes, saw that the face and the smile belonged to him, and that for whatever reason—destiny, pheromones, the fulfillment of childhood dreams—it had always been that way between them. He folded her in his arms again, tighter than before, and they kissed.

16

He wished he were in his Dart. He was used to more laid-back driving—power steering, power brakes, automatic transmission, nothing to do but fiddle with the FM reception. The rustbucket Toyota he found himself driving had no working radio, and the manual transmission was giving him fits, bucking every time he let the clutch out and stalling twice before he made the entrance ramp to I-75 and began the cruise toward downtown. It had bucket seats. He hated bucket seats. Too much back support, like sitting with a brace on.

The car didn't even belong to Janet. It was a loaner from her older brother Harold in Indiana, with Indiana plates, while Janet's Omni was having its third transmission put in. He drove carefully, staying well within the speed limit. The last thing he needed was to be pulled over by a cop. He had no idea where the car's registration papers were.

When he pulled onto the Central Bridge to Newport, he could feel the tug and pull of the tires along the metal grooves. Or was it the wind pushing the little Japanese car around? He cracked the window, quickly rolled it shut again. It was a cool blustery night, early autumn in the air, and a sky so clear that a few stars actually pierced the nimbus of downtown lights. Below, the river was churning from the wind, white scallops fanning across black water.

He was wearing his navy-blue blazer, the microcassette in his right inside pocket, the gun in his left. The uneven weight distribution made him nervous, so that he kept shifting his shoulders as though his body were askew. He didn't feel half so sure of himself as he had fifteen minutes ago, when he was holding Janet. After they had kissed, she had stepped back and looked at him. It was a look that could only be described as faith. Faith in him.

"You'll be back," she said. Statement of fact.

On Monmouth Street he found a space between two pickup trucks in front of a secondhand furniture store, almost directly across the street from the Kentuckian Cafe. He backed in, fighting with the rack-and-pinion steering and maneuvering in and out several times before snugging the curb. With the engine still running, he pulled the emergency brake and, without thinking, let out the clutch. The Toyota lunged; he slammed the brakes and the car promptly stalled.

"Damn!" He wanted to swear in Japanese.

He sat for a moment, collecting himself. He looked down at his coat, saw the oblong bulge the .38 made just under the hanky pocket. Somebody was sure to notice. Then he thought of a trick he'd seen in the movies. He pulled the gun out of his coat, leaned forward, and tucked it behind him in his pants. At least the bartender wouldn't see.

It was almost ten P.M. Cruising traffic was beginning to build on Monmouth Street. Red-necks in pickups, stenciled vans, monster four-wheelers, and macho machines with the rear ends jacked up. Suburban swingers, too, on the prowl in big Buicks and Olds, bigger Cadillacs. He waited for a break in traffic, crossed the street, and found the front door of the Kentuckian wide open. Scraps of litter blew down the street and swirled inside.

The Kentuckian had all the ambience of a parking-garage stairwell—dark, quiet, reeking of port and stale urine. Patrons sat widely spaced at the bar or alone at small tables, nursing glasses of wine. No music, no conversation. Nothing to interfere with the sweet rush of alcohol through arteries and veins. Wino heaven.

He went to the far end of the bar, away from the street,

and sat on a stool in front of the bartender, who was wiping glasses with a sloppy gray towel, setting them bottom up along the rail. He wasn't what Decker had expected to find. He was cheerless, almost studious-looking, with wire-rim glasses like Stein's. And young, too, not more than thirty. He was trim and well-groomed, with his dark hair balding front and back. He looked like an ex-priest instead of a bartender. He went on with his wiping until Decker said, "I'll have a draft."

"No beer," he said, flipping the wet towel over his shoulder.

"Make it a bourbon and water."

"What we sell here is wine," he said, pointing to a shelf full of dusty gallon jugs behind the bar. Rosé, port—red or white—and a generic selection labeled, quite simply, "Red Wine."

"A rosé, please."

"Large or small?"

"Small."

He plunked a beer glass in front of Decker, reached back for one of the jugs, and unscrewed the metal cap. He stopped pouring at the half-glass mark and returned the rosé to its shelf, where it was sure to stay good and warm. He held out his hand for the money. No tabs kept here. Decker pulled out his wallet and put two one-dollar bills in the man's waiting palm. The bartender slapped one bill back onto the bartop, took the other to the mechanical register, and returned with two quarters in change. He slapped that, too, on the bar.

"Thanks," Decker said, pushing the change back toward the bartender. He ignored the tip and returned to wiping glasses. Decker wondered what kind of bartender ignored tips. The poor and the proud, maybe. The loose coins didn't escape the notice of an old wino sitting on his right. He was wearing a blue yachtsman's hat with a torn bill, a red Hawaiian shirt, and a pair of dark brown pants bunched at the waist. There were streaks of brown tobacco juice in his gray beard. He looked quizzically at Decker, then at the coins. Decker slid the two quarters down the bar and the old man politely tipped his hat.

"Roger," the old man said to the bartender, "gimme another."

Decker put his elbows on the bartop, lifted them again, and felt his jacket cling to the sticky surface like Velcro. He stayed hunched over his glass anyway, wanting to look like the rest of the patrons. In a minute or two, after casing the joint, he would make a move. For now, he took a sip of the warm rosé and let it slide down his throat. The stuff was as sweet and thick as cough syrup.

Above the register was a sign hand-lettered on a shoebox top. "Rooms. $2.50 a night. Clean sheets $1.25."

Yep, Vernon went first-class.

He thought again about the possibility of a trap, but there was no use dwelling on it. He finished the wine in three or four gulps, trying to bypass his taste buds. He pushed his empty away and signaled for Roger, now at the other end of the bar. Roger nodded without turning his head, taking his time with another patron. In a minute or so he went to the shelf and put his hand on the big jug of rosé.

"Another?"

He nodded, and while Roger was pouring, Decker said, "Vernon Walker said I might find him here."

Roger didn't say anything until he'd filled the glass halfway again and put the jug back on the shelf. Gripping the edge of the bar, he leaned in close. Decker could see himself doubled in the man's wire-rim lenses.

"What do you want Vernon for?" he whispered evenly, and stepped back as though he were sizing up Decker, trying to see how much trouble he'd be.

"He said he needed to talk to me."

"You the reporter?"

He wasn't sure if he should answer, so he didn't. But Roger smiled anyway and said, "You reporters don't hide your heat very well."

"Heat?"

Roger pointed to a spot behind his own back.

"Oh, that . . ." But there was no need to explain. Roger went to the cash register, stuck his hand behind the machine, and returned with a key. "Take the stairs past the men's room here. Turn left. It's the last room on the right. Number seven. Be sure and knock."

The hallway leading to the stairs was long and dark, almost pitch-black, except for the slivers of light that slipped through the cracks around the men's room door. Decker kept his hands out in front of him, like a kid walking through a fun house. He tried not to breathe too deeply. The closed space reeked of urine, and the darkness made the smell all the more keen.

He found the first step by tripping on it, and crashed up the stairs, landing hard on his right shin and forearm. He heard the gun clatter down the steps and onto the floor. He stayed put a moment, breathing deep from the pain but more concerned about the racket he'd just made. He listened a moment, heard no response, then retrieved the gun and stuffed it inside his jacket. He started up again.

At the top of the stairs, light peeked from below a door. He fumbled until he found the knob and gave it a soft twist and a shove. Stuck. He pushed with both hands. Still no good. He was about to use his shoulder when the possibility dawned on him that the door opened inward. He turned the knob and pulled. The hunch was right.

The second floor, too, was unlit, but there was plenty of alley light falling through the back windows. He turned left and walked down a short hallway. The only sounds were his own footsteps crackling on the uneven linoleum and the muffled hacking and coughing behind the numbered doors. He turned left again at the end of the first hallway. Room seven was at the front of the building, right-hand corner. He was about to knock when he heard heavy footsteps on the stairway. He pressed his back flat against the wall, reached inside his coat. The footsteps continued up the stairs, slow and heavy, and around the first corner. A lock scraped, a door creaked, then slammed shut. No more footsteps.

Door number seven was covered with rusted sheet metal and fitted with a U-hook and bracket for padlocking. Like a store-and-lock compartment, only for people. He rapped softly and waited. No answer. He knocked again, harder this time, and pressed his ear against the cool metal. He heard the slow creak of bedsprings.

"Who's there?"

The voice was so faint Decker wasn't sure if it was coming from room seven or the door behind him. The question was repeated, louder and more insistent this time, and he recognized the nasal twang of the man he had spoken to on the phone.

"Decker," he answered.

"Who?" the voice demanded.

"Rick Decker," he said, not much louder.

"Use the key."

He fumbled in the dark until he could slide the key into the lock. The deadbolt scraped as it turned, then snapped free, and the heavy door swung open into a cramped, unlighted cubicle. There was a single window at the front of the room. Streetlight angled across a mattress to the right, where a pair of bluejeaned legs and bare feet lay one over the other. The man's face was hidden. Decker searched for the glint of a gun.

"Mr. Walker?"

"Yeah," he answered listlessly, "come on in."

He stepped inside and closed the door, and that's when the smell hit him—the sweet-sour odor of cooped-up flesh, stale booze.

"Lock the door," Vernon ordered. "We don't need no company."

Decker did and returned to the middle of the room as Vernon got up slowly and sat on the edge of the mattress. Decker could see his hands now in the slanting light (there was no gun) and his grimy white T-shirt. Vernon reached for a bottle on a folding tray next to the bed and drank long and hard as he signaled Decker to take a seat.

There was an old metal-legged kitchen chair by the window next to the head of the bed. Decker positioned himself in the light and waited while Vernon took another swig of Jim Beam. A quart, two-thirds gone.

Outside, just below the window, was a flashing neon sign. It bathed the room in soft green, then red, then green again. It was flashing green when Vernon's face came into the light. He held out his bottle to Decker.

"No, thanks."

"Suit yourself," Vernon said, setting it down on the floor. He was hunched forward on the mattress edge, elbows on his knees, feet barely touching the floor. He was a little man, lean and wiry, which made it hard to guess his age, although Decker guessed mid-forties from the way he greased back his dark hair, à la Elvis.

Vernon had the face of a troll: pointed chin, big ears, and bulbous nose, as though they were the only parts of his body to reach full growth. And as if he didn't have enough problems, there were the awful scars—down his throat to the neckline of his T-shirt, and from his fingertips halfway up his forearms.

It was eerie how the neon played against the scars. In the red, they almost disappeared; in the green, they showed darkly, like a cancer.

He stared at Decker, sizing him up the way Roger had, and finally smiled in mute derision. He shook his greasy head and reached for the bottle.

"So you're the goddamn reporter got everybody scared." He let out a quick harsh laugh.

"Just doing my job," Decker said. He set his micro-cassette on the window ledge, making sure the built-in mike was pointed in Vernon's direction.

Suddenly Vernon turned pensive, looking out to the street as the wind pressed against the window pane, rattling the loose frame, whistling through the cracks. Dogged, penetrating.

"First off," he said, pointing at Decker with his bottle, "I gotta tell you something right now, and you gotta believe me. I never meant to kill nobody. Not Greenburg, not them boys on the football team. Not even that fat nigger lady in the kitchen. *Nobody*, you hear me?" He was drunk, but not so badly that his speech was slurred. Decker was glad of that.

"So you set fire to the *River Queen*?" He wanted it on the record.

"Hell, yes I did. They paid me to do it. Damn good money, too. But they didn't tell me there'd be anybody on that goddamned boat. They patted me on the ass and said, 'Now Vern, don't you worry about a thing now. The boat's closed on Sunday nights. Won't be a soul on it.'" He threw his head back, as far as the neck scars would allow, and burst out laughing.

When he finished, he stared out the window again, his troll face long and pensive. "Then I read the papers the next day about them boys burnin' all to hell. My God almighty Jesus . . ."

Decker checked the Sony's recording light. Still bright red. He was taking detailed notes, too, as backup.

"Who paid you to do it?"

"A good question, and a hard one to figure exactly," Vernon said, sounding tired and subdued now. "About a month ago, Joe Ricci gives me a call—he's one of Carbone's boys, his bookkeeper or somethin' like that. Anyway he asks me if I'd be interested in a job that paid twenty grand. I said why hell yes. I'd burn down City Hall for that kind of money. So then he tells me to meet him at the Brass Donkey Lounge later that night and we'd talk over details.

"Well, when I show up, I find he ain't alone. There's this other guy with him—a real dude, in a three-piece suit and all. So I ask Joe, 'Who's this guy anyway?' And Joe says, 'Don't you worry about names. He's the one puttin' up the money, and he wants to see exactly what he's buyin' into.' So I says to Joe, 'Tell him, Joe. Tell him I'm the best goddamn torch in Kentucky. More than two dozen jobs and never been caught.' And Joe says, 'Hell, he knows all that. He just wanted to be here hisself, close to the action, you know.'"

Decker interrupted. "Did you ever find out who the other man was?"

"Hold on. I'm gettin' to that. I want you to know all the particulars, because this may be the last time we talk." Vernon turned his head and looked out the window again to collect his thoughts. Then he narrowed his eyes and fixed their gaze on Decker as he continued.

"I didn't know his name at first, and I didn't really care. Not back then anyway. He's the one that tole me nobody'd be on that boat. The stupid sonuvabitch. I drop my matches and there she is, bigger 'n life, this big fat nigger mama in the kitchen. She starts screamin' her head off at me. I told her to jump ship, but she just stood there in the flames cursin' and swearin' at me like a crazy woman."

Vernon's eyes pleaded. "You gotta believe me on that. I ain't no murderer."

Decker nodded, scratched in his notebook. "Tell me more about the man with Joe."

"I'm gettin' to all that. So here's what happened. The man hands me five thousand in neat hundreds, all tucked inside an envelope, and says there's fifteen grand more where that came from just as soon as I finish the job. Only I never saw that fifteen grand. And I wouldn't've seen the man neither if I hadn't gone lookin' for him. I found him, all right, a couple days later, struttin' around like a little boy in a brand-new suit, comin' out of a jelly-roll house on York Street. I followed him to where his car was parked around the corner, then stuck a knife in his ribs. Not clear through, just enough to give him the message. Like this."

Vernon stuck half a thumbnail between his fingers, to show how far. "So I ask him, where's my money? He's says he don't know. He says he don't even know who wanted the job done. I push the blade in a little harder, real persuasive like. And then he says to me, you got to see a lawyer. I say I don't need no lawyer, I need my fuckin' fifteen grand. He says that's what he means. I got to talk to some lawyer over at the Hamilton County Courthouse."

"Ethan Nottingham," Decker said matter-of-factly.

"You got it. So I call this Ethan fellow's office, and that's when I find out he's some muckety-muck in the prosecutor's office. *Je-e-e-esus* Christ." Vernon reached for his bottle again.

"Wait a minute," Decker said, remembering something Kristi McLain had told him. "You knew all along about Ethan. Kristi said you told her Ethan would take care of you."

"Shit, did that bitch talk to you?" He shook his head in disgust and threw back some Jim Beam.

"For two bills," Decker said.

Vernon almost choked in mid-swallow as he laughed. He wiped his mouth with a bare forearm and said, "Whew! That

Miss Kristi. Like a jukebox—she don't play no songs without no money."

"She's been a friend of yours for some time, I understand."

He turned his head and spat on the floor. "A friend as long as I got the cash. She spent most of my five grand—mostly on cocaine and smack. Then when she found out I was a marked man, she didn't want nothin' to do with me."

"A marked man?"

He put the bottle back on the floor. "Just let me finish my story. When I find out this Ethan asshole is an assistant DA, I call Joe Ricci and I say, 'Joe, what the hell am I gonna do? How do I get the rest of my money?' Joe says he'll go to bat for me, see what he can do. Only he says it won't be easy, because word's out that I fucked up, see. I killed people. Wasn't nobody supposed to get killed. I says, Joe, you was there. They told me nobody'd be on that goddamned boat. He says, it don't matter. He says somebody's goin' to have to take the rap, and that's when I smelled big trouble."

"So you're the fall guy," Decker said.

Vernon gripped his knees and rocked forward, a wry grin on his face. "You got it, baby. And all because of you asshole reporters. Joe says the *Eagle's* got everybody edgy as hell. Both sides of the river. Carbone, Orsini, the boys down in the Hamilton County Courthouse—"

Decker looked up from his notes. "You haven't heard then."

"Heard what?"

"Orsini killed himself two nights ago."

"Oh, shit," Vernon said quietly. His eyes widened with some awful realization. He picked up the bottle again. There was a corner of Jim Beam left, and he drained it. "That explains a lot," he said, wiping his mouth with the back of his hand.

"Like what?"

"Let me get to all this in my own good time. You rush me and I'll forget somethin'." He tossed the empty bottle on the mattress. It rolled to the foot of the bed.

Decker was getting impatient with the pace of the interview, and increasingly nervous about his safety. With one ear, he listened for footsteps in the hallway. "You mentioned the boys in the courthouse. Are you saying Krieger is part of this, too?"

"Yes," Vernon answered dully, and then with more force, "no, I mean maybe. Hell, I don't know for sure. Joe says he is, but I don't know. But I can tell you this. Ethan wants somebody to take the heat, and with Orsini gone, that means me. Joe told me all about it. Carbone's got a snoop right in police headquarters, and this snoop told Joe the word came out of Ethan's office today: I ain't supposed to make it to trial. The first cop that finds me, I'm dead meat. I asked Joe if Carbone would give me some protection, and he says, no way, because it would look like Vic put me up to the job."

"Why don't you just get out of town?"

"I can't," Vernon said, looking out the window.

"Why not?"

"Because . . ." He broke into a wry little smile, a smile that declared himself a knowing fool. "Because they'll kill Miss Kristi, that's why."

Decker smiled a little, too, musing a moment on the awful mysteries of love. Then he asked, "And who are 'they'?"

"Another good question. Ever hear of a group called the Pendulum?"

He was about to shake his head no when he remembered what Barrett had stumbled onto. "You mean The Pentagram?"

"No, the Pendulum. Hell, you don't have any idea how deep this shit is, do you? Reporters, why hell—" He spat on the floor. "You guys don't never know the half of it."

"Just tell me about the Pendulum."

"I don't know the particulars, but I know they exist. It's some kind of fancy-ass secret society, like the Klu Kluxers, only they don't cotton to red-necks. Joe told me about it back when them two abortion clinics got torched last spring. Wasn't any of my doin', but it was first-rate work. I asked Joe who done it. He said the Pendulum was behind it. I asked him what the Pendulum was, and he got this scared look on his face like they was zombies or somethin'. Can you imagine? Carbone's right-hand man and he looks so scared I thought he'd shit his pants just talkin' about it.

"And I'll tell you why. It's because the Pendulum makes Carbone and his boys look like kid stuff. They got members in the fire department, in the police department, in all levels of city government. And you know who they say is at top, pullin' all the strings? Joe says it's Krieger hisself."

Decker raised a hand for Vernon to stop so he could catch up on his notes. His head was pounding with a thousand questions about Krieger and the Pendulum. Questions he wouldn't have the chance to ask.

"Hey," Vernon said, "come here a second." He was crouched to the right of the window, looking north on Monmouth Street. A hard gust of wind rattled the window frame as Decker got up from his chair.

Vernon pointed to a white Toyota across the street. "I saw you get out of that car, didn't I?"

"Where?"

Decker knelt where Vernon had been, caught a glimpse of the action, and felt his stomach knot. It was like watching your own body being violated. He saw a man deep inside the Toyota's hood, working fast and purposefully, while a second man's outstretched legs showed under the front bumper. In a second, the man under the car rolled out on a dolly wiping his hands with a grease cloth. Both men were dressed in dark blue mechanic's suits. The second man scooped up the dolly while the first shut the hood, and then they walked together up Monmouth Street to an unmarked white van. They hopped in back and closed the doors. The van didn't move.

He turned from the window with a sudden, sickening realization—Rick Decker, reporter, was no longer observer, seeker of truth, protected party. He was now participant. A part of the action. A target.

"I've got to find a phone," he said, snatching his tape recorder from the window sill.

"Don't be crazy." Vernon caught him by the arm. His breath was sourish and stale, like the odor in the room, only five times worse. "The phone is at the bar. You go down there, they'll be layin' for you."

"What the hell do I do, then?"

"Sit tight for a spell. I got a few more things I got to tell you. Then I'll slip you down the backstairs and into the alley."

"What if they come up here?"

"Roger won't let 'em."

"Roger?"

"The bartender. He's been lookin' out for me."

"All right," Decker said impatiently, setting the recorder on the sill again. "Let's do it."

Vernon sat on the mattress with his back against the wall and started talking slowly and evenly to make sure Decker got it all down.

"Tomorrow afternoon they'll have a whadyacallit—press conference—in the Safety Building. Joe says they're going to announce a new *River Queen* investigation. Some bullshit or other about new evidence. You got that? Okay, the police will be there, too. Captain Schaeffer—he's supposed to be big, too, in this Pendulum thing. Schaeffer is going to say the police are looking for a man by the name of Vernon Walker. That's right, yours truly. Wanted for questionin' only. They're

going to lay out a real good description of me—and that won't
be hard because there ain't too many human bein's what look
like this." He held out the insides of his forearms to show the
scars. "According to Schaeffer, I am armed and dangerous and
not to be dealt with lightly." He winked broadly.

"Only there's one thing they won't count on," Vernon
said. He smiled like a man at peace with himself. "The *Eagle*
is going to print the real honest-to-God truth about the *River
Queen*. Isn't that right?"

Decker closed his notebook. "If I can get out of here
without being killed."

"I'll get you outta here," he said matter-of-factly, then
pointed at the bulge inside Decker's blazer. "You plannin' on
usin' that thing?"

"If I have to," he said. He picked up his recorder and
stuffed both it and the notebook inside his jacket.

"You know somethin'? You're gonna need a bullet for
every cop in Cincinnati."

Decker saw the wry twinkle in Vernon's eye. He was
right. It was no good. He pulled out the .38 and tossed it
lightly on the mattress next to Vernon. "You probably need it
more than I do."

Vernon glanced at the gun and grinned. "You ain't got no
bazooka now, do you? At least a bazooka'd be fun."

Vernon got up and handed the gun back to Decker and
walked him to the door. He gave him a look uncannily like the
one Janet had given him before leaving her apartment. A look
of faith.

"There's only one thing goin' to save me," he said, staring
Decker hard in the eye. "The truth. You just make sure you
print the truth."

Decker smiled a little. "Isn't that what reporters always
do?"

Vernon laughed and took him by the elbow into the

hallway, where he whispered in the gloom. "That last door there on the left goes down to the alley. Stick to the alleys and the backstreets, but head for the bridge just as fast as your two feet can move. If they're gonna kill you, they'll do it here in Newport. That way they can make it look like Carbone's doin'. I'm tellin' you, get your ass across that river, and don't waste no time."

Decker put out his hand, but Vernon refused to shake. Instead, he pointed down the hallway. "Haul ass, buddy."

"Thanks, and I mean that," Decker said, walking backward down the hall.

"Just print the truth. You tell 'em now. Tell 'em Vernon Walker ain't no murderer."

17

There was a flight of covered wooden stairs that ran down the side of the building to the alley. Decker jumped the springy planks two at a time, reached bottom, and stopped to look around. It was an old-fashioned back alley—a narrow cut between shabby brick buildings, covered with loose tarmac, potholes, clusters of hardy weeds. Vapor lamps created domes of light every half-block or so in either direction. He saw no one. Nothing but windblown trash scraping over the tarmac like tumbleweed.

Upstairs, through the open hallway windows, he heard quick pounding on one of the metal doors.

"Walker, open up!"

There was a rush of heavy footsteps in the hallway, and then a loud metallic crack—or was it a gun shot? Decker sprung from the last step and broke into a sprint down the alley, his loafers slipping on the oily gravel, his heart pounding in his throat.

Near the end of the second alley, he slowed to a trot and looked behind. There was no one at his heels. No cops, no red-neck thugs. Only the echo of his own panting, raspy and hoarse, chasing him down the alleyway. He was disgusted with himself. Two weeks without swimming and he was pathetically out of shape.

He wondered now if he should have gone back to help, if he had done the gutless thing by running. But there was nothing he could have done for Vernon anyway. Not if the Pendulum had made its move.

He looked at his watch. It was 10:40. In twenty minutes,

if he didn't call Janet, she would call Stein, and Stein would come looking for him. But where? It would be like shooting at a moving target, blindfolded. He picked up the pace again, kicking his knees high to keep his thighs from cramping. All he cared about now was getting across the river and finding a pay phone.

The alleys were uncharted territory. No street signs, no door numbers, no familiar landmarks. He assumed he was moving parallel to Monmouth Street, heading north to the river about six or seven bocks away. That he knew from the pink-yellow fringe of sky ahead, the telltale nimbus of downtown Cincinnati. What he couldn't remember was the direction to the Central Bridge. East or west? He would have to go clear to the levee and look.

From the bridge, it would be a half-mile across the Ohio, maybe another half-mile to the nearest pay phone. And if he was caught with the tape . . .

It would have to be ditched.

He scouted hiding places as he ran. Nothing seemed safe enough. Garbage cans (might be dumped), drain spouts (what if it rained), a missing brick in a cracked wall (too obvious), a broken window in a garage (a car might back over it). At last a promising prospect—a rusty old commode propped against a telephone pole. But when he lifted the cover on the water tank, the bottom was busted out.

At the start of the fourth alley, in the limestone foundation of a small apartment building, there it was: a torn screen over a basement window. He stopped just long enough to make sure no one was watching, and slipped the tiny cassette inside the screen. He ran across the street and kept going.

The alleys came to an end at Big Daddy's used car lot. It was as bright as the Resurrection. Row after row of waxed cars gleaming under strings of hot white lights. At the rear of the lot was the levee, thirty feet of concrete above which nothing showed but sky. Until he looked off to the west. There, hovering above the wall as though suspended in air, was the superstructure of the Central Bridge, a floating silver behemoth with a triple-humped back.

He walked to avoid attention. Past Big Daddy's was a stretch of ramshackle storefronts, the fringe of the Newport business district, well lit but deserted at that hour. On the glass door of an insurance office ("Jack O'Reilly, He's There When You Need Him") he found a stenciled street address. 151 E. Third. He passed a cinderblock Elks lodge, a family pool hall, a greasy spoon with lace curtains and smeary windows. All closed.

Suddenly he felt eerily alone. It was like walking into an Edward Hopper painting. In the cold artificial light, even the shadows seemed empty. Storefronts and windows were vacant, black, soulless. A ghost city without ghosts, without sound, save for the hum of neon and vapor lamps, the whisper of wind through the telephone lines.

He shivered once and snapped to when his eyes were drawn ahead to the corner. High above the sidewalk, a red neon hand flashed off and on. *Halt. Turn back.* He shut his eyes for a second, and the afterimage burned green, then faded to violet behind his lids. He opened his eyes again and read the lettering below the neon: MADAM SHEBA. PALMIST. SPIRITUAL GUIDE IN ALL MATTERS OF LIFE.

He thought of his mother and how she would have gotten to her knees and prayed for help, for strength. He crossed himself like a child and whispered, "Please, just get me over the river."

Enough, if it meant anything at all.

A gust of head wind rushed down the street. It blew cool through his hair, caressed the outlines of his face and hands, soothed his jangled nerves like a gentle massage. Part of him believed it was a sign. Why not? Divine assurance delivered on a breath of wind. And as he walked under Madam Sheba's flashing palm and looked around the corner, he found the entrance to the Central Bridge. A long sloping approach led into a cavern of thick iron struts and bulging rivets. A massive, ugly bridge, yet somehow more reassuring in its crude strength than the modern, more elegant designs.

He walked quickly across the empty intersection toward the bridge walkway, a narrow stretch of metal grating wide enough for one. There was a low cement wall on his left, a guardrail against traffic on the right. Both walkway and bridge were clear as he started toward the other side.

A steady wind blew downriver and into his open jacket, chilling the sweat under his arms. He looked back just once. No one. And then for the first time since leaving Vernon's room, he felt relaxed, optimistic. He squared his shoulders and loosened his stride. He was going to make it after all.

Through the grating under his shoes, a hundred feet or more below, the black water of the Ohio rushed and tumbled, driven by the breeze and its own swift current. He looked up and across the river. The downtown lights were dazzling in the crystalline air; they shimmered like distant stars pulling Decker toward some overwhelming destiny. For a moment, he felt himself at the center of it all—the bridge, the river, the breeze, the lights—all revolving around him like swirling matter in a galaxy.

Yes, Stein had been right. They could make a difference here. "Shed light, and the truth will be found." In a tiny tape hidden now in a Newport alley was the light to blast through a darkness so complete no one could imagine the evil that lurked there.

Then came the blast of a bargehorn. The sound was low and mournful, starting far upstream and echoing from bank to bank down the valley before disappearing into the night. He looked upriver. A towboat's search light scanned the water, slowly rotating in its socket like a huge cyclopean eye.

He glanced at his watch—it was almost eleven. He picked up the pace again. The Coliseum landing was the pot of gold at the end of the bridge. He remembered where he could find a bank of pay phones there. He checked his pants pockets. There was a single quarter among the useless pennies and nickels.

In the next instant the bridge hummed with the sound of tires. He snapped his head around. A Toyota pickup quickly overtook him on its way into Cincinnati, followed by a red Skyline taxi hot on its tail. He watched until they disappeared.

A few moments later he was approached head-on by some good old boys in a beat-up red Buick, the radio blaring Hank Williams Jr. over the din of a missing muffler. The car slowed and one of the good old boys leaned out the back window and launched a beer bottle at Decker's head. He saw it coming and ducked. The bottle shattered harmlessly against a girder behind him.

"Fuck you, fucker!" one of them shouted. The car crept by at the same speed, the occupants daring Decker to say something, anything, to make their day. He was tempted (he had the gun), but he walked on, feeling a bit full of himself in the knowledge that he had spared the unsuspecting. After all, there were larger scum to fry.

At last he crested the hump of the bridge. He was looking down toward the Coliseum when a pair of headlights bounced and entered the bridge from Cincinnati. He wasn't much concerned until he saw the third beam, a searchlight on the passenger side, probing the recesses of the walkway. He stopped in his tracks.

There was nowhere to run. Not toward the cruiser. Certainly not back to Newport. He did what he could; he dropped flat to the walkway, hoping the guardrail would hide him.

He lay still, spraddled facedown on the waffled grating. The metal pressed cold and hard against the weight of his body, dug into his crotch and cheekbone. But it was the view that caused him the most discomfort. The dark water roiled a hundred feet below, as though he were suspended over a black abyss, a plunge into eternal gloom. He closed his eyes to stop his head from spinning, his stomach from sinking.

The cruiser closed in. He could feel the vibrations in the grate, the tingling becoming sharper and sharper, resonating with his fear. In a minute he could hear it. The whine of the tires, then the smooth rumble of the big V-8, and closer still, the sound of radio transmissions, thin and crackly from inside the cruiser.

The noise and vibration reached a crescendo, and for a breathless instant he feared the cruiser would drive over his body. He dug his fingers into the grate, held his breath, and in a second or two, the sound of the tires, the engine, the radio began to recede, and so did the vibrations in the grate. He lay still a minute or two longer, until the tingling had ceased and he was certain the cruiser was gone.

He congratulated himself with a smile and got to his feet, rubbing his cheek where the grate had dug a gridlike impression.

"Enjoying the view, Mr. Decker?"

He wheeled round and saw the two men with guns. The cop in the beige trench coat he knew instantly: Ellway, his bald head and wan ugly face shining like a skullbone under the bridge lights. The bearded partner, small and wiry, took a second longer. Then he remembered: the mountain man in Kristi's dressing room. The one with the lunatic blue eyes.

But it was Ellway who drew Decker's cold, reasoned hatred. Ellway, who had asked so many questions about his tape recorder the night Barrett was killed. Ellway, who had popped up at the Christian Unity League rally just as Turk was about to have his head cracked. It was all clear to him now. He put it in words: "You son of a bitch . . ."

"Uh uh uh," Ellway said, wagging his gun and stretching his pale meaty lips into a smile. "Let's show a little respect for an officer of the law. Now I suggest you get those hands in the air."

Decker raised his hands but kept his eyes fixed on Ellway, who embodied now all the ugliness and horror of what had once been a faceless abstraction—the Pendulum.

Ellway nodded to the mountain man. He was wearing a black bowling jacket, the satiny zippered kind, with JAKE stitched over the heart in red. What he lacked in size, he made up in firepower: a big Western-style revolver, a Colt maybe, with a long, nickel-plated barrel. Jake stepped forward, a head shorter than Decker, and spun him toward the cement railing with the force of a man twice the size.

"Spread 'em!"

He was frisked. The gun was pulled first, then the notebook and Sony. Decker was bent over the railing, face down into the abyss again. He closed his eyes. The cool wind rushed over his back and neck, chilling the sweat there, and he shivered violently.

"Give *me* the recorder," Ellway snapped at Jake. Decker heard the casing pop open. Then a moment of silence.

"*Where* is the tape, Mr. Decker?" Ellway was exasperated.

Decker turned his head. "No, you tell me something, asshole. Who murdered Barrett? You or Grizzly Adams here?"

Something jabbed so hard into his left kidney his head snapped back from the pain.

"The tape, Mr. Decker? We're running out of patience."

He was close to passing out as Jake rammed the gunbarrel

deeper into his side. He had a sudden, strong urge to urinate. "I hid it in Newport," he said through clenched teeth.

"Careful," Ellway said to his partner. "Mr. Decker here will need his strength to accompany us to Newport. Won't you, Mr. Decker?"

Suddenly, the pressure on the kidney was gone, and Decker was grabbed by the shirt collar and shoved past Ellway. Newport lay ahead now.

"Move it!" Jake said. Decker began to limp down the walkway, his bruised kidney burning in his side like a hot lump of coal.

"Don't even think about running," Ellway said.

He couldn't run anyway, not with the burning pain in his side. He tried to think. He couldn't take them to the tape. But where? Maybe lead them back to the Kentuckian Cafe, somehow keep them there until Stein came looking.

He could almost feel the spot in his back where the Colt was aimed. He still had the sharp memory of its barrel there when a bargehorn blast set all his nerves firing at once. He jumped and snapped his head around at the same time. The tow was about a half-mile above the bridge.

Jake laughed derisively. "Gawd, is he some kind of nervous!"

"Keep it moving," Ellway said.

The idea had taken shape in the same instant his head had spun around and his eyes had seen the barge. It was crazy, totally preposterous. Which was exactly why it had a chance of working: he would jump from the bridge.

He glanced over the railing, a split second was all, enough to draw his scrotum into knots. The plunge would be scores of feet downward into blackness and—*pow!*—onto the choppy surface like a sack of bricks. If he wasn't killed or knocked unconscious on impact, he'd have a chance. He was a damned good swimmer. Out of shape, maybe, but good for at least a quarter mile.

How deep was the water? He had no way of knowing. Maybe not deep enough. Maybe nothing but muck at the bottom. He saw himself pinned under the fast-moving current, struggling like Houdini to pull his feet from the sucking mire.

Could he? He looked over the railing again, longer this time, and got the same gut-wrenching response. But what choice did he have? The moment they had the tape, he was as good as dead.

He tried now not to think about the fall, but how to execute the jump.

He turned his head around. Only Jake had his gun out. Ellway's hands were deep inside his pockets.

"Listen," Decker said, "I've got to relieve myself."

"No surprise," Ellway said. "But it can wait."

"No, it can't. Unless you want me to piss my pants."

"Be my guest," Ellway said evenly. Jake giggled like a schoolkid.

"Listen, I hid the tape in a friend's house. They'll goddamn well know something's wrong if I piss in my pants."

Jake giggled again, and Ellway told him to shut up.

"All right, dammit. Stop here."

Decker stopped and cozied up to the cement railing and took a sidelong glance at Jake, who stood watching with the big Colt in his hand, an expectant grin on his face. Ellway was behind Jake, staring off downstream, his hands still stuffed in his pockets.

Decker unzipped. "How 'bout a little privacy, please?"

"For Christ's sake, shut up and piss!" Ellway snapped. Jake threw his hand back and laughed out loud, and that's when Decker put both hands on the railing and, in one smooth motion, swung his legs up and over and straight down.

He heard the crack of the gun, but it didn't matter. He was already falling, his stomach in his throat, his feet aimed toward the blackness below. Down, down, down—the cool rush of air whistling in his ears, working into his eyes, whipping around his pantlegs, and the rippled blackness below pulling closer and closer. He kept falling when he thought it was no longer possible to keep falling, always toward the blackness but never breaking into it, never touching anything but the cool wind that whipped around his body and burned into his eyes.

In the next instant, he was falling through a different kind of darkness, colder and thicker. Fast at first, then slower, until the falling was over and his body was suddenly weightless, then buoyant. And, yes, he was rising slowly upward through the current. His hands clawed at the water, groping upward through the darkness, trying to break to the surface where the night air was waiting. He clawed and clawed and still, it seemed, the surface was no nearer. His lungs and chest began to burn, his head pounded. He had to breathe. Water or air, it didn't matter. And when it seemed he couldn't hold his breath another fraction of a second, his left hand burst into the icy air, then his head, and he was suddenly there. He threw his head back, mouth open wide, and groaned to fill his lungs.

He took a moment to savor his victory, floating on his back and gulping air into his hungry chest. The shimmering panorama of city lights reflected all around him. He was free now. Saved by the dirty waters of the Ohio. He rolled to his stomach and started toward shore—the public landing was dead ahead.

Something was wrong. His right arm was floating loose from the shoulder, like a piece of sodden driftwood. He found a small tear in his jacket just behind the right shoulder. Strangely, he felt no pain. Just an icy numbness deep behind the shoulder blade.

He panicked for a moment, thinking in rapid sequence—blood loss, shock, unconsciousness, drowning. But he didn't think long because there were gunshots from the bridge. He dove under, not trying to swim this time, but letting the current take him downstream. He stayed under until his lungs were on fire, came up for air, and quickly submerged again. Surfacing a third time, he found himself perhaps a hundred yards downstream, well out of handgun range, halfway between the Central and Suspension bridges.

Decker prided himself on his swim stroke, but it was another thing to cross a river with only one good arm and a wet suit of clothes weighing you down. He kicked off his shoes under water, but left his jacket on, afraid of injuring the wound. Then he rolled to his left side and began a slow, easy sidestroke, his right arm trailing in the water.

It was maybe an eighth of a mile across river to the city marina, where Decker could see houseboats and cabin cruisers bobbing along the floating deck. But it was slow going against the current. He wondered how much blood he was losing. Wondered, too, if what they said about drowning was true. That it was quick and peaceful if you didn't panic. Like lying down to sleep.

He had gone twenty yards, struggling to a point just past midstream, when he saw the tow coming. It was the same one he'd spotted from the Central Bridge—open hoppers of coal, three across. Now it was about fifty yards upstream and bearing down on him at a slow, but inexorable pace. From surface level, the oncoming rakes looked enormous, like a drifting wall of steel.

Decker treaded water and watched. The barges would miss him by at least ten yards, but the towboat far at the rear was angling toward midstream in preparation for the bend beyond the Suspension Bridge. It would be too close for comfort. Decker had heard stories about deckhands falling overboard and being sucked into the huge propellers, chopped into sirloin. He rolled to his back and started kicking toward the Kentucky shore. It wasn't long before the first of the wake hit, and he bobbed in the water like a cork, the water rushing over his face in oily waves. He kept kicking and pulling away.

The coal barges, five deep, slipped by in succession like a floating island of rolling black hills. And then came the towboat, a white triple-decker, with its big diesel engines humming and throbbing. From a safe distance Decker was treading hard to keep his head above water. His legs, his one good arm, were cramping. The water seemed suddenly chilled.

Through the windows of the mess hall, he could see three men standing together in the fluorescent brightness—talking, laughing, safe, and cozy. But no one to hear him shout.

The first two rows of barges were beyond the Suspension Bridge as the towboat veered still farther into midstream to negotiate the bend. The boat's stern came slowly around, engines groaning against the crosscurrent, the big propellers thrusting out a rolling current of their own.

At the rear of the towboat, in the light of an open door, a mechanic was leaning against the frame smoking a cigarette.

Decker thrashed to keep his head above the wake. He shouted like a madman for help.

The deckhand stepped outside for a closer look, and dropped his cigarette.

"Jesus Christ. Hold on, buddy!"

He ran forward along the starboard deck, pulled something from the wall, then ran back to the stern. With both hands, he heaved the lifesaver like a gigantic white frisbee. It sailed out over the water—Decker could see it spinning and wobbling as though in slow motion—and splashed softly about ten feet to his left.

* * *

When he tested bottom, his feet sank to the ankles in squishy silt. The water came just above his waist. With his one arm, he lifted the lifesaver and managed to toss it weakly back out, hoping to leave evidence of his own drowning.

He braced the wounded arm and sloshed through water and muck the rest of the way to shore. The numbness in his arm and shoulder was now full-blown pain, throbbing, insistent. The wound burned in the cool night air.

He stood a moment on the muddy shore and took several deep breaths. He felt lightheaded, nauseous. He was on a curved outcropping just downstream from the Suspension Bridge. There were thick bushes and tangled trash leading into a small woods. Beyond that he had no idea.

He was exhausted, but he had to keep moving. There were probably patrols now on both sides of the river.

A phone. He needed to reach a phone.

The wind rustled through the treetops, calling him to sanctuary. With his arms folded in front, he trudged into the woods where the cool night air was even cooler and the darkness complete. He crouched low under tree limbs, stepped high to avoid trash and underbrush, and each time his bare feet jarred on rocks or uneven ground, the pain shot up his shoulder and clear into his skull like a current of electricity.

He stumbled once on something slick and hard, like a log, and went down on his knees in the soft ground. Instantly, he got to his feet, afraid of losing momentum, afraid of losing consciousness.

The woods continued up a levee strewn with bricks and chunks of asphalt and cement. He climbed a slow step at a time, careful of his footing and his balance on the loose, uneven slope. When he reached top, he was grasping for air, but heartened by what he saw in the open distance. Flood-lights, a row of warehouses, and above them, a giant billboard: SANTINI & SONS INC. WHOLESALE PRODUCE.

He moved quickly over a double set of railroad tracks, the sharp gravel stabbing the bottoms of his feet, and then stopped to rest for a moment. He was dizzy and thirsty as a nomad. He shut his eyes for a second to keep them from crossing.

Ahead of him was a long stretch of asphalt leading to the rear of the warehouses. There were four buildings, each one-story and constructed of cinderblock. Between the middle two was a wide break, a passage no doubt to the loading docks. And maybe, just maybe, a pay phone.

He broke into a trot across the asphalt. It seemed like an old friend after the river muck and the railroad gravel. Suddenly his legs felt light and springy and powerful. He soared upward in a huge moon leap, defying gravity, arcing through the air like a gazelle, and then touching down again, lightly, gracefully, as though he was nearly weightless. He laughed with the exhilaration of it all, took another glorious leap, and another, before gravity reasserted itself and he pitched forward and crashed hard on his hand and knees.

He lay gasping on his left side, his wind knocked out and the pain in his shoulder like hot sharp metal driven deep into his side. When he could catch his breath, he got to his knees. He gripped the swollen forearm with his hand, feeling how cold it was now, how separate from the rest of his body. The fingernails had turned a bluish-gray. He had visions of gangrene and rot and amputation. Still, he could move the fingers, just a little, and that seemed a good sign.

He stood and forced himself to keep moving. One foot fell in front of the other until he reached the opening between the warehouses, and there it was, like something he had willed into being, bolted to the far end of the left wall—a pay phone.

He checked both his pockets. The change was gone. It didn't matter. He tucked the receiver between his ear and shoulder and, in a second, there was a dial tone. He pressed zero, waited. There was a sharp clicking noise, and then the woman operator answered with a nasal, "Ycll-o."

He tried to say something, but the sounds caught in his parched throat like bugs on flypaper. He started coughing instead.

"Can I help you?" The voice was impatient now.

"Yes," he croaked, "this is an emergency." He almost laughed he was lisping so badly. His tongue was swollen and sluggish, like something alive but not his own lodged inside his mouth. His upper lip, too, was badly swollen, probably from the fall. He gave the operator Janet's number to dial.

"Are you sure you don't want the police or fire department?" the operator asked.

"No!" he said, with enough force to buckle his knees. He shook his head to keep from blacking out. "Just the number . . . please . . ."

The operator dialed, and in one ring, Janet's voice was on the line, frantic and filled with concern.

"Rick, is that you?"

He couldn't speak for a second or two. His head was suddenly balloon-light, his tongue had disengaged. Finally he said, "Ycs," and chuckled.

"Rick, where arc you?"

"Let me see . . ." He was lisping like a drunk. He tried to swallow, but there was nothing in his mouth to swallow. Nothing but the oily residue of the river, mingled with his own dried blood.

"Rick, are you hurt? Speak to me!" Janet's shouting sounded faint and echoey, as though she was trapped at the back of a cave and he was standing outside wondering how to find her.

"Yes," he answered, his voice trailing off. "I'm uh . . . I've, uh, been shot . . . in the shoulder."

"Oh God, Rick. Tell me where you are. Think!"

He licked his lips and clamped his eyes shut and tried to

make the gears spinning in his brain mesh with whatever drove the mouth. When the words came at last, they came in uneven spurts, like a car bucking uphill. "Santini and Sons . . . warehouses . . . down by the river . . ."

"Santini and Sons?"

"Yes . . . next . . . near stadium—"

"Rick, listen to me! I'll find you. I'll bring help. Just stay where you are—"

"Janet! he rasped, trying to raise his voice above a dry whisper. "No cops . . . The cops, they shot me . . . please, no cops . . ."

"Rick, I'll be there. Stay warm. Try to stop the bleeding. Do you hear me? Apply pressure to the wound."

"Yes . . ."

"I'm leaving now, okay?"

"Yes . . ."

And the line was dead.

He dropped the receiver and watched it swing loose by the cord, like his dangling arm.

"Hey . . . you too?" he whispered, and smiled.

He wrapped his left hand around his right shoulder and pressed as hard as he could against the wound, mumbling to himself, "I pledge 'legiance to the flag . . ." He giggled and pressed harder, holding his breath against the pain. But he couldn't keep it there more than a minute or two, not because of the pain, but because he was too weak to hold his hand in place.

He wanted more than anything to lie down, to curl up on his side on the asphalt and sink into painless oblivion. But he was afraid he might bleed to death before Janet found him, or that he might not be able to stand again, and then how would Janet get him into a car?

Poor Janet.

He stumbled away from the pay phone and out into the broad expanse that fronted the loading docks. The lot was empty, save for a pair of tractor trailers and a pickup truck parked side-by-side in the distance. Well beyond the lot he could see a road, empty now, with a wide paved access leading back to the docks.

Giant vapor lamps, tall as redwoods, stood in rows up and down the lot, droning with their own consciousness. In the steady light, bits of broken glass glinted here and there like fresh-fallen snow. A peaceful scene. A place of rest and quiet.

Suddenly he felt himself let go. His heart went fluttery inside his chest, his legs began to sway. He fought back, pitting mind against body, mumbling in a kind of willful mantra, "I will not die . . . I will not die . . . I will not die . . ."

He continued to sway, and worried that he might fall, decided to walk to the nearest loading dock and sit with his back against a wall. He was about to turn when he saw the headlights moving along the empty road. The car slowed and started to turn onto the long access.

Deliverance. He closed his eyes, whispered a prayerful thanks, and raised his hand to wave. "Janet! . . ."

But the moment the car pierced the outer glow of vapor light along the access, he could see the white paint job. The red and blue bubble lights completed the picture.

He needed darkness, and the nearest he could find lay directly behind him, in the recesses of the warehouse doors. He shuffled to the loading platform. It was chest-high. He looked for steps, found them at the far end of the docks. It was too far to go.

The headlights were about to enter the lot when he braced his arm and threw himself headfirst at the platform. His knees slammed into the wooden bumper, but the forward momentum sent him skidding on his face and chest across a slimy layer of produce.

He was still conscious. With his left hand, he clawed the slick cement and dragged himself the remaining foot or so to the warehouse door. He lay in the shadows, his back snug against the corrugated metal. He watched the cruiser as it started a slow circle around the edge of the lot, its spotlight tracking across the empty fields and railroad tracks. Then it turned sharply and started toward the center of the lot, stopping behind the two trailers and the pickup.

He quit watching. A queer sensation—something light and ticklish—was brushing the fingertips of his left hand. He twisted his head around, chin resting on the cement, and squinted down the length of his arm. In the gloom, he saw a rat sniffing here and there at the knuckles of his open hand. A healthy, happy rodent, plump from the pickings at Santini & Sons. It was making contented little rat noises. *Freet, freet, freet.*

Decker wiggled his fingers a little, and the rat backed off to a corner of the door. It arched its spine like a cat's, worked the air with its pointy nose. Decker could sense the rat's anxiety. Inside the tiny brain a tough debate was raging: food or danger . . . food or danger . . .

He flipped his hand over, palm-side up, and wiggled the fingers again, beckoning. "Come here," he whispered through cracked lips, "come on, little buddy."

The rat edged forward in cautious little leaps and started sniffing at the fingertips. When the razor-sharp teeth sunk into the tip of his forefinger, there was no pain, only a hot tingle and then the warm ooze of blood. The rat chewed a while, took another nibble. Decker could feel its happiness in the taking of a warm meal. It stretched out its quivering forepaws and pinned them on his open palm.

"Yes," he whispered like a patient lover, "relax . . . enjoy."

And then he clamped his fist around the plump hairy little body, and watched it squirm as he squeezed and squeezed and squeezed. . . .

18

No matter how hard he tried, he couldn't shut out the light. It beamed through his eyelids, filling his brain with hot shades of pink and orange. He was naked. He could feel that, and he could feel something brittle, too, something hot and scratchy on his skin from toes to chest. He wanted to push that thing away, off of him, but he couldn't move his arms. His whole body was pinned flat to something cold and hard.

Then he heard voices, laughter. No, he didn't hear, he could *feel* the voices, soothing and gentle, seeping into his skull. He tried to open his eyes, blinking fast against the light, but it stabbed clear to the back of his brain. He rolled his head to the right, away from the glare, blinked again, and opened his eyes. The light came streaming in, but without form, without shadow. Nothing but a bright, snowy blur, flat and dimensionless. Was he blind? He blinked some more and felt the sticky glaze on his eyes began to break and clear. Slowly the world took shape.

Something warm fell lightly across his right cheek, pressed against it, and his head rolled slowly to the other side. He blinked again, and in the soft focus, there was Janet's face, smiling, like a vision he'd summoned into existence.

"Greetings," she whispered, "from the Twilight Zone."

He smiled and felt the corners of his lips crack and burn, like stretched sandpaper. Janet leaned over and, holding back her glasses with one hand, kissed him lightly and pulled away, still smiling. He licked his lips, disappointed. There was nothing there but the coppery taste of dried blood.

"Well, big boy," she said, "you made it. *You* are home safe and clean."

Then he heard the other voice, a man's, whiny and brittle. "Yeah. *He's* safe, and *we'll* probably go to prison. I'm telling you, Janet—"

She rolled her eyes. "Everything will be okay, Bruce. You're such a nervous twit."

Her long hair was pinned loosely behind her head, and gold wisps of it hung about her neck, which Decker wanted badly to kiss. She was wearing her white physician's jacket over one of his blue button-down shirts. Gently she lifted his left eyelid, then the right, staring into his pupils with one part affection, two parts medical analysis.

"Don't you worry, either," she whispered. "You're in good hands now. Bruce Lapchinski is the best ER man in Cincinnati."

Bruce overheard. "Yeah, but I'm no orthopod. And that's what this man needs. If that shoulder doesn't set right, he'll never pitch for the Yankees again."

"That's all right," Janet said, grinning down at Decker. "We'll settle for the Reds. Won't we, Rick?"

He smiled and then Janet went away to where he couldn't see her.

His neck was stiff and sore, but he tried to turn his head a little to see his surroundings. It was a small room, with an overhead surgical light and walls that were very white and very cold. There was an IV tube dripping a clear liquid into his left arm. The wounded arm, his right, was bandaged from elbow to shoulder and pinned to his side by strips of tape that circled his chest. He felt no real pain, just a heavy numbness in the right shoulder, until he tried to move his arm inside the bandages, and the pain shot like a current into his neck and skull.

Janet returned with a medicine cup in her hand. "This is

water," she said, then added teasingly: "Think you can handle it?" He nodded and she put the cup to his lips. He gagged on the first cold swallow, but the second was better, the coolness seeping all the way into his chest.

There was a clatter of metal trays and cabinet doors. Then Bruce came up to Janet and stood where Decker could see him. He was a short, pudgy man, about thirty-five or so, his dark curly hair receding toward the top of his skull. He didn't look like a doctor. He wasn't very commanding. Just nervous. There were small beads of moisture on his forehead and upper lip.

"Janet," he whispered intensely. "I've dug out enough police bullets to know a thirty-eight Special when I see one. Now, if this friend of yours is in some kind of deep shit, I don't want *any* part of it."

"Bruce, I'm the one signing the ER report," she said. "You've got nothing to worry about."

Bruce pointed to himself. "But *I'm* in charge of this goddamn department. *I* will be held fucking responsible if the police find out we aided and abetted this—this *fugitive* from justice."

"No," Decker croaked, "don't tell the police." He lapsed into a small hacking fit.

Bruce looked at him in thin-lipped disgust and stepped away.

"No one is going to tell the police anything," Janet said. She smiled mischievously for Decker's sake. "You've had a nasty kitchen accident. That's all." She gave him more of the water.

"Right," Bruce snorted somewhere in the front of the room, "you were shooting a pot roast with a thirty-eight Special."

Janet shushed him, only half-serious, and explained to Decker: "The ER report says you tried to force a stuck patio door with your right shoulder. The glass shattered and you suffered deep lacerations."

Decker licked a corner of his mouth. "My shoulder?"

"Yes, your shoulder. You see, Mr. Domestic, you were carrying a tray of burgers outside to be grilled."

"Beautiful," Bruce sneered, "Beautiful. If the police buy that, they'll buy anything."

Janet put her light-blue stethoscope in her ears and wrapped a blood-pressure belt tight around his bicep and started pumping until the Velcro seal began to crackle. Decker watched her eyes follow the needle around the dial.

"One-twenty over eighty," she smiled, dropping the stethoscope around her neck and ripping the Velcro loose. "You won't be needing this anymore." And the IV line came out.

Bruce walked over to Janet and placed something in her hand. She rolled it in the flat of her palm, a mushroom-shaped bullet, its hollow lead tip flattened where it had smashed into Decker's collarbone.

"You keep it," Bruce told her. "I don't even want to see it again." With that, he moved crisply to the door and swung it open. Bustling hospital sounds poured in from the hallway.

"Bruce." Janet called, before he stepped outside. "Thanks," she said, quietly, sincerely.

"Anytime," Bruce snorted, and was out the door.

"Janet," Decker said. "The *Eagle*. I've got to—"

"I know, I know," she said, gliding her fingertips over his temple, "you have to call the office. But not at four-thirty in the morning. You need some rest first. You've lost an awful lot of blood."

He frowned in protest, but recognized the weakness of his position.

She teased him by frowning back, her lower lip pushed out like a child's. He would have burst out laughing if he hadn't feared for his shoulder. He lifted his left hand to stroke her cheek, but found the fingers buried in a mound of bandages. Janet took the bulbous hand in both of hers.

"You know," she smiled, "this hand is in much better shape than the rat I found in it."

He managed to laugh a little through his nose. So he'd gotten the fat little bastard after all.

"You laugh now, mister, but you won't be if you need rabies shots. Your furry friend is undergoing tests at the health department lab."

She stopped smiling as she looked around the room. He saw the deep circles under her eyes, the slackness in her mouth.

"You haven't slept," he said.

She smiled again. "Of course I haven't. Residents don't sleep; they run on rechargeable batteries."

She kissed him softly on the cheek and stepped away to a corner of the room. She returned with a wheelchair.

"Come on, big boy. You're coming home with me."

When he woke, he found himself in a single bed, the flowered sheets tucked to his chin. Janet was fast asleep in a rocking chair at the foot of the bed, a thick textbook spread across her lap and a reading lamp shining behind her head like a halo. He looked at the clock-radio on the nightstand. It said 10:58—A.M. or P.M.? A streetlamp was burning outside the window. Impossible. His brain started wrestling with how long he'd been out when another thought popped into his head: call Stein.

He threw off the sheets, dangled his legs over the side of the mattress, and slowly raised his torso until he was sitting on the edge of the bed. There was pain in his shoulder and down his right arm—a new kind of pain, not sharp, but dull and throbbing, like a giant abscess under all the bandages and tape.

He tried to heave himself to a standing position and fell backward just as quickly, his behind thumping resoundingly on the mattress. He would have smiled at himself, but he was in too much pain. He tried again, more slowly this time and leaning forward from the waist. Reaching a steady crouching position, he straightened himself and was at last on his feet.

His head was as light and empty as a lampshade. He put one foot in front of the other, pushing his toes along the hardwood floor as though he were doing a ballroom-dance step. The pain alone kept him moving.

Standing naked against the kitchen counter, he picked up the wall phone and dialed Stein's number. Barry answered on the second ring, alert and calm as always.

"Boy, is it good to hear your voice," Decker said.

"And likewise. How's the grazed wing?"

"A real pain in the neck, so to speak. How did you know?"

"Janet called earlier today. Gave us a rundown on most of what happened, but not many details. She sounds like quite a woman."

From the open kitchen, he could see her through the bedroom door, her head still drooped to one side in the rocking chair. "That she is."

"Listen, Rick, the new interim fire chief—a guy by the name of Chalmers—held a press conference this afternoon—"

"Let me guess," Decker interrupted. "The *River Queen* investigation is being reopened in light of new evidence."

"And so how did *you* know?"

"I'll get to that later. Go on."

"Thurston wrote the story for first edition. It's not much. Chalmers refuses to say what the new evidence is, or whether it has anything to do with our own investigation."

"It doesn't matter now, Barry." His hoarse voice cracked

with excitement. "We've got the bastards by the balls. I talked to Vernon Walker last night, and he told me things that will turn this town upside down—"

"Whoa, there," Stein said. "I can't wait to hear, but maybe I should tell you a few things first. The Newport police say a man was shot and killed early this morning behind the Kentuckian Cafe. They won't give us an ID yet, but they say the man was wanted for questioning in a string of recent arsons. They're hinting he was the leader for some kind of arson ring. Does that sound like our man Vernon Walker?"

"Oh, Jesus." Decker rubbed his forehead with his bandaged hand. He felt a stab of pain as he recalled the little man sweating in the dark grubby room, a cornered animal who could smell impending death.

"There's more," Stein said. "Police on both sides of the river say they want *you* for questioning."

Decker smiled. He wasn't surprised, only amused and a little curious. "So what's the charge?"

"No charges—yet. But they're saying you were the last person seen with this arson character before he was shot."

"Fuck the police, Barry. They tried to kill me last night. A Cincinnati cop named Ellway and some sleazoid low-life named Jake. Hell, maybe they were both cops. Jesus Christ . . ."

"I know," Stein said calmly, trying to cut the outburst short. "Janet told me. They dug out a thirty-eight Special. But it will be our word against theirs. It's not impossible for your average thug to buy that kind of ammunition."

"All right, forget the goddamn bullet," Decker said, realizing the truth of what Stein had said, but not very happy about it. His anger only increased the throbbing in his neck and shoulder.

He calmed himself and began to tell Stein everything he could remember from the Walker interview. Vernon's meeting with Joe Ricci and a go-between to plan the arson. Vernon's insistence that he thought the *River Queen* was deserted. His hearsay on the torching of the two women's clinics. And behind all of these machinations, a murky group of conspirators known only as the Pendulum.

Even as Decker recounted Vernon's words, their import seemed utterly fantastic. A secret society penetrating all levels of local law enforcement? With the venerated Fritz Krieger at the helm? It didn't seem possible. Not in the real world. Not in the world that newspapers wrote about.

But then what about his mangled shoulder? Wasn't that proof enough of a nether world? Didn't the throbbing pain testify to what Vernon had said? That the powerful play out their own secret drama, by their own rules, while reporters are handed a whole other script to put before the sheep. But that wasn't the saddest part. At least not for Decker. When he thought about the great media "plays" of the twentieth century—the Kennedy murders, the Bay of Pigs, the Gulf of Tonkin, Watergate—the saddest part was that the script had been enough for most reporters. Only a handful of the best saw the shadows on the stage and tried to pull the curtains back.

When Decker finished, Stein said nothing for a while. He could almost hear the computer mind whirring and clicking, processing an information overload, then finally spitting out the one question: "Can we trust Vernon Walker?"

Decker answered emphatically. "More than anybody we've talked to. Vernon knew his number was up. People don't lie in that situation."

"Unless Carbone was pressuring him to lie," Stein said.

"Well, there's no way to ask him now, is there?" Decker snapped. He quickly apologized. "Forget it. I'm frazzled. This shoulder is starting to drive me berserko."

"I won't keep you much longer," Stein said. "Did you get the interview on tape?"

"You bet. But I ditched it. It's hidden in an alley behind Monmouth Street. What scares me, Barry, is that they *know* I ditched it. The cops were taking me back to Newport to look for the damn thing when I bolted. I just hope to God I hid it well enough."

He told Stein where he could find the tape. Stein said he and Thurston would hunt for it first thing that morning.

"Better go while it's still dark. They may have the whole area under surveillance."

"Will do."

Decker thought of one other thing. "Barry," he said, "Turk's funeral—did I miss it?"

"Not until three tomorrow. Basilica of the Assumption."

"The basilica? Turk was never Catholic."

"No, but his sister from Detroit found a last will-and-testament among his things. For some strange reason Turk wanted a funeral mass with all the pomp and frills. The will mentions something about the basilica organ."

"Oh my God, yes," Decker said, caught between laughter and tears. He remembered Turk dragging him to an organ concert at the basilica one Sunday afternoon in the fall. The deep-throated pipes had shaken the pews, rattled the stained glass. Turk had come away ecstatic.

"And how is the archbishop taking this?" Decker asked.

"Not so well at first. Until someone made a rather generous donation to the basilica maintenance fund."

"Let me guess. Was the donor perchance Jewish?"

"Well, I wasn't the only one."

"Listen, Barry, I'd like to be there tomorrow."

"You'd better stay away, Rick. My guess is the police will be staking out the place. Lay low for a while. Let's see what Krieger has up his sleeve."

"Plenty, I'm sure," Decker said. He pressed hard against

the back of his neck, trying to divert the pain. "So what about Thurston? Has he found anything new on the crash?"

"Nothing." It was one of the few times Decker had heard a note of despair in Barry's voice. "Thurston has knocked on doors all over Mount Adams. Nobody saw the accident, nobody saw Turk's car leave the Blind Lemon. The coroner released his report yesterday afternoon. It's not good, Rick. He says Turk's blood-alcohol level was close to point-two—well over the intoxication limit. Although it beats hell out of me how they can test a burnt corpse for alcohol. The police have already closed the case. No foul play."

"Dammit, Barry, I can't swallow that. They tried the same thing on me while I was talking with Vernon. These two assholes in mechanic's suits started working over my car. Vernon and I saw it from his window. 'No foul play.' Jesus, Barry, is the entire police department in on this shit?"

"Let's hope not," Stein said, back to his upbeat self. "In the meantime, I better retrieve that tape."

"Barry, call me as soon as you get home—"

"No, you need your sleep. You call me first thing in the morning at the office. Use my private line. I wouldn't trust the trunk lines. Not now."

Suddenly, the enormity of what they were up against washed over Decker like a cold wave, and he shivered.

"This whole thing is pretty damn scary, isn't it, Barry?"

Stein laughed it off, but Decker knew he felt it, too.

"The truth is always frightening," Stein said evenly.

When he hung up, his awareness of the pain came flooding back. The entire length of his arm was throbbing in unison now, from fingertips to shoulder, threatening, it seemed, to burst through the tape and bandages.

At that moment he would have gladly consented to amputation, anything to end the pain. He decided he would have to wake Janet and ask about the pills. But it wasn't necessary, because when he turned, she was standing in the entryway to the kitchen, arms folded and a bemused smirk on her face. That's when he remembered he was buck naked, save for the bandages around his arm and chest.

"Do you always strip before phoning?"

"I was just going back to bed."

"Would you like a bathrobe?"

"Yes," he said demurely, "that would be very thoughtful."

She went to the bedroom and returned with a blue terry-cloth wraparound. "You know, from the waist up, you would make a good mummy," she said. Holding the robe in her outstretched arms, she started toward him, teetering on her heels like Bela Lugosi.

"Extremely funny. Poking fun at a wounded man." He snatched the robe from her hands—a bad move on his part, because the pain traveled straight to his brain.

Janet winced in sympathy. She pulled a small brown bottle from her front jean's pocket and quickly drew a glass of water from the sink.

She handed him the glass and three white tablets. "It's the strongest prescription I could write. Dilaudid."

"No heroin?"

"We'll save that for your final days."

"Which are right now, I think."

He started shuffling out of the kitchen. Janet tried to help, but he wouldn't allow it.

"I'm not your grandfather, goddammit."

"I hope not. You're in far worse shape—and temper, I might add."

Reaching the bedroom, he saw again the lonely twin mattress pushed sideways against the wall. It belonged in a monk's cell, not the boudoir of a healthy young woman.

"And where might you be sleeping tonight?" he asked.

"Don't worry. The living room sofa and I are old friends."

"Good, because the only person I'd share this bed with right now is Kathleen Turner."

Janet poked his sore arm. He winced.

"Kathleen Turner couldn't write you a prescription," she said smartly.

He laughed so hard he lost his chance for a comeback. Then he noticed her standing quite close beside him, a shy smile on her face like the little Janet he knew as a kid, dressed in blue jeans and a saggy white T-shirt. Only the T-shirt and the jeans were filled out now. In this new light, the situation seemed to call for more than an affectionate hug. So he wrapped his arm around the small of her back, just above the spot where he really wanted to reach, and pulled her tight. He was about to kiss her when she broke into an impish grin and said, "What about your shoulder."

"What shoulder?"

When he woke the next morning, she was gone. There was a note on the nightstand. "I'm in OB catching babies today. Back at noon to change bandages, fix lunch. Pain med is in the nightstand. Call if you need anything."

It was signed "Kathleen Turner."

Cute. Then he checked the clock-radio—it was past ten. He grabbed the pill bottle from the nightstand, the robe from the floor where Janet had tossed it the night before, and stumbled into the kitchen.

He didn't know if the shoulder was better, or just his attitude, but he was feeling less pain. He thought about last night and smiled. He didn't know where among his near-depleted resources he'd found the energy to make love. Maybe it had been all the fear and tension of the last few days finding a natural release. Or maybe an expression of gratitude, an outpouring, as it were, for just being alive. Or maybe, too, gratitude for Janet. Sweet Janet Shoemaker, who pulled him off the loading dock at Santini & Sons, like the lovely maidens who found Odysseus washed ashore, and took him home to bathe him, to rub his body in fragrant oils. And then like Calypso, to make slow, easy love to him.

He filled a tumbler from the sink and was about to take his pills when he noticed a second note on the kitchen table. "In case you're worried about Harold's car, don't. I pick up the Omni this morning. We'll rescue the Toyota later."

Oh God, that was right. He had forgotten all about leaving her brother's car in Newport. The cops would probably impound it. That is, if it hadn't been blown to bits. Janet would have to call her brother, before the police traced the tags and started asking questions.

He turned his attention to the *Cincinnati Times* Janet had left unfolded on the kitchen table. A banner headline screamed: "Bizarre *River Queen* Case Reopened." He picked up the paper and raced through the story, amused at first, but with every advancing line, his pique grew toward rage. After leading with Chalmers' press conference of the day before, the *Times* simply rehashed a history of "the bizarre case" from stories that he and Turk had pieced together with their own sweat and blood.

Nowhere in the story was the *Eagle* given a word of credit.

He got on the phone to Stein.

"Those fucking SOBs!" he shouted. His arm and shoulder were throbbing, but he didn't give a damn. He was pacing all over the kitchen, stammering into the receiver. "We give our, our—we give our *lives*, for Christ's fucking sake, Barry— we give our lives to break this goddamn story, and those bloodsucking bastards come along and pull a stunt like that. . . . It's like—it's like we don't even exist in this goddamn town, Barry. We don't even fucking *exist* . . ."

When he finished, there was a long silence on the other end.

"All right," Stein said. "Is it out of your system now?"

"No!" he screamed. "Let's sue. Let's take the bloodsucking bastards to court. Goddammit, Barry, I can't believe they can get away with this . . ."

"Rick, you and I both know this isn't the first time—"

"I know it isn't the first time, Barry, and that's what makes me so goddamned mad. When are they going to stop taking credit for every fucking story we break . . ."

"Okay," Stein demanded, "enough. That's enough. We have other things to talk about. Are you sitting down?"

"No," he snapped, "there's no place to sit in this fucking kitchen."

"Then find a chair."

He grabbed a chair from the table just outside the kitchen and sat. He could feel the blood pounding in his upper arm now, as though someone were squeezing through the flesh, trying to cut off the circulation. "All right. What is it?"

Stein started out slowly. "I went out this morning looking for the tape. Your directions were excellent, by the way, and I had no trouble finding what I believe was the hiding spot. Only one problem—no tape."

"Oh God." He closed his eyes and pinched the bridge of his nose. He felt his head go light and fuzzy.

"Now wait," Stein pleaded, "let's not lose all hope. I have an idea." Decker winced as Stein put on a show of enthusiasm. Some editors excelled at playing cheerleader for their reporters; Stein had never been one of them. "What about a first-person piece? You know, an *Eagle* exclusive by 'someone who was there.' You can dictate it over the phone. Say how you met with Vernon hours before he was killed. How he confessed to torching the *River Queen*. Who paid him for the job, and why. Then the clincher—how you were shot at by two men who wanted the tape. We don't come right out and say they were cops, but we drop plenty of hints. Last but not least, tell readers why you're in hiding—"

"But, Barry, I don't even have notes—"

"Explain that, too. The whole piece will be a recollection of dramatic events, to the best of your abilities."

"But what about Finch? Will he go for it?"

"Good question." And Stein's voice lost a good deal of its enthusiasm. "I think I can persuade him simply on reader appeal. What the hell, this is the old-time journalism Finch cut his teeth on. Real rock 'em, sock 'em stuff. There's a chance he'll go for it."

"A chance . . ."

"Yes, a chance."

Decker took a deep breath and sighed. "What the hell, Barry."

"Good. There's a couple other things. I think the time has come to contact the local FBI—"

"With what? We've got no tape, Barry. No notes, no nothing. It's my word and a dead man's against the biggest names in Cincinnati law enforcement."

"I know. But we should at least make contact. Let them know what we're working on. We may need their help. And besides, the feds could be conducting their own investigation. It can't hurt."

"What if they tip off the *Times*?"

"Come on, Rick. You know the FBI is more savvy about the media than that."

Decker said he hoped so, then invoked the name of Griswald for all their troubles.

"Griswald may come through yet," Stein said. "Especially if we can get this first-person piece into the paper. If he has any social conscience at all, he's got to come forward—"

"Dead men don't come forward, Barry."

"Don't give up so easily," Stein said. There was a touch of anger in his voice.

Decker switched the subject. "You think you'll make the funeral this afternoon?"

"I'd like to. But if Finch says okay, we'll both be tied up on your first-person piece."

"Let's hope so," Decker said in his best Stein imitation.

When they hung up, he returned to the sink where he had left the pain medication. He spilled three tablets onto the counter, thought a moment about taking more, and heeding Janet's advice about turning into a drug-store junkie, settled on the recommended dose. He picked them up one at a time between his thumb and bandages, and kicked each back with a half-glass of water. He followed with an orange juice chaser and crawled back into bed, where everything still smelled of Janet.

He tried not to think about the missing tape, or the pain, or about anything except the morning with Janet, and other nights and mornings to come. He lay on his left side and closed his eyes, but it was no use. He was a stomach sleeper, but now it meant crushing his bandaged arm. He settled on his back, feeling like an invalid in a nursing home, and waited for the medication to do its work.

He struggled to capture Janet in his mind, the fierce, willful intensity on her face as they made love, the changing smells of her skin, the taste of her mouth. But the more he tried to escape into dreams of Janet, the more Krieger and Ellway and Nottingham intruded into his thoughts. They were a clever bunch. They could put two and two together. They would look through the emergency-room records, figure out who had treated him, who was hiding him.

There was nothing to do now but wait for the loud knock at the door. As Vernon had waited. As the Jews in Germany and Holland and Poland had waited.

It might be Ellway and Jake, or it might be a whole SWAT team. It didn't make much difference. They would move the neighbors out first, cordon off the street if they had to, so there would be no witnesses, and then bust down the door. In the ensuing ruckus, shots would be fired. Lots of them. They'd be sure to hit him from the front. And afterward they'd plant the gun in his hand—the Taurus he'd bought in Covington—then squeeze a couple of rounds into the wall. Make it look good for the ballistics people.

"His" gun, he snorted. He'd never fired a gun in his life. Not even a BB rifle. His parents had told him what every parent tells a kid who wants a BB gun. "You'll shoot somebody's eye out." Only it was true. He remembered Sharon Clancy. The day she returned to fifth grade with the shiny glass eyeball in her empty socket, and all the kids squirming in their seats trying to get a look at it, making faces at each other like they were going to be sick. Kids. The cruelest monsters on God's earth. Especially in packs. Like the Pendulum . . .

At 11:20, the phone rang. He went to the kitchen, groggy now from the medication. Stein said hello and asked, "The pain any better?"

"Get to the point, Barry." Decker knew by the tone it was bad news.

"The big man says it's no go. At least for now. The libel implications are enormous. If we go to court, it's your word against Kreiger's and Nottingham's. I don't have to tell you how we would fare with a jury."

Decker tried the reporter's last and always unsuccessful resort. "Barry, if they don't let me tell my story, I quit. Now. This very second. Tell that to Finch."

"Fine, Rick. But think a minute. If you leave the *Eagle*, who else will see this story to print? Who else knows the background? Listen to me. The *Eagle* is the *only* place your story has an ice cube's chance."

Stein was right, he was always fucking right. "But goddammit, Barry, how long can I sit like a duck—a wounded duck—in this goddamn apartment?"

"You'll have to be patient. Something could break in a day or two. Or Finch may give in—"

"When? When they've killed me? Like they killed Barrett and Turk and everybody else who ever got in their way?"

"Just listen a minute. I have more. I called the FBI and they say they're willing to talk to us. I don't know how much of this they'll believe. But they should be willing to give you some kind of protection—"

"They better make it soon, Barry, or they'll be protecting a corpse."

"I'll impress them with the urgency of the situation."

When Stein hung up, Decker felt suddenly exhausted, emotionally drained, as though his energies had been sucked into the phone and dispersed into a dial tone. He barely had the strength to hang the receiver on the wall. In a narcotic stupor, he slumped in a chair by the kitchen table, thinking he had no reason to sit up, to walk, to do anything but sit there and listen to himself breathe. The world as he knew it no longer had any reason or justice or meaning. There were only men like Krieger—tyrants, egomaniacs, controlling the world from the shadows.

"*He's* going to get away with it," he said to himself. It felt good to say it out loud. Somehow it didn't seem so bad when he could voice the monstrous fact of it. He laughed and said it again, the words rolling off his tongue like a metered poem. "The *fuck*ing *bas*tard is *go*ing to *get a*way."

He stood and went to the cabinet above the sink where his pills were. There were three tablets left. He swallowed all three and began searching the other cabinets. He flung doors open and ransacked dishes, bottles, boxes until finally, in the bottom cabinet next to the oven, he found an unopened fifth of Dewar's. He broke the seal and started chugging.

He took the bottle into the bedroom, set it on the nightstand, and sat across the bed with his back against the wall. He drank the Dewar's, more slowly now, and after a while felt the warmth of it radiate from his stomach into his chest, then to his head, and eventually to his throbbing shoulder, which no longer throbbed but seemed now to hum and tingle with an excess of blood.

He nursed the bottle a few more times and slumped down the wall until his back lay on the bed and his feet were on the floor. His eyes began to follow the maze of basement pipes— fat ones, skinny ones, rusty ones—zigzagging across the ceiling like exposed entrails. In a minute or so his head began to spin and he arched his spine and pressed his skull into the unyielding mattress. The walls were closing in around the bed. He rolled onto his side, made himself small so that all of him would fit on the mattress. But still the walls closed in. The Pendulum. The pit and the pendulum. He was trapped. Trapped and no way to fight back. Just like the miserable fucking rat he'd crushed in his fist. Only now he was the rat and Krieger was the hand, squeezing, squeezing, squeezing.

"Well, I'm glad to see you're not comatose."

Janet was standing in the bedroom doorway, her back against the frame, a sack of groceries in her arms. She glared at the half-empty fifth on the nightstand and walked out.

He got to his feet, swaying a little, and grabbed the bottle. He seemed to float into the kitchen. Janet was there, taking things out of the sack, stacking them on the counter. She wasn't smiling. She wouldn't look at him.

"Do you think that's very smart," she said, "drinking on your medication?"

"No, but then I was never very smart. Or very sensitive—not like you, Doctor Shoemaker." He kicked back a long chug on the Dewar's, more to make her mad than anything else.

"He's going to get away with it," he said with dramatic finality. He slammed the bottle on the countertop, steadied himself. His mouth twisted into a smirk. His lips felt slippery and numb and his speech was slurring. "Krieger is going to get away with it. And you know what?" Janet busied herself emptying the bag, still not looking at him. "You know what, Doctor Shoemaker? Nobody in this town'll give a shit. Not even one lil' shit."

"So what happened?" she said, stashing carrots, celery in the bottom of the refrigerator.

"What happened? I'll tell you what happened. They got my tape, that's what. They got the one goddamn thing I could fight back with. They shoulda just cut off my balls."

He laughed and touched off a coughing fit. When it stopped, he grimaced and clutched his shoulder, and started in again. "And Finch," he sneered in disgust. "Alexander Finch, that gutless wonder. No tape, no story, he says. Who cares if it's only the biggest goddamn story of the decade? Why, gee golly willikers, the *Eagle* might get sued."

He inspected the Dewar's. He was a quarter of the way from emptying the bottle. He considered tossing back the rest, then thought better. "I'm dead," he said evenly. "The tape is gone, and I'm dead. That's all folks. I'm just a dead fucking rat."

He popped the Dewar's into his mouth again, and Janet pushed him aside to put some cans away.

"So now," she said, returning to her grocery bag, "you're going to kill yourself by mixing alcohol and narcotics. Is that it?"

"No," he said, "now I'm getting out of this fucking town and never coming back. I'm going to Chicago. Just as soon as I can walk. I'm going to Chicago and work for the *Tribune*. And you know why?"

When she wouldn't answer, he shouted, "You know why?"

"No," she said barely above a whisper, "why?" She was standing frozen, expressionless, staring into the empty bag.

"Because nobody here cares about the fucking truth, that's why. Because nobody here even wants to *hear* the truth."

When Janet wheeled around, he saw the eyes of someone he didn't know. Narrow and angry and flashing blue.

"The truth!" she sneered. "Let me tell you some truth." Her face seemed inches from his. There were dark circles under the eyes, no color in the skin. "Two hours ago I delivered a baby to a couple who've been trying for three years—three years!—to have a child of their own. For twelve hours that woman was in labor, and for twelve hours she refused any medication. She groaned and she pushed and she groaned. And for what? So she could produce this, this . . ." She stretched her hands apart and stared into the empty space between. "This thing. This monster with no brain. Yes, a baby without a brain! And if this woman and her husband are lucky, their little monster will die. In a day. Maybe two. And then they can go back and try again for another little bundle of joy."

She pointed toward the door and shouted. "Now you go over to that hospital! You go over there and you ask that woman if she gives a damn who set fire to the *River Queen*. You ask her if she cares who prints your story of the decade. Ask her if she cares if Rickie Decker gets the Pulitzer Prize. Go! Go and ask her!"

And then she was sitting in one of the dining-room chairs, not sobbing or even crying, but rubbing her forehead with the tips of her fingers and staring into the table as though she wanted to cry but there were no tears left. He put his hand on her shoulder, and felt her shudder.

"Janet," he said softly. "I'm sorry—"

She jumped from the chair. The eyes that were someone else's burned again.

"Just stop pretending," she said, and turned away. She walked fast to the door, where she stopped and said, her voice under control now, "Go to Chicago. Go to hell if it will make you happy."

And she was gone.

For a long time, he stood there in the kitchen, swaying and staring at the open door. He seemed to feel nothing, nothing but a kind of emptiness buzzing between his ears.

He looked at the door again. It was still open, but Janet wasn't there.

He put the bottle on the table and slumped into a chair. He stared at his ghostly reflection in the window and smiled. Yes, that's me. It's always been me. Me, me, me—poor little ole me. He broke into a laugh, and suddenly the self-pity seemed to drain out of him like a poison. He belched, loudly, and smiled again.

"All right, Janet Shoemaker. All *right*."

He got out of the chair and stumbled to the sink, where he poured the rest of the Scotch down the drain. He ran the tap, filled a tall glass with cold water and gulped it down. He belched again.

He shuffled to the door and closed it and returned to his chair. He had to think. He had to think like a reporter. Like a man.

Who would know if Krieger had the tape? Nottingham, surely. But who would be willing to help? Of course—Victor Carbone. Carbone had everything to lose if he was blamed for the *River Queen* fire. Krieger would call in the feds. He would demand the rats' nest in Newport be cleaned out and Cincinnati made safe again.

He stood from the chair and nearly lost his balance. He picked up the kitchen phone and called Stein.

"Barry, what about Carbone?"

"What about him?"

"Couldn't we make a deal? Couldn't we say we'd print the truth about the *River Queen*—that it was Krieger's idea, not Carbone's—if he could get us the tape."

Stein was silent for a moment. "Yes. Maybe. Assuming, of course, he could get us the tape."

"Come on, Barry. It's worth a try. Carbone has people everywhere, for God's sake."

Stein thought on it a while. "It's like making a deal with Lucifer to catch Satan, but maybe you're right. It's too bad we can't get to someone closer to Krieger."

The idea shot into Decker's brain like a rush of adrenaline.

"Charlotte!"

"Who?"

Decker tried to calm himself. The blood was pounding in his ears.

"Charlotte Krieger! Fritz's daughter. She hates him. I know she does. She was one of the counterdemonstrators . . ."

"Rick, wait. Slow down. What are you talking about? How do we even know how to reach this girl."

Decker racked his brain. Their conversatin at the pool party. "Mother of God. That's it. Mother of God Academy. I gotta go, Barry. I'll call you back in a jiff."

"All right. In the meantine, I'll be on the phone to Carbone's office. And one more thing."

"What's that?"

"Calm down. You'll have a stroke to go with your busted arm."

He fumbled through the phonebook on the kitchen counter and found the number for the academy. He took a deep breath, cleared his throat, and dialed the number. A secretary in the principal's office answered.

"Yes, hello," Decker said in his deepest, most commanding voice. "This is Mr. Krieger calling. I would like to talk to my daughter Charlotte. It's rather urgent."

"Why, of course, Mr. Krieger. I'll have someone get her out of class right away. Please hold."

Decker smiled. It was working. He took a deep, measured breath, then another. It seemed forever before Charolotte came to the phone, but then a tiny voice said, "Hello?"

"Charlotte?"

"Yes, who is this?" The voice was perturbed now. The jig was up.

"Charlotte. Listen, don't hang up. This is Rick Decker, the reporter from the *Eagle*. Remember we met at your father's place last Friday night?"

"Yes?" It was his summons to go on.

"I need your help with something. Something very important. You remember how we talked about your wanting to be a reporter someday? Well, now's your chance."

"I don't understand. I'm not looking for a job."

"That's not what I mean, Charlotte. I need your help. I think your father has a tape, a *very important* tape, of an interview I did last week . . ."

"I'm sorry, Mr. Decker. I can't talk to you just now. I'll have to call you later."

"Wait, Charlotte. You don't have my number!" But the line was already dead.

"Damn!" He slammed the receiver into the cradle, leaned against the counter, and felt his head begin to spin. Suddenly, he was exhausted. The adrenaline had worn off and the drugs and alcohol were taking hold again. There was nothing he could do but wait. Wait and sleep and hope. And maybe when he woke again, Janet would be there beside him.

19

He woke and found himself on the sofa, tucked underneath a long black overcoat. It smelled faintly of perfume.

"Janet?"

The phone was ringing. He slipped off the sofa, got to his knees, stood. He didn't know which pained him more—his head or his shoulder. Both were pounding, both were on fire. He expected the phone to stop ringing at any moment, but it didn't. It wouldn't. Each ring seemed to tighten the band around his scalp, causing his head to pound all the harder. He had to make it stop. He lurched to the kitchen, made a grab for the receiver. But it fell off the wall and flopped around the kitchen counter like a decked fish until he slapped his hand over it. He brought it to his ear and grunted "Yes?"

"Rick, you all right? I wasn't sure you would pick up."

It was Stein again. "I'm okay. Just a little groggy from the medication, that's all. What time is it?"

"Almost three. You're sure you're all right?"

"Yes, yes," he said, every spoken word a monumental effort. Almost three, yet it seemed much later from the gray-yellow light coming through the kitchen curtains. He couldn't see outside, but he guessed it was a typical rainy mid-September afternoon, full of deep grays and greens and maybe the first leaves turning.

"What's up, Barry?" He tucked the receiver in the crook of his neck and pulled down a glass from one of the cabinets.

"I just received a very strange phone call. From Charlotte Krieger."

"Charlotte?" Then it came back to him. "Oh, yes,

Charlotte Krieger. Promised to call back. I didn't believe her. What'd she say?" He started searching the cupboards and drawers for some aspirin.

"She said she had to talk to you—"

Decker panicked. "You didn't tell her where I was?"

"Of course not. How much medication are you on?"

"None—right now. That's the fucking problem." He gripped the front of his skull, squeezed until he thought he might crack something. Which would have been a blessed relief if only it would stop the pounding. "Can't even find an aspirin in this goddamn place."

He began slamming cabinets and drawers. "You'd think a doctor would have some goddamn aspirin—"

"Have you tried the bathroom?"

"Oh, sheesh—" He gripped his skull again.

"Listen closely, Rick. I don't know if this Krieger girl is a crank or if she's laying a trap, but she claims she has your tape."

Decker froze. "The tape with Vernon?"

"Yes. I suggested she bring it to the *Eagle*, but she thinks she's being followed. I said I would meet her, then, but she insists on meeting with you."

"Did you give her my number?"

"No. I said you would contact her. She wants you to call right away. She's waiting by a pay phone in a restaurant." Stein gave him the number. It was somewhere in Hyde Park.

"Keep your line clear, Barry. I'll be right back."

He tagged the wall phone cradle, got a dial tone, dialed the number for the pay phone. A girl's voice answered on the first ring. She spoke in a whisper, urgently but politely, as befitted a Krieger.

"Hello, who is calling, please?"

"Decker, from the *Eagle*."

She let out a small sigh of relief. "Yes, Mr. Decker. I

| 304 |

found your tape." He could tell her hand was cupped around the receiver; the sound of her voice was hollow and sibilant. "The problem is, I don't know how to get it to you. I'm being followed."

"Who's following you?"

"Wait a minute. Please." There was a loud clunk and a rattle as the receiver dropped. In a second she was back on the line, her voice more urgent than before.

"They're sitting by the door now. I think they're friends of Father's. They suspect I have the tape."

If she wasn't genuinely scared, he thought, she was putting on a damned good act. Her voice grew more frantic with every sentence. He asked calmly: "Tell me, how did you get the tape?"

"Late last night, I heard Father and Ethan listening to the tape in Father's study. I didn't hear everything that went on, but I know what they've been up to. I've known for a long time now. After you called, I went home on my lunch period and stole the tape from his desk and drove back to school. I don't know how he found out it was missing. But I know he thinks I took it, and that's why they're following me."

Decker was rubbing the back of his neck, only vaguely aware of his pain now. "I want to believe you, Charlotte. But how do I . . ."—he didn't know how to phrase it tactfully— "how do I know this isn't a trap?"

"Oh, believe me, it's not a trap," she said. "I'll do anything to get away from him—".

"Him?"

She was stiff, assertive, a chip off the old Krieger block as she explained. "I was going to steal the tape, even if you hadn't called. I intended to use it as a kind of—how should I put it?—blackmail, I guess. To win my freedom. I simply can't tell you any more than that right now. You have to trust me, Mr. Decker."

He was ready to believe, but he pressed on. He wanted to understand. "And you changed your mind about the blackmail?"

"I know I couldn't hide the tape from Father. Not for long. He would make me tell. I know he would. You have no idea—"

Torment and confusion flooded her voice now. Decker was convinced it was no put-on. No one, not even an overwrought teenage girl, was that good an actress.

"We have to meet," he said, and then to himself more than to Charlotte, "but where?" He ran cold water into a glass and gulped it down—with instant regret. The water churned like acid in his stomach.

"Are you still there, Mr. Decker?"

"I'm thinking, I'm thinking." He palmed the back of his skull. He wanted to kick himself for guzzling the Dewar's. Stupid, childish. Just when he needed his wits . . .

Certainly they couldn't meet at the *Eagle*. The two tails would cut her off before she reached the lobby door.

They would have to meet on neutral ground. Somewhere public, somewhere a gun couldn't be pulled without people noticing.

"The funeral . . ."

"The what, Mr. Decker?"

"Never mind. What time is it now, Charlotte?"

He heard the payphone door squeak and crunch. "The clock here says three-fifteen."

"Good. Charlotte, can you find your way to the Basilica of the Assumption in Covington?"

"Yes, Father knows the archbishop there quite well."

"All right. Meet me inside the basilica just as soon as you can. There's a funeral Mass going on there right now. Just act as though you belong there. Go in the front door and take a pew with all the others. Mix with the crowd. But look for me first. If I'm there, slide into the pew next to me. Have you got all that?"

"Yes. But please hurry. I'm afraid they'll tell Father where I am."

"I'll be there. And another thing, Charlotte—"

"Yes?" she said in a voice so small and frail he thought he was talking to a child.

"Don't panic. Drive slowly and stick to the main roads. Act like everything is perfectly normal. Okay?"

"Yes. I'll try."

He hung up and suddenly realized that Janet may have taken her car. His heart stopped until he looked at the wall hook next to the door. The keys were still dangling there.

He phoned Stein.

"Barry, I'm meeting the Krieger girl. But I want you to be there, too. I've got a plan."

Driving was no simple matter, he discovered, with one arm taped to your side and your only hand wadded in bandages. Shifting into drive was the first obstacle: he went through painful contortions in the Omni's bucket seat in order to reach across with his left hand and push back the automatic floor stick. He decided to forget the seat belt. Gripping the steering wheel proved a slippery problem, so he used his teeth to tear off the bandages on his left hand, and was surprised to see dozens of tiny stitches—no doubt Janet's painstaking work—zigzagging across his reddened fingertips.

From Clifton, he picked up I-75 and headed south toward downtown and Covington. It was a wet dusky day, the roads slick and the clouds so low that even the modest skycrapers of Cincinnati were socked in like mountaintops. It was a good day for a funeral. Or a killing.

He arrived at the basilica just after 3:35 (if the dashboard clock could be trusted), and parked in a two-hour slot on

Madison Street, a half-block from the main entrance of the church. He skipped the meter, crossed the street, and walked up the cathedral steps—fast, but not frantic, like someone late for a funeral. He lowered his head through the spitting rain.

He needed all his strength—and weight—to tug open the basilica's enormous carved oak door and slip through before it closed with a reverberating thud.

He waited a moment inside the vestibule. While his eyes adjusted to the dark, he breathed in the long-remembered church smells of candlewax, wood polish, incense. A smell synonymous in his mind with pious souls.

He tucked in his shirttail as best he could and buttoned his sportcoat. He was a little embarrassed that his Oxford shirt was half-unbuttoned and his shaved chest was showing; there had been no other way to cover the bandaged arm. He hadn't thought of taking one of Janet's T-shirts until he was out the door.

He walked slowly up the long main aisle, gawking as he always did in magnificent churches. It was a cavernous Gothic structure, with tall, stained-glass windows rendered in moody colors of lavender and rose. At the front of the aisle stood the coffin, set on wheels and draped in the Stars and Stripes, as he supposed coffins were for every veteran, although he had never thought of Turk that way. "Veteran" was obituary talk, a label reserved for the dead. Or near-dead.

He genuflected quickly from some past instinct and slipped into an empty pew on his right behind the other mourners. It was a disappointingly small turnout, scattered in the first four or five pews on either side of the coffin. Even so, he couldn't find Stein or Charlotte on first glance, until the faithful began filing out of their pews for Communion. Stein was to his left, directly across the aisle, looking stiff and embarrassed as the others stepped around him. His round frizzy mane looked planted on top of his dark suit, as though someone had mixed up heads at a mannequin factory.

Decker crossed over, genuflecting again on the way. One of the altar boys flanking the priest at the Communion rail gave him a blank stare. He was a sight, he knew. Two days of stubble. His shirt wide open. An empty jacket sleeve dangling down his side.

Stein smiled to see him and slid over to make room in the pew. He leaned close and whispered. "Is she with you?"

"No," Decker whispered back, "she's meeting us here."

"Good. In the meantime, explain this arcane ritual to one who is not saved."

"Don't ask. I've been a heretic for years."

He spoke too loud. An old woman returning from Communion shot him a nasty look as she stepped into the pew ahead. Her wizened mouth was still working on the Host. Decker knew the type. A funeral groupie, feeding on dead souls. It was the shabby overcoat, the sanctimonious air.

He whispered to Stein. "What about the FBI?"

Stein shrugged. "They said they'd try to send an agent. He may be outside."

Decker looked over his shoulder to the back of the church. No FBI agent. No Charlotte. He wasn't overly concerned—not yet anyway. It was a long drive from Hyde Park, and she was probably following his instructions, taking it slow, trying not to look panicked.

He checked out the rest of the crowd. There were only two or three other reporters from the *Eagle*, and no editors, save Stein. Certainly no one had ever accused journalists of being a sentimental lot. But he was touched to see Darrell Thurston there, second pew on the right, and towering next to him Rebo Johnson, like some Old Testament figure in his beaded dreadlocks, dabbing his eyes with a lavender hankie.

When the last communicant was served, the priest

retreated to the altar and began to busy himself cleaning trays and chalices. Everyone knelt.

Decker looked over his shoulder again. Still no Charlotte.

He began to worry.

"Let us pray," the priest said, holding his arms out to his sides and spreading his surplice like the wings of an enormous black bird. Everyone stood. In a deep monotone, he chanted: "We are waiting for our Savior, the Lord Jesus Christ; He will transfigure our lowly bodies into copies of His own glorious body."

The congregation answered "Amen."

They were still standing when the sound of footsteps echoed from the back of the church. Decker and Stein turned their heads at the same time. Charlotte Krieger was stopped in the middle of the aisle about three pews behind, nervously scanning the crowd. She was the essence of girls school beauty in her fresh white blouse, plaid skirt, little white anklets. A discreet but telling portion of leg showed between anklet and skirt, and her long blond hair was pulled back into a loose ponytail, unleashing the healthy glow of her face. Our Lady of the Schoolyard. But without the blessed serenity. She was clutching a small black satin handbag in both hands.

He caught her eye and waved her toward the pew. Her whole body seemed tensed as she sidled in close to Decker, and when she nodded toward the back of the church he knew why. Two men materialized from the shadows of the vestibule like a pair of gargoyles come to life. They started briskly up the aisle. It was Ellway again, and with him this time a younger detective. A lumbering redhead, tall and thick-boned as a farm boy. Both were in dark blue suits.

He nudged Stein. "We've got trouble."

Stein took a quick look around. "Sure it's not FBI?"

"Nope. The one on the right took a shot at me."

The cops genuflected in unison and Ellway went first into the pew directly behind them, the farm boy on his heels. Decker could hear their labored breathing, and guessed they had sprinted from their car and up the church steps, afraid of losing Charlotte.

The priest stepped down from the altar—full of himself in a priestly way—and stood rocking on his heels in front of the coffin, his small hands touching at the fingertips.

"Brothers and sisters in Christ," he announced, "the family of the deceased has asked the organist to perform a rather lengthy piece at the conclusion of this Mass. The music is a special favorite of Mr. Nystrom's. We will delay the procession from the church until the music is finished. I ask your patience."

Then he spread his arms before the standing congregation and chanted: "The Lord be with you."

Decker saw Charlotte zip open her handbag and dip a hand into its jumbled contents. He knew the eyes behind them were watching, too.

"Wait," he whispered.

Her hand came out of the bag with a folded sheaf of white Kleenex. She began dabbing her eyes.

The priest remounted the altar, then turned again to the small congregation. "May almighty God bless you, the Father, and the Son, and the Holy Spirit."

They sang a half-hearted, "Amen," and the priest said, "The Mass is ended. Go in peace."

Suddenly, people in the pews turned toward each other and began shaking hands in a ceremonial way. The old funeral groupie offered a limp black-gloved hand to Decker, and when he didn't respond, she spotted his empty coat sleeve and broke into an embarrassed smile. "Go in peace," she said, and turned quickly away.

Then Charlotte got into the act, taking Decker by surprise

at first by grasping his left hand in both of hers. "Go in peace," she said, pressing something small and flat and hard into his open palm. Her worried smile held his eyes for a moment and he knew then what she had put in his hand. He smiled back and closed his fist around the tape. It felt good there.

While Charlotte turned round to shake hands with Ellway and the farm boy, Decker turned to his left to Stein, who seemed a bit baffled by all the instant congeniality. Decker smiled and held out his left hand until Stein put out his own. When they shook, a glimmer of comprehension showed through Stein's wire-rims as he felt the tape against his palm.

The organist began to play, and from the first two haunting notes—a low moan of fervent desire, barely audible, swelling up from the bass pipes—Decker recognized the Passacaglia. Turk had gone on and on about it once after an organ concert. About how Bach, obsessed with the mystical significance of numbers, had underpinned the piece with an eight-measure theme that changes voice again and again, but survives to the end.

Six more couplets followed, rising, cresting, then falling, like hope lapsing into despair, and ending with a final elongated note that was neither hopeful nor despairing, but having surrendered all doubt, resonated with a perfect tranquillity. That single note seemed to speak to God Himself, crying out its tormented faith, its belief in belief. And so on through all twenty variations, the same eight-measure catharsis, a never-ending search, then acceptance, then search again.

Charlotte looked at Decker, her eyes pleading for direction.

He whispered reassuringly: "Just stay close."

Safety wasn't the only reason. As long as Ellway and his partner suspected Charlotte had the tape, she was the main attraction. And with any luck, he and Charlotte could divert the two cops long enough for Stein and the tape to reach the *Eagle*.

He worked it out in his head. When the service ended, Charlotte and he would join the procession, lose themselves among the faithful, and once outside, make a run for his car. Unless Ellway and the farm boy were total lunatics, they wouldn't dare shoot from the crowded church steps. Decker would then take the pair on a wild goose chase through Covington, across the river, and into downtown Cincinnati.

And ending where? Ah, yes, a touch of irony. At the courthouse, of course. Where he would race into Krieger's office and deliver the bad news to Fritz himself: the tape was already in the hands of the *Eagle*, and the mighty power of the press was about to do him in.

The Passacaglia began building to its majestic climax, a swirl of notes in many voices, chasing one another toward the vaults of heaven. The windows rattled, the pews vibrated, and, surely, Decker thought, the coffin would burst open and Turk would rise from the dead.

In the end, the voices came together to form a single reverberating note. A note not of acceptance this time, but of triumph. A thundering transcendence that cried out, "I will there be a God!"

The organist held the triumphant note, and held it, and when he stopped, the voices that had been one scattered in all directions and disappeared into the farthest reaches of the cathedral.

"Amen," Decker said, not realizing he had spoken aloud until he saw the funeral groupie glance over her shoulder.

One of the altar boys handed the priest a gold bucket filled with holy water and a silver pestle, and the priest began to circle the coffin slowly, mumbling incantations and flinging water from the pestle. The spray fell with a soft patter on the flag. When he finished, he waited with the altar boy until the four ushers appeared, two on each end of the coffin, and started trundling its weight up the aisle. The priest followed, then the altar boys, and then the front pews began to empty, one at a time, as the congregation formed a slow procession from the church.

When it was their turn to fall in, Decker took Charlotte by the elbow and they stepped together into the aisle, genuflected, and turned. He held Charlotte back until Stein could step out and walk ahead.

Ellway and the farm boy stood motionless in their pew; they would be the last to join the procession. Their faces were blank but alert, the two sets of eyes fixed squarely on Charlotte's handbag.

Decker whispered in Charlotte's ear. "Take it slow. Let Barry get a good lead." Having guessed the plan, Stein was already weaving ahead through the procession. In a second or two, his dark suit had vanished into the crowd.

Decker took Charlotte's hand, and with the procession a good ten feet ahead, they started up the aisle and past the sidelong glances of the two detectives.

He leaned in toward Charlotte. "When we reach the door, we run for my car. Got it?"

She nodded and they picked up the pace. But with their next step, Charlotte let out a muffled cry. When Decker turned, a hand was clamped over his mouth and a knife pressed at his throat.

"Make a sound and I'll unzip your neck," Ellway snarled in his ear. "Now walk backward, and keep it slow."

He did, watching the last of the procession disappear into the vestibule. Stein, he knew, was with them and on his way.

"All right, turn around. No quick moves."

Ellway twisted Decker's arm behind his back and pressed the flat of the knife blade hard against his Adam's apple. He wanted to gag from the pressure. Meanwhile Charlotte was just ahead, struggling with the big farm boy, whose hand was still clamped over her mouth and nose. She must have been biting down, because the farm boy was kneeing her from behind and whispering through clenched teeth, "Cut it out, dammit! Cut it out!"

Charlotte and the farm boy fell behind as Ellway led Decker through the Communion rail gates and across the slick marble floor of the sanctuary. They veered sharply to the right, through a doorway and into what Decker recognized as the vestments room. It was an odd, gloomy place, a triangular room with windows of frosted glass and a pious odor of candlewax and starched linen. One wall, the longest of the three, was covered with an assortment of dark walnut drawers, cabinets, closets, fitted together like pieces in a puzzle. In the left corner of the room, down a short set of steps, was a passageway. Perhaps to the archbishop's quarters.

Ellway, who must have guessed Decker's thoughts, pressed the knifepoint into his chin. "Scream and your tongue gets spiked."

They waited as the farm boy and Charlotte entered the room. She was gagged now with a necktie, and her wrists were tied behind her back with a belt. The farm boy was holding her handbag in one hand, gripping her by the collar with the other as he pushed her roughly into the room.

"Is your partner always such a gentleman?" Decker said.

Ellway gave his arm an extra twist. "Just shut up and start down the stairs."

He almost said, "What stairs?" when Ellway shoved him toward a small door camouflaged among the cabinets and closets. Decker pulled it open and stooped under the low clearance. With Ellway's knife centered in his back, he stepped carefully down an unlit winding staircase. The tired metal creaked with every step.

At the bottom Ellway stood him in a lighted clearing next to the staircase and, slipping his knife into a sheath on his belt, pulled a standard issue .38. "Just stay put."

Decker shivered. The air in the room was cool and somehow dead. They were deep inside an underground vault, where in every direction as far as the light would allow, Decker could see the rolling stock of Catholicism. To the right, an army of candleholders and life-sized plaster statues; straight ahead, rows of old kneelers and lecterns, with a narrow path cleared to a freight elevator; and to the left, beyond a row of brick pillars, dozens of dismantled pews, stacked like kindling and disappearing into the gloom. The cement floor was dry and dusty. A parched odor stung the nostrils, like the air in a long-closed attic.

The farm boy literally carried Charlotte down the stairs, his arms in a bear hug around her waist, the purse strap in his teeth. Charlotte kicked and whimpered all the way. At the bottom he dropped the purse and planted Charlotte hard on the floor. His face was still red with exertion as he unbuckled her wrists and loosened the gag.

She turned on him instantly. "You wait till I tell Father," she snapped. And by the way the cop's face blanched, you knew it wasn't an idle threat.

"Bring her over here, Mike," Ellway said. Mike shoved Charlotte into the clearing next to Decker. Ellway held the gun on both of them while Mike recovered the purse.

"You won't find the tape in there," Decker said.

"Shut up," Ellway said, snatching the purse from Mike. He lifted the revolver and took aim.

"You kill us and you'll never find the tape," Decker said. "Just look in the goddamn purse."

Ellway tossed the purse back to Mike. "Do it."

Mike crouched low, unzipped the bag, and dumped its contents. A brush, a powder case, a credit-card holder, a small change purse, and some wadded Kleenex spilled to the floor. Mike dropped the bag and sifted around with his hands.

"Nothing, Lieutenant."

Ellway glowered impatiently. "Check the coin purse."

Mike unsnapped it. "Nothing, sir."

Decker was about to speak up when a commanding voice, somewhere in the surrounding shadows, beat him to it.

"That will be all, gentlemen."

Krieger stepped from behind a statue of the Virgin Mary and, in the dull penumbra of light, presented himself as though at military attention—chest out, chin high, feet spread apart. He held his left hand behind his back, the other gripped the handle of a gleaming nickel-plated Army .45, the hammer cocked. He looked calm and distinguished, a feat that only Krieger could have managed with a small cannon in his hand.

He pointed the .45 at Ellway. "*That* will be all, I said. I can handle this affair from here on out."

"Yes, sir."

Ellway motioned to Mike, who stood transfixed, staring at Krieger as though at a beatific vision. When the farm boy continued to gawk, Ellway grabbed his arm and tugged him toward the stairs. While Mike started up, Ellway turned to Krieger and bowed. "I'm sorry, sir. I mean, if we offended your daughter—"

"Just go!" Krieger roared. Ellway bowed again and skittered up the stairs.

And then it was just the three of them. Charlotte and Decker drew together, shoulder-to-shoulder, facing Krieger across the room. He marched slowly toward them until he was a yard or two away and the lightbulb shone directly above his head. In the yellow glare, his face looked bloodless, almost waxen, like a devil's mask, with shadows underscoring his eyes and cheekbones and coming to a point under his nose. He aimed the gun off to Charlotte's right, at a spot Decker could almost feel in his diaphragm. Krieger flicked the barrel upward; Decker raised his one good arm.

"The tape, please," Krieger commanded. He took several short steps forward and held out his palm, the curled fingers flexing in a come-hither gesture. His eyes traveled first to Charlotte, then to Decker, and settled at last on his daughter's upturned defiant face. Krieger's eyes seemed to glaze over, not with anger, but with disappointment, hurt.

"Charlotte, I know you took the tape," he said softly. "Please stop the nonsense and give it to your father."

"I don't have your tape." Her eyes were icy with contempt.

"Charlotte," he said, his voice filled with perplexed hurt and sadness, "why must you always torment me?"

He advanced another step toward his daughter, his palm still extended. Keeping his eye on the gun, Decker began an almost imperceptible retreat, sliding his feet backward inches at a time.

Father and daughter were face-to-face now in silhouette. Hovering behind them was the statue of the Virgin, her hands folded in silent prayer, her unseeing eyes peering down at the increasingly surreal drama.

Decker riffled through the options. The staircase was directly behind him, maybe ten or fifteen feet. Even if he made it, he would be target practice on his way up. He might have a better chance among the stacks of church pews to his left. The choices: he could run and be shot, hide and be hunted, or wait and be executed. None seemed very wise. Yet every muscle in his body seemed to quiver with the need to run, to fight, to do anything but just stand there.

"Charlotte," Krieger said. His pained expression shifted to a gently pleading smile. "Can't you forgive something that happened years ago?"

"Forgive, yes," she said, narrowing her eyes and shaking

her head, "forget, no. Not while I have to be anywhere near you."

Decker looked at the two, the one pleading, manipulating, the other cold and impregnable, and suddenly it became clear.

Krieger's voice exploded. "Charlotte, listen to me! This is *not* the time . . ."

But Charlotte gave it right back. "Yes it is time. How do you think I feel every time some boy even looks at me . . ."

"Enough!" he demanded. And then the pleading again: "Don't you see, dear Charlotte, that I must be about my Father's business."

Krieger took another step toward his daughter and the gun wavered just long enough for Decker to take his cue. In a burst of pure adrenaline, he sprang—straight for Krieger's head, his left hand reaching for the .45. They crashed forward in a heap, tumbling across the cement as the gun clattered away. They were still rolling in tandem when Decker knocked his head against a pedestal, and the statue of Mary toppled and shattered across the floor.

Decker was flat on his back when Charlotte cried out, "Father, *no!*"

He turned in time to see Krieger scuttling for the gun on his hands and knees. He threw himself on Krieger's back. The gun just inches from his hand, Krieger groped and strained, his fingers clawing at the dusty floor. Decker grabbed Krieger's elbow and pulled back. It was like trying to break a tree limb in half, but he kept Krieger from reaching any farther. Decker was operating on more than adrenaline now. Something primal, something never before tapped. He heard himself snarling in Krieger's ear.

Like a kid playing bronco, Krieger tried to throw him off, twisting and heaving against his weight. Decker held on with his knees, and finding the back of Krieger's ear, bit down as hard as he could. Blood oozed into his mouth—warm, slick, salty—and he clamped down all the harder, deep into the rubbery flesh, snarling and hissing through clenched teeth. Krieger wrenched his neck and screamed.

"Charlotte!"

She had retrieved the gun and was holding it in both hands, her loose aim somewhere over Decker's head.

"Stop it!" she screamed at Decker. "Stop it!"

He stopped, but only because Krieger had suddenly blacked out. The left side of the silver head was an explosion of red. Krieger was stretched flat on his stomach, lying next to the shattered remnants of the Virgin, like lovers on a cold hard bed. Remarkably, the statue's head was in one piece, severed at the neck so that the hollowness inside showed.

Decker got slowly to his knees. He clutched his bandaged arm, and, yes, it was still connected to his shoulder, but it was completely numb. No pain, no tingling. A ghost limb.

Charlotte stared at him in horror. Sweet Charlotte with her pleated skirt and white anklets and golden hair. With one hand she kept an unsteady grip on the gun, with the other she clutched her mouth.

He wiped his chin: the blood was already cold there. He touched his mouth. Something protruded from the lips. He spat the thing into his palm, and discovered an ample chunk of ear. Only now it didn't look much like an ear. He dropped it on the floor by Krieger and stepped toward Charlotte.

"Give me the gun," he said evenly. But she backed away, still holding a hand to her mouth, her eyes wide with fear and revulsion.

"Charlotte," he pleaded as calmly as he could, "everything's cool now. Just hand me the gun." He took a few more steps and she retreated until the stacks of old pews blocked her path.

"No!"

Decker turned in time to see the resurrected head of Mary about to come crashing down on his skull. Suddenly, the room exploded in light and sound, and Krieger flew backward from the impact. Decker was still standing when Krieger hit the floor.

There was no writhing, no death throes. He lay on his back with his arms outstretched like wings, staring upward at his own vision. His face glowed with the true-believer's inner tranquillity, a look Decker had seen on Krieger's face so many times before. He had never known what hit him. There was a hole in his chest the size of a quarter, and blood had splattered as far as the wall.

The gun slipped from Charlotte's hands and clattered to the floor. She slumped into the pew behind her, not crying or sobbing, but in a silent daze, staring, it seemed, at the empty pedestal where Mary once stood.

Decker retrieved the gun, put the safety on, and stuffed it through his belt. Then he sat beside Charlotte.

"It's all right now," he said softly, laying a hand on her rigid shoulder. She shrank away from him to a corner of the pew. He didn't blame her.

He slouched and let his head fall back over the pew. He breathed deeply, almost contentedly, as he listened to Charlotte's sobbing echo through the vault. It was an eerie, tormented sound, like the wailing of some wretched soul that had lost its way from here to there and was looking for a way back, or a way beyond.

The calvary arrived in a belated charge. Stein and an FBI agent came racing down the staircase. The agent had his snub-nose revolver drawn and pointed in the air. Very professional-looking. They stopped at the bottom of the steps, surveyed the scene. Stein's eyes popped behind the wire-rims. He looked like a little boy in the front row at a creature feature.

Decker grinned and felt the crack and pull of dried blood around his mouth. Suddenly the absurdity of the scene overwhelmed him. He threw his head back and laughed like a demon.

"Welcome," he intoned, "to the House of Horrors."

20

At least a dozen times that evening Thurston stopped typing in order to ask Decker to slow the hell down. Decker itched to hit the keys himself, and if he could have done it with one hand, he would have. He hardly needed his notes for the dictation. The story, word for word, seemed to be in boxes of neat type already assembled in his head. In two hours, they had their first and final draft to show Stein. It was enough to fill a complete page of the *Eagle*.

Stein read through the story on his screen while Thurston and Decker watched over his shoulder. Stein made small changes here and there, mostly typo corrections, nodding vigorously with each paragraph he read.

When he finished, he said, "I won't cut a word."

The story's credibility was beefed up considerably by Thurston's interview with Griswald. Yes, Lieutenant Milton O. Griswald, who had been alive and well and in the protective custody of the FBI. For three weeks the feds had kept him holed up in a motel outside Nashville with a couple of agents to keep him company. Not even his wife had known.

The *Eagle* wouldn't have known either, except the paper refused to hand over its information until the feds were forthcoming with their own.

The FBI had begun following several low-echelon members of the Pendulum—what they described as a neo-fascist, quasi-religious cult among a small group of Cincinnati law enforcement officials—soon after the abortion clinic bombings in the spring. (The name itself, they believe, referred to the group's quest to "swing the social pendulum" back to "Christian" values.)

An anonymous caller had tipped them off to the organization, possibly someone in Greenburg's operation. But the feds admitted they had no idea the Pendulum reached into the city's highest offices—to Krieger himself—until the *Eagle* began its own investigation.

And what of poor Charlotte? Soon after questioning, the agents had placed her in the care of her mother, whom one agent said was in "a mild state of shock" after learning what had happened to her husband. She would probably need to be hospitalized, Decker thought, when she learned the whole story.

That afternoon, while the team had pieced together the story, Lafferty had been holed up as well—in his own office. He putzed around with paperwork and made some calls. Later, Decker saw him slink out of the newsroom, head bowed and battered briefcase in hand.

"Exit Bozo, stage left."

Thurston laughed and Stein looked up from his editing and smiled. "Hear, hear men. No cheering. The poor bastard is bleeding."

Decker glanced at the wall clock. It was a little after five. In Chicago, just after four. He excused himself and went back to his desk. He called the number for the *Tribune* and asked for the metropolitan editor. Decker told him he wouldn't be taking the suburban bureau job. He had certain commitments in Cincinnati.

"Well, you might continue to send us your clips from time to time," the editor said, sounding a bit put off by Decker's decision. "But I can't guarantee any openings in the near future."

Decker hoped the *River Queen* story would finally propel

Stein into the city editor's slot. Finch could hardly ignore him now. And maybe Bozo could be kicked upstairs to write editorials or something innocuous like a gardening column.

The Boss made his grand newsroom appearance during the final editing of the story. He gave it his characteristic quick read and then congratulated the team in front of a half-dozen reporters who had stayed late to follow the day's developments. They clapped and cheered.

The story was in the can by nine P.M. The FBI had agreed to release nothing to the other media until the *Eagle's* first edition hit the streets the following morning. Which was the least the feds could do, Stein said, seeing as how the *Eagle* had saved them months of investigation.

The team gathered round while Mullins, the slot man, typed a momentous sixty-point headline across the top of his screen: KRIEGER CONSPIRACY ENDS IN BLOODBATH.

Stein read it aloud and cocked a skeptical eyebrow. Mullins wheeled in his chair: "Goddamnit, Barry, a sensational story deserves a sensational headline."

Decker and Thurston nodded heartily. The matter was settled.

When both story and headline had finally disappeared into the *Eagle's* electronic innards, the team members allowed themselves a round of backslapping.

"We did it!" Thurston said, raising his hand for a high five. Stein was on tippytoes as the smack reverberated across the newsroom. "We nailed ass like nobody's business," Thurston said.

"Yeah," Decker concurred, his voice subdued, "we nailed ass, all right." And then he trailed away from Mullins' desk and returned to his own, where he began to busy himself shuffling papers and filing things away.

There was Turk's old desk in the corner. A new night reporter, a kid fresh out of college with horn-rim glasses and his hair parted in the middle like Herbert Hoover's, was sitting there now, talking politely into the phone, taking meticulous shorthand on a yellow legal pad. One of the new breed. Educated, polished, polite almost to the point of timidity. Like me, Decker thought, only more so. He could almost hear Turk growl: "A newsroom full of wimpy-ass college boys, afraid to get their hands dirty."

Three desks over from Turk's, below the newsroom clock, he was reassured to find Barrett's old station still piled high with notebooks, old papers, foolscap. Just the way she had left it.

In a moment, Stein came over and half-sat with his leg over a corner of Decker's desk. The pipe was clamped in his mouth and he was looking around the newsroom at everything, nothing. Neither said anything for a while.

Then Decker leaned back in his chair and softly broke the question on both their minds.

"Was it worth it, Barry?"

Stein puffed and ruminated. When he was ready, he popped out his pipe, and was about to hold forth when he stopped himself short. He shook his head.

"How do you ever know?"

Decker unlocked the inside door and stepped quietly inside. The fluorescent light over the kitchen sink was all that was on, casting a soft glow about the white formica. There was a hushed orderliness about the room, an air of expectancy. Janet was curled up on the sofa, sleeping where a different Rick Decker had slept, it seemed, a million years ago. Her cheek was resting on folded hands, her mouth open and moist like a child's. She was still dressed in her white hospital jacket. A tired stethoscope lay on the floor where it had fallen from her pocket.

All the grief and worry of the last week—what had been

in it for her? He knew now what she meant to him, but he was confused more than ever as to what he meant to her. He only hoped . . .

He walked to the sofa, knelt on the carpet, and put his face close to hers. Her slow breath was warm and sweet. With his fingertips, he lightly brushed her hair aside and kissed her cheek. It tasted of salt. From tears?

Her eyes blinked a few times and opened. She smiled sleepily, without surprise, without stirring. As though she had expected to wake from a long slumber and find him there beside her.

"I'm home," he whispered.

DATE			